Everything the girl said had the ring of truth. He had no doubt she believed everything she had just told him. But whether she had been programmed thus, or had simply chosen to omit some things, would require deeper questions.

But she was yawning, and he wondered how long it had been since she'd slept. She was so young, younger than his youngest child. He suppressed a parental urge to suggest she rest now. Illogical, and self-defeating. Nevertheless, if she was overtired, her answers would make no sense. Only one more question, for now.

"Are you a member of the Tal Shiar?"

For the first time she laughed outright. It would have been a pleasant sound, if it hadn't been laced with sarcasm. "You mean, am I a spy? There are no spies on Romulus, don't you know that? There is no need for spies, because everyone is a spy."

"Answer the question, please."

That made her angry. She leapt out of her chair, almost knocking it over.

"I am nothing! Don't you understand? I don't exist. On the way here, Cretak and I went past two sets of sentries and three sensor arrays inside the space hub. The sensors recognized Cretak, but they never even registered me, because I don't exist. You're aiming in the dark."

"Are you a member of the Tal Shiar?" he asked again, unperturbed by her outburst.

Did he notice that she hesitated for the space of half a breath? *No*, Zetha told herself, watching sidelong as the impassive face revealed nothing. *He has not noticed.*

"No," she said carefully. "I am not."

STAR TREK®
THE LOST ERA
CATALYST OF SORROWS

2360

Margaret Wander Bonanno

Based upon STAR TREK
and STAR TREK: THE NEXT GENERATION®
created by Gene Roddenberry

STAR TREK: DEEP SPACE NINE®
created by Rick Berman & Michael Piller

and STAR TREK: VOYAGER®
created by Rick Berman & Michael Piller &
Jeri Taylor

POCKET BOOKS
New York London Toronto Sydney Romulus

An *Original* Publication of POCKET BOOKS

POCKET BOOKS, a division of Simon & Schuster, Inc.
1230 Avenue of the Americas, New York, NY 10020

STAR TREK is a Registered Trademark of Paramount Pictures.

ISBN: 0-7434-6407-9

First Pocket Books paperback edition January 2004

10 9 8 7 6 5 4 3 2 1

Cover design by John Vairo, Jr.

Manufactured in the United States of America

For information regarding special discounts for bulk purchases, please contact Simon & Schuster Special Sales at 1-800-456-6798 or business@simonandschuster.com.

For Jack, ever and always.

And in memory of Alan Ravitch,
who never met a pun he didn't like.
The world's a sadder place without you.

ACKNOWLEDGMENTS

Special thanks to Rick Sternbach for technical advice par excellence (and for using nice small words, so I could understand it). . . .

To Susan Shwartz for helping me to see Aemetha. *Jolan tru.* . . .

To Alex Rosenzweig, Big Jim McCain, daedalus5, and everyone else at psiphi.org and the trekbbs.com who got me back on the radar when it was most important. . . .

To Marco Palmieri, an editor with a deft touch and a prince among men, for welcoming me aboard. . . .

And with homage to the master, John Le Carré, for providing the template, and for teaching me how.

HISTORIAN'S NOTE

This story is set in the year 2360, sixty-seven years after the presumed death of Captain James T. Kirk aboard the *U.S.S. Enterprise*-B in *Star Trek Generations*, and four years before the launch of the *Enterprise*-D in "Encounter at Farpoint."

Sometimes we have to do a thing in order to find out the reason for it. Sometimes our actions are questions, not answers.

—John Le Carré: *A Perfect Spy*

Prologue

No border, however hostile the forces on either side of it, is ever impermeable. Even after almost fifty years of silence, the Romulan Neutral Zone was no exception.

Cretak grimaced as she and her attendant passed the sentries on either side of the no-man's-land between the designated Romulan and Federation sections of the space station. It wasn't the presence of the guards that disturbed her. She had the proper credentials, and they scarcely noticed her. It was the filth.

The station lay nominally within what humans called the Neutral Zone and Romulans the Outmarches—the two sides unable to agree on even that much—at one of several points where inhabited planets with allegiance to neither side had made it necessary for the mapmakers to do a bit of gerrymandering. Succinctly, the Zone ran rather narrow here, and more species than not pretended it did not exist, traveling within the Zone with impunity, as long as they didn't venture into either Federation or Romulan space. The station itself was run by a consensus of those species loyal to neither side, and functioned primarily for those myriad other species, allowing Federation and Romulan presences as long as neither "started something." Thus the need for sentries between the two areas designated specifically for them.

Apparently no one in the consensus, Cretak thought crossly, *is acquainted with the merits of a mop and broom!*

The walls were smudged, the floors sticky beneath her boots. Exposed bits of circuitry blinked feebly where fixtures had apparently been ripped out and never replaced. There were whole sectors where lighting was dim or nonexistent, and atmospheric control sporadic, creating pockets where it was hard to breathe. Stray clumps of *something* rolled sluggishly along the curve of the corridors, propelled by the ambient breeze whenever an airlock opened and closed, and in the darkest corners other somethings moved more rapidly, hissing and squeaking when disturbed. It was said they would eat anything that didn't move.

The areas immediately surrounding the guard posts were properly maintained, and Romulan personnel kept the corridors leading to their designated berths in pristine condition (Cretak could only assume the Federation did likewise), but the rest of the place, even the few bedraggled shops selling trinkets and replicated food in the main hub, clearly showed the disdain the unallied species felt for both sides.

It was a crossroads, a waystation, the kind of place where as many species as were known to travel across two quadrants—and even some who weren't—could be seen intermingling in the crowded, dirty corridors. At the moment, an air of watchfulness pervaded the place as well. Three Romulan ships were currently in port, effecting a transfer of diplomats on their way to a conference on a remote colony world. The rest of those on the station would be grateful when they shoved off. It was said that, while Klingons were given to brawling and breaking the furniture, Romulans were humorless, and that was worse.

Ordinarily a Romulan senator would have remained on the ship and sent one of her attendants on whatever errands might need doing in such a place, but Cretak had been overheard complaining about cabin fever and, since no one told a senator what not to do, she was free to explore the common areas of the station, attendant in tow, as long as she returned before the evening's first round of meetings and receptions began.

Someday, Cretak mused, *I shall have to learn to be more circumspect. But if this adventure is not successful, will there be a someday?*

Once far enough around the curve of the station's outer rim to be invisible to the guards at the warbird's airlock, she threw back the hood of her travel cloak, and nodded to her attendant to do the same.

"Is this wise, Lady?" the younger woman questioned. "I see no other Romulans here."

"It's as wise as your ability not to act like a Romulan!" Cretak said abruptly. "Has your training taught you nothing? For our purposes here, you are vulcanoid, allegiance unspecified. Comport yourself accordingly!"

You might begin, Cretak thought, *perhaps unfairly, by not staring wide-eyed at every non-Romulan you see.* She reminded herself that the girl had never been outside the Capital in her brief life, much less offworld and so far across the Marches, where Romulans were the minority. A little giddiness was to be expected. She herself had hardly been a model of decorum the first time she met a human.

"Forgive me," Zetha replied, lowering her eyes and her voice and walking behind Cretak as she had been taught. Nevertheless, she continued to scan her surroundings, as Cretak did. The only difference was that Cretak knew what she was looking for.

Zetha studied the unfamiliar text on the Departures padds beside each airlock, memorizing the scrolling symbols in several languages out of force of habit, even though she had no notion what they might mean.

"Wait here!" Cretak commanded, and went to talk to an

unpromising-looking humanoid slouching against a particular bulkhead, in a language Zetha did not recognize. She studied tone and gesture, intrigued. She already knew what the conversation was about, anyway.

"My attendant has been visiting family in the Zone," Cretak would say, or something to that effect. "She requires passage to the Alpha Quadrant. She will sleep anywhere, eat whatever your crew eats. She does not speak your language and owns nothing worth stealing. You will have full payment when I receive word she has arrived safely."

Some manner of delayed-activation currency would be exchanged, and the humanoid, no doubt the skipper of the battered merchanter Zetha could glimpse, partly lit by an overhead but mostly in shadow, just beyond the airlock, would take her aboard.

"Speak as little as possible," Cretak had warned her. "Most of them can't tell the difference between Romulan and Vulcan, but don't test them."

"Especially since I'm not Romulan," Zetha had reminded her, only to earn one of Cretak's cutting looks. Whoever said brown eyes could not go cold had never angered Cretak. "What if I am missed?" the younger woman had said to change the subject. Why did she care what the senator thought of her, when they would probably never meet again? Yet, for some reason, she cared. "If someone notices you have one attendant fewer . . ."

"Someone might notice if I went missing," Cretak had answered dryly. "But my staff are interchangeable as far as anyone else is concerned."

"What if I encounter a Vulcan?" Zetha asked, ignoring the insult. "What if I'm asked—"

"Once you're on the Federation side, it will not matter," Cretak said.

Zetha could not imagine what it would be like not to constantly be questioned about one's identity or origins.

That alone might be worth the adventure, even if her survival was reckoned only in days.

While she had been reliving the conversation in her mind, Cretak and the humanoid had apparently reached an agreement. The humanoid sized up this last-minute addition to his cargo under eyebrows that all but met in the middle, muttered something that didn't sound encouraging, and gestured for Zetha to follow him.

Cretak had raised the hood of her cloak and was already walking away. For some reason she turned one last time to see the question in the youngster's eyes.

Poor you! she thought. *What a shock this all must be. Your first offworld flight, and you didn't even get space sick. Your first look at the stars up close, and all you did on the first leg of the journey was stare at them all through the third watch when you should have been sleeping, as if they would vanish if you didn't watch them! Poor child, have I put too much responsibility on those narrow shoulders?*

None of it showed on her strong-jawed face, she hoped. "What is it?" she asked in the same imperious tone she had adopted since she had wheedled Zetha away from Koval expressly for the purpose that had brought them to this godsforsaken place. "I have not much time before I am missed. Speak!"

"Am I to return, Lady?" was all Zetha asked.

"I try not to predict the future," Cretak said. "Nor should you, if this is the life you want."

Zetha hesitated for only a moment, then shrugged. "Any life is better than no life."

"Then go!" Cretak ordered her, thinking: *And what little faith I have left in the future go with you!*

Chapter 1

Not every crisis, Admiral Uhura believed, *begins with exploding planets or even a starship battle. Sometimes it is the things we cannot see that cause the greatest harm.*

"Joshua Lederberg," McCoy said, glowering at her from the comm screen in her office at Starfleet Intelligence, "Twentieth-century Earth geneticist. Said something to the effect that the single biggest threat to man's continued dominance in the universe is the virus. They were here long before us, they'll be here long after we're gone."

"So you will help us, then," Uhura said.

"Yes. Repeat: No."

Uhura frowned back at him. "Now what is that supposed to mean?"

"It means, young lady, that I can't help you with this one. I've gone fishing."

Uhura counted to ten before she trusted herself to speak again. Age hadn't mellowed Leonard McCoy one iota; he was as ornery as ever. He was pretending to ignore her, puttering with something just below the comm screen's sightline, and she wondered what it was.

"What if I told you it's urgent?" she asked.

"It's *always* urgent!" McCoy grumbled. "Is Starfleet so devoid of decent medical personnel these days that every time there's a crisis you have to drag an old warhorse like me out of the barn? Dammit, woman, I'm retired! Leave me in peace!"

He had a point, Uhura thought. He was at least a decade up on her, and every other week she thought of retiring. Not that Command would let her.

She supposed if she insisted they'd get someone else to cover her class at the Academy, but she *liked* teaching! It was being head of Starfleet Intelligence that Command wouldn't let her wiggle out of. The C-in-C would have her believe that she was the only one in the quadrant who could handle that.

Meaning no one else is crazy enough to take the job, Uhura thought wryly. *Also, the theory is I know too many secrets to be trusted to take them with me to some quiet country retreat and be relied upon to keep my mouth shut.*

But McCoy had no such burden. He was legitimately retired . . . again. But every time he stepped down, someone or something lured him back in. A man of 130-something ought to be allowed to enjoy a little leisure. Maybe she'd leave him in peace after this assignment, but right now Uhura really needed his expertise.

"I already have a team in place," she explained, wishing he'd stop fidgeting and pay attention. "All I'm asking you to do is consult by remote. I've got some excellent people working on this already, but I need your wisdom and experience, Leonard."

"Flattery will get you nowhere . . ."

"You won't even have to get off the porch," Uhura wheedled.

"Then you don't need me!" McCoy grumped. "You've got all of Starfleet Medical at your disposal. How many Vulcan physicians are there in the fleet these days?"

"It's not just about Vulcans," Uhura said.

"Affirmative, Admiral," Dr. Selar had told her, after no doubt staying up all night to run the algorithm. "I am investigating all reported cases of unusual illness on Federation worlds bordering the Neutral Zone."

"And—?" Uhura prompted.

"Ruling out an outbreak of neo-hantavirus on Claren III, which was self-limiting and contained in a single sector, and a previously unidentified aerobacter found in the soil of Gemus IV, which caused flulike symptoms in 1,700 children in two of the three settlements before it was isolated, and for which a vaccine has since been developed, there are so far seventy-three cases in seventeen different locales proximate to the Neutral Zone which potentially fit the parameters."

"Demographics of the victims so far?" Uhura asked, jotting notes on a padd for a memo to her Listeners on the ships that patrolled the Zone.

"Thirty-one Vulcan, twenty-three Rigelian, nineteen human."

"All fatal?"

"Affirmative."

"Did they infect anyone else?"

"Unknown at present, Admiral. All of the Rigelians were from the same extended family, but the Vulcan and human casualties were isolated and, apparently, unknown to each other. The last confirmed case occurred three weeks ago, so it is assumed the current outbreak was self-contained."

"Which is not to say that there couldn't be further outbreaks," Beverly Crusher chimed in from the other screen on a three-way conference call. She was across town from Uhura at Starfleet Medical HQ; Selar was parsecs away aboard a Vulcan research vessel on its way to Earth from the Beta Quadrant. "It could be something geographic, something seasonal or cyclical, something that occurs every few years or even centuries."

"And except for the Rigelians, none of them knew each other?" Uhura said. "Traveled between worlds? Had a friend or relative in common? Ordered supplies from the same source? Ate at the same restaurant?"

"Admiral," Selar said, "may I respectfully point out that we do not yet know, purely on symptomatology, whether this is the same illness in each case?"

"I realize that, but—"

"Nevertheless, I am attempting to establish a commonality among the victims," the Vulcan physician added primly. "As for ordering supplies from offworld, irradiation procedures at point of origin and point of arrival would have precluded the possibility of any known disease organism—"

"I know, Selar." Uhura sighed. "It's the unknown disease organisms I'm concerned about. Dr. Crusher, suggestions?"

"I'd suggest Selar expand her algorithm to include all Federation worlds." On her screen, the Vulcan nodded, unperturbed by the amount of extra work this would require. "In the meantime, I'll need tissue samples, or at least readouts, from as many of those seventy-three cases as possible to run a comparison. I'm still trying to isolate an organism in the samples you gave me from . . . the other side. There isn't very much to go on. I'm doing my best."

"I'd expected nothing less," Uhura said warmly. "Carry on, Doctors. Keep me informed."

"My people are already working on it," she told McCoy now, preparing a data-squirt about "it" even as she spoke. Her talented fingers ticked over the controls like a concert pianist's. "There's this weird fever that's been cropping up in some of the colonies. Starfleet Medical thinks it might be similar to something that my sources tell me may be happening inside the Romulan Empire. I'm sending you the readout now."

"Readout on what?" McCoy demanded, intrigued in spite of himself.

"Medical's initial analysis of Romulan tissue samples," Uhura said concisely.

"Did I hear you say 'Romulan'?" McCoy asked. "My God, that's not a word I thought I'd hear again within my lifetime! How the hell did you—?"

"Not at liberty to say," she replied. "Not even on Scramble."

"That hot, huh?"

I've got him! Uhura thought. *He can't resist a mystery. As soon as he sees this data . . .*

"Let's just say there could be . . . political ramifications. The colonies affected are very near the Neutral Zone."

"Cloak and dagger stuff," McCoy muttered. "Your bailiwick, not mine. All the more reason why my answer's still no."

Just then Uhura's Andorian aide stuck her head through the door, antennae twitching, whispering, "Admiral? You'll be late."

Uhura waved her away. "The class is not till 10:00, Thysis. I've still got thirty minutes."

Uhura's lifelong ambition was to be able to do one thing, just one thing, at a time. As if this were the only crisis on her desk—! As if she didn't have to monitor hotspots across the quadrant, know the whereabouts of every one of her operatives at any given time, not to mention staying awake at staff meetings and—

"It's not just the class," the Andorian hissed. "You have a press conference scheduled beforehand. It was last-minute. I thought you might have forgotten."

"Leonard, hang on a minute. No, I haven't forgotten, Thysis. Tell them I'll be with them in five. Now, shoo! Go away!"

The floss-white head popped back out through the door as quickly as it had popped in.

In those few seconds, McCoy had turned his back to the screen, rummaging for something on a worktable in the background, returned, pointedly ignoring Uhura, as if that would make her and her troubling news go away. At last she could see what he was doing. He was tying trout flies, one eye half shut, his tongue caught between his teeth in concentration.

"You still here?" he demanded at last, tying and snipping, examining the finished product with something like disgust, then scowling at her.

"Rigelian fever can cross species," was Uhura's response.

"Wiped out for more than twenty years," he shot back. "Last known case recorded in 2339. Samples kept in stasis on Starbase 23 just in case. Any new outbreaks, they can replicate a vaccine from there."

"Worse," Uhura cajoled him.

"Not interested." McCoy examined the lure in his hand one more time before rejecting it. "Hands shake too much!" he reported, starting over. "Dammit, you're ruining my concentration. Go away now. This conversation's over." He made shooing motions toward the screen. "Come back when you want to just chat instead of always picking my brains."

"The Gnawing," Uhura said.

That got his attention. "Say again?"

"The Gnawing. At least that's how the translator renders it out of Romulan. Know anything about it?"

"Just rumors. Something Spock said once about..." Uhura watched the transformation on his wily old face. One minute he was blustering, the next he got that kind of glaze-eyed look which meant he was running permutations through his mind, calling upon more than a century of past experience, tempted to get to a lab and start running tests, just as she'd hoped he would be.

"Now, wait just a goddamn minute!" McCoy snapped, breaking the spell. "I know what you're up to. Trying to reel me in with some rumor about a disease that's only legend. It won't work!"

"Apparently it's not a legend anymore," Uhura said, coding and scrambling the data-squirt while she talked. *Multitasking is my middle name!* she thought, sending it before

McCoy had a chance to block it. "We have first-person reports of what amounts to a small epidemic. Not in Federation territory. Yet. But it may correlate with something similar that's crept over to our side. As I mentioned, we do have tissue samples. And I've got agents in the field double-checking the veracity of the reports. It's all there. If you'll just read what I'm sending you before you—"

"I hear Starfleet Medical's developing some sort of new-fangled android or hologram or something that's supposed to replace living beings in high-risk areas . . ."

How the *hell*, Uhura wondered, had he found out about the Emergency Medical Hologram project? Starfleet was at least a decade away from so much as a working prototype, and even that was classified. Parsecs from nowhere, Leonard McCoy still heard all the scuttlebutt.

". . . get yourselves one of those, you won't need me!" he finished.

Uhura sat back and waited, casually drumming her perfectly manicured nails on the surface of her desk while her screen bleeped: *Message Received*. She knew once he read the first few sentences, McCoy's curiosity would get the better of him. She buzzed Thysis while she waited.

"Tell the media people I'm on my way."

"Yes, ma'am."

McCoy never could read as quickly as Spock did, but he skimmed the report, his practiced eyes picking out the pertinent data. Outbreaks of high fever and wasting sickness in Romulan and Federation space, signs and symptoms, failure to respond to standard treatments, mortality rates, projected outcomes if the disease spread unchecked. Uhura almost regretted involving him when at last those tired blue eyes found hers; the look on his face was stricken.

"Where the hell did you get these figures? Especially the Romulan data?"

"I'm not at liberty to say."

"One hundred percent mortality?" he asked incredulously. "That can't be accurate. Is this thing bacterial or viral?"

"I don't know," was what Dr. Crusher had said after the preliminary lab work. "We don't know enough about Romulan genetics to distinguish damaged genes from healthy ones. There are some bacteria that can disguise themselves as viruses, and some viruses that can mutate and integrate themselves at the genetic level so they look like a normal part of the DNA sequence."

She'd tucked a strand of bright red hair behind her ear and sighed in frustration. Uhura could see Dr. Selar nodding agreement.

"As soon as I get readouts on all the samples from the colonies, I'll compare them," Crusher said. "But it could be weeks before we can find a match, Admiral, if at all. I'm sorry."

"All right," Uhura had replied, not expecting it to be good news, not this soon. "Do your best. There's someone else I need to talk to in the meantime."

That was when she called McCoy.

McCoy was talking to himself. "Can't be bacterial. The bubonic plague by most estimates only killed twenty-five to forty percent of the population of Europe and Asia." He glared at Uhura, annoyed at being drawn into something she'd known he wouldn't be able to resist. "Gotta be viral. Even so, those numbers . . . the Ebola virus's mortality rate was eighty-eight percent at most, but it was transmitted person-to-person, and it was self-contained. It didn't go hopping across solar systems."

"What if it's airborne?" Uhura asked. She'd been learning more than she wanted to know from Medical ever since this thing first crossed her desk.

"Then the spread would be faster, but mortality would be

much lower," McCoy pointed out. "Ever hear of the Spanish flu?"

"No, but I'm sure you'll enlighten me."

"Earth, 1918. End of what some historians at the time took to calling the Great War. Now, there's an oxymoron if there ever was one . . ."

Uhura glanced at the chrono, trying not to be impatient. Thysis would be back any minute pestering her about the press conference. She could picture the roomful of reporters from half a dozen worlds clearing their alimentary canals and shifting their appendages restlessly.

". . . theory is that those who didn't die in the trenches brought this bug back home with them. Or it could have come from Asia, which is where most flu bugs came from at the time. It killed more people within a year than the Black Death did over several centuries. Lowered the life expectancy in the industrialized world by ten years. People would keel over in the street with a high fever and not last the night."

"Which sounds very much like what we're dealing with here," Uhura suggested. "And that's exactly why we need your help."

McCoy ignored that last remark. "Except that the mortality rate for that particular strain of flu—which thank God was never replicated, at least not on Earth—was only 2.5 percent. Millions of people got sick, but most of them recovered. Even in 1918, with no vaccines or even palliative treatments like antibiotics. Not that antibiotics work against a viral infection, but—"

"Leonard, this is fascinating, but—"

"—but I'm dithering, and you've got work to do," he finished for her. "All I'm saying is you can't have every single one of your patients dying from a possibly viral, possibly airborne infection. Either this isn't viral or these numbers are wrong."

"Then help me make them right," Uhura challenged him.

"A one hundred percent mortality rate?" McCoy was

talking to himself again. Uhura sighed. She'd wanted him onboard, but wished he'd get off the pot. "No response to treatment, and across species? How do you know these numbers from inside the Zone are accurate? And why are you in charge of this instead of Starfleet Medical?"

Good thing this is a secured frequency, Uhura thought. It was past time for her to take control of this conversation.

"Are you finished?" she asked quietly. "The reason this was brought to my attention . . ." *Well, not the entire reason,* she thought, *but he doesn't need to know that now, if at all.* ". . . is because—and Leonard, we never had this conversation—those numbers suggest that whatever this is, bacterial or viral, airborne or direct contact, it's not a natural phenomenon. That it's been manufactured, either by the Romulans or by someone from our side. It's my job to figure that out before this becomes more than just a particularly nasty flu bug killing a few thousand people on a half-dozen worlds and becomes an Interstellar Incident, uppercase. It's your job, if you decide that saving lives is more important than trout fishing, to assist my medical team with the microscopic stuff, lowercase."

"If you'd—" McCoy started to say, but Uhura rode right over him. She was slow to anger, but once there, she was dangerous.

"I've got two of the best MDs in the fleet doing the lab work, agents in place on the other side attempting to confirm the reports of outbreaks there, and I'm gathering a team to go in and investigate this on the ground. But nobody has the decades of experience you have, and Dr. Crusher asked for you specifically . . ."

Thysis's antennaed head appeared in the doorway again; she heard the tone in the admiral's voice, and vanished again without a sound. If Uhura had so much as noticed her, she gave no sign.

"I'm not asking you to go hopping galaxies, just to consult," she told McCoy, building to a crescendo. "And if

you're going to balk, I'll get someone else. Someone probably not as good as you, but a lot more cooperative. I do not
have the time or the patience to coddle your ego or put up
with your carefully nurtured idiosyncrasies. Now, are you in
or are you out?"

There was a long moment of silence while McCoy
waited for her to cool off.

"Are *you* finished?" he asked carefully. It wasn't everyone
who could bite his head off from across the quadrant.

"Yes, I am."

"Tell me about the tissue samples," he said doggedly.
"What kind of tissue samples, and from where?"

"I'd rather not discuss that unless I'm sure you're in." She
knew that would get a rise out of him.

"Are you saying you don't trust me?" he demanded.

"You know, you're probably right," she said, suddenly
changing course, pretending she hadn't heard him, shuffling
datachips on her desk, watching him out of the corner of her
eye. "Someone younger, more up-to-date on current pandemic
management techniques, would probably be a better choice."

She saw his ears perk up at the word "younger."

"Someone who?" McCoy demanded. "These youngsters
today can't be bothered doing hands-on lab work. They
think you just push a button and the computer does everything for you. This thing I'm looking at here isn't going to
yield to that kind of slapdash technique. There are times
when a good, old-fashioned empirical approach—"

"Leonard, I'm sorry, I've got a press conference," Uhura
cut him off. "It would have been great to have you on board
to help us stop this thing a little sooner, maybe save a few
extra lives, but I'll tell Beverly you're not available for consult. She did say you were one of her role models in med
school, and she was hoping you'd help fill in the gaps in her
knowledge. She'll be disappointed, but never mind. Sorry to
have bothered you. Uhura out."

"Beverly?" McCoy ruminated, not noticing that Uhura hadn't closed the frequency yet. "I wonder—? No, couldn't be the same one. You might recall I gave a series of guest lectures at the Academy a few years back. So well attended Command asked me to do it again the following year. Told them no, too. Nobody listens."

Yes, I do remember, Uhura thought. *It's part of my job to forget nothing.*

"There was this sweet young thing who cornered me after the first lecture, asked me questions for about an hour. Got shipped out and couldn't attend the rest of the series, though. Pity. Stunning-looking woman. Tall drink of water, legs up to here, flaming red hair . . . wanted to do more than just *teach* her anatomy, I can tell you. Young enough to be my granddaughter, but there's something about red-heads . . ."

While he was woolgathering, Uhura had sent him Crusher's holo on a quick squirt.

"Well, I'll be damned!" McCoy said as the picture arrived, genuine pleasure lighting his face for the first time. "There she is! Her name was Howard back then, though. Beverly Howard. I remember now. Married, I suppose."

"Widowed," Uhura reported. "With a young son. I'll send her and Dr. Selar your regrets."

"You've got Selar on this, too? Now, her I know by reputation. Wouldn't mind sharpening my wits against a Vulcan's again. It's been way too long." McCoy frowned. He suddenly realized he'd just been dismissed. "Wait a minute. Do you want my help on this or not?"

"Yes, repeat: No." Uhura said, throwing his own words back at him.

"You said I can consult on remote."

"Correct."

"Don't have to leave my front porch."

"Affirmative."

"Get to interact with bright, attractive women and maybe save a few lives in the bargain."

"Affirmative."

"You've talked me into it."

Uhura gifted him with one of her dazzling smiles. "Welcome aboard!"

Only after she'd closed the frequency did she let her face relax and show what she was truly feeling, which was a bone-deep exhaustion. This mission had occupied her attention 24/7 ever since Cretak's message had reached her from inside the Empire. In that time she'd done all the things she'd just told McCoy—put the medical team to work, gotten through to her operatives inside the Empire with instructions to track down every rumor of unusual illness anywhere in Romulan space, and scanned her files to determine who she had available to send into the Neutral Zone for what could at best be an exercise in futility, and at worst mean a death sentence.

Because if this was just some unusual bug, the potential was bad enough. But if, as her source suggested, it was an artifical pathogen designed to kill everyone it affected, the potential was too horrific to contemplate.

It had been almost fifty years since the infamous Tomed Incident, fifty years in which Empire and Federation had turned their backs on each other, shunned each other, withdrawn their diplomatic embassies from each other's soil, and metaphorically glared across parsecs of space at each other in stony silence, neither side willing to take the step across the void that separated them and start again.

Which was not to say that the silence was absolute. Starfleet Intelligence had Listeners inside the Empire, just as Uhura knew the Romulans had operatives in Federation space. Occasionally one side or the other was able to turn one of their counterparts into a double agent. There was always some question about what could or could not be believed. But sometimes the source was so well established it predated Tomed and the silence, and in that respect it could perhaps be trusted more.

Would the messenger have been sent at all if someone other than Uhura had been head of Starfleet Intelligence? What if she had stepped down this time last year, or even last week? Retirement was always on her mind, and yet—

No more! she told herself. *Just this one more mission, then I'm stepping down.*

She said the same thing every year. And every year, when the winter rains began to sweep across San Francisco Bay and her birthday came around, she pulled up the resignation letter she'd kept on file since the day she took this job, updated it, and thought: I'll submit it on New Year's Eve. Secure all my agents-in-place, give the C-in-C my recommendations for who should replace me, help groom that person for the job, and, before the year is out, quietly step aside.

And then what? she wondered every time. *When do I decide it's enough, that someone else can take my place, and it's time for me to do what, exactly?*

She supposed she could always retire to the country house near the ruins of Gedi, and sit under the jacarandas watching the blue flash of *agama* lizards flitting through the leaves and the giraffes making their stately parade through the clearing, or sling a Vulcan lute over her shoulder and hitch a ride on the first freighter headed toward a star beyond Antares, or write her memoirs. . . .

Ah, now, there was the rub. There was so much she couldn't tell, and so many biographies and autobiographies and historical overviews and intimate portraits had already been written by and about the crew of *Enterprise*, but what the historians and biographers knew about Nyota Uhura was the tip of the proverbial iceberg. And because she couldn't talk about so much of what she knew, they would more likely than not sum up her career as being nothing more than "Hailing frequencies open, Captain." No, that wouldn't do. There was still good work that she could do here.

Besides, she'd miss the parties. The Klingon flagship *K'tarra* would be in town next week, and Starfleet was holding a reception for her senior officers. Sarek of Vulcan would be there trying to maintain his dignity while Thought Admiral Klaad and Curzon Dax drank bloodwine and swapped tall stories all night, and she wouldn't want to miss that for the world. Retirement from Starfleet Intelligence meant a special kind of retirement. It meant either you submitted to having your memory selectively erased, in which case you ended up smiling vacuously when people mentioned missions you were on because you truly didn't remember them, or else you stepped out of the limelight altogether and lived somewhere quietly, probably under a new identity and no doubt under observation, because there were things you knew that could be extracted from your mind and used with terrible consequences. They never told you that when you entered intelligence work, only when you tried to leave.

I'd miss the parties, Uhura thought. *And the sense that once in a while what I do makes a difference to the cosmos at large. I don't want to give that up just yet. But all the rest of it . . .*

Oh, hell! Uhura thought. *I'm a long way from being able to retire. But this will be my last hands-on case, I swear. From now on, I delegate. This will be a fitting swan song, the final sentence in a conversation that began in an unlikely spot on Khitomer almost seventy years ago . . .*

"Admiral Uhura," a stringer for the Altair Information Syndicate wanted to know, "is there any truth to the rumor that you're planning to retire at the end of this year?"

"I'll tell you this much," she said seriously. "I do not intend to die at my desk."

By now she could play the reporters like a string quartet. She wondered why they came back year after year, just as the academic year was starting, to ask her the same questions again and again, plead for a chance to sit in on the most popular class ever taught at the Academy, pester her for insights into the workings of SI that were retina-scan classified and that she couldn't possibly give them.

But Command said interaction with the media was necessary. Keep the public informed, Academy personnel were told; let them see that Starfleet is their friend. So Uhura played along, poised and in control at the speaker's podium, her rich contralto voice with its three-octave range caressing their auditory receptors regardless of their species.

What did they see when they looked at her? A petite human woman of African ancestry, well past the century mark, with a single wing of jet-black hair sweeping back from her brow into the aura of white hair that framed her face like a cloud, accentuating her upswept amber eyes and what at least one old admirer had once called "cheekbones to die for."

Her heritage was Bantu, from among those tribes whose tradition was matrilineal, where sons inherited from their mothers and every woman was a queen. She held herself like a queen and moved like a dancer, and it was not unknown for her male students to fall all over themselves with schoolboy crushes trying to impress her. Nor were they alone. Part of her skill at moving among the influential of many worlds was her ability to attract the appreciation of males from a multitude of species.

She was at peace with herself, comfortable in her own skin, and it showed.

"So how did you get involved in intelligence, Admiral?" a Benzite asked, his aerator huffing between phrases.

Uhura smiled her careful official smile, no less dazzling than the range of others she possessed. Her voice went low and conspiratorial, and her eyes went hooded with mystery.

"I could tell you but, as the saying goes, I'd have to kill you." She waited for the translators to render it, for the requisite laughter that followed, then added: "If you'd asked my grandfather, he'd have said I was born to it . . ."

The old man sat watching the sunlit pattern of the leaves at his feet. The morning was quiet enough for him to hear the chirring of insects, the squawk of the go-away birds, the sough of the breeze through the feathery leaves of the jacaranda whose powerful branches arched above him. He shifted his bony frame on the bench, his long-fingered hands clasped contentedly on the knob of the cane he used more as a symbol of his dignity than as an aid in walking for, even at 120 years, he was still straight and limber and strong.

The silence and his contemplation were broken by the sound of something wild running breakneck through the bush.

A blur of skinny arms and legs shot out of the trees, zigging left and right, but headed toward him. He could hear her labored breathing, see the terror in her eyes, and could only imagine what was pursuing her. When she was almost past him, the old man snaked out one remarkably quick hand and snagged her by the shirttail.

Nyota jerked to a halt, her bare feet kicking up dust, and ducked behind the old man, making herself as small as possible.

"*Polepole*, my girl!" the old man chided her in kiSwahili, trying not to laugh at the sight of her. Her little ribs were heaving; there were twigs stuck every which way in her halo of small braids. "Slowly, child. Where do you think you're going so fast?"

"They're after me, *Babu!*" she wheezed. "They're going to get me!"

"Who is?"

"Juma and Malaika." Her ten-years-older cousin and his girl.

"And why would they be doing that?"

Nyota took one deep breath and calmed herself, drawing

herself up to her full height, looking very serious. "They were *kissing*," she reported, saying the word with a *frisson* of intermingled disgust and delight.

"And you were spying on them," her grandfather suggested.

"I was not!" she said, indignant at the very thought. She settled herself on the bench beside the old man, legs swinging, confident he would protect her. "I was only climbing the old mangrove tree. They just happened to be kissing under it."

"The same place they go every afternoon, and you know it," the old man said dryly. "You were spying. So. What happened?"

"The branch I was sitting on started to crack. I was falling, but I caught myself. I wasn't hurt, but they heard the snap and they saw me. Malaika was laughing so hard she fell off the big root where they were sitting. But Juma said he was going to get me. So I ran."

"Ah, I see," the old man said, just as the young couple emerged from the bush, holding hands and laughing, and looking not at all as if they were chasing anyone.

Most of the year, Nyota lived with her parents in Mombasa, a coastal city of high-rises and traffic and noise, where her entire childhood was regimented into school and after-school and music and dance lessons and swimming classes and gymnastics and languages, and it was only during the height of the January heat, just after her birthday and the holidays, when her parents packed her off to the country for a month to be with her grandparents and a raft of cousins, that she felt truly free. The happiest memories of her childhood were here.

But Babu was right; she had been curious from the day she was born.

"You're a terror, you!" the old man told her more than once. "*Tumbiri*, monkey-child, climbing trees and spying through windows and listening on the stairs. Asking questions ever since you could talk. 'Why, Babu, why?' You are

uhuru. Independent. Free as the wind and completely un-
tamed. But someday your spying is going to get you into
trouble, and I may not be around to save you . . ."

She was the same age now that Babu had been then,
Uhura realized with a start, hoping the lapse had only been
in her mind and not something the reporters might have noticed. They were still smiling up at her expectantly.

"I have an idea!" she announced, as if it were something
that had just occurred to her, and not the same suggestion
she made at the end of the press conference—she could see
the veterans already nodding—every year. "How would you
all like to sit in on my class this morning?

"It's called Communications 101," she explained, leading
them down the corridors. "It's been called that since the
Academy was founded. When I took over, the deans suggested I could change it to whatever I wanted, but I've kept
the designation. After all, if you think about it, the secret to
understanding the universe is communication . . ."

Just this mission and then no more, she thought, the disease vectors she'd passed on to McCoy still active in her
mind, resonating with visions of death and more death. *Because if in fact my source inside the Empire is correct and this
is not a natural phenomenon, but something someone has created for whatever hideous reasons, and if I and my "shadow
people" can't resolve it, it could be yet another excuse for war.*

*I went into intelligence work for one reason only, because I
believe that the military solution must be the last and not the
first choice. This has always been my philosophy both as a
Starfleet officer and as a private person. Consequently I must
use all the Starfleet resources at my disposal to try to stop this
thing before it's too late!*

Chapter 2

When Crusher had completed the first round of tests at Uhura's request, she had asked the same thing McCoy would ask a few days later. "Where did these tissue samples come from?"

"Inside the Romulan Empire," was all Uhura said.

"How did—?" Crusher started to say, then realized she wouldn't get an answer. She thought of a different question. "How can you be sure they're genuine?"

"I trust the source. I've also got my Listeners trying to get confirmation."

Uhura's Listeners were many and varied, the backbone of Intelligence under her command, from sleepers who committed themselves to a lifetime on the inside—Vulcans passing as Romulans, humans surgically altered to resemble a dozen other species that bore watching—to troubleshooters thrown into crises while they were happening, who landed on their feet and did their best at damage control, to dozens of communications officers on Starfleet ships flung across the quadrant who, in between their assigned duties, monitored every stray frequency that passed through their consoles, listening for . . . anything. A sudden flurry of trade agreements in an Orion-controlled sector which meant the pirates were smuggling arms again, a rumor that a Coridan ambassador's death by food poisoning might not have been food poisoning at all but a carefully planned assassination or, now, a tale from the heart of the Empire of a disease thought all but eradicated a thousand years ago which in its latest incarnation killed everyone in its path—there was little that escaped the eyes and ears of the Listeners, even after half a century of "official" silence.

While Crusher had been running preliminary tests, Uhura had been fielding any number of transmissions that began with "Admiral, this might not mean anything, but . . ." Her job was to pull all the strands together and weave them into a tapestry of information that presented a coherent picture, however long it took.

"Is there enough there to go on?" she asked Crusher now.

"I don't know yet," Crusher said. "The tests I've run so far indicate this thing is particularly virulent. And it doesn't respond to antibiotics, known antiviral agents, or even household bleach. Radiation will kill it back temporarily, but only in amounts that would kill the patient. Turn the radiation off and the bug regenerates."

"Is there anything you can do?" Uhura asked.

"I'll need to grow a big enough batch of it in culture to run some more tests. If we had time, we could work on cracking the genetic code, then developing an antigene to combat this."

"What kind of time are we talking about?"

Crusher shrugged. "Weeks, maybe months, maybe not at all without samples from healthy Romulans to compare this with."

"Could you compare what you've got with samples from similar species?" Uhura asked. "Rigelians, let's say, or Vulcans?"

"Theoretically I could compare normal specimens from any vulcanoid species with the disease specimens, but the match wouldn't be exact," Crusher said. "Romulans, I gather, from what little there is in the databanks, are different. And I'm still not clear on why I'm doing this."

"Need to know, Doctor. I can't tell you that now, but it's urgent. Can you give me an ETA on when you'll have those additional tests completed?"

"As soon as I can get this thing to grow in culture," Crusher responded. "Even I can't hurry Mother Nature."

"Keep me informed," Uhura said, and moved on.

Something one learned as a comm officer in a crisis was what Uhura called operational triage. Overwhelmed with multiphasic transmissions and often under fire, you had to decide in a heartbeat which messages were most important. Very often the voices yelling the loudest were the ones you could most safely ignore. It was the whispers you had to pay attention to.

This mission had begun with a whisper.

The fog in the Bay Area was particularly heavy that morning, and Uhura walked the winding paths of the gardens on the academy grounds more by familiarity than by sight, nodding to Boothby, who was dead-heading a row of rosebushes in front of the C-in-C's office, and silently saluted her with the trimming shears as she passed. By midday, she knew, the marine layer would burn off, leaving a brilliantly sunny day, but for now the world existed only as far as the eye could see, which was only a meter or two in any direction.

By rights she could have had a groundcar bring her from home, or even beam directly in to her office as she did during emergencies, but unless it was raining she preferred to get off the monorail one stop early and walk to work, even on a day like today. If she had to be stuck behind that desk all day, at least she could start with a morning walk. It kept her young.

In retrospect, whoever sent the messenger must have known even that much about her. And if the messenger had been anything other than a messenger—an assassin perhaps, or even someone who thought kidnaping the head of Starfleet Intelligence might affect the balance of power on any number of worlds—Uhura shuddered to think. She would never know how the messenger got through the Academy's security cordon, which was supposed to be one of the best on the planet.

The fog played tricks with sound. Footsteps and voices might sound close but in fact belong to those few cadets and instructors who had braved the weather and were passing between buildings on the far side of the quadrangle. At the same time, nearby sounds were muffled, hard to distinguish. The messenger made no sound, but simply fell into step beside her.

"You are Admiral Uhura." The voice was female and seemed young. The words were in carefully spoken Standard, with only a trace of some offworld inflection. The figure, swathed in a hooded Vulcan-style travel cloak, was no taller than Uhura herself, who only made people think she was tall by the way she carried herself. "I bring you a message from Romulus."

As Uhura turned, startled, a pair of jade-green eyes beneath the characteristic dark upswept brows met her own. A delicate face with a wide, expressive mouth, a smattering of freckles across a high-bridged nose, a stray lock of chestnut hair fallen across her brow, were all that showed beneath the hood. The first impression was of a child playing dress-up. Nevertheless, Uhura felt the hair on the back of her neck prickle and found herself thinking of phasers.

A Romulan? On Earth, after all this time? And here on the grounds of the Academy without anyone stopping her?

"Who are you?" was all Uhura could think of to say, in a voice much calmer than she felt.

"Pandora's box," the messenger said.

It was a code spoken by another in a time long ago, and Uhura decided to trust her.

* * *

"Pandora's box?" a very young Romulan subaltern named Cretak had repeated Uhura's words. "What an interesting expression. What does it mean?"

She and Uhura had met under unusual circumstances at a place called Camp Khitomer, where an interstellar peace conference had almost been derailed by a handful of militarists from the three major powers plotting to kill the Federation president.

"It's from an old story about a woman to whom the gods entrusted a beautiful box, but with instructions never to open it," Uhura explained. "Naturally, her curiosity got the better of her and she opened the box, letting all the evils inside escape into the world. But when in her despair she glanced into what she thought was an empty box, she found that a priceless jewel still lay within. That jewel was hope."

Cretak tilted her head like a bird, considering this. "A moral, no doubt. There are many such tales in my culture as well."

"Which shows we're more alike than different," Uhura suggested.

For the first time, the young Romulan smiled. "If only it were that simple!"

In the intervening years, Khitomer itself had been left a smoking ruin following a Romulan attack, for the usual reasons Romulans and Klingons carried on their multigenerational antagonisms: honor, as well as an inflexible attitude of absolute superiority, from each toward the other. As for the Romulans and the Federation, there was Tomed, always Tomed. Yet though their governments might posture and throw stones or, more recently, ignore each other's existence, two resourceful individuals could get messages through the static if the need were great enough.

"From across the parsecs and across the years, I send my greetings," the message began, composed in the traditionally flowery language of the Romulan court but, once

Uhura and the messenger were ensconced in her office, delivered in Earth Standard. No need to translate from any of the Romulan languages, much less to decode it. Considering the source of the message and its means of delivery, Uhura was surprised, to say the least, but only for a moment. Cretak was, above all else, resourceful. There had been other third-party messages down the decades, but none so direct as this one.

"With satisfaction I report that I am well, and hope that you are also. I have, as much as possible in this turbulent weather with its recent storms—" A reference to the Neutral Zone, and to the supposedly ironclad silence between the Federation and the Empire since Tomed. "—followed your career with much interest, and wish you continued success . . ."

Even if my actions sometimes work against your own people, Cretak? Uhura wondered, holding up one hand to stop the message while she digested this much of it. *No, let's be clear: What I and my operatives do is not against any people, but is a means of checking and balancing those who would presume to make decisions in their name. Decisions like Tomed and Narendra III and a hundred lesser incursions that are enacted "for the good of the Romulan people," meaning the good of those who stay in power by feeding off the fear of the populace, creating imaginary enemies to keep the war machinery in motion. My goal is to sniff out those plots in either Empire or even among my own kind before they gather momentum, and nip them in the bud.*

I warned Command about Narendra III but, alas, not in time to save the Enterprise. *If Cretak, who travels the corridors of the Romulan Senate and knows things none of my operatives can get near without losing their lives, sends me a message by way of a living messenger, it's important.*

"Go on," she told the messenger.

"I could wish that this were merely a social call, but the

very form my message has taken may suggest to you that it is in fact a matter of some urgency."

Again Uhura stopped the message and studied the messenger.

"How much of this do you understand?" she asked carefully in Romulan.

"Nothing, Lady," the messenger replied in the same tongue, masking any surprise at hearing her own language spoken by a human. "I do not understand your language. I only repeat what I have been told."

"Told to you by Cretak," Uhura prompted her. She could see the young woman's eyes flicker, as if she were searching the corners of the room for hidden meanings. No doubt she had been told only to repeat her message, and given no further instructions, not even any indication of what was to become of her once the message was delivered. Uhura remembered something else she had learned about Romulans, something which any good Federation spy ought to be mindful of as well. Romulans don't trust walls. Nor, even in the office of the head of Starfleet Intelligence, should they.

She had made a point of bringing the girl to her office initially, to make certain she hadn't brought company, and so that the security sensors could scan her for concealed weapons or listening devices. Now that she was determined to be "clean" and acting alone, she could safely be moved elsewhere.

Uhura got up from her desk and surveyed the grounds below her window. As she'd anticipated, the fog had burned off and the day was radiant. Cretak's messenger had had enough faith in her to allow herself to be brought indoors for the preliminaries, but now it was time for a change of venue.

"It's a beautiful day, and I need some air," Uhura said. "Walk with me."

The young woman hesitated. Did she think she was going to be imprisoned, even executed, once she had delivered the core of her message?

"Sometimes the walls have ears," Uhura suggested.

"Indeed," the Romulan said, and instinctively pulled the hood of her travel cloak up over her own.

"You know my name," Uhura began after they'd walked in silence for a while. "May I know yours?"

"Zetha," she replied at once.

"Zetha," Uhura repeated. "That's your family name?"

"It is my name," the young woman said tautly. "I was born in Ki Baratan. I have no family."

And that, Uhura realized, was all she would get out of her. But it told her a great deal. Romulan society was built on kinship lines. A Romulan without family had no identity, and legally did not exist.

"I see," Uhura said. They were in a remote part of the grounds few frequented. A pity really, since it was some of Boothby's best work. Dewdrops sparkled on the glossy leaves of the gardenias, and a maze garden of carefully trimmed yews and azaleas beckoned to them, but Uhura deliberately kept them out in the open, amid the groundcovers and low-growing flowerbeds, so that Zetha could see they were not being followed.

Which was not to say they couldn't have been monitored from across the quadrangle or across the sector, Uhura thought, mindful of some of the equipment her field agents and their Romulan counterparts had at their disposal, which could listen through fortress walls or starship bulkheads or photograph the rank pips on a subcommander's uniform from a system away as he strolled the streets of the Capital on market day, but the gesture was necessary.

And if the occasional passing cadet noticed the two in conversation, they made nothing of it. Tomed had happened decades before any of these youngsters was born. Even the battle simulators were no longer programmed for Romulan scenarios, which Uhura personally thought was a mistake.

On any Federation planet, someone like Zetha would be taken for a Vulcan, no questions asked.

Out of the corner of her eye, Uhura watched her young charge react to the weather and her surroundings. San Francisco had rewarded them with one of its better sunny days, and the girl had lowered the hood of her cloak and turned her face up to the sun like a flower, breathing deeply of the warm, scented air. But even then she did not relax. She watched and listened, absorbing everything.

No, not a child playing dress-up, Uhura decided, studying the grimness of the mouth, the stubborn set of the chin, but a child who never had time to be a child. It had occurred to her from the outset, code words or no, that Zetha might not have been sent by Cretak at all. What she learned about her in the next few hours would be vital in deciding that.

She had already noted several things. Zetha lacked the pronounced upswept brow ridges that so many Romulans, including Cretak, possessed. But there were as many Romulans, Uhura thought, mindful of Charvanek and Tal and the smarmy, double-dealing Nanclus, who did not. She also wore her hair longer than the rather unflattering unisex pageboy that the Romulan military, at least, seemed to favor. Her movements were quick, wary, catlike, as if she were accustomed to always being on guard; the impression, to Uhura's experienced eye, was that this was not just a result of training, it was hard-won and from life.

She would submit her young charge to a more formal debriefing after this, but for now, a walk in the garden would win her confidence and make it easier for her to talk.

"So it's about an illness," Uhura said carefully. "Something that resembles the Gnawing, which once killed half your people. How did your . . . employer . . . get this information?"

*   *   *

"Our own doctors cannot analyze this, cousin," Taymor told Cretak, his breath coming short. "Or else they will not. You know the situation."

"Of course," Cretak said. "If your governor decides to spend the medical budget on new uniforms for his personal guard, he tells the people that suffering is good for the soul. In the larger scheme the Praetor buys warbirds, and our medical technology remains primitive. To suggest he do otherwise is deemed disloyal. You do not look well, cousin."

"I am not, Kimora. Those who contract this die within days. I'm at the country house, and I've sent the servants away. I wanted to tell you while I was still coherent. I have already sent you the evidence, in the diplomatic pouch so it will not be scanned or irradiated. You'll get it on the next incoming courier. It's all I can do."

Cretak struggled to keep her distress from showing on her face. In childhood she and Taymor had been as close as siblings. To think that she would never see him again . . . she placed her hand on the screen beside the image of his face, as if that would offer him comfort.

"Who else, Taymor? Kaitek, the children—?"

"So far, no. I am apparently the only one from my family so affected. Which is why I say this smacks of something unnatural. The Gnawing is legend, two thousand years old and, with what we know now, curable. But this . . . this is evil . . ." Taymor was overcome by a paroxysm of coughing. There were flecks of green on his lips when he could speak again. "All my love, cousin. Farewell . . ."

Cretak stared at the blank screen in despair.

"She did not tell me that, Lady," Zetha replied, remembering her dignity and turning her face away from the sun and back toward her questioner. "Only sent me to tell you what she knows."

"So I'm to accept her word, from your mouth, that an ancient illness which once killed almost half the Romulan people has been reawakened in a form that kills everyone it affects, and which may be artificially created?"

"Not my word, Lady," Zetha reached her small hands inside her cloak and took a chain from around her neck, "but this."

"Hold out your hand," Cretak had said abruptly, holding something in both of her own.

Instinct said *don't*, but Zetha did anyway. The object in question was a locket on an intricate chain, a death locket. She had seen such in the display windows of the pawnshops on Jenorex Street when times were hard, cleverly disguised as medallions bearing a family crest, but with a secret compartment in the back to hold some relic of the deceased, most likely a lock of hair, sometimes braided like a bracelet. Some of these lockets were quite ornate, crusted with gemstones, others unadorned but intricately wrought, their value in the workmanship. This was one of the latter.

"Put it on," Cretak instructed her in the same cool tone. "Be careful with it."

Poisoned? Zetha wondered. *Or, more likely, wired, fitted with a small transceiver that will record my every sound, every move.* Nevertheless, something about the strength of this woman, her self-confidence, made her obey. Where with the Lord she had questioned everything, with Cretak she obeyed.

"It stays with you until you arrive where I am sending you. You give it to one person and one person only. No subordinates, no intermediaries, no helpful fellow travelers. If anything happens to keep you from this person, that object goes with you, day and night, until death do you part. If you open it you will die, and I will instruct you in what to say when you deliver it so that it is not opened too soon. If you are in harm's way and know you are about to die, you destroy it, and I will tell you how. Any questions?"

"I am to tell you not to open it except within a medical steri-field," Zetha said now, in the careful singsong she adapted when reciting the words Cretak had taught her. "It contains biomedical material from those who have died, which may still be highly contagious."

The locket was beautiful, almost as big as the palm of Uhura's hand, but the touch of the cold metal coupled with Zetha's words about contagion made her hand tingle, and she had to suppress an urge to fling the object into the bushes as if it were a scorpion. She waited for common sense to overcome fear, then enfolded the locket in her fingers, her mind racing.

Operational triage: What to do first. Get this to Medical at once. Entrust it to Dr. Crusher, with instructions. Attempt to verify everything she'd just heard by contacting her Listeners on the other side. And then—

And then figure out what she was going to do with Pandora's box now that she'd delivered her message that there are evils loose between the stars, and the head of Starfleet Intelligence must attempt to stop them. Uhura took a deep breath and steadied herself.

"Are you hungry?" she asked Zetha.

Ravenous would have been a better word. Uhura and Lieutenant Tuvok watched from behind the mirror wall as Zetha polished off a meal that would have done a longshoreman proud, then went back to the replicator for seconds.

"What do you make of her, Mr. Tuvok?" Uhura asked quietly, always interested in the Vulcan perspective. Early in his Starfleet career, Tuvok had done some undercover work for Intelligence, and Uhura was familiar with his credentials. He had also come to her with Hikaru Sulu's highest recommendation, and that was worth its weight in latinum. Examining his record since his return to Starfleet, Uhura could see that even his long leave of absence to pursue *Kolinahr* had not dulled his skills or tarnished his loyalty. He would be a strong asset for her team.

Tuvok canted his head slightly as Vulcans did when they were studying something, his usual seriousness deepening into a slight frown.

"Female vulcanoid, age approximately twenty Earth years. Height approximately 1.6 meters, weight approximately forty-eight kilos. Color of eyes, green, color of hair, dark brown, distinguishing marks, none apparent . . ."

Was it only Uhura's imagination that as Tuvok spoke, the young woman stopped shoveling food in with both hands and raised her head imperceptibly, as if she sensed another, and nonhuman, presence? There was no question she had known at once that the mirror wasn't just a mirror, and that she was being observed from the other side. But did she also sense by whom? *No*, Uhura thought. *That much I'm imagining.*

"Freckles," she said when Tuvok was done, watching Zetha finish her second helping and, with a sleight of hand almost too quick to see, secrete an apple and two uneaten spring rolls in a pocket of her travel cloak against future contingencies, conditioning, perhaps, from not always knowing where her next meal was coming from. "Surely you noticed the freckles. And she's built like a Balanchine dancer."

She could see Tuvok searching his memory for the reference and coming up blank. Vulcans, she knew, hated to admit they didn't know something.

"I am not familiar with the reference," he said at last, grudgingly.

"Nor should you be, Lieutenant. George Balanchine was a ballet master on Earth a few centuries ago. He believed the perfect female body for the dance was one that was exactly the height and weight you described, but with legs proportionately longer than the torso. Balanchine would have adored this one."

"Indeed."

"But you said 'vulcanoid,' not Romulan."

"Is she Romulan, Admiral?"

"I'm asking you."

"Uncertain merely on appearance. If I could engage her in conversation, I might be able to learn more. A mind-meld, of course, would ascertain her identity definitively."

"I doubt the latter will be necessary," Uhura said, moving away from the mirror wall and indicating that Tuvok should do the same. "But she came to me from the other side of the Zone, and the person who sent her used the code words 'Pandora's box.' "

This was a reference Tuvok recognized. "Indeed?"

"I'm not saying she's a security risk, but I'm asking you to debrief her with your usual thoroughness, and take her in hand for the course of this mission. Not so that it's obvious, but—"

"Understood. Now, as to the nature of the mission—?"

Uhura motioned him out of the anteroom and let the door lock behind them. "In my office," she said.

She offered him coffee, real brewed arabica, not synthe-sized, ground fresh every morning from beans grown on the slopes of Mount Kenya, not far from her grandparents' sum-mer house. Tuvok accepted, tasted, nodded appreciatively. Uhura put her own cup down and got to the point.

"Tell me what you know about something the Romulans call the Gnawing."

"An ancient illness," Tuvok said carefully. Vulcans were always careful in addressing anything to do with their distant siblings and the reasons for their separation. "Rumored to have arisen among those who chose to leave Vulcan at the time of the Sundering. I know no more than that."

"It killed upwards of fifty percent of those who settled on Romulus," Uhura told him quietly.

"Indeed?" Tuvok's eyebrow went up. He seemed about to question the number, but decided against it. "Nevertheless, to my knowledge, it is an ancient illness. There have been no serious outbreaks since the Sundering."

"There are now," Uhura said.

Chapter 3

History, it is said, is written by the victors. But what of a war where there is no victor? Who writes the history then?

The pundits refer to the split between Vulcan and Romulan, between the followers of Surak and those who could not accept his teaching, as the Sundering. As if it were as quick and clean as an amicable divorce, the two parties deciding that, no longer having anything in common, it was time for them to part. Or, perhaps more likely from the Vulcan perspective, as if severing a diseased limb from a healthy body and casting it aside.

It is no dishonor to the memory of Surak to say that he and his philosophy were less than perfect. And it is a lesson of more than one planet's history that even the most inspired of reformers cannot foresee all possible long-term outcomes of their reforms.

Outworlders know of Vulcan only what Vulcans wish them to know. Vulcans speak in lofty phrases of a history "shrouded in antiquity . . . savage, even by Earth standards," and few who are not Vulcan presume to question them further, grateful perhaps that beings of such intellect and physical strength—and telepaths at that—have chosen to suppress all that potential for violence beneath a veneer of logic and civilization. Easier to assume that those who could not tolerate Surak's reforms simply boarded their ships without a glance back and quietly, if bitterly, left the planet.

But did they go all at once or over decades, years, generations? Was there only a handful of ships, or did vast armadas fill the skies above the arid and unforgiving mother world? Did all who went go willingly, or were some forced into exile, and by what means? Were families, friends, lovers torn apart?

And what of those who stayed behind? Did they buy the official story, that both sides would be the better for it, that it was not an end but a beginning? Or did some, even as the ships departed, too late, have second thoughts?

Postulate a civilization that had spaceflight technology millennia before humans did, but almost lost it all to the terrible violence that led to the rise of Surak. Rebuilding from a fragmented culture—the shattered statues at Gol speak eloquently in their silence, their offspring extant in the masked and ax-wielding entourage that accompanies every traditional Vulcan marriage ceremony—surely they vowed to employ whatever means necessary to guarantee that such destruction would never occur again.

Beware of those who think and speak in absolutes. "Never" is a very long time, and at what cost? The *ahn-woon* and the *lirpa* remain. Vulcans may murmur of ritual and custom, but small wonder so few outworlders are invited to the wedding. The scowling, bare-chested guards with their faces obscured by beaklike masks are impossible to ignore, difficult to explain.

Were they present at the departure as well, these guards, ranks of armed and uncompromising sentries, making certain everyone who was meant to get onboard the ships of the Sundering did so, with no opportunity to turn back? It is a thing no outworlder may know.

Because the question remains: If the Sundering was amicable, by mutual agreement, why was all communication severed once the ships were gone? Why were the distant siblings sent off into the void and never heard from again? Was it their choice to turn their faces from the mother world and never look back? Or were they so instructed?

There is an obscure novel of the last century, written by a non-Vulcan, which purports that the ships of the Sundering were fitted with no means of communication beyond simple short-range radio for ship-to-ship communication. Some sources say they lacked even that. Yet given the resourcefulness of the Vulcan mind, could they not have jury-rigged something with which to communicate long-range, back to the world they had departed?

Unless they had been forbidden to do so. Or any attempt to communicate with anyone back on Vulcan was jammed at the source.

In any event, the silence was absolute, and the Sundered, whether over the course of months or generations, whether free and clear to navigate or beset by ion storms, food shortages, hostility from those whose space they blundered into, internecine squabbles, ended their journey on Romulus.

Did all of the Sundered get that far? Did some perish along the way? Did some venture off in other directions, find other worlds, or disappear without a trace? This can only be conjectured. What is known for certain is that those who remained on Vulcan saw the ships off into the sky, returned to their houses, and went about their lives under the aegis of logic, a logic that did not dwell overmuch on what might have been.

Perhaps they spoke of those who had departed, perhaps not. But it is interesting that such a characteristically curious people were so remarkably incurious about what might have happened to their distant brothers in the centuries between. Was the silence, indeed, absolute, or did their ships sometimes pass in the night? Or if, when Romulus and Earth were at war, the Vulcans looked down their noses when asked and replied, "We don't know who these people are," was it at least partly true?

* * *

What drove the distant siblings away? Perhaps nothing more than fear of the monolithic society Surak's teachings would inspire. They knew the Vulcan mind. Did they fear that, having decided to embrace logic, Vulcan would become some great monochrome sand-colored boredom, which they could not abide?

For how was one to define emotion against logic? Were only the "negative" emotions like anger and sorrow included in the roster of what it was now necessary to suppress, or were all emotions suspect, dangerous, in need of suppression? And was the individual to be trusted to take charge of her own emotions, or would there be outside enforcement, thought police patrolling the streets searching for violations, coworkers spying on their colleagues, children on their parents?

What about literature, art, music? Who was to decide whether a piece of music was "logical," a painting "emotional"? Or were those forms to fall under blanket interdict as well? As it turned out, they did not, but how were the early dissidents to know? The definition of what was deemed "illogical" was too broad, and thereby too narrow, for some to bear.

Humans who suppress all emotion become either mystical or mad. Had the Sundered tried the way of logic at first but, seeing too many of their fellows fall to madness, decided it was better to leave? Was there nowhere on the world that they could live in peace? Whose idea was it to pack themselves off on a trajectory to nowhere, and forever?

Doubtless there are histories on Romulus, at least, which record that part, but they are not accessible to the average citizen. And if the Vulcans knew, they were not sharing. "Lost when the ships were lost," is the official story even today.

Whereas the history of life on Romulus seems to have begun, and almost ended, with the Gnawing.

* * *

There are plenty of brave little children's stories about the early settlers in their hand-me-down clothing who stood on a rise overlooking a valley burgeoning with green and growing things beneath the light of a gentler sun, the stars of a different sky. The artwork accompanying these stories is often quite evocative.

The stories tell of the brave pioneers using the hulls of their ships as shelters from the too-frequent rains on their strange new world as they learned to forage the native materials to build rudimentary housing and supplement their dwindling food supply. Some of the teaching materials deemed acceptable for adolescent readers are a little darker, featuring epic struggles with native predators, unforeseeably indigestible plants, lightning and floods and deadly windstorms, through all of which, of course, the Indomitable Spirit of the Romulan People inevitably triumphed, leading naturally to the Dawn of the People's Empire. But if one reads carefully, one notices a considerable gap of years between those early days and the ascendancy of that almighty Empire.

That gap is not spoken of. It holds too many horrors. Too many things went wrong.

There was the climate, for starters. Why did they choose to settle here, when it was so different from the world they'd known? Did they choose, or was it chosen for them? Had they run out of fuel or gone off course, had their instruments told them this was the only habitable world in their path and they had best make do? Was there damage from the Jeltorai asteroid belt that meant they had to make landfall, and soon?

There is some suggestion that they didn't even know at first that there were twin worlds. Perhaps they landed here and thought it was all there was. Was there debate or even revolt, one group who said "We will land here," who simply shouted louder than the ones who said "But what about the weather"? If it was recorded anywhere, no one knew where to find it.

Where Vulcan was hot and dry and rain was such a rarity that, even in their logic, Vulcans would stop what they were doing whenever it fell to go outdoors and marvel at it (apparently, as more than one human wag had put it, not having sense enough to come in out of the rain), it rained overmuch on most of this new world for the well-being of those whose origins were desert.

There were doubtless some among the early settlers who rejoiced in pointing out the benefits—a longer growing season, no need for irrigation, no food shortages regardless of how their population increased. It had not occurred to them that lungs evolved over millions of years for the desert might find breathing difficult in a place where the weather alternated between hot and humid and cold and damp. It was difficult to grow food and build cities or even walk about when you were battling fungal infections, skin rashes, and airborne allergens, and felt most of the time as if you were drowning. Trudging about under an alien sun or, more often, finding it obscured by ominous cloud cover, wiping runny noses and scratching dermatoses, few noticed the symptoms of the Gnawing, until it was too late.

First came the headache and shortness of breath, followed by an annoying dry cough and loss of appetite. Light and sound became painful, clothing chafed the skin. There was dizziness, sometimes double vision, always chills and fever. Even the strongest were unable to work or think or even stay on their feet; they took to their beds and tried what cures they knew, but nothing worked.

The cough became persistent but still nonproductive, meaning it did not free the throat or lungs of whatever was attacking them. As the lung tissue broke down, some coughed up blood. They were the lucky ones. Eventually their lungs would fill with fluid and they would slowly drown, spared the symptoms of the later stages.

Those whom the cough didn't kill faced nausea, vomiting, agonizing joint pain, a rigidity in the muscles and the spine that made it impossible to bend, to turn the head. Contemporary physicians described some victims' flesh as literally stiffening to the consistency of wood.

By now the fever was so high it boiled the brain; victims babbled and raved, had to be tied down to keep from harming themselves or others, assuming they had not been abandoned by those fearing the contagion themselves. Some died then, others when the lymph nodes in their necks enlarged so greatly that their throats closed and they strangled, all this within a day or two of the first symptoms. Those who survived beyond this faced the worst of all: the rash.

It wasn't really a rash, but the pooling of blood beneath the skin, signifying that the capillaries were disintegrating, internal organs liquefying. By then the only hope was for death, and soon.

Worst of all was the solitude. The rudimentary clinics the settlers had been able to set up before the illness struck were soon filled to overflowing, with medical staff dying almost as quickly as their patients. Those stricken in their homes were abandoned there; no one wanted to risk contamination. Whole families were sometimes sealed up in their houses, the living along with the dying and the dead. Corpses were dumped in common graves until there was no one left with the strength to bury them; the last of the dead were heaped up and burned or left to the scavengers where they lay.

When it was over, one out of every two healthy adults had died. The incidence of death among infants, children, elders, and the sickly was never accurately measured. Later statisticians estimated that if fewer than one hundred more of the entire population had died, the Sundered would have gone extinct, lacking enough viable members to breed a new generation.

When it was over, it was referred to simply as the Gnawing, a demon which inhabited the body and consumed it from within. Those few who survived it passed like wraiths among the healthy, possessed of a hunger that could never be satisfied. No matter how much they ate, they never recovered the strength and muscle mass lost to the fight against the disease.

The etiology was eventually traced to a bacillus native to the soil of Romulus whose spores, like those of tetanus on Earth, could lie dormant, encapsulated, surviving extremes of temperature in the driest soils for a century or more, until activated. Had the simple act of turning over the soil to plant crops disturbed them? Or was it that combined with the amount of wind and rain that year, the temperature, the angle of the sun, the position of the planet in its orbit, evil spirits, the wrath of unknown, offended gods?

And once disturbed, infiltrating the lungs of the farmer in his field, absently rubbed into a minor cut on the hand of a clerk in the village, ingested by an infant crawling along the floor, how did it become contagious, passing from host to host?

Perhaps if they had studied this more closely, those early Romulans might not have suffered from the fear of the thing millennia later. But once the Gnawing was over and the last victim disposed of, a kind of societal amnesia took hold. No one took the trouble to develop a cure, much less a vaccine, no one followed up on the anecdotal realization that some very few of their number were immune, and could pass among the suffering without so much as a cough.

When, down the centuries, an occasional outbreak was reported in a rural area, usually among school-age children, antibiotics were administered, and no one died. Grateful for that, the average Romulan followed the news report and then moved on, unaware.

Unaware that the parent bacteria could under certain circumstances mutate into a virus. Unaware that that virus could mutate further and integrate itself into a survivor's

DNA. Unaware that that DNA had further mutated down the millennia so that some descendants were immune, carriers of something that might by now be benign, or not.

Some precautions were taken. Whenever new plots of land were cleared for farming they were first examined for the bacillus which, mysteriously, could no longer be found. Samples of the original organism were kept in stasis in medical facilities in the most secure locations, just in case. In case of what, no one dared say.

The Gnawing is not written in the children's stories, but every child knows it as they know their own fingerprints, the color of their eyes, the caste they were born to. It isn't just a matter of hearing it from the adults ("Eat up all your *viinerine*, there's a good child; if you don't eat, you won't be strong, and you might catch the Gnawing"); it is simply known. It is in great measure what makes Romulans what they are.

Some Earth historians insist that the Renaissance in Europe could never have occurred without the Black Death to reduce the population ahead of it. No telling on how many other worlds something similar might be true.

Those who survived the Gnawing beheld the universe with a jaundiced view in more ways than one. The disease had atrophied the nictitating membrane which had protected their eyes from solar flares on Vulcan, and literally changed the way they looked at color. To the alien eye, Romulan cities seem gray, Romulan clothing drab. Among the genes the virus altered were those governing visual perception. Where a human or Cardassian might see gray, Romulans now saw many colors, which meant that bright colors often disturbed them. Only certain shades of red could soothe, not unexpected for a species whose blood was green.

As for the psychological impact of all of this, if the survivors were xenophobic, could they be blamed? Thereafter anything which approached from the outside might be construed as an attack. When there is no off-switch for the fight-or-flight mechanism, one becomes a Romulan.

Other species found them arrogant. Were they not entitled? Take a Vulcan's intellect and send it into exile, alone in its own company for however long, set it down on a world entirely different than anything it has heretofore known. Allow it to barely establish itself on its new world, only to be all but buried alive in corpses. Task such a species with a sickness, seemingly out of nowhere, which kills every second person it touches, and you frighten it, humble it, grind its face in the dust. When the sickness passes, those who remain, the taste of dust in their mouths, the stench of death in their nostrils, will never be the same.

Now observe as these people burn their dead and shake off the ashes and establish a civilization, only to find themselves bracketed by the rapacity of Klingons on one side and the sloppiness that is humanity on the other, and dare call it arrogant? Or only Romulan?

"There are really only two kinds of Romulan, you know," Pardek told Cretak once, in one of his frequent avuncular teaching moods. She was very young then, and one of his newest aides, eager to please him in whatever way she could. Pardek had been married seemingly forever even then, so it wasn't a matter of that. He was one of those men who cherished power above all else, even wealth and sex. What he really needed was a pair of young, unspoiled ears to listen to him.

"Truly, Lord?" Cretak had responded, humoring him, but also curious. "And what are they?"

"There are those who like things just the way they are and will stop at nothing to keep them that way, and those who understand that change is the natural order of the universe, and one must change with it."

"I see," she said, amused at the very idea that it could be so simple. "And which are you?"

"Why, the latter, of course! I am a simple man, Cretak, so lacking in guile it's a wonder I ever made it into politics. I shift with the tides and follow the times, always. There is no mystery to me at all. But you, you are the mystery. Which kind of Romulan are you?"

She didn't even have to think of an answer. "I believe I am as committed to growth and change as you are, Lord."

Pardek had smiled indulgently. "Ah, but you're young yet. We will see if age and experience have their way with you."

Her conversation with Pardek was still fresh in Cretak's mind a few mornings later when she awoke beside Koval.

She propped herself up on one elbow and studied his face. He was feigning sleep, but she knew him well enough by now to tell it was only pretense. He was so seldom himself, it was safer to assume he was always pretending.

He has a weak chin, was her first thought. *Why did I never notice this before? Then again, even the kindest of my kin say my jaw's too strong. If we had had children, would they have favored him or me or something halfway between?*

The match would have been an acceptable one. She and Koval were of the same caste, children of the intellectual and military families who made up the outer circle that protected the inner circle of the imperial court and who, of course, aspired by either marriage or accomplishment to be permitted into that inner circle someday. When and how had their society ossified into these rigid little boxes? Vulcan society, while nominally a meritocracy, also had its subtle class distinctions; it was a given that the old, propertied families wielded most of the true power. But Romulan society had subdivided into castes within castes, each ringed about with customs, laws, and taboos which made it all but impossible to escape from one into another.

Was this, too, an outcome of the Gnawing? Had the Sundered begun as a communal entity, with everything shared equally, or had they brought the concept of the Old Families with them from Vulcan? And with half their number gone, did the wealth shift to the survivors? Did they, anticipating a future Gnawing, build shields and fences of class and caste around their possessions, so that even if they died, their offspring would be safe?

Lost to the mists of time and revisionist history. No way of knowing in the here and now.

In the event, Koval and Cretak had recognized each other, at least by type, before they ever met. Though they came from different sectors, they were of the same caste, and had gone to the same sort of exclusive schools, studied the same subjects, been imbued with the same familial and societal expectations designed to shape them into good little apparatchiks in the service of the Empire, and both had followed form, each in their own way.

Their affair was discreet, and might have led to marriage, but after the initial blush of passion, it had become ordinary, predictable. The first thing to go had been anything resembling real conversation, and now Cretak understood why.

Koval was one kind of Romulan; she was another. He had accepted his role by moving smartly from his caste's mandatory military duty into a low-level position with intelligence, and slowly climbed the ladder, stepping on hands or necks as necessary, but always carefully. Now that he was halfway up that ladder, it was said behind his back that Koval didn't so much serve the Tal Shiar as much as it served him.

Most Romulans looked sideways and whispered whenever they said the words *Tal Shiar*. It could accurately be said that no one, not even the Emperor himself, for whom the organization was named, was safe from them, and there was no Romulan living whose life had not been touched by them, who did not have a relative or sometimes an entire branch of the family gone missing in the night, all their possessions confiscated. Everyone knew of former prisoners who had returned from detention in distant places with hollow eyes, silenced voices, empty souls, looking like nothing so much as survivors of the Gnawing.

To actually want to be a part of that . . . Cretak shivered, and not only because the room was cold. Koval was one of those who would do anything, to anyone, at any cost, to preserve the status quo and his place in it.

Has he ever been offworld? Cretak wondered, still studying that weak-chinned face. *His masters have probably sent him on all sorts of secret missions that I would never know about, even if we wed. What kind of relationship would that be?*

His breathing was far too regular to be natural. Was he watching her under his eyelids? Difficult to tell. His eyes were so small, so hidden behind over-large eyelids and prominent brow ridges that it was hard to tell what he was looking at even when he was awake, something his employers no doubt cherished in him.

Cretak had been to other worlds in Pardek's train. Those outside the Empire assumed that Romulans only interacted with Romulans, that all their worlds were the same, but nothing could be further from the truth. The Empire might not have the multiplicity of species that comprised the Federation, but there were wide variations in race, language, culture, technology. Ironically, the homeworld, ruled by suspicion and the assumption that everyone was watching everyone else, was backward in comparison to some. It was hard to be innovative when you were always being monitored, hard to keep the machinery repaired when the budget went first to the military.

The constant state of war, with others and with the paranoia within themselves, was to blame. Even a simple letter to a friend, a stray remark to a family member, could be read as seditious. Progress does not flourish in an atmosphere of dread. There was so much more they could become, if only they could set aside their fear.

Had Koval ever harbored thoughts like these? Could he see beyond his own nose, or did he truly subscribe to the credo that the Romulans had created the perfect state and simply look no farther?

Cretak was not looking at him now, but at the view beyond the gauzy curtains. It was the cold season, the trees bare, the sky as gray as the city they had left behind. They were staying at one of his family's houses, a grand old multi-roomed estate complete with servants in one of the better suburbs. Still, grand as it was, it was cold.

Sensing that her attention was no longer focused on him, Koval at last opened his eyes.

"You're pensive," he said.

"I was thinking of futility," she answered.

"A suitable topic for a winter's morning. It must be the weather. I will have one of the servants build a fire. That should perk you up."

"Do you know how many we could feed and clothe and educate if we weren't always at war?" Cretak said with sudden passion, ignoring his desultory attempts to placate her, sitting up abruptly but keeping the coverlet wrapped around herself, and not only against the cold.

"Why would we want to do that?" Koval wondered indolently, suppressing a yawn. "They'd only breed that much faster." He stretched and seemed about to reach out for her, but changed his mind.

Was he always this shallow? Cretak wondered. *Why have I only now noticed that, too?* She rose from the bed, her back to him, and began to dress.

"Where are you going?" Koval asked, suppressing a second yawn.

"Away" was all she said, terminating the relationship with no more fanfare than that.

As if she could ever truly have gotten away, she thought ruefully a lifetime later. For all the millions of them streaming through the streets of the Capital, they of the blood could not avoid bumping elbows, and more than once had she felt Koval's eyes on her in public places. Should she have remained in his bed a little longer, to learn a little more of him? All she really knew was that she did not trust him, and that is far too little to know about Koval!

"I am no medical expert, Admiral," Tuvok said gravely, studying the locket Uhura had given him, "but it is my understanding that it is not unusual for illnesses once believed eradicated to recur decades, even centuries later. However, with the exception of Rigelian fever, I know of no such organism that crosses human/vulcanoid bloodlines. Nor am I aware of any disease which kills everyone who contracts it."

"And if you were thinking like a spy . . ." Uhura suggested, letting him finish the thought.

"One logical explanation might be that this disease had been deliberately created. But by whom, and why?"

"Exactly what it's our job to find out. For security reasons, I'd like you to deliver this to Dr. Crusher personally. Then have a chat with our little friend."

Tuvok studied the locket gravely. " 'Security reasons,' Admiral? Even on the grounds of the Academy?"

Uhura made a wry face. "Yes, I know. It's made it all the way from Ki Baratan to here untampered with, but I can't help thinking, now that it's my responsibility . . ."

"Understood," Tuvok said.

Chapter 4

"This is not intended to be a formal interrogation," Tuvok began. "Merely an attempt to establish the veracity of the information you have given us."

"Of course," Zetha said in a tone which suggested she believed just the opposite. The tone was not lost on Tuvok.

The disciplines of *Kolinahr*, even unfinished as Tuvok's had been, left resonances. While all Vulcans were touch telepaths, he had learned to augment his innate skills to such a degree that often touch was not needed. In addition, his years among humans had instructed him in the nuances of body language. The angle of a head, the tension in a spine, the nervousness of a gesture, a dilation or contraction of the pupils, changes in respiration, pulse, body heat, all told their tales. The ability to read them was a vital part of his armamentarium as scientist, security officer and, where necessary, interrogator.

Feral child, was his first thought, watching Zetha once more through the mirror wall. If she was in fact a trained intelligence operative, she was relatively inexperienced. Or very, very good.

The room Uhura had consigned to her was windowless and secured from the outside but, in all other respects, as comfortable and well-appointed as an officer's billet aboard a starship, complete with a sleeping alcove, a replicator, sanitary facilities, a library computer, even a wardrobe containing several changes of clothing in the correct size.

Tuvok noted, however, that having satisfied her hunger with several trips to the replicator, Zetha seemed content to leave the other amenities untouched, and to wait until someone told her what to do next, however long that might take. In the meantime, she had curled up in one of the overstuffed chairs with her feet tucked under her, and was devouring matter of a different sort, running several information programs on the computer simultaneously.

No doubt, Tuvok thought, she realized that everything she was reading could be monitored, and attempts to access sensitive materials would be blocked. His supposition was confirmed when, seeing him in the doorway, Zetha sat up and put her feet on the floor like a child interrupted at her homework, but made no attempt to hide what was on the screen. Tuvok heard the drone of a basic Romulan/Standard language program in the background.

"A wise choice," he commended her in Romulan. "Learning our language will facilitate your time with us."

"You're a Vulcan," she responded by not responding. "How do I silence this thing without losing what I'm reading?"

"Computer, mute program," Tuvok said, and it did.

" 'Computer, mute program,' " Zetha mimicked him, almost perfectly.

Tuvok watched her process a multitude of impressions, not least of which was the surprise of meeting her first Vulcan, without any overt reaction, though he detected an increase in her pulse and respiration.

"I am Tuvok," he said. "Admiral Uhura has asked me to make certain you are comfortable, and to speak with you."

"Tuvok," Zetha acknowledged, glancing at his insignia. "You are less than an admiral."

"My rank is lieutenant," he acknowledged. "You are observant."

She shrugged.

"Shall we begin?"

She shrugged again. He activated the universal translator and the recorder.

"Zetha," she said, before he could ask. "Born in Ki Baratan, or so I am told."

Tuvok's eyebrow rose. "You do not know for certain? There is no record of your birth?"

"None that I am aware of. So I can't tell you how old I am, either."

If Tuvok found the answers unexpected, he gave no sign. "Known relatives?"

"Didn't I just answer that?" she said impatiently, and Tuvok noted a tension in her muscles, a barely controlled hostility. "No family name means no family. If what I know about Vulcans is true, you should understand that."

Bravado, Tuvok noted. Hiding what? He sat back in his chair and softened his approach. "Perhaps you should tell me what you know about Vulcans," he said, as if he were addressing one of his daughters.

"I've heard things," she said diffidently. "Rumors. We of the Sundered talk of our distant siblings often, even though you choose not to acknowledge us."

It was at this point that Tuvok began to wonder who was interrogating whom, and he knew he would get no further on that topic.

"How were you raised, then, if you have no family?"

"What's the first thing you remember?" Tahir used to ask her, whispering in the dark while they waited for a contact who might or might not show up.

"A voice," she would say. "Screaming at me. Or, no, the first thing I remember is the hands."

"Hands—?" he would prompt her, his breath warm on her face, his own hand brushing her cheek.

"Yes. Grabbing me by the hair. Then the voice . . ."

The feeling of her hair being pulled out by the roots, to the accompaniment of shrieks, her own and those of the creature doing the pulling. "I'll snatch you bald-headed! Ruined my life, demon spawn!"

Slam! The eye-smarting pulling stopped, if only because the claw-like hands had released her and flung her against the wall. She skidded on the slick tile floor, trying for purchase, to gain her feet and run. Not far; she knew from past experience that the door was locked. There must be earlier memories, then, interchangeable with this one.

Smack! The impact of an open hand against her jaw. She hadn't seen it coming, so at least had not clenched with fear. No teeth chipped this time. She dropped and rolled, barely clear of the boot-toed feet kicking at her shins. But she'd forgotten about the ugly divan in the middle of the room, and found her small body trapped against it; it was too low for her to crawl under it. The kicks came faster then, striking anywhere soft. Zetha curled into a ball, feeling the blows against her ribs, her spine, knowing there would be fresh bruises over the old ones, the familiar ache in every muscle that by now seemed more normal than not.

"Get up!" the woman said at last, breathless from the effort. "On your feet and out of my sight!"

Mother, grandmother, caretaker? Old, young? Was she even Romulan? Or was it she, not the absent paternal parent, who had polluted the "pure" bloodline with her alien genes? Try as she might, Zetha could never see the face, only the clawing, hurting hands and the tiny booted feet. The voice might have been Romulan, might not; the accent was colonial pretending to be citified. But who or what she was or had been, no knowing. Because a time came when the screaming stopped, and the hands and little booted feet went away.

After that, what seemed a very long time when it was dark and I was hungry, Zetha thought. *It was probably only a sin-*

*gle night, but to a child it would seem longer. Two women in
healers' uniforms came and took me away. I didn't know if the
one with the claws and the little booted feet had abandoned
me or if someone had reported her. I didn't know if she was
dead or alive, and never cared.*

*But tell all that to the Vulcan? Never. What was it the
Lord used to say? Dazzle them with details. When I think of
what I could tell him, about what goes on in back alleys and
abandoned buildings and in catacombs deep below ground, of
splinter groups and Vulcan runes and mutters of reunifi-
cation . . . but no. I never told the Lord. Why should I tell
him? Hold back. Make him work for it.*

"I was brought up in . . . a House. I don't have a better
word for it. A place where the unwanted are fed and clothed
and trained to do tasks that are considered worthy of them."

"An orphanage or foster home," Tuvok suggested. "Run
by the state?"

Zetha shrugged. "A place where the unacceptable are
housed and taught a trade. A place I was ill suited for. I
stayed until I learned all they could teach me about working
in a factory or cleaning a rich man's toilets, then I left."

"Left?"

"I ran away. Aemetha took me in."

And leave it there, she told herself, *because how I escaped
from the House, and who Aemetha is is none of their business.
Much less the rest.*

"Then Cretak gave me the locket and taught me what to
say and sent me across the Outmarches, and now I'm here."

"Indeed," Tuvok said, as if that part were inconsequential.
"Who is Aemetha?"

Think! Zetha told herself. *Is he only plodding through this
for the sake of thoroughness, or is there something I'm missing
here?* The very connection between Cretak and Uhura told
her that the Federation's reach could extend into the Em-

pire as easily as the reverse was true. But could they harm Aemetha? Would they, because of something she might let slip? She'd thought she was on slippery footing with the Lord, but this was different.

"My godmother," she said with her usual diffidence, hoping Tuvok would consider it insignificant. But she used a word that was common to both their languages, which meant more than merely "godmother," implying teacher, guardian, surrogate parent, and Tuvok caught the difference.

"Tell me about her."

Decide! Zetha told herself. *The Lord knew everything, and either he acted against Godmother after you were gone or he didn't. No way of knowing. Surely this Vulcan or his Starfleet cannot have any more control over you than the Lord had.*

Dazzle them with details, she thought. She took a deep breath, shifted around in the chair to bring her knees up almost to her chin and clasp her arms around them, and began.

"She taught me how to read. Then she taught me what was worth reading, and how to read between the lines on what wasn't. She dressed me and fed me, and at the same time taught me how to dress and how not to eat with my fingers . . ."

"When a people are always at war, child," the old woman said, not wheezing for a change because she was sitting down for once and not trying to do three things simultaneously, "the war need not ever touch the homeworld to affect every person living there. When a civilization is predicated on the assumption that the best and brightest of every generation must be swept offworld into warbirds flung to the far reaches of its territories, there perhaps to perish, when a world's best resources, be they in manpower, technology, or simply the expectation that the best foodstuffs, the best boots, the finest-wrought metals and strongest fabrics and even the optimum works of art and music and literature are relegated to the military, what is left for those downworld?"

"I don't know," Zetha said when the old woman finally paused for breath.

"Scraps, that's what! Scraps and tatters and making do. Schools that teach children to chant and salute and march about smartly, but not to read and reason and appreciate the finer things. But why am I telling you what you already know?"

Zetha shrugged. "Because I'm here. And because you know I won't betray you to the Tal Shiar."

"*Child!* Don't ever say those words, not even in jest. You really don't know what you're saying."

You'd be surprised at what I know, Godmother! Zetha had thought at the time, but let it go. Her most pleasant memories were here in this crumbling room, her belly full with whatever she and the other scroungers, some of them huddled and snuffling in the corners, had managed to "organize" that day, a few bits of scrap wood in the ornate but crack-flued enameled stove a hedge against the chill and damp outside. The villa was ancient and had no central heating. It stood for the very things Aemetha talked about—an Empire which could conquer distant worlds but didn't care to keep all of its citizens warm.

Aemetha was old and talked about the past. Tahir, Zetha's fellow scrounger, talked about the future, a future he was not clear about, yet knew somehow would be better than the present. And Aemetha remembered better times, so perhaps it was possible. But Zetha, caught between the two, could only deal with the now.

If anyone had told her this would be the last night she would spend listening to Aemetha's stories, she'd have shrugged and feigned indifference. No one, not even she, would know what she was feeling inside.

"Godmother?" she'd called out that morning, sunlight over her shoulder, bracing the creaky outer door with her back so it wouldn't slam. Her arms were busy with a box that needed to be held level so as not to damage its contents. "I'm back!"

"Rag manners!" someone chided from three rooms away, barely audible. "In the salon, child. The civilized don't shout."

"Whatever you say," Zetha muttered, finding the old woman sorting hand-me-down clothes for her foundlings as usual. There were several of the littlest ones gathered around her, keeping quiet and waiting their turn in Aemetha's presence, far different from their usual fidgeting and squabbling and rolling about in the gutters biting and scratching, fighting over everything.

Zetha waited until they had scattered like leaves before the wind, clutching garments that the average Romulan wouldn't use for dustrags, before she set her treasure down on a rickety side table and let Aemetha open it.

Barter, Zetha thought, *is so much more creative than stealing. Stealing is easier, but both, in this time and place, are equally dangerous. I'll be caught one of these days, and probably disappear. But the satisfaction of seeing old Aemetha's eyes widen with surprise is worth the risk.*

"*Kalia* jellies! Goodness, child!" Aemetha cried, having threaded her way down the narrow alley between the heaps of castoff garments higher than her head in the dank-walled room. The effort made her wheeze; she pressed one hand against her side where it ached. "I'm not even going to ask where you acquired these! Or how," she clucked, touching one of the shimmering purplish sweets gently with gnarled but no less sensitive fingers.

"Perhaps better not," Zetha suggested wryly. The last thing she wanted to do was to get Tahir in trouble. She liked Tahir, and was certain he liked her, and that could have possibilities down the road. Like her, he had no family, which meant he was free to mate where he chose. But what future could be made by two who had no past? She would ask Aemetha's advice about that later.

Aemetha had counted the jellies and saw that there were two more than the usual allotment per box. She hesitated only a moment before popping one into her mouth. She closed her eyes, savoring every atom of flavor, letting it melt on her tongue and trickle leisurely down her throat, an expression nearly orgasmic on her mapped and storied face.

"Oh, child!" she sighed at last, swallowing the last remnants. "There have been times when I'd have killed for less!"

Zetha helped herself to the other extra one, gulping the treat down with less fervor. Food was food, sustenance to keep one going until the next meal.

"There's nothing mortal I would kill for," she remarked, licking her fingers, knowing that both her bad manners and her words would earn one of Aemetha's cutting looks. They did. She shrugged. "I've never been that hungry."

"Then you've never been hungry enough" was Aemetha's opinion. Her fingers reached for a second jelly, then stopped. She sighed. "Mustn't. We can give these to Blevas in part payment for mending the roof. Though where we're to get the tiles . . ."

"Way ahead of you," Zetha said, more than a little smugly. "The jellies go to Rexia in exchange for a bolt of good quilted brocade."

"Stolen, no doubt, from the uhlans' stores," Aemetha offered.

Zetha shrugged. "Where she got it is Rexia's business, as is how." Rexia, they both knew, had a weakness for officers, though she could be friendly to a uhlan if need be.

"And what are we to do with the brocade thus acquired?" Aemetha wondered, though she had a fair idea.

"I've promised that to Metrios in exchange for a partial shipment of roof tiles. His wife wants it for winter jackets for the children. She'll dye it with blue-bark and turn it inside out so no one will know it's military-grade, hence stolen. Metrios will deliver the rest of the tiles after I procure him two tickets for the heptathlon semifinals."

"Which you will acquire how, exactly?"

"You probably don't want to know that, either."

Aemetha sighed. "Very well. Let us assume Metrios does deliver the other half-shipment of roof tiles . . ."

"No need to wait for that," Zetha assured her. "Blevas has agreed to start working on the roof as soon as the first shipment arrives. With luck, the roof will be finished before the winter rains."

The roof in question was the roof of Aemetha's ancestral villa, a great drafty shell of a building which was the only thing her family had left her before having the bad taste to back the wrong side in an old senatorial election and disappear in the small hours of one morning. That Aemetha had been allowed to keep the villa was indicative of how little she or it meant to the Powers That Were.

Aemetha kept to the old religions, and repaid the gods for their beneficence to an old woman without offspring by using her ancestral home as a not quite licit hostel for Ki Baratan's street urchins. Barter, outright theft, and the odd anonymous donation by the occasional aristocrat with a conscience kept the walls standing and, usually, the children fed. The roof had been another matter, until now.

Aemetha's eyes were moist, from more than just the gift of *kalia* jellies. "You do more than you should for me, child!" she said now.

"It's not for you, it's for all of us," Zetha said practically, repacking the jellies to keep them moist. Sentimentality made her nervous. "I have to deliver these."

"Take something with you," Aemetha fussed. "I set aside a tunic and some trousers for you. They may be a little large, but they're almost new . . ."

She pulled herself to her feet and went searching.

"Here you are. The trousers are decidedly too wide, but that can be amended. And they'll need washing."

Zetha examined the tunic thoughtfully, making no mention of a split seam she could mend when the old woman wasn't looking, and held the trousers up to her waist.

"They'd fit two of you!" the old woman clucked.

"I'll tie them with the sash you gave me," Zetha said. "They're fine. Thank you, Godmother."

"Grateful even for that trash!" Aemetha sniffed, her nose running more from emotion than the morning's chill. "You're too grateful, child. That's your problem."

"Grateful to be alive, and no longer beholden to a House, thanks to you," Zetha said, bundling the clothing under one arm and leaning down to kiss the old one's furrowed brow. "I have to go now."

"Be careful!" Aemetha whispered.

"Always," Zetha said, slipping through the door curtain and away with no more motion than a breeze.

Life is a game, she thought, threading her way through back alleys, avoiding the sunlight (mindful of the Scroungers' First Law: Never run when you've stolen something), *a game whose stakes are nothing more than the game, which is life itself.* She lived in shadow, blending herself with the crazed stone walls, slipping from light to shadow and back again.

There was so much to do. Stop at an unmarked door, slip a broken datachip under it. The person on the other side would have the matching piece; spliced together they said: You can trust me, and another transaction would be begun.

Or slip a calling card that said "The poet Krinas holds a recitation in the Square today. All are welcome." It meant "The uhlan on the third watch at the North Gate is a friend." A different card, "Music canceled on account of rain," meant "They've posted extra guards. Avoid."

Those who are born between worlds live in the between world. They are as comfortable in this neither/nor as in their own skins, and sometimes even more so. They learn to slip between the cracks of time and space, to be where they are not and not be where they are.

But those who live this way of necessity, who learn by doing, cannot always anticipate the wiles of those who live this way by choice.

Even as she watched, Zetha was being watched. Koval saw her shadow slipping between the shadows, and made note.

"How did you come to be in Cretak's employ?" Tuvok asked carefully.

"You mean how did a street urchin with no identity come to the attention of someone so important?" Zetha stalled. This was the question she had to answer most carefully, the answer she had been rehearsing since the skipper of the freighter had shown her to a makeshift pallet behind some containers that reeked of dried fish and left her alone—she'd had to find the communal shower and the food dispensers on her own—rehearsing it until it sounded not rehearsed but spontaneous and totally true.

"Godmother had friends. Old family connections despite what had become of her family. There was one rich patron who came every year at the same time and left enough currency to support the entire household through the winter. I never saw his face or learned his name, but he had a beautiful voice." *And have wondered ever since who he was, and whether it was guilt money he left,* she thought, confident in her storytelling, because every word, so far, was true.

"Was this patron related to Cretak?" Tuvok's voice did not change, but some nuance suggested he knew she was stalling.

"How can I know that if I don't know who he was?" she shot back.

"Then what is his relevance to my question?"

Damn you! Zetha thought, though whether the thought was aimed at Tuvok or at herself, she wasn't sure.

"Only by way of explaining that Aemetha knew people. She used to tell us stories about the dinners her family gave. Half the senior officers in the Fleet used to attend, she said. She was old enough to remember the time when your people stole our cloaking device."

"And Cretak?" Tuvok persisted.

Now, Zetha thought. *But carefully.*

"She intends to run for reelection at the next session. I shouldn't be telling you this, but it's common knowledge in Ki Baratan, at least. She will require more aides than she already has, and was looking to train a new one. Aemetha recommended me."

Tuvok weighed this against what little anyone in the Federation knew about the workings of government and social caste and custom within the Empire. On that basis alone, it was impossible to know for certain if Zetha's answer was truthful. However, he had noted no change in her pulse or respiration. Again, the veracity of her answers depended on whether she really was what she appeared to be—a rank amateur telling the truth as she understood it—or an operative so skilled she could lie with impunity.

"On what basis did she recommend you?"

"I have an eidetic memory," she replied, as if it were nothing special.

Cretak handed her the locket. "Any questions?"

Zetha hesitated only a moment. "What else?"

For the first time, Cretak smiled. "Much more. But first . . ." She took the locket back. "You have to be prepared for this. How good is your memory?"

"Perfect," Zetha said, her eyes narrowing. She disliked being toyed with, even by someone who could snuff her life out without a thought. Especially by someone who had that much power. "You were testing me."

"Wouldn't you, in my place?"

The very thought that she could ever be in Cretak's place gave Zetha pause.

"I suppose I would."

"Even so. A perfect memory, you say. You're overly confident."

Zetha shrugged. "Just accurate. If I hear something, I can play it back in my mind like a recording. If I read it, it scrolls across the inside of my eyelids."

Cretak tilted her head like a bird, skepticism written in every plane of her handsome face. She tapped something into her personal comm and turned the screen so that Zetha could read it. Zetha did. Then closed her eyes and recited it verbatim.

Even Cretak, it seemed, could occasionally be surprised. "Impressive," she said, "but that puts us only halfway there. Try this."

She coded a sequence into the keypad on her desk and a voice recording began to play. Zetha listened intently. After a moment or two, Cretak stopped the recording.

"What language is that?" Zetha asked.

"Inconsequential. If your memory is what you claim it is, you can reproduce it."

Again Zetha shrugged, and began to speak the foreign tongue, though she understood not a word of it, perfectly.

Cretak seemed to have been holding her breath. Now she let it out in a great slow exhalation. "Eidetic!" she breathed. "No wonder your lord treasures you. This may make matters more complex rather than simpler."

"How so?"

"Not for you to know." Cretak opened a wall safe and handed Zetha a datachip. "Your lord has given you to me for now. I will provide you with a room and a listener. You will memorize everything on this chip, however incomprehensible it may seem. You will recite it for me so I am certain you have it right, then you will not speak it again until you reach the person to whom you are also to entrust the locket."

Something thrilled in Zetha's blood. Who was this person, on what side of the dilemma of good and evil? If she refused this mission now, would she be killed? It seemed apparent, considering the amount of information she'd just been given. *This*, she thought, *is where you must decide*.

"Who is this person? Where?"

In answer, Cretak had one more bit of media to display, a grainy visual full of static and flutter, the audio fading in and out. Zetha lacked the sophistication to recognize that what she was looking at was an intercept of a long-range comm signal, but didn't care. She had seen vids about humanoids and had a vague idea what they looked like. And she knew that there were hundreds of other species to be found in known space. She had simply never seen so many in one place before. Her mouth opened in awe, and stayed open.

The setting seemed to be a classroom. Zetha's own experience with such venues was limited, but she recognized that the person in the center of the room was instructing those around her. Most of them appeared young, and most of them wore some manner of uniform. Holoscreens around the room showed other listeners from an even wider range of species in attendance.

"They are so confident of their own security that one of our officers was able to register for the course by posing as a Vulcan," Cretak mused, shaking her head in disbelief. "That is how we were able to intercept this transmission. Do you understand how long-range communication works?"

Zetha shook her head, and managed finally to close her mouth.

"No reason why you should." Cretak froze the screen. "If

I explained that this transmission is several years old, but we received it only yesterday, will you understand?" She saw the younger woman's skeptical look. "No matter." She brought the image in close on the instructor's face. "It is this one. She is Admiral Nyota Uhura, head of Starfleet Intelligence, yet she teaches a basic-level course in communications to cadets. Can you imagine the head of the Tal Shiar doing likewise?"

Zetha had no idea who the head of the Tal Shiar even was. She could only shake her head, transfixed by the different faces on the screen.

No one spoke the words "Federation" or "Starfleet" or even "human." A kaleidoscope of broken bits of information knit together in a patchwork quilt in Zetha's mind.

"How am I to find this person?"

"Memorize what I've given you. You will be gotten to where you need to go. The fewer questions you ask . . ."

After she had committed the contents of the chip to memory, Zetha knew no more about the mission than she had before. No point in asking: *What happens to me after I give this information to the one called Uhura? Am I alive, am I dead? Am I in exile or must I return to Ki Baratan? Am I to do this for the rest of my life, or only this once?* No answers to these questions now. Just get the job done.

"I've cleared it with your lord. No, don't ask me how. Just go and get whatever personal belongings you can carry in one hand, and come back here at once."

Zetha laughed wryly. She had a flat polished stone Tahir had given her stashed in a pocket; she caressed it whenever she was cross or tired or confused. The sash she wore around her slender waist in lieu of a belt was something Aemetha had given her that no one had managed to steal. There was nothing else.

"I'm already carrying it," she said. "Where am I going?"

"I don't suppose there's any way of knowing ahead of

time whether you're going to be space-sick," Cretak mused, almost to herself. "You're going with me."

Tuvok frowned slightly. Everything the girl said had the ring of truth. He had no doubt she believed everything she had just told him. But whether she had been programmed thus, or had simply chosen to omit some things, would require deeper questions.

But she was yawning, and he wondered how long it had been since she'd slept. She was so young, younger than his youngest child. He suppressed a parental urge to suggest she rest now. Illogical, and self-defeating. Nevertheless, if she was overtired, her answers would make no sense. Only one more question, for now.

"Are you a member of the Tal Shiar?"

For the first time she laughed outright. It would have been a pleasant sound, if it hadn't been laced with sarcasm. "You mean am I a spy? There are no spies on Romulus; don't you know that? There is no need for spies, because everyone in a spy."

"Answer the question, please."

That made her angry. She leapt out of her chair, almost knocking it over.

"I am nothing! Don't you understand? I don't exist. On the way here, Cretak and I went past two sets of sentries and three sensor arrays inside the space hub. The sensors recognized Cretak, but they never even registered me, because I don't exist. You're aiming in the dark."

"Are you a member of the Tal Shiar?" he asked again, unperturbed by her outburst.

Did he notice that she hesitated for the space of half a breath? *No*, Zetha told herself, watching sidelong as the impassive face revealed nothing. *He has not noticed.*

"No," she said carefully. "I am not."

Chapter 5

"Okay, what have we got?" McCoy demanded, rubbing his hands together, exhilarated by the chase in spite of himself.

"A bug of unknown etiology which can affect humans and Vulcans, kills everyone it infects, and may have been artificially created," Crusher reported grimly.

"And a possible disease vector," Selar chimed in from aboard the science vessel whose ETA at Spacedock was 1900 hours that evening.

"This is new," Uhura said from the center seat. "Let's hear it."

She had "assembled" all three of them in a holoconference in her office. Each of them, wherever they were, experienced the presence of the other three *in situ*. This level of holo technology was not yet Fleet standard, but was something Uhura, working with the Starfleet Corps of Engineers, had been instrumental in developing. It not only gave the impression that she and the three doctors were actually, three-dimensionally present in four locations at once, but the transmission frequencies were virtually impenetrable by at least current Starfleet technology. At the moment the prototype could be transmitted only from her office at SI, though she knew that some of the newer starships were being fitted with holodecks employing the same principles.

For now, Crusher, looking tired but no less groomed in her characteristic blue smock, her waves of bright red hair barely contained in a practical ponytail at the nape of her neck, had arranged three empty chairs in a clear space between the countertops and autoclaves in her lab at Medical HQ. Dr. Selar, for her part, had arranged some low couches in a space in her vessel's sickbay, confident that, on a Vulcan ship, neither she nor the confidentiality of the meeting would be disturbed.

McCoy, in his favorite rocker on the porch of a retreat so remote only Intelligence had been able to track him down, was enjoying the company of three beautiful women seated in a semicircle of cushioned Adirondack chairs on his back lawn, under a starlit sky and accompanied by the sound of crickets. Uhura, hosting all three of them in her office had, just to be whimsical, seated his flannel-shirt-and-old-Levi's incarnation on a windowsill overlooking San Francisco Bay, where the sun was starting its late-afternoon slide down the sky beyond the Golden Gate Bridge. McCoy had refused to shave for the occasion and, with his tousled white hair and three-day stubble, looked like nothing so much as a wild-eyed mountain man.

"First things first!" he blustered now. "We've got to know what this thing is before we start trying to figure out where it came from."

Uhura shot him a *Who's in charge here?* look and turned to Crusher. "Dr. Crusher, you have the floor."

"Right." She took a deep breath and began. "Assuming this is actually a variant of the disease the Romulans call the Gnawing, its original source is a naturally occurring bacterium found in the soil of the Romulan homeworld.

"Bacteria, for our purposes, Admiral, are 'big' germs, easy to see under a microscope, fairly easy to kill. Just for show and tell, I'll give you some examples. . . ."

Three images, projected from a fifth locus of the holoprogram, materialized in the middle of their field of vision.

Each was about a foot high and floated in mid-air; each was a many-times magnified three-dimensional realization of what would be visible under a microscope. One was a bright red-orange podlike shape containing five orange ovules that could have been peas or soybeans but, in fact, as the readout beside it attested, were the spores of botulism. The second, a methane-blue sphere with a fluid, coruscated surface, from which smaller, seedlike purplish spheres were escaping like solar flares, identified itself as bubonic plague. The third and central one featured scatterings of purple rods like the sprinkles on an ice cream cone, though with the characteristic drumstick knob at one end which identified the "sprinkles" as tetanus. As Crusher spoke, the images pirouetted slowly to 360 degrees and back again, displaying themselves in all their deadly glory.

Uhura, to whom this was all new, watched transfixed. The others, who had seen these maleficences and others before, still found them strangely compelling. When she thought they'd seen enough, Crusher made all but the tetanus image vanish, and brought up a new image whose "drumsticks," interspersed with vague, shapeless blotches, looked very similar to the tetanus, except that they were yellowish-brown in color.

"What you're looking at here," Crusher said, "is a specimen, taken from the locket Admiral Uhura delivered to Starfleet Medical yesterday, of something that we have been told is killing Romulans on some of their colony worlds, and which may be related to the historic Romulan plague known as the Gnawing. If this is in fact the same entity, it's very much like tetanus and, like tetanus, it's a killer, a killer that can lie dormant for decades, even centuries, until the soil is disturbed by plowing or building roads, or even by a child playing in the dirt. And, like tetanus, the original form is only dangerous if ingested or if it infiltrates an open wound. It's not contagious. It can't be passed from person to person like a head cold."

"Further," Selar chimed in. "It would be most unlikely for an identical bacterium to be found in the soil of as many different planets, spread across as wide a region of space, as have thus far yielded casualties of this disease. The bacterium that resulted in the Gnawing has thus far never been found on any world other than Romulus."

"With you so far," Uhura said, hearing a resonance of the shared Vulcan/Romulan it-is-not-a-lie-to-keep-the-truth-to-one-self behind Selar's words. Later she would take Selar aside privately and ask her how much she'd known about the Gnawing, and from what sources, before this. But now was not the time. "But if it's not contagious, how did it kill up to fifty percent of the population of Romulus nearly two thousand years ago?"

"We do not know that for certain, Admiral," Selar said. "History is often replete with exaggeration."

"Nevertheless, Selar, it did kill enough people to make it into the histories. I can't believe they all contracted it from soil samples."

"There might have been an airborne version," Crusher suggested. "Which might have been contagious, transmitted by a cough or sneeze. As could an animal-to-Romulan form, like the bubonic plague on Earth, which was transmitted from rat to flea to human. Or by eating the meat of an infected animal. While we know that Vulcans post-Surak generally don't eat meat, modern Romulans do."

No one actually looked to Selar for confirmation or denial. The question, like the holos, hung in the air unanswered.

"Even so," Crusher said after an uncomfortable silence. "Bacteria, as I say, are incredibly easy to kill. If that was all we had here, we could develop a vaccine from the killed strains, inoculate anyone in a hot zone, maybe share the vaccine with the Romulans as a good-will gesture, problem solved. But . . ."

With the flick of a toggle, she made the tetanus bacillus vanish and moved the Gnawing bacillus to one side.

"Some bacteria can mutate into viruses, which is what we think was the case with the prototypical Gnawing," she said as several new images slowly materialized. "We can only conjecture, because we don't have records from the pandemic two thousand years ago. And I imagine it might be very difficult to send someone to Romulus to gather soil samples in remote areas in the hopes of finding an unadulterated cluster of Gnawing microbes."

Difficult, Uhura thought, *but probably not impossible*. She had in fact sent one of her Listeners to do just that, but the Listener had not yet reported back.

"Now, viruses are much, much smaller than bacteria, more difficult to detect, and much more mutable, hence difficult to cure," Crusher was saying. She had conjured up six new images by now. "I've selected just a few examples that have plagued humans in the past . . ."

She highlighted each image as she identified it: "Herpes" was an orange, sponge-shaped orb with a spiked multicolored ring around it. "Polio" looked like nothing so much as an attractive blue-green sea anemone. "Smallpox" was a rusty-looking ovoid with an hourglass shape inside. "Hantavirus" looked like land masses on a planet, sickly pink, dotted with malevolent-looking little black seeds around the edges of each "continent."

"Ebola," Crusher continued. This looked like an aerial view of a series of crop circles in a wheat field. "Skorr pox." This was a series of gray concentric hexagons. "And finally human immunodeficiency virus, or HIV."

Glanced at quickly, this one was formless, a spider's nest, a tuft of cat hair, something that might have rolled out from under the bed. But Crusher dismissed all the other images except the Gnawing, which still lingered on the periphery, and began to slowly enlarge the HIV virus. Gradually it became an elliptical shape with another shape inside it like an inverted tear drop, with a third, cylindrical shape within that. All of the shapes were studded about with strange artifacts that the readout identified as "surface glycoproteins," "HLA I and II," "core proteins (modified by AT-2)."

"I chose this one," Crusher said, "Because it seems to most closely mimic the end stage of the bug we're dealing with. Or, at least, one of the end stages."

"One of them?" McCoy echoed her, scowling.

"I'll get to that in a minute," Crusher said.

"Go on," Uhura encouraged her.

"Let's take another look at our prime suspect," she said. The HIV, rather than disappearing, simply moved slightly away from center stage at her instructions and the Gnawing bacillus moved in to hover beside it.

"I started with the specimens from the locket," she explained. "There were four distinct compartments inside with blood, skin and hair samples from four victims. They were collected so meticulously I was able to classify them by gender and blood type. Whoever put this together was very skilled."

She looked pointedly at Uhura. The question she wanted to ask was one Uhura still couldn't answer. Were the samples themselves faked? Was this all a ploy to spread false rumors about an epidemic that didn't exist, to divert Starfleet energies into pursuing a phantom, even to create an interstellar incident based on accusations of biological warfare? No way to answer any of that yet. Uhura wondered what progress Tuvok was making with Zetha.

"Go on," she told Crusher.

"I grew each of these specimens in culture, and compared them with specimens from healthy Romulans kept in stasis on Starbase 23—and while we're on the subject, I got a lot of flak when I requisitioned those. Mind telling me what we're doing with Romulan blood specimens?"

"Left over from the Earth-Romulan War," Uhura said tightly, watching Crusher's and Selar's eyebrows go up si multaneously. "And . . . other sources. On the rare occasion we've taken a Romulan prisoner alive, we take blood samples. They do the same with captured humans."

She was avoiding McCoy's eyes, though she could see him in her peripheral vision, scratching his stubble and looking uncomfortable. They both knew of at least three captured Romulans from their early years together, a commander accidentally beamed aboard *Enterprise*, and two of her guards who had started out as exchange prisoners but had not been returned until long after *Enterprise* had beaten a hasty retreat out of the Neutral Zone with a stolen cloaking device.

"Go on," she told Crusher again.

"When I compared the normals with the disease entities, the results were almost too good. There was the bug, all right. So I knew it would grow *in vitro*. I ran simulations based on several terrestrial and Vulcan life-forms."

"Quite logical," Selar commended her.

"Anyway," Crusher went on. "There it was. But then I thought, 'It can't be this easy.' And I was right. Because within two hours of regrowth, it had mutated into a viral form."

Slowly she enlarged the Gnawing specimen image until the yellow-brown rods and vague blotches almost blotted out the empty space between, and some of the blotches showed bright green patches of something else. The entire entity moved, replicating inexorably as they watched, seeming almost to pulse malevolently.

"This is why it took me twenty-four hours to report," Crusher explained. "Because we had to rule out the possibility that this might be a totally separate entity, so we observed isolated specimens of the bacillus until we actually caught them mutating into the viral form. What you're looking at here is a time-lapsed version, ten hours compressed into less than a minute." She froze the image. "And right about here seems to be the point at which the virus then mutates into a retrovirus."

She paused. Her fellow MDs were looking grim. Uhura looked puzzled.

"Now I'm going to have to ask you to explain to me the difference between a virus and a retrovirus," she said. "Use nice, simple words, please. As if you were explaining it to your son."

The mention of Wesley, who'd just turned eleven, made Crusher smile.

"I think Wes is a lot more interested in physics than medicine. I guess most kids want to find themselves instead of following in their parents' footsteps. Still, it isn't really that complicated. A retrovirus is a virus that can infiltrate at the genetic level, become part of the patient's DNA. HIV is a classic example. And I believe this thing is, too."

"Okay," Uhura said. "Still with you."

"Now, we have the technology to not only identify every known virus, but to develop algorithms to identify unknowns. It might take a while, but we'd eventually catch the thing. Then we'd work backwards to create a decoy and—"

"A decoy," Uhura repeated.

Crusher nodded. "I'll use the HIV as an example, because it's old news and we know exactly how it behaves and how to circumvent it: The virus attacks healthy cells by finding a way to get inside them and kill them. In the case of HIV, it does this by infiltrating a protein embedded in a T-cell membrane.

"T-cells are the Good Guys," she said helpfully before Uhura could ask. "But HIV invaded the T-cells by attaching itself to the CD4 receptor located on the surface protein, and deactivated the T-cells. Without enough healthy T-cells, the patient had no defenses against a host of opportunistic infections and even certain cancers, and wasted away and died. With me so far?"

Not about to ask what a CD4 receptor was, Uhura nodded. "So far, yes."

"Now, one way to distract the HIV virus and keep it from attacking the T-cells was to create a decoy cell. Decoy cells are genetically engineered molecules which look exactly like normal cells. They fool the virus into attaching to them instead of to the patient's naturally occurring cells. The decoys grab onto the virus before it can do any harm, flush it out through the liver and kidneys and *voilà*."

"So can we do that here?" Uhura nodded at the prime suspect, the Gnawing bacillus-turned-virus and, as if on cue, Crusher made the HIV disappear.

"We might," Crusher said. "If this were only one virus."

"Uh-oh," McCoy murmured.

Crusher manipulated the image, creating a duplicate. As they watched, one model developed small splashes of orange, while the other continued replicating in green. When Crusher created a third image, it showed no growth at all and, in fact, the yellow-brown rods began to disappear. A fourth image showed no rods, but splashes of orange and green, interspersed with round gray nodules.

"Are we looking at the four distinct specimens from the locket?" Uhura guessed.

"I wish it were that simple," Crusher said. "No, these are all time-elapsed shots of the same specimen. What I thought was just one bug became two. Or was it three? And did I just imagine it, or had the first bug mutated into two new bugs? Or had it vanished altogether? This damn thing won't hold still. It's a moving target. Every time I look at it, it's something else. Sometimes it moves so fast even the instruments can barely detect it. Nothing natural can do that."

"At least nothing with which we are familiar," Selar suggested.

"Copenhagen theory . . ." McCoy muttered, scratching his chin. "If it works for quantum physics, why can't it work for medicine?"

All three women gaped at him. Selar's fingers stopped moving.

"Indeed," she said. "Why not?"

"Okay," Crusher said. "Now I'm the one who needs nice, simple words."

"The wave-versus-particle theory of quantum physics was first described by the Nobel physicist Niels Bohr in Earth year 1927," Selar said. "Bohr was born in Copenhagen, hence his theory is referred to as the Copenhagen theory. Prior to this, physicists could not understand why quantum matter appeared in the form of particles, but behaved like waves. Bohr suggested that quantum particles function as waves as long they are unobserved. Each quantum particle is equally distributed in a series of overlapping probability waves. But when observed, the waves revert to particles."

"What's that got to do with—?" Crusher began.

"If a tree falls in the forest and no one is there to hear it, does it make a sound?" Uhura suggested.

"Oh, now we're talking magic—!" Crusher protested.

"Like the placebo effect?" McCoy countered.

"Not the same thing at all," she shot back.

"In English, please," Uhura said.

"C'mon, Bev, think about it," McCoy argued. "Every MD knows that every time you introduce a new medication, outcomes are always influenced by the fact that some people get better just because they're taking a pill. You give a hundred people a sugar pill when they think they're getting the actual medication, and ten to thirty percent of them will report that they feel better. Except with antidepressants, where up to sixty percent of patients given a placebo report effectiveness, just because someone's listening to their troubles, patting their hand, and giving them a magic bullet."

"If you're talking about human patients, sure," Crusher acknowledged. "But that doesn't apply to all species across the board. Vulcans, for instance."

"Oh, well, Vulcans!" McCoy dismissed them with a wave

of his hand, then seemed to remember that Selar was there. "Sorry, Selar. No offense."

"None taken, Doctor."

"And anyway," Crusher went on heatedly. "We're talking about a virus here, not a patient or a tree. What the hell does the Copenhagen theory or the placebo effect have to do with—"

"Time out!" Uhura said sharply, and they subsided. As if on cue, her intercom sounded.

She'd sent Thysis home early and diverted all incoming calls to other offices. Only her Romulan Listeners and Tuvok had authorization to interrupt.

"Uhura," she said, touching a contact on her console and settling an earpiece in her ear.

"Listener Tau-3," said a voice through the static.

"Go ahead."

"Confirming presence of disease entity designated colony world . . ." the voice said shakily. Male or female, and of what species, impossible to tell. The voice was deliberately filtered to foil attempts to intercept it or trace it back to source. "Have visual . . ."

"Project when ready, Tau-3," Uhura said crisply. She nodded toward Crusher, who turned off the medical holos with the snap of a toggle. In their place appeared images out of several species' infernal places.

The source was obviously a vid unit secreted on the person of someone walking through a hospital or clinic or quarantine station, then coded and transmitted on a piggyback frequency across parsecs of space, and the quality of the image was commensurately bad—shaky, in and out of focus, the lighting sometimes so poor the image was lost altogether. What came through was a jumble of ghostly figures, and a great deal of sound.

The figures were Romulans of all ages, some packed together on rows and rows of medical cots, the overspill milling about, propped up in corners, lying on the floor. Healers, some of them looking as ill as their patients, moved hastily among them offering whatever little comfort they could. A no-doubt dangerously obtained close-up of a group of children showed them huddled together, some coughing uncontrollably, others retching helplessly, great running sores on their faces, virid blood running from their noses or flecking their parched lips. Those whose lungs still worked howled or whimpered with pain. The others could only gasp helplessly, their eyes frightened, their little sides heaving with the effort to draw breath.

The Listener with the hidden camera, probably a Vulcan passing as a Romulan, moved with difficulty past a steady stream of incoming patients until the camera showed daylight, and a line of sick and dying Romulans, some too weak to stand without holding themselves up against the outer wall of the building, waiting for admission to the clinic. The line extended as far as the camera could project before the image was lost.

"Confirmation . . ." the Listener's voice said once the image disappeared. "Estimate ten percent of the population of . . ." The code name for the city was lost in static, but Uhura knew the Listener's location anyway. "Among the sick, no survivors. This is no rumor."

"Message received, Tau-3," Uhura said, putting far more bravado into her voice than she felt. "Get out of the hot zone now. Your job is done. Report back to base for some leave time, and—"

"Negative, Command. Evidencing the symptoms myself. Estimate less than one hour before delirium ensues. Terminating now . . ."

No one spoke for some moments after the transmission ended. Finally McCoy cleared his throat.

"Just when you think you've seen everything . . . guess there's no question now whether this is real or not."

"Or that it's manufactured," Crusher added sharply. "This isn't a natural phenomenon. It was created. How, why, or by whom—"

"We can assume the why," Uhura said. She would deal with losing a top operative, and also a friend, later. "The three of you are going to find out how, and I'm going to find out by whom. Dr. Selar?"

"There is a traceable disease vector, Admiral," Selar reported evenly, the best among all of them at disguising her reaction to what they had just witnessed. "If all of your Listeners confirm what your original source provided . . ." Now it was Selar's turn to use the holo program to draw up a star map highlighting a sector which included several Romulan colony worlds, a segment of the Neutral Zone, and a cluster of Federation worlds on the other side. Four of the Romulan worlds were highlighted. ". . . we can be certain that the disease has occurred at selected sites on these four worlds. In addition . . ."

She manipulated the map to show more of the Federation side.

"Beginning with the seventy-three seemingly isolated cases on these seventeen worlds, I have developed an algorithm which would not only analyze any reports of similar symptoms anywhere within Federation space, but also analyzed any undiagnosable illnesses within the same field."

"Anyone sneezes, she's on it," McCoy offered, trying to shake them all out of the mood the Listener's video had plunged them into. "Clever girl!"

"Indeed," Selar said, accepting the compliment. She either was in awe of the senior physician or simply had a far greater tolerance for McCoy's humanity than most Vulcans. "Such variables as reports of increased numbers of headcolds, absenteeism from work or school, antiviral prescriptions, and use of native remedies or vitamin supplements are included in the algorithm."

"Throughout the entire Federation?" Crusher marveled. "You have been busy!"

"And—?" Uhura prompted, glancing at the chrono. Selar's ship would be requesting docking clearance at Spacedock in less than thirty minutes, and they'd have to terminate this meeting beforehand so the discrete would not interfere with ship-to-shore transmissions.

"Two hundred seven cases reporting symptoms such as we have just seen on the Romulan colony, on eighteen Federation worlds and two outposts along the Neutral Zone," Selar reported. "Given the number of worlds surveyed, there are not many cases, but there have been no survivors. If in fact it is the same entity, the vector is here."

The map rotated, and a bright red line superimposed itself over known space, connecting the dots on the Federation side. A concomitant green line connected the four Romulan colonies. The two lines stopped at the Neutral Zone, but seemed almost to be reaching toward each other. With a little bit of imagination, one could draw a dotted red and green line, connecting a scattering of inhabited worlds between the two.

"I am continuing to run the algorithm as new case reports come in," Selar concluded. "However, as of yet I am unable to determine how this has been able to spread among these distant worlds. All persons transporting from ship to ship or ship to surface are screened for disease entities, all goods are irradiated."

"Not all, Selar," Crusher said. "Someone got these specimens across the Zone to Admiral Uhura."

All eyes turned to Uhura. "Only persons or objects passing through a transporter are screened," she said, and left it at that. "And even that's about to be remedied."

"Meanwhile, this thing is spreading!" McCoy voiced what they all feared. He really was too old for this. "Unchecked, it could hopscotch from every world where we've found it clear across two quadrants. Even if it doesn't, it could potentially create panic, put a stop to interplanetary travel, bring commerce to a standstill, quarantine the affected worlds, turn them into charnel houses . . ."

"Then we'd better get busy," Uhura said with more enthusiasm than she felt.

"If it is manufactured," McCoy said, almost to himself. "It will have a signature."

"A signature?" Uhura echoed him.

"Mad scientists are like mad bombers or computer hackers," he explained, his eyes very far away, as if he were scanning his own personal memory banks for a datum that was just out of reach. "They leave a signature, a calling card, some little sarcastic fillip encoded into the virus that says: 'This is mine.' It stokes their egos, makes them feel important . . ."

He drifted off for a moment, lost in his own thoughts. Finally he said: "You leave this sonofabitch to me. If he's ever done anything even remotely like this before on any scale, I'll track him through the database, and I'll catch him!"

Uhura said nothing, but she knew he knew this was why she'd wanted him on the team.

Crusher was off on her own train of thought. "What I wouldn't give for one living Romulan to run some background tests on—!" she said.

Uhura's intercom beeped again. It was Tuvok.

"Sorry to interrupt, Admiral. You said you wanted a preliminary report."

"I did. Go ahead."

"Our subject is sleeping at present. The first phase of our interview is concluded."

"And—?"

"And, as discussed earlier, I believe, as you do, that either she is exactly what she says she is, or she is under such deep cover that, barring a mind-meld, I cannot further confirm her veracity."

Uhura sighed. "All right, Tuvok. Let her sleep for now. I'd like your report on my desk by tomorrow morning."

"It is on its way to you now, Admiral."

Uhura suppressed a smile, seeing the tell-tale blinking on her console. "Figures. You're off-duty for tonight, Mister. Get some shut-eye yourself. I'll call you when I need you, and I want you sharp when I do."

The three doctors had listened silently to Tuvok's report, and they remained silent now. Selar's maps, like all the previous visuals, had been terminated, and the space between them was empty, except for McCoy's, which still held stars and crickets. Uhura drummed her fingers on the desktop for a moment, thinking.

She'd been wondering what to do with Zetha from the moment the girl appeared. She still wasn't sure, but she was beginning to get an idea.

"Dr. Crusher, I think I can provide you with at least one healthy Romulan for your tests. You can see her tomorrow after she's had a good night's sleep. She'll need a physical before we go any further, anyway."

Crusher's eyes widened. "You have a Romulan, here? Why wasn't I informed before this?"

"We need to find the link between those two disease vectors," Uhura said succinctly, adjourning the meeting without actually answering the question. "To do that, we need to look at this thing from the ground. I'm sending an away team into the Zone. Dismissed."

"Pretty grim stuff on that visual feed," McCoy remarked after Crusher and Selar had signed off. "And it means you've lost one of your Listeners. I'm sorry."

"So am I," Uhura said, keeping her voice level. She would grieve later. "Just when I think I've seen everything . . . Tell me, Leonard, how do you ever get used to it?"

"Who says you get used to it? It's just as grim the hundredth time you see it as it is the first. I'll tell you, though, it's the sounds that get to me more. The sound of a child in pain, no matter the species . . . you hear it in your sleep; you never get used to it. If you do, it just means you're too hardened to be a good doctor, and it's time you cashed it in."

"I'm sorry I dragged you back in for this," she said.

"Oh, the hell with that!" McCoy dismissed it with a wave of his hand. He studied her face and didn't like the expression he saw there. She could have terminated their transmission at the same time she'd dismissed the other two, but she hadn't. "Nyota? Can I ask you something, just between us?"

"Sure."

"What're you going to do if we find out this is manufactured? And since most of the casualties so far seem to be on the Romulan side, well, what if it's someone from our side?"

Her chin came up. The look in her eye was deadly. "I'd like to personally track them down, point a phaser between their eyebrows if they have any, and force them to inject themselves with their own disease."

McCoy waited. She closed her eyes, took a deep breath, exhaled.

"However, I probably won't be allowed to do that. Let's find them first. And then we'll see."

"I need help with this!" the voice said, cracking around the edges. "I told you we shouldn't wait too long. There's a delicate balance between letting this spread just so far and having it reach pandemic proportions. You promised me—!"

"If you can possibly keep your mouth shut," Koval said icily, annoyed at being interrupted during his daily soak in his own personal hot spring, "you will hear me once again tell you that nothing will go wrong. Did you hear me? Nothing will go wrong."

Chapter 6

"I sometimes think," Uhura told Ambassador Dax that evening, "that there were only two events of significance in the universe, the Big Bang and Camp Khitomer. My cadets may think I'm old enough to have been present at the first, but I will admit to being present at the latter."

"What's the saying? 'All roads lead to Khitomer,'" Curzon Dax said with a twinkle in his voice as well as his eyes. He was flirting with her as usual, for all the good it would do him. "And this one is no different. There's something on your desk and on your mind that has you thinking of the past. Tell me everything."

Uhura and Curzon had met for a drink in the officers' lounge on Spacedock in orbit above Earth, a tradition whenever he was in town, and were watching the big ships going to and fro like so many gigantic stately birds, while shuttles flitted among them like dragonflies.

Uhura looked at Curzon under her eyelashes. "As if I could!"

"You know you can," he coaxed her. "I've got the same security clearance you do. Over the course of several lifetimes, I've probably done more covert work than you. In this instance, I have a fair idea what's going on. I just need you to fill in the details."

Two can play at this game! Uhura thought. She smiled at him.

"Why don't you start by telling me how much you know, so I won't have to repeat myself?"

"I know you received a, shall we say, interesting little special-delivery package from the other side that set this whole thing in motion."

"Well, then," Uhura said, shaking her head "no" to the Quallorian bartender when he gestured toward her empty glass, "it sounds to me as if you know as much as you need to know."

"I'm primarily curious how the, ah, other side—" Curzon did not say "Romulans." Out of long experience, he knew that the noisier the locale, the easier it was for someone to be listening. "—knew to send their little gift directly to you."

"I'm head of Starfleet Intelligence, Curzon. It didn't exactly require rocket science."

"But why would you accept the messenger so willingly?" he persisted. " 'Beware Romulans bearing gifts,' and all that, especially after we've each spent nearly half a century pretending the other doesn't exist. How could you know that the gift was genuine? How did you know it wasn't a trap?"

"I didn't," she said. "I still don't. Know whether or not it's a trap, I mean. But I'm reasonably certain it's genuine, considering the source . . ."

Oops! she thought, *too much information.* She waited for Curzon to pounce on it.

" 'Considering the source'?" Curzon pounced.

Uhura realized what he was doing and stopped. "Oh, no you don't! That much I won't tell you."

"You don't trust me." It was not a question. He managed to look like a hurt child.

What was it about him? Uhura wondered. How this frail-looking man had ever found the nerve to walk out on the Klingons at Korvat was beyond her, yet something about him made

her believe that he could, and it was only one of the diplomatic
ploys he was famous for. She was among the few non-Trills who
knew enough about them to understand the concept of the
symbiont, physically vulnerable outside of its host body but,
safely joined, virtually immortal. And this immortality lent Dax
a vast and deep-running wisdom. But while the Curzon part
was appealing enough, by himself he was truly rather unprepos-
sessing—bookish, white-haired, with a certain elfin twinkle, but
really, he was not her type. Unless, of course, it was the spots.

Most Trills had those leopard spots, starting at the hairline
and going all the way down to . . . where? Any non-Trill who
knew a Trill always had to wonder how far the spots went. But
while there was an almost overwhelming desire to connect
the dots and see where they would lead, in Curzon Dax's case
it was something more. Was it the synergistic blending of the
two personalities that made him all but irresistible?

"I trust Curzon," Uhura said, wanting more than anything to soothe the little-boy pout off his face. "But I don't
really know Dax. I don't think anyone does. Trills are like
elephants; they never forget. A hundred years from now or a
thousand you could let something slip—"

"My lips are sealed," he said, still twinkling at her.

"Sorry."

"Maybe there's something I can do to help," Curzon suggested.

"Not unless you can join Starfleet by tomorrow afternoon
and learn how to run a ship all by yourself," she joked.

Curzon smiled. "Maybe I can't," he said. "But I can recommend someone who can. I believe he's already on your
short list."

Once more Uhura didn't ask him how he knew, but she
took his recommendation. The following evening at the reception for the senior officers of the K'tarra, Curzon found
her in the crowd.

He had, as she'd predicted, been drinking blood wine

with Thought Admiral Klaad all evening, but while Klaad was drowsing in a corner and the reception was winding down, Curzon managed to look as if he'd been imbibing nothing but Altair water and was ready to start a new day.

Maybe that's the secret, Uhura thought. *You don't have to outshout a Klingon, just outdrink him.*

"Well?" he greeted her. "Any luck in talking my hard-headed young protégé into joining your mission?"

"I gave him twenty-four hours to think about it," was all Uhura would say.

"I warned you it wouldn't be easy."

"So you did," she acknowledged. "But one way or the other, I did want to thank you."

"You can do that better in private," Curzon suggested. "I'm staying in my usual suite on Embassy Row. I have an unopened bottle of a rare aperitif from Izar that will spoil you for anything else, and some recordings of Hamalki 3D string music you'll never see or hear anywhere else. The composer is a dear friend who wrote several pieces just for me. We could . . ."

At her wry look, he stopped. They danced the same waltz every time they met.

"Just as friends," he suggested. "Two intelligent people who share the same tastes in the finer things. It doesn't have to be anything more than that. I know you need to keep your mind occupied now that you've set this thing in motion."

Uhura glanced at him sharply. She didn't know how much he picked up through diplomatic channels, how much just on hearsay. If he asked her anything further, security clearance or no, there was only so much she could tell him. But he was right. Very soon, depending on the cooperation of the assistant engineer from the *Okinawa*, she would send a team on a very dangerous mission inside the Neutral Zone that, whether it succeeded or not, officially never happened. After that, there was nothing she could do but monitor the situation and wait. Shuffle documents on her desk, teach her class, give the occasional press conference, field the crisis or crises *du jour*, and wait. Go home at night to an empty house built into a hillside overlooking the Muir Woods, and wait.

Or spend at least one evening in good company while she waited.

"Spend the rest of the evening with me," Curzon asked again. "I promise not to ask you anything more about the mission. Just two friends having a little private visit. Anything else is up to you."

It wasn't as if Uhura hadn't considered other things. Curzon Dax was urbane, witty, and charming, and if he had been anything other than a Trill, she might not have been able to resist him all these years. But it was the thought that, however brief or extended their relationship might be, he or at least his symbiont would carry the memory—and no doubt the urge to gossip; she knew Trills—into subsequent lives, possibly forever, that put her off.

"Just as friends," she agreed finally. "After all, I do owe you a favor."

"Oh, you mean talking Captain Leyton into lending you young Benjamin Sisko?" Curzon waved it off. "That might not prove to be much of a favor. He can be incredibly stubborn. The lieutenant has a natural command ability, but anything beyond the theoretical scares him. He really has no idea who or what he is, so he loses himself in diagnostics and hypotheticals. But once you bring him around, he'll give you the best he's got."

"I understand humans have an expression about 'hiding your light under a bushel,' " was how Dax broached the subject with Benjamin Sisko once he knew Sisko had gotten Uhura's summons. "One of these days, Benjamin, you're going to take your head out of your technical manuals and notice the universe at large."

"Yes, sir," Ben Sisko remarked by reflex. At the time he'd had his head inside a reflux manifold making an adjustment. It was cramped and hot and airless, and he was feeling light-headed and not a little claustrophobic. "Whatever that means, sir."

"It means, among other things, that you can drop the 'sir,' " Dax said dryly. "This is us, Benjamin. There's no one else down here but you and me. No one's listening."

"Sorry . . ." Sisko made the final adjustment and eased his head out, dusting off his hands, sliding the manifold back into place, activating it, and securing his tools in his belt kit. Everyone else had gone ashore, but he'd volunteered to take a tour in engineering during the layover. ". . . Old Man. It's great to see you again, and I appreciate your putting in a rec-ommendation for me, but whatever this is about, I'd really rather not. The yard crew's going to be crawling all over this ship at 0800 sharp tomorrow. I promised the chief I'd super-vise while he spends some time with his family. And there's Jake's first day of kindergarten . . ."

Just then Dax had touched his shoulder, Sisko thought, to brush some of the dust from the filters off his uniform. There was something askew in *Okinawa*'s environmental controls that created static and caused some of the filters to collect an inordinate amount of dust; Sisko had been puz-zling over it for weeks but hadn't solved it yet. It was one of the things he intended to work on during the refit. He was about to make some comment about the dust when he real-ized Dax was tapping his Starfleet insignia lightly.

"What's this, Benjamin? Just some scraps of metal? Or do they mean something to you?"

"Oh, come on, Old Man! Don't go all Duty and Disci-pline on me! Yes, I'm a Starfleet officer. A Starfleet officer assigned to this ship. And if I'm assigned to another ship, or to a starbase, I'll go. That's what I signed on for. And I will bring my family with me. But being recruited by Intelligence and put on standby for a 'special assignment' while *Okinawa* sails without me? I didn't sign on for that."

"You don't know that's what this is about," Dax suggested.

"Oh, yes, I do. Admiral Uhura keeps a file on everyone who ever took her communications class who showed what she calls 'exceptional skills.' She's not above drafting people from those files for special missions. And you recommended me. That's exactly what this is about."

"And if you know that, you also know you can refuse," Dax said quietly. "But I think you need to at least find out what it's about first. Then talk it over with Jennifer, and—"

"Talk what over with Jennifer? How much can the admiral tell me if I don't agree to sign on?"

Dax gave him a thoughtful look. "You've already got your back up, Benjamin, without knowing anything. You owe it to yourself as much as to Starfleet to keep an open mind here."

That had given Sisko pause.

"What does that mean? Have you been reading tea leaves again, Dax? I didn't know Trills could foretell the future. Wait, where are you going?"

Dax had turned on his heel and started to walk away. "Planetside," he said over his shoulder. "Thought I'd do a tour of some of Earth's wildlife preserves. I hear the bird sanctuaries are extraordinary. I'm especially interested in parrots. Expect I might have a more intelligent conversation with one of them than I'm having here."

Sisko loped down the corridor after him. He towered over the deceptively frail-looking Trill. "Old Man, listen. Captain Leyton's ordered me to speak with Admiral Uhura. He told me you spoke to him on her behalf. You've as good as seen to it that if I do refuse, it won't sit well with Captain Leyton."

"Benjamin—"

"Let me finish. If Admiral Uhura wants me for some special communications project on Earth or aboard ship while we're on layover here, fine. But if it's something that's going to take me off the ship and away from Jake and Jennifer . . ."

Curzon had given him a look then that Benjamin Sisko would remember for the rest of his life. "I don't read tea leaves, Benjamin. Why don't you wait until you know what the assignment is? Then discuss as much as you can with Jennifer. She's a lot more sensible than you are."

"I always do that anyway," Sisko said to Curzon's departing back.

"Benjamin Sisko loves three things, in reverse order of magnitude," Curzon warned Uhura now as he decanted the Izarian aperitif, pouring it into two balloon snifters, waiting for its inner glow to change from iridescent blue to a deep ruby-red before he placed one in her hands. "Good food, his work, and his family. You're proposing to take him away from all three. Don't expect that to go down easily."

"Curzon, he's a Starfleet officer," Uhura said quietly, but not without a bit of steel. "He'll go where he's ordered. But one of my weaknesses, and unfortunately one that I'm known for among the younger generation, is my inability to force a junior officer to accept a commission he doesn't want. I've found out the hard way that an unwilling agent makes a careless agent. And careless agents cost unnecessary loss of life."

Curzon made himself comfortable on the deeply cushioned divan beside her and waited for her to taste the Izarian nectar.

"Curzon, this is exquisite!" she said, smiling for the first time since she'd arrived. She sipped again and settled back among the cushions, the sleeves of her flowing *kikoy*, with its red-brown-black pattern known as Footsteps of Fire, arranged like the folded wings of some exotic butterfly.

"So are you," Curzon replied.

As if on cue, the Hamalki string music began its appearance on the small holopad built into the low table between them, filling the air with sounds and visuals that dopplered softly off the walls and wrapped around the two listeners in innumerable pastels and sprightly sparkles, guaranteed to soothe the soul and stimulate conversation and, perhaps, other things. Curzon touched the rim of Uhura's glass with his own.

"To Benjamin Sisko's greater enlightenment," he suggested. "And to no unnecessary loss of life."

Earlier that day, Uhura had kept Lieutenant Sisko waiting while she pretended to peruse his service record, aware of the impatience all but oozing out of his pores as he sat at attention on the other side of her desk.

Yes, sitting at attention was the only way to describe what he was doing, because when he'd first arrived and she'd told him to take a seat he'd said he preferred to stand. When she advised him he might be here longer than he'd want to be standing he'd sat, but reluctantly and on the edge of his seat, as if ready at the slightest provocation to spring out of it.

It's all about communication! Uhura reminded herself. She'd been about to start communicating when Lieutenant Sisko jumped the gun on her.

"Permission to speak candidly, sir?" he said in that soft, almost musical voice.

"That's why you're here, Lieutenant," Uhura said, closing the file she'd had memorized before he stepped through the door and folding her hands on her desk expectantly.

"Admiral, I'm assuming you asked me here to take part in a special assignment."

"And why would you assume that?"

"Because I know you keep a file on each of your students who show exceptional ability, and I know I was one of them."

Uhura suppressed a smile. "Humility doesn't seem to be one of your problems, Mr. Sisko. And your communications skills will be an asset to this mission. But it's your all-around ability to handle multiple stations and situations that I'm more interested in."

"So you intend to commandeer me from *Okinawa* and assign me—temporarily—to another ship?" Sisko said quietly. "May I ask where?"

"You may not. If I decide to use you, once you're sworn in, you'll have sealed orders fed into your vessel's conn. Essentially the ship will tell you where to go."

"You're giving me command of my own ship?" Sisko asked, puzzled. This was the last thing he'd expected.

"Temporarily," Uhura said. "Just for the duration of this mission. And it's a very small ship."

"May I ask what ship?"

"Not at liberty to tell you that yet, either," Uhura said.

"But I can safely assume the mission will be covert, and it would mean leaving my family behind. With all due respect, Admiral, I'd prefer you found someone else."

"I wasn't asking, Mr. Sisko," Uhura said, her voice even quieter than his.

She saw his jaw working, knew he was trying mightily not to let his temper get the better of him. Like many a big man, he had learned very young that he didn't need to shout or threaten; his mere presence was usually enough to get him his own way.

He stood up to his full height, not intending to intimidate, simply prepared to refuse the assignment and leave. He hadn't counted on having the wind knocked out of his sails by The Look.

"I want to tell you, Commander, it was the expression on your face more than the phaser that backed me into that closet," Lieutenant Heisenberg had told her a lifetime ago, Spock's lifetime to be precise, when she had volunteered to man the most remote transport station in the Sol System in order to help Kirk and company steal *Enterprise* out of Spacedock and bring Spock's *katra* home.

"What are you talking about?" she'd said, suppressing a chuckle, though she knew darn well.

She'd been hoping to have the station to herself that night, but not a half hour before Kirk and Sulu broke McCoy out of the loony bin and stormed out of the turbolift onto the transporter pads, this big galoot had shown up.

"Heisenberg, Scott, here to assist you, ma'am," he'd said, fuzz-faced, tall, and gangly, with a knack for putting his foot in his mouth.

"I don't need any assistance, Lieutenant." She'd frowned. The duty roster had indicated this to be a one-man station. Did someone upstairs suspect something? All of Kirk's crew had felt Command's eyes on them since leaving Spock behind on Genesis. Had Heisenberg been sent to keep an eye on her? "I'm supposed to be assigned here alone. There must be some mistake."

Heisenberg, meanwhile, had been sizing up his new assignment. "Oh, this is great, just great! I wonder whose toes I stepped on to get relegated to this dump?"

"Do you frequently step on people's toes, Mr. Heisenberg?" Uhura pretended to busy herself with a Level-1 diagnostic, probably the first one these battered controls had had in ages. She wished the big lunk would sit down and stop prowling around. Everything depended on timing. If Scotty and Chekov had infiltrated *Enterprise* by now, if Kirk and the others showed up on time, every second she spent trying to sidetrack her unwanted assistant could put the mission in jeopardy.

She'd secreted a phaser under the edge of her console when she came on duty, just in case. Just in case of what, she hadn't been sure, but anyone trying to stop Kirk from getting to *Enterprise* once he was here would have to get through her first. She contemplated the back of Heisenberg's head and wondered if she could just stun him while he wasn't looking. Just then he finished scowling at the charred and battered walls and swung around toward her.

"Yeah, that's me. Open mouth, change feet. Bad enough they used to call me Uncertainty back in the Academy—you know, as in Heisenberg's Uncertainty Principle?" he'd explained, and this time Uhura almost did burst out laughing. "—but bad luck follows me everywhere. Not that I mind being here with you, ma'am, a Starfleet legend and all that, but—"

"Well then, why don't you light somewhere before you trip over those feet as well?" she asked him. Nothing made her feel older than when the younger generation started that Starfleet legend nonsense. "Since you're here, you may as well help me with this diagnostic."

He'd parked himself in the empty chair at the duty station, but made no effort to assist her. Then he'd made that remark about her career winding down, and she'd frozen him in his tracks with what would become known as the Uhura Look.

It wasn't much. Just a pause for about the length of a breath while she stopped whatever she was doing and slid her eyes sideways under those long eyelashes, fixed her victim with them, and raised her head slightly, as if to say "I know you didn't say what I just heard you say."

She'd sworn she could hear Heisenberg's jaw snap shut. She would have liked to see how long that would last, but then Jim Kirk had burst through the door, giving Heisenberg something else to think about.

Months later, after Spock had been restored, and they'd saved the whales and Earth in the bargain, and the flood waters had receded and the "Trial of the *Enterprise* Seven," as the media dubbed it, was over, she'd run into Heisenberg in a corridor at HQ. That was when he'd told her about the Look.

"It's like lasers," Heisenberg said. "You turn those highbeams on a man, you can cut his heart out."

"Best you remember that next time you have dealings with me, young man," Uhura had said, poking him none too gently in the shoulder. "How long were you in that closet, anyway?"

"Couple of hours. I thought my kidneys were going to give out. Earned a nasty reprimand from my CO for letting you get the better of me, too."

"I'm sorry, Heisenberg," she'd said sincerely. "I'll have a word with your CO about that. After all, we both know you were defenseless against The Look."

Many a junior officer had felt the power of that look in the intervening years. Every time she had call to use it, Uhura thought of Heisenberg and resisted the urge to smile.

She turned the Look on Sisko now, and he felt his ears starting to singe. He opened his mouth and nothing came out, found himself shifting his feet, something he only did when he didn't know what else to do. Uhura, barely masking her amusement, let him stew for a few seconds longer, then relented.

"As you were, Mister," she said very quietly, and Sisko returned to his seat. *"Liya na tabia yako usilaumu wenzako."*

"Sir?"

" 'Don't blame others for problems you have created yourself.' I didn't think you spoke kiSwahili. But now that I have your attention . . ."

She cleared her throat, folded her hands on the desktop once again, and began communicating.

"I'm not going to flatter you by telling you're the best theoretical engineer or the most versatile young officer in the fleet, because you're not. What you are is the most versatile young officer in the fleet who has also excelled at my Special Communications course, and who happens to be available in this sector at this time. There are at least three other people I could tap who qualify on the first two counts, but you're here, they're not. And I don't have the luxury of waiting for someone halfway across the quadrant to rendezvous with the rest of my team, which is here, in place, and good to go on a mission where time is of the essence, because lives are being lost with every minute's delay. Am I getting through to you, Mr. Sisko?"

"Loud and clear, sir." Sisko was looking at his boots.

"Good. Now I will give you until 0800 tomorrow morning to reach a decision. If your decision is 'no,' then I will go to the next person on my list. If your decision is 'yes,' then you will see your son safely launched on his first day of kindergarten, and then you will report to me."

She watched his head come up at the mention of Jake.

"A child's first day of kindergarten is a milestone his father shouldn't miss. But there are sacrifices we sometimes have to make, Mr. Sisko. You see Jake off on his very important mission. Then I'll trust you to make the right choice about yours."

"You actually let him walk out of your office without committing?" Curzon was surprised.

"He said he wanted to talk it over with his wife," Uhura explained. "Technically, I suppose I could have ordered him to report for duty straight from my office, but I didn't. Part of what makes my job so hard is not being able to do things like that. But I'm hoping he'll come around."

"If I have to knock him down and sit on him," Curzon said, "he'll come around. Although I think we can count on Jennifer to save us the trouble."

The Hamalki string music had ended. Uhura was looking exceptionally pensive, and the mood Curzon had tried so hard to create was in danger of dissipating.

"Another drink?" he asked her, though she'd barely touched the first one. She shook her head. "More music? I have a number of new pieces that—"

"Thanks, Curzon, but I really should go."

"Without telling me what really happened to you at Khitomer?" Curzon asked. "Isn't that what you came up here for?"

"You know it isn't!" Uhura said, smiling in spite of herself. "But it's as good a place as any to start."

Chapter 7

"I'm not easily embarrassed," Uhura began. "But some of the things that led up to the peace conference on Khitomer left me feeling very much ashamed of myself, personally and professionally." She knew Curzon didn't need to be reminded of the events on Khitomer from nearly seventy years ago; he'd been there himself as part of the Federation delegation negotiating the Accords. But she also knew the side of the story she was about to impart wasn't one he knew.

"First of all, there was the bigotry we all felt toward the Klingons after Praxis exploded. Kirk seemed willing at first to simply let the Klingons reap what they'd sown, and while not all of us felt that strongly, the idea of forming an alliance with them was, at best, unsettling. And while I didn't share the concerns of some at the Starfleet briefing that we'd have to 'mothball the fleet,' as one of the brass put it—I know enough about history to know that as soon as you make peace with one adversary, there's always someone bigger and scarier ready to take his place—I was, shall we say, less than open to the idea of having the Klingons feel they owed us a favor for coming to their aid. That's not a healthy state of affairs for a species obsessed with honor. Not that I need to tell *you* that.

"But that aside, you know what really embarrassed me? The fact that I didn't know enough Klingon to get past the guard post on the way to Rura Penthe. I speak several Earth languages, and know how to cuss in several offworld ones. I've even, for reasons I won't go into here, had reason to make myself understood in basic Romulan from time to time. But beyond knowing how to call someone a *petaQ*— which is not something I'd do on an open frequency—I'd been relying on the universal translator on the rare occasions when it was necessary to deal with a Klingon ship, but this time, that wouldn't do. . . ."

When it was all over, and *Enterprise* moved out of Listening Post Morska's sensor range and slid into warp, Uhura let the dictionary fall to the deck with a thud. "Well, *that* was mortifying!"

Regaining her composure, she gathered the stack of reference books her crew had scrounged from everywhere on the ship, including Kirk's quarters, to try to convince the very sleepy Klingon at Morska that they really were just a passing freighter. The books had saved them from attack; she ought to have a little more respect for them. Always with one ear on passing comm chatter, she braced for the next crisis.

Oddly, the battle with Chang's ship was such a case of déjà vu that it hadn't rattled her. It had been a while—assigned planetside, chairing seminars at the academy—but once the shooting started, she'd even remembered the best places on her console to grab onto when the incoming fire battered the shields and the ship began to yaw. It was a standing joke between her and Scotty.

"Every time there's a refit, the lass sneaks aboard a day early just to see what changes have been made to her station," he'd say with a wink in her direction. "And I'll catch her rehearsin' which handholds worked best under what conditions. Space battles didn't faze her in the least, long as she's got somewhere to grab on to!"

It never once occurred to her that the ship, or she, might not survive. In the event they didn't, well, she hoped it would at least be quick.

However, beaming into the thick of things on Khitomer wasn't something she did every day. Yet there she was, right behind Chekov as they formed a flying wedge through a moil of panicked diplomats to get at Admiral Cartwright and the Romulan ambassador Nanclus while Kirk threw himself between the Federation president and harm's way and Scotty took out the assassin on the upper level. Her adrenalin pumping, there was no time to think. It seemed to be over before it had begun, and if she needed to fall apart, she'd do it later. Even as Azetbur and Kirk were congratulating each other and everyone was lining up for the applause and the photo op, all Uhura could think was: *At least give me a minute to comb my hair!*

Only after security had asked everyone to clear the conference room so they could remove Colonel West's body and clean up the blood, and everyone began to drift toward the buffet a little ahead of schedule, did she manage to excuse herself to find a restroom and try to restore order.

Even as she wove her way down the unfamiliar corridors, past well-wishers from a dozen worlds gesturing, touching her arm, murmuring their gratitude in as many languages, sliding past in a blur of good thoughts and feelings, she was remembering how primitive Klingon facilities tended to be. There had been a single cubicle on Kruge's bird-of-prey, which once upon a time had brought them back to Earth in search of whales, containing little more than a hole in the floor. She couldn't imagine, Khitomer having been chosen as the site for the interplanetary conference, that the same would be the case here. She hoped.

And of course she couldn't remember the Klingon word for "rest room," either, she thought ruefully, approaching an exceptionally serious young Klingon security officer, who saw her puzzlement and offered his assistance. She mimed something which he somehow understood, and pointed her toward the proper door.

Behind which, mercifully, someone had seen to the provision of facilities to accommodate females of all species present at the conference. In fact, the appurtenances proved to be quite luxurious—marble basins, polished brass fixtures, real wood paneling, even a shower and sauna. She sighed with pleasure, her heart rate finally returning to normal.

She didn't dare look at herself in the room-wide mirror above the basins until after she had washed her face and hands and straightened her uniform. She was choosing a comb from the dispenser when a muffled sound from one of the booths told her she was not alone.

At first she was annoyed, mostly with herself. She'd assumed she wasn't the only one in need of a fresher, and had cased the joint, looking for telltale feet under the doors of the booths as soon as she entere¹ But all the doors were at least partway open, and she'd heard no sounds and seen no feet, so she'd assumed the place was empty.

Now she pretended to work on her hair while she used the mirror to scan underneath the doors behind her once more. Nothing. But she definitely heard breathing. Whoever was in there was deliberately hiding, waiting to do—what?

Her nerves still jangling from recent events, Uhura had her phaser out before she realized it.

"Who's there?" she demanded, whirling around, activating her translator and trying to keep her voice steady.

The response was silence, as of someone holding their breath hoping not to be discovered.

Too late for that now, Uhura thought. *Whoever you are, I've got you!*

"Come out of there," she ordered quietly. "I'm armed. I won't harm you if you show yourself, but you've got to come out *now.*"

Still nothing. Phaser at the ready, she moved quickly, pushing doors open randomly, her eye on the second-to-last booth. By now she could hear labored breathing, as if whoever was in there was no longer attempting to hide, but rather was coiled, ready to spring. Pushing the final door open with her phaser hand, Uhura made a grab at a bundle of quilted fabric, found a limb underneath, wrapped her hand around flesh and bone and yanked, hard.

She swung her captive around, out of the booth, and against the wall, casually frisking her for concealed weapons, finding only a small honor blade, which she palmed and slipped into her uniform belt before really taking stock of what she had on her hands.

It was a very young Romulan female, wearing the livery of the diplomatic corps. She was ashen, and not only from the effects of having a phaser pointed at her throat. Her face was smudged with tearstains, and fresh tears started in her luminous brown eyes.

"A-are you going to kill me?" she stammered.

She was just a child, Uhura realized. Probably some diplomat's daughter, frightened by all the shooting, needing to empty her bladder and wash the tears off her face before she disgraced herself. And here was a Starfleet officer scaring her all over again. So much for diplomacy! Chagrined, not for the first time that day, Uhura put her phaser away.

"I'm sorry," she said. "No, I'm not going to kill you. But after what just happened in that conference room, I thought maybe *you* were planning to kill *me*."

As if remembering, the girl started to tremble, and Uhura resisted the urge to put an arm around her and comfort her. She *was* Romulan, she reminded herself. How would someone from her culture handle it? In a gesture of complete trust, she held out the honor blade and, when the girl did not take it, pointedly placed it in her hand and turned her back to her, returning to the mirror.

"It's my guess," she said, addressing the mirror, watching the girl's reflection, "that you've never seen anyone killed before. It's horrifying. I know."

"You are a Starfleet officer," the girl said seriously, weighing the blade in the palm of her hand for a moment before concealing it within her quilted tunic. "You must be accustomed to it."

Uhura put the finishing touches on her hair and dropped the comb in the disposal. She contemplated the choices of lip color in the dispenser as she continued to address the girl without looking directly at her. "Believe me, honey, even if you're trained for it, you never get used to it. And *you* certainly weren't expecting it. My guess is you came here with your family, expecting nothing more than an offworld adventure, a chance to mingle with other species, enjoy some exotic food in alien surroundings—"

She watched the girl's spine stiffen.

"Do not mistake me for some sheltered child. I am an aide to Senator Pardek. I—" She as quickly snapped her jaw shut, angry. "You are a spy! You are trying to trick me!"

"Oh, for pity's sake!" Uhura exploded, turning on her. "May I remind you that you're the one who was hiding from me?"

That seemed to back her off. Uhura programmed in her makeup choices, powdered her nose, touched up her eyebrows, applied the lip color she'd chosen, all in silence, watching the Romulan the entire time. Finally the girl sidled up to the mirror beside her. She ran some water into the palms of her hands, splashed her face. Uhura handed her a towel, which she took after only a moment's hesitation.

"Forgive me," she said at last, watching Uhura's reflection in the mirror as well even though they were all but standing shoulder to shoulder. "You are correct. This whole event has been . . . not what I expected. I rushed in here because I was feeling ill. I had hoped no one would find me until I had regained my composure." She disdained the choice of combs in the dispenser, and began running her fingers through her helmet of dark hair. "That is the only reason I was hiding. And then for you to take me for a child . . ."

"That was presumptuous of me," Uhura said. "Guess I owe you an apology as well. Here, you've got the part all crooked. Allow me . . ."

With that she selected a fresh comb from the dispenser and began to groom the Romulan's short, dark hair; the girl permitted it, and seemed to relax with the added attention.

"There, now, that's much better!" Uhura announced when she had done, leaving the young woman to wonder if she meant the apology, or the repair to her person. "You okay now?"

The girl listened to the translation, then nodded.

"If it's any consolation," Uhura said, disposing of comb and makeup, and wiping the water spots off the basin before disposing of the towel, "the first time I saw someone killed, I also lost my breakfast."

She waited for the translator to render that into an analogous Romulan idiom before she offered her hand and said, "My name is Uhura. Nyota. May I ask yours?"

"Cretak." The girl's handshake was firm and decisive. "Kimora."

"Kimora," Uhura repeated, smiling. "That's lovely. But I will of course call you Cretak until we know each other better."

"Will we?" Cretak withdrew her hand, tucked both hands into her sleeves; it made her look very dignified. "I do not see how. After what happened in that conference chamber, no doubt our peoples will consider each other enemies for a very long time."

"Why? Because some on both sides turned out to be traitors not only to the peace process but to their own people?" Uhura waved it away. "Either we're all implicated with the traitors or none of us are."

"Truly?" Cretak considered it. "How ironic!"

"What?"

"That I am in training to be a diplomat, yet this is an aspect of diplomacy that I had never considered."

"There's a jewel in the bottom of every Pandora's box."

"Pandora's box? What an interesting expression. What does it mean?"

Uhura told her.

Cretak tilted her head like a bird, considering this. "A moral, no doubt. There are many such tales in my culture as well."

"Which shows we're more alike than different," Uhura suggested.

For the first time, the young Romulan smiled. "If only it were that simple!"

"It can be," Uhura said. "Azetbur and Kirk have just made peace. And so have you and I."

"And so with that the two of you became lifelong friends," Curzon suggested dryly.

"Hardly," Uhura sighed. "You know how they say timing is everything? Just then a whole flock of Andorians came fluttering through the door and, as if we'd rehearsed it, Cretak slipped outside, I checked my hair in the mirror one last time to give her time to put some distance between us, then I went back to join my crewmates."

Whom she found, just on a hunch, diligently working the buffet, rounding up traitors having had no noticeable effect on their appetites. The only one missing was Spock, whom she couldn't find at first in the crowded room. Escorting Valeris into custody, Uhura assumed, not wanting to think of what that scene must have been like. It really was a shame. Such a bright young woman, her whole career ahead of her . . .

Two things happened simultaneously. First, Uhura spied Spock at last, talking rather seriously to a portly Romulan senator at the far side of the room. Among the senator's staff, most of them female, most of them young, she caught a glimpse of Cretak, who, as if sensing she was being watched, glanced briefly in Uhura's direction, and as quickly looked away. Or had she been watching her, Uhura wondered, ever since she'd entered the room?

The second thing was that she suddenly found her path blocked by a very tall female officer with captain's bars whom she didn't know but who seemed to know her, and who didn't waste time on formalities.

"Commander Uhura? Unfair of me to stop you on the way to the buffet after the day you've had, but a word alone?"

They beamed blind onto a ship whose identity Uhura never did learn but which, judging from the fact that there were only two transporter pads, she surmised to be about the size of a scout or a frigate. The transporter room was empty. So was the small soundproofed briefing room directly off the transporter room, which was all she ever got to see.

Without being invited, she took one of the two chairs on either side of a bare table in the center of the room and watched, fascinated, as the captain, who still hadn't given her name, ran a hand-held debugging device over the bulkheads (on her own ship?) before she spoke again. In that amount of time, Uhura studied the captain.

Humanoid, but not Earth human. Judging from her pallor and the shape of her skull, possibly a Rhaandarite. Uhura scanned her memory for all the captains whose names she knew, and none of them was a Rhaandarite. Maybe she shouldn't have accompanied her so readily.

"There's no need to look for escape routes," the captain said as if reading her mind, setting the debugger to scramble and putting it on the table between them. "If you can't trust me, it's too late now."

Uhura said nothing, just watched and waited. The captain produced two porcelain mugs and a thermos from somewhere, and took the chair on the other side of the table.

"I'll make this simple. Before the night is over, the command crew of *Enterprise* will be formally debriefed on the events of the past twenty-four hours, but I'm due elsewhere by then, and I wanted to talk to you personally before I left. We've had a listen to your conversation with the Klingons on the way to Rura Penthe—and yes, against orders, in violation of treaty, et cetera—and, no, this time you're not in trouble. Command's long since given up trying to keep Jim Kirk on a leash, but even after he came up roses yet again by saving the president today, there'll be some very big names who'll sleep easier once he's retired."

The captain poured coffee as she spoke. Uhura, remembering the coffee plantations near her grandparents' house, recognized the aroma of real brewed arabica roasted to perfection, and it set her radar tingling. Was the coffee just a coincidence, or had someone learned enough of her background to have supplied it to make a point?

"All that aside," the captain said, setting a steaming mug in front of her, "we're impressed with your handling of the Listening Post and . . . is something funny, Commander?"

"It is now," Uhura said, suppressing a bubble of laughter, "it wasn't then. It was one of the most embarrassing moments of my recent career." She grew suddenly serious. "And I doubt very much that that's the real reason you brought me here. What I'd really like to know is how the hell—begging the captain's pardon—you were able to listen to that conversation?"

"And we were wondering—'we' meaning my superiors and I—" the captain continued as if Uhura hadn't spoken, "now that your ship's about to be decommissioned out from under you—again—whether you really would be content chairing seminars at the Academy for the rest of your life, or if you'd like to join us. How's the coffee?"

Uhura had been holding the mug between both hands, but hadn't tasted the contents. The mundane question superseded a dozen others, and helped her focus.

"It's probably delicious," she said, pushing the mug slightly away from her. "And you expected me to say that, because it's brewed exactly the way I like it, which you know because you've investigated everything that's known about me, probably right down to my DNA, and you didn't do that in the time it took us to get here from Rura Penthe. Are you special ops, SI, or from some other branch of intelligence that we don't talk about?"

"There is no other branch," the captain said evenly. "Yes, I am with Starfleet Intelligence."

"And you know my likes and dislikes, my entire personal and professional history, probably my IQ, my shoe size, and the fact that I love real coffee," Uhura said, also evenly, but there was fire in her eyes. "And you somehow managed to monitor transmissions made while we were deep inside Klingon space and on silent running. And much as the rest disturbs me, it's that last part that really bothers me, because I thought I could detect any bug Starfleet could produce."

"Who said it was Starfleet issue?" the captain asked ingenuously. Uhura had nothing to say to that. "Intrigued? Want to know more? Want to think about joining us?

"This latest escapade shows what we've known about you for a long time, Nyota, which is that you can think on your feet, always essential in an undercover operation," she went on. "But I won't pretend your feeble attempt to master the complexities of Klingon grammar at a moment's notice was what decided us. As a matter of fact, we've had our eye on you for quite some time. It's just that the opportunity to recruit you presented itself here and now because you and I were both in the same place at the same time, and I've decided to act upon that.

"Before you say anything, think about it. Who better than a comm officer to simultaneously work in intelligence? You're *in situ* anyway, monitoring every whisper and string of code incoming and outgoing on a vessel anywhere in two quadrants. Who better to keep her ears on for things outside the parameters of the job?" The captain sipped her own coffee. "Mm, this is good. I wish you'd try it. We can trade mugs, if you think yours is drugged."

"And end up ingesting something Rhaandarites are immune to but Terrans aren't?" Uhura snapped back, not sure whether she was finally starting to fray after the events of the day, or was just annoyed at the cavalier way in which she'd been virtually kidnapped in order to be given this recruitment speech, or whether it was something else entirely.

Because the truth was, the offer sounded like just what she was looking for. There was a tendency in Starfleet to keep kicking people upstairs until they were so brass-heavy they could barely move, then mothballing them behind a desk on a remote starbase somewhere. She wanted to be on a ship. No other ship would ever be *Enterprise*, but she wanted to be on a ship.

The captain's smile widened. "Oh, you are good! And that's why we'd love to have you aboard. But only if you're comfortable with it. All we ask is that you think about it. I promise you won't have to compromise your principles or put your life on the line any more than you've had to under Kirk's command." She coughed. "This isn't some antique spy movie. There's no combat training, you'll not be issued a license to kill or anything silly like that. We just need you to do what you do anyway, which is listen. But listen for us. The opportunities for promotion are . . . interesting. It would be a wise career move for someone with your skills."

"How long will you give me to think about it?" Uhura said after they'd both let the silence go on for a while.

The captain finished her coffee and got to her feet.

"As long as you need to. Let me get you back to the party before you're missed. When you've reached your decision, you can contact me here."

She handed Uhura a communicator of a type she had never seen before.

"It's a one-way, single-use comm unit," the captain explained. "Activate it within one year's time, and it'll find me wherever I am and tell me you're good to go. If I don't hear from you within a year, it'll deactivate itself, you can toss it out the airlock, and you and I never had this conversation."

"That was the whole sales pitch?" Curzon asked, taking the empty brandy snifter from her hands.

"Pretty anticlimactic, wasn't it?" Uhura said. "Oh, and by the way, there was no Rhaandarite captain in the fleet. I checked. But I did a little investigating of my own once I was inside SI, and managed to track her down, just to return the favor."

"Who was she?"

"That I can't tell you. She's dead now, so it doesn't really matter, but she had her reasons for remaining anonymous. And, the truth is, I was at a crossroads; I wanted to jump at her offer. But I was annoyed with the way she'd approached me, so I kept her waiting until after Kirk disobeyed orders one last time and we took the old girl for a spin out Thataway. When I came back, I said yes, and here I am."

"So all those years, even when you had command of your own ship—?"

"Yes. And before you ask, no, I never spied on anyone in Starfleet. Mostly what I did was what I always did, monitored every layer of multiphasic transmission that we passed through on our way from Here to There."

"I'm sure there was more to it than that," Curzon suggested.

"Well, yes, then there's learning to interpret what you hear. What sounds like two merchant captains having a conversation about ion storms could really be a code for safe smuggling routes. What sounds like random static could be a Tholian numeric code revealing an attack plan on a Romulan outpost. If Starfleet is able—circuitously, of course—to get word to the Romulans so they can abort the attack before it happens, at some point that's going to count in our favor."

"Which brings me back to Cretak. Surely you two haven't been incommunicado all this time?"

"No," Uhura said thoughtfully, wondering if the years had been as kind to Cretak as they had been to her. "We never met face-to-face again. But we kept in touch. Sometimes not for decades, but we kept in touch. There are always ways to punch a message through, if you know how. Just a word now and then, a specially coded transmission that only the other would understand, which says 'I'm still here, and you?' And that's all I can tell you on that subject, even here."

"And eventually you ended up running the whole show," Curzon inferred, returning to sit beside her on the overstuffed divan.

"Something like that," she said, feeling his arm slip around her shoulders and deciding to let it stay there.

Not surprisingly, Benjamin Sisko couldn't sleep that night. He tried not to toss and turn too much, but Jennifer was so attuned to him she knew something was wrong even when he was lying still. Finally she said into the darkness: "Want to talk about it?"

Sisko groaned and put the pillow over his head, as if that would make it go away.

"Ben? Ben, come out of there and talk to me," Jennifer bossed him, laughing and tugging on the pillow. She heard him mumble something, then sigh, then surrender. "Ben?

You were at HQ today. My guess is it was something important. Is that what this is about?"

"Can't a man have any secrets?" he wondered.

"Not when a shuttle comes all the way from San Francisco to retrieve you personally."

He'd planned to wait until breakfast to tell Jennifer as much as he could about his meeting with Uhura, trying to figure out a way to tell her just enough but not too much, but now he thought: *Wait a minute. What exactly is there that I can't tell her, since Uhura told me not much of anything? Jennifer's as much bound by Starfleet regulations as I am. She knows whatever we say about this never leaves this room.*

He sat up and told her everything.

"And—?" Jennifer prompted when he'd finished.

"*And*, I don't want to go off on some open-ended assignment and leave you and Jake."

"And you told this to Admiral Uhura without even knowing what the assignment was?" Jennifer said carefully.

"Jennifer, I don't want to leave you. Not for a day, not even for a minute. Can you understand that? I think I'm more in love with you than I was the day I met you. I feel as if every moment away from you is a moment lost forever."

"Every moment except when you're up to your eyebrows in engine specs," Jennifer said dryly. "If I really believed that, Benjamin Sisko, I'd think you were a man obsessed, and I'd tell you you need to have your head examined."

There was a silence between them, a silence where he lost himself for a moment in the liquid depths of her eyes and forgot everything else.

"You think I'm being silly," he said at last, a little sheepishly.

"I wouldn't put it in so many words, but—"

"—but I'm being silly. I should at least find out what the assignment is before I say no. Curzon said something about it helping me to see the world beyond an engine room, but—"

"And how often is Curzon wrong?"

"Curzon is a poet," Sisko grumbled, rolling over on his side and clutching the pillow beneath his head in case Jennifer tried to take it away from him again. "I'm a pragmatist. I don't have the patience for—"

"An assignment with Intelligence can only help your career, Mr. Pragmatist," Jennifer suggested.

Sisko rolled over and scowled at her. "That's *Lieutenant* Pragmatist to you. Are you saying you don't think I'm being promoted fast enough? Are you saying I'm a trophy husband?"

Jennifer laughed and punched him on the shoulder, not entirely playfully.

"I'm saying you married another pragmatist. Someone who's interested in seeing you become your best self."

"No, that would be Curzon." Sisko turned away from her again. He sighed. There'd be no sleeping until they got this settled. "Why is it everyone knows what's best for me better than me?" he asked of no one in particular.

There was no answer from Jennifer, who lay there smiling secretly to herself.

"You want me to go back there tomorrow and tell Uhura I'm in," he suggested. "Without even knowing what it's about."

"Oh, far be it from me to tell you what I think you should do!" was Jennifer's answer.

This time it was Ben who said nothing.

"Ultimately, it's up to you," Jennifer said at last, kissing his elbow, which was the part of him closest to her. "But let it be about you, not about Jake and me, because we're not going anywhere." She kissed his arm where the bicep bulged, then his shoulder, then his neck, then his ear. "Wherever you go, however long you're gone, when you come home, Jake and I will be right here. And I hope the same thing would be true of you if I were the one on special assignment."

"Of course it would!" Sisko said plaintively, turning toward her, stroking her cheek, cradling her head tenderly in one of his big hands.

He kissed her then, and for a long time neither of them said anything.

"You said yourself you don't know where you want to go in your career," she murmured later, snuggled against his shoulder. "Maybe this mission will help show you the way."

"I just miss you," he said, much calmer, settling down toward sleep at last. "Even when I'm with you, I miss you."

"A man obsessed!" Jennifer repeated with a smile. She waited until his deep breathing told her he'd gone to sleep before she too closed her eyes.

The next morning, Benjamin Sisko scooped Jake up in a bear hug and danced him around the room.

"And how is Captain Jake this morning?"

"Going to kiddergarten!" Jake announced seriously in spite of being spun around and in grave danger of being tickled.

The elder Sisko stopped spinning and matched Jake's seriousness with his own.

"Kiddergarten, eh? That's a very important assignment," he said, lowering Jake to the floor. "Are you fully prepared, Captain?"

Jake stood up as tall as he could. "Aye, sir!"

"Well, then, we'd better get you there at warp speed!" Sisko announced, scooping him up again and carrying him out of the kitchen at a run, amid much whooping and giggling.

Chapter 8

She'll never get out of dock! was Sisko's first thought. As he brought the shuttlepod around to view the ship in all her ugly entirety, he tried not to let his despair show on his face.

She was a merchanter, of a class that he thought had been decommissioned nearly a century before, mainly because its designers, desperate to maximize interior space for cargo, had routed far too much of her workings to the exterior, making her vulnerable not only to weapons fire, but even to casual space debris.

She looked like a gigantic horseshoe crab, her engine nacelles tapering aft from the curve of the forward hull into ridiculously narrow finials which, Sisko recalled from a tech manual subheading on how not to design a ship, also doubled as weapons ports. Now there was a brilliant idea! Run your plasma weapons off the same outtake conduits as your matter/antimatter flux and hope every time you fire you don't blow yourself up in the process. But Sisko assumed the weapons had been deactivated, possibly even removed, for the sake of cover. They were supposed to be peaceful merchants dealing in dry goods and machine parts, not the contraband runners these ships were clearly designed for. Somehow the distinction didn't cheer him.

Sisko maneuvered the pod under the hulk's keel, shaking

his head in dismay at the number of conduits, holding tanks, and jury-rigged components he could identify, right out there in the open. Talk about a soft underbelly! A kid with a slingshot could damage this ship. It was a flying bomb. Couldn't Starfleet have done better? Or was that the point—to make this ship seem so hopeless she wasn't worth investigating?

"Permission to speak candidly, Mr. Sisko," Uhura said quietly beside him. She'd been watching the play of emotions on his expressive face, and could sense the steam rising under his collar.

"Those stabilizers have seen better days, Admiral," Sisko remarked tightly, containing himself, his expert eye noticing hairline fractures that would have to be sealed before this thing went anywhere. "And if I had the time and the resources, I'd customize the retro bafflers and do something about streamlining her prow."

"But since you have neither, you'll make do," Uhura said dryly. "You also don't want to defeat the purpose of this mission by making this thing look like anything other than a hunk of junk. Which, as you've obviously surmised, is what it's meant to be. We want any Romulan who picks her up on long-range and comes alongside for a look to dismiss her as not worth getting his hands dirty. Shall we go aboard?"

It took Sisko a moment to find the docking port amid all the shadows and odd angles and, once he did, he eased the pod up to it as gently as he could, as if afraid a sudden jolt would cause the entire ship to cave in and disintegrate into flakes of rust. Not surprisingly, the airlock groaned when he activated it.

Uhura led the way, and Sisko followed her into the cargo bay, glancing wistfully forward toward the conn, which he'd wanted to check out first. Alternatively, he'd have liked to head straight for the engines, which would be where he'd want to spend most of his time before departure. But for whatever reason Uhura wanted him to see the cargo bay first. Well, all right; it was her show.

At least the cargo bay, unlike the gangway, was big enough for him to stand upright without ducking his head. But when Uhura stopped in the middle of one of the narrow aisles formed by several rows of monolithic gray containers as if awaiting his approval, Sisko didn't know what to say.

"Look around you, Lieutenant," she said off his puzzled expression. "What do you see?"

"Containers, ma'am," Sisko answered, hoping he didn't sound sarcastic. Obviously he was being tested. He glanced at the padd readouts on the nearer ones. "Containers whose manifests tell me in Standard and what I assume is Romulan that they're carrying grain and bolts of fabric and machine parts."

"And, being a pragmatist," a voice issued from the direction of a narrow, rusting catwalk Sisko just now noticed running around the upper perimeter of the cavernous space, "you believe exactly what you're told. No one would ever accuse you of uncertainty."

The voice belonged to a lanky older man with snow-white hair, dressed in civilian clothes but with a vaguely Starfleet air about him. He took the treacherously narrow steps down from the catwalk lightly and with extraordinary speed for a man of his apparent age and strode jauntily down the narrow aisle to join them. He had an infectious smile, and that smile was directed at Uhura, though he was sizing up Sisko as he approached.

"He's young," he remarked as if Sisko weren't there.

"So were you once, Heisenberg," Uhura replied warmly. It was obvious these two had known each other for a long time. "Care to show him what you've got here?"

Activating a device about half the size of a communicator concealed in the palm of his hand, Heisenberg pointed it toward the manifest padd built into the side of a container near the end of the aisle, and the container began to move. Actually, it unfolded. The top slid sideways and down, fitting snugly against the rear wall of the container. Then all four sides lowered gracefully to the deck like the petals of some huge metallic flower, revealing not the machine parts the manifest declared, but what looked like a section of a modular medical laboratory.

Countertops slid into place, lights lit up, instrument panels continued a conversation with each other that they'd obviously been conducting in the dark, rows of beakers and retorts evidenced bubbling activities Sisko could only guess at. Transfixed, he barely noticed that Heisenberg, with a spryness that belied his age, was moving among all the containers in the bay, though effecting the same magic on only some of them.

"Some of them are empty," the old man was explaining, his voice echoing as he periodically disappeared from view, "designed to telescope into themselves to make room for the lab modules, which have been randomly distributed among containers that actually do contain what they say they do . . ."

As he explained, the containers, as if on cue, did exactly what he said they would do. The choreography was so complicated that even to Sisko's engineer's eye it looked like magic.

"I'll provide you with a schematic, Mr. Sisko, which you will commit to memory before departure," Heisenberg was saying, his voice nearing and fading as he hopped out of the way of each opening container like an antic spider. "You'll also guard this little gizmo—" Indicating the tiny control unit. "—with your life. From my hand to yours, and no one—repeat, no one—else's."

"Yessir . . ." Sisko said vaguely, unable to keep himself from gawking as the transformation was completed. An ordinary cargo bay inside the ugliest ship in Federation space had become a compact medical laboratory, its components fitted into a single module, as complete as that of any starship's sickbay. The whole thing was an engineering and logistical marvel.

"Dr. Selar will be continuing her research on the virus while you're in transit," Uhura was explaining. "You and Lieutenant Tuvok will be collecting air and soil samples on the planets you visit, looking for contaminants in the water, the food supply, anywhere, while Selar attempts to get tissue samples from anyone reporting an unexplained illness. All of that comes back here at the end of the day for analysis. There are facilities to set up a small field hospital, including a reversed air-flow room and a full-spectrum decon beam to screen incoming personnel for anything contagious that might be clinging to their skin or clothes."

"I see," Sisko said, half listening, moving not quite as quickly as Heisenberg, examining the internal configuration of each container in growing amazement. Uhura, pleased that he was now with the mission in soul as well as body, let him woolgather.

One last module opened to reveal an apparatus even Sisko couldn't quite identify. He was about to examine it when he suddenly realized who had created all of this.

"Dr. Heisenberg?" he said, not even attempting to keep the awe out of his voice. "*The* Dr. Heisenberg? The man who single-handedly kept refining Starfleet's sensors to counter improvements in the Romulan cloaking device?"

"The same, I'm afraid," the white-haired gent acknowledged, containing his admiration for his own work long enough to join his guests. "Although we have little knowledge of what improvements have been made in the cloaking device since the Tomed Incident. Love to get my hands on one. Damn clever, those Romulans."

Sisko turned slowly, absorbing the whole *gestalt*. "This is incredible, sir! I've studied some of your designs, but I've never before seen one in action. But, I don't know how to say this, sir . . . I thought you were dead."

"Ah, well . . ." Heisenberg began, scratching one ear contemplatively. "There are reasons why we want the universe at large to believe that I am." He and Uhura exchanged glances, and Sisko thought he understood. Heisenberg was an SI operative, designer of brilliant gadgetry for agents to use in the field, whose notoriety in a previous career made it necessary for him to be invisible.

"Of course, sir," Sisko said, a trace of hero worship lingering in his voice. The urge to tell Jennifer about his encounter would have to remain just that, an urge. "These modules are incredible!"

"And the beauty of them," Uhura explained with a kind of maternal glow at Heisenberg, "is the double reading. Go over them with the most sophisticated scanner, and they'll show you what you think is inside them."

"How—?" Sisko started to ask Heisenberg, then examined the thickness of one container's sides and figured it out for himself. "False walls. You've installed bafflers in the intramural space."

"Programmed to emit molecular readouts mimicking what ought to be inside each container," Heisenberg acknowledged.

Sisko grinned. "Brilliant!"

"Heisenberg is, shall we say, an expert on enclosed spaces." Uhura added with a twinkle.

It was obviously an in-joke that Sisko didn't get. Did Heisenberg actually look embarrassed?

"I assume, Mr. Sisko, that you'll want to see what makes her tick?" he said.

Sisko's face lit up. "I would indeed, sir."

The engine room was as grimy and rundown as he'd expected, but he found himself rubbing his hands together in anticipation. Jennifer was right; he spent too much time in the realm of theory. Here he would finally get a chance to practice some of the things he'd only dreamed about. He would take this hunk of junk apart and put her back together and have her purring like a kitten in no time.

Sisko stopped himself. *Only if you can do it on the fly, fool! The fact is, you have no time. According to the briefing Admiral Uhura gave you on the way up here, you've got to get this beast up and running and out of here by tomorrow and fly her into the Neutral Zone, if you have to hold her together with spit and paperclips in order to do it.*

As he poked and prodded her, grimacing at the cramped space he'd have to work in, hearing sounds he didn't like, aware that one of the atmospheric converters was overheating even sitting in dock, and wondering where that drip was coming from, he saw that Heisenberg was watching him appreciatively.

"How fast will she go?" Sisko asked at last, wiping his hands on a rag he'd found wrapped carelessly around an atmospheric conduit, ducking his head and following Heisenberg forward to the conn. Admiral Uhura was no longer with them, and he assumed she'd stayed behind in the cargo bay, possibly receiving more incoming from the rest of her team.

"Guess," Heisenberg said with his characteristic twinkle.

"I'm guessing warp 4 flat out," Sisko said.

Heisenberg was scratching his ear again. "Not quite."

"You mean she's slower than that? With all due respect, sir, why don't we just paint a target on her side and have done with it?"

"Actually," Heisenberg said diffidently, "she can manage warp 7 or even a tad more if you speak to her nicely."

That rocked Sisko back on his heels. "You can't tell me this ship can go that fast."

Heisenberg shrugged. "Don't need to tell you; I can show you. Computer: Engine specs, code 'Uncertainty.' " A schematic appeared on the heretofore blank forward screen. "Modifications here, here, and here."

Sisko whistled appreciatively.

"I'm hoping no one but an engineer would notice them," Heisenberg said. "There's also a set of blind controls double-rigged on her impulse controls to conceal her special skills from prying eyes. But I guess, being a pragmatist, you'll have to take her out and discover all that for yourself."

"But she's not built for it," Sisko objected. "And with all those exterior components, she'll rattle apart."

"Will she?" Heisenberg seemed surprised at the thought. "She didn't the last time I took her for a spin."

"You've reinforced her bulkheads as well," Sisko guessed. "How, without it showing up on scanners?" He thought about it. "Oh. The same way you've double-hulled the containers."

"Bright lad!" Heisenberg said. "Truth is, with all the modifications, she weighs almost twice what she's supposed to. But unless the Romulans—or even one of ours—can actually haul her into a spacedock and put her on a scale . . ."

"One of ours?" Sisko repeated, but Heisenberg was headed back to the cargo bay.

"The outer hull is also equipped with bafflers programmed to feed back the same readings as the manifests on each individual container. Scan the ship from the outside, and you'll see rolls of Tholian silk in the most alluring colors, replacement parts for Romulan food replicators, a consignment of blue corn destined for the Draken colonies, assorted cams and stem bolts. One container actually holds medical supplies, but none worth stealing. More of the take-two-aspirin-and-call-me-in-the-morning variety, but they may come in handy for trade."

The lab modules continued their humming, blinking, bubbling conversation with each other. As Sisko had guessed, Uhura was waiting for them here, sitting primly on a stool behind a medical console that twinkled like a Christmas tree, looking like a schoolgirl on the first day of biology lab. Heisenberg, still in lecture mode, concluded his talk.

"Someone would actually have to board the ship and manually breach the containers—since you won't let anyone take the control unit from you—to find the lab modules or the transmitter."

"Which brings me to a question, Doctor," Sisko said. "If we are stopped and boarded, by the Romulans or, as you say, someone from our side—because once we cross the Zone we'll be in violation of treaties on both sides—but someone with enough clout comes aboard and demands to see the cargo bay, how quickly can these modules—"

He never finished his sentence. In the time it took Heisenberg to wink at Uhura, who, knowing the floor plan, wisely stepped out of the way, the containers began to reverse their initial opening dance, refolding and sealing themselves with such rapidity that Sisko almost didn't know where to duck first. When the show was over and everything had been put back into place in an uncannily brief amount of time, he tried to recover his dignity.

"And what if someone's inside one of the modules at the time?"

"We're assuming they'll hear the commotion you and Mr. Tuvok are creating in the control cabin trying to keep the invaders out, and manage to step away in time," Heisenberg explained. "If not, I've programmed in just enough space for an average-sized person to conceal themselves—not comfortably, but safely—and enough breathable oxygen for about thirty minutes. If you can't subdue your attackers in that amount of time, the assumption is they're going to take over the ship and your cover will be blown and your crew captured regardless of what I've done to prevent it. The bottom line, Mr. Sisko, is that technology can only do so much. The rest is up to you. And now, just one more thing . . ." Heisenberg motioned toward the mystery apparatus in the final container. "A little joint venture on the part of the admiral and myself. This one amazes even me."

It was the module that had mystified Sisko when he first

saw it. Heisenberg allowed him to puzzle over it for several minutes.

"I give up!" Sisko said finally. "What is it?"

"Only the most amazing holotransmitter not yet known to modern technology," Heisenberg said. "It's a little bit of transporter technology grafted onto a great deal of communications wizardry. With this, the admiral and her medical team will be able to accompany you on your journey."

With that Dr. Selar "appeared" at one of the lab consoles. She glanced up at the three of them as if it were they who had appeared in her space and not the other way around.

"How goes it, Selar?" Uhura asked.

"Progressing, Admiral. We have been able to track some samples of the pathogen by sound using wave transmitters, and consequently to increase the accuracy with which we detect mutations."

"Excellent . . . I think," Uhura said. "I'll get back to you on that. We're just testing the holotech at the moment."

"Understood," Selar said as she shimmered out of sight.

"Holograms," Sisko shrugged, unimpressed for the first time. "Fun to play with at close range in real time. But impractical for long-range transmission. They'd be detected immediately."

Heisenberg and Uhura exchanged glances.

"He's young," Uhura admitted.

"O ye of little faith . . ." Heisenberg shook his head. "You did not hear me say what I'm about to say, but SI's best comm people and I have created a kind of piggy-back technique that rides existing carrier waves and is virtually undetectable."

"It's only a prototype," Uhura explained. "It'll be decades before it's standard issue, but what we've developed so far will be tested on this mission. You, Tuvok, and Dr. Selar will physically be on the ship inside the Zone, but with the help of Heisenberg's wizardry, Dr. Crusher and Dr. McCoy will 'go along' as consultants. And I'll be popping in from time to time as well."

Sisko looked from one to the other of them. They seemed to think this was the most brilliant bit of technology aboard this old ship, but he was still unimpressed.

"I can't see how that's going to help," he began tentatively. "Or how it can go undetected . . ."

Heisenberg motioned him toward the controls. "Run a diagnostic right now and tell me if you detect any stray transmissions."

Sisko did as he was told and, not surprisingly, came up with nothing. "Not now, sir. You've shut down the transmission to Dr. Selar. There's no reason why there should be—"

"Tsk, tsk, tsk!" Uhura said as she shimmered out of sight.

"What the—?" was all Sisko could manage.

Heisenberg was chuckling. "You reported to her office, walked together to the pod bay, got in the shuttle and came all the way up here together. Or so you thought."

Sisko said nothing.

"She's been walking through the choreography in her office, son. She was never here. And neither am I."

Now it was Heisenberg's turn to disappear.

"But . . ." Sisko suddenly had to sit down, but he wondered, if he did, whether any seemingly solid surface around him might not also disappear. If the entire ship suddenly vanished out from under him at this point, he wouldn't have been surprised.

"All right, that may have been a little over the top," he heard Heisenberg's voice behind him. The old man—or his holo; who could tell anymore?—came toward him, the same smile on his face, the tiny control for the containers still half-concealed in the palm of his hand. "No more tricks, Mr. Sisko, I promise. This is the real me."

He held out his hand and Sisko shook it.

"The real me has been running this from the forward cabin until now."

"But Admiral Uhura—?"

"Never left Earth."

As if on cue, she reappeared, beaming at them both.

Sisko didn't realize he'd been holding his breath. He let it out now in a great sigh of exasperation. Then he began to laugh.

Heisenberg was fiddling with the holotransmitter. "I think that means we did good," he told Uhura. He handed Sisko the tiny control unit. "She's all yours, Lieutenant. Be good to her."

With that he winked, gave Uhura a sloppy half-salute, and made his jaunty way along the gangway, ducking his head to get through.

There was a long moment of silence as Sisko studied the control in his hand and considered everything he'd just seen. Uhura was so quiet he all but forgot she was there, until he remembered she wasn't. This comm thing was going to make him dizzy if he thought about it too hard.

Uhura watched him glance up at the deck plating above them, assessing conduits, listening to the old hulk breathe. Finally he found his voice.

"Does she have a name, Admiral? The ship, I mean?"

It was something Uhura hadn't considered. "Not as far as I know, Lieutenant. Registry's got her listed by number, but I don't believe she ever had a name."

"Well, she does now," Sisko said with a grin. "I hereby dub her *Albatross*, because while she's not exactly hanging around my neck, I know she's going to come to haunt me. How long can I spend with her before departure?"

Pleased at his enthusiasm, Uhura smiled back. "The away team meets in my office at 0800 tomorrow. You're set for departure at 0900. I expect you'll have this bird in shape to fly by then."

"Yes, ma'am!"

With a spring in his step, grinning like a kid with his first treehouse, Sisko headed for the engine room.

"Numbers," Koval said. "Give me numbers."

"How am I supposed to do that?" the voice on the other end protested. "They're changing literally by the hour; where the seeds have been activated, entire populations are dropping in their tracks. Why are you asking me? The transmitter you gave me doesn't have that much range; you've got access to more accurate numbers than I possibly could."

"Not the numbers of dead, you fool!" Koval snapped. "The numbers of seedings necessary to achieve critical mass."

"Oh, forgive me. This thing is getting on my nerves. I thought by now we'd . . . here . . . Green Sector, one hundred four, all activated, Blue Sector, forty-one released, eight activated so far. Inside the Zone—"

"Make that forty-two," Koval said.

"Say again?"

"Forty-two on the Federation side. One little seed has escaped the main pod all by itself and drifted across the Zone without any help from us."

There followed a long silence.

"Should I be pleased at that information?"

"Considering where it landed, you should be thrilled," Koval said, then interrupted before the other could speak. "You won't lose your nerve now, I trust? I have not cared for the tone in your voice of late."

"I'll be fine as soon as I can release my data. When can I release my data? If this thing spreads too far, even the medication won't stop it, and knowing the Federation, they'll spend months questioning my data until somebody important dies . . ."

"Are you squeamish?" Koval wondered half to himself. "Does the thought of all that death weigh on your conscience? Or is it just that you're greedy for all the accolades that will come your way once you announce your cure? Remember, the disease has to have a name first. It has to kill enough people to be seen as a threat before you can offer a cure."

"How much longer do you intend to let this go on?"

"Don't question me." Koval's voice, never warm, went colder still. One finger hovered over the toggle that would terminate the transmission. "I find it unpleasant. I don't believe I need to remind you that you don't want to give me the least bit of unpleasantness."

"It wasn't supposed to happen this way," Cinchona muttered to himself, forgetting how acute the woman's hearing was. "If he'd targeted a planetary leader, someone visible. It should be over by now . . ."

Boralesh paused in her kneading. "What's that, husband?"

"The universe, my sweet," he answered quickly. "The universe is against us. Some of us believe that there is an innate rightness in the way things work. That all we have to do is work hard and we will be rewarded for our labor."

Boralesh dusted her hands with more flour and began to work the dough anew, repressing any rude comments she might be inspired to make. "Work" and her husband were not two words she could put together in the same sentence.

"The universe will reward you as you deserve, husband," she said dryly, knowing her subtlety would elude him. "Give it time."

"Got to release my data," he murmured. "He has to understand; I've got to release my data . . ."

Boralesh smiled secretly. The morning light in her cheerful kitchen was kinder to him than it ought to be, softening his chronically furrowed brow, his lipless mouth and suspicious squint into something almost attractive. She reminded herself that if he hadn't wed her no one would have, and she ought to be grateful. And yet, she'd grown up among the healers of her own country and had seen how their work shaped them. They became more open, more beautiful as they became more evolved in the practice of their craft. The saying "heal others and you heal yourself" had proven true among her own kind.

But the more her spouse labored over his mysterious methods in the cave below the village, the harder, the more shut down, the more furtive he seemed to become. He thrashed and moaned and ground his teeth in his sleep, his digestion troubled him, and even her best herbs had no effect.

She had crept to the mouth of his secret cave more than once and heard him speaking in tongues. Sometimes he seemed to be communing with some god or gods, because there would be silences and then he would answer. Whenever he returned to the house after one of those sessions, he was silent, moody, more impatient than usual with the children, and he couldn't eat or sleep at all for days.

Did she love him? Boralesh wondered. Or did she cling to him because without him her children's lives and her own would be meaningless? It was not a question she could answer. As her hands worked the dough for the homemade bread he loved so much, she added some herbs from her secret store and bided her time.

Chapter 9

The arrow whizzed past Tuvok's right ear, tearing foliage off the trees behind him. Unperturbed, he drew the bowstring back as far as his left ear, and let fly.

"Incoming at five o'clock, husband," Selar reported beside him, crouched below the tumble of rocks Tuvok had chosen as a defensible position when the attack started. She was picking up life-form readings on her medical tricorder, since Tuvok's hands were occupied. "Bearing 13 degrees azimuth."

Careful to aim above their attackers' heads, Tuvok let a second arrow fly. It was greeted by a spatter of truncated Sliwoni arrows, released from short bows held sideways at the waist, making them far less accurate than Tuvok's longbow. Two fell short, skidding to a halt in the dirt, another overshot the Vulcans, two more struck the rocks very close to them, sending stone chips flying, but doing no more damage than that.

Taking advantage of their assailants' inferior weaponry, Tuvok responded with a third arrow, then a fourth, a fifth, a sixth in rapid succession. The response was two more shots from the attackers, then nothing.

"They are dispersing," Selar reported before Tuvok's last arrow had even struck home, embedding itself, they discovered as they made their way back to the ship, a hand's-breadth deep into one of the old-growth trees in the grove from which their assailants had tried to cut them off from the ship.

Their arrival on Sliwon had been uneventful enough. The Sliwoni had a taboo against orbital vessels and so, against Sisko's better judgment ("I just hope I can get her off the ground again!" he'd muttered), *Albatross* had followed the authorities' instructions, crossed atmosphere, and come to land.

Sisko had set her down in a clearing not far from the highway leading to one of the larger communities, backing her around so that her stern was all but flush with a sheer cliff face dropping more than fifty feet to the sea. Because of Sliwon's exceptionally large moon, the tides here were extreme, varying as much as thirty feet from low tide to high. That and crosscurrents and quixotic winds made the cliff face virtually unassailable even by the local hovercraft. All the same, Sisko stayed with the ship, content to tinker with his engines while the others went about their research in town. Their cover story that they were traveling merchants had, just as on the two previous worlds, been readily accepted.

But something had happened while the Vulcans were away. Rumors arrived with the great rumbling convoys bringing produce to and fro, or beeped and chattered along each citizen's personal comm unit, worn permanently affixed to the left ear for constant communication. Something heard from somewhere else had turned the Sliwoni suspicious, and hostile looks followed the outworlders. Tuvok and Selar had wisely decided to curtail their visit, only to find that a party of villagers armed with traditional weapons had gotten back to the clearing before they did, and cut them off.

It had been agreed from the beginning that the away team would not carry phasers, which was not to say that Tuvok was unarmed. Though they were advanced enough to have in-system spaceflight and fairly sophisticated communications and transportation technology, the Sliwoni held an anachronistic reverence for knives and archery as personal weapons. Tuvok had fashioned a longbow and some arrows from native materials, and found he had need of them now.

Clearly not expecting that one lone outworld archer could outfire them, the villagers had retreated.

"My thanks for your assistance, wife." Tuvok lowered the longbow, which was almost as tall as he was, to his side, but nocked another arrow at the ready, just in case.

"What you need is an infrared scope," Sisko said, opening the *Albatross*'s hatch, which he'd sealed off when the attack began, and seeing them safely aboard. "Or maybe heat sensors embedded in the arrowheads."

Tuvok waited while Selar stepped through the decontamination beam, then repaired to the lab with the day's specimens, before stepping off the transporter pad and out of the beam himself.

"Since it was my goal *not* to hit any of the villagers, I fail to see how a heat-seeking sensor would be of benefit," he said dryly. "I assume you are joking."

"Yes and no," Sisko said. "But you have to admit the infrared scope would be a good idea."

"Indeed, given a warm-blooded species." Tuvok headed for the sleeping quarters to put the bow and his few remaining arrows away. "But it would not work for Gorn, for example."

"Granted," Sisko said, following him to continue the conversation, "but give me the specs, and I could probably design one that could read even cold-blooded species . . ."

"Boys and their toys!" Tuvok heard Uhura murmur.

"Well, no one had the courtesy to give me an exterior visual to watch the fight," McCoy grumped. "But from what I hear, that 'toy' may have just saved your away team."

"Has the ship sustained any damage?" Tuvok asked, ignoring both Uhura and McCoy. Unless they were holding an official briefing, the away team was so accustomed to the holos' background chatter by now that they usually worked around it.

"She's fine," Sisko reported of *Albatross*. "They may have been intent on vandalizing her, but they didn't get very far before you all arrived. I just battened down and waited until I picked you up on sensors. May I?"

Tuvok un-nocked the last arrow and handed Sisko the bow. Not for the first time, Tuvok noticed the human admiring the craftsmanship.

"Not bad for a southpaw," he said, handing it back. "How'd you learn to shoot like that?"

"In ancient times, many Vulcan tribes were skilled archers." Tuvok stored the bow beneath his sleeping compartment. "The arid climate is conducive to accuracy over great distances, though the heavier gravity also presents some challenges. Nevertheless, if one can learn to shoot an arrow on Vulcan, the skill is commensurately easier on other worlds."

"That's the long answer," Sisko said with a slight smile. "Is there a short one?"

"I have taught the principles of archery at the Vulcan Academy of Defensive Arts," Tuvok replied. "And to assume that one who is naturally left-handed is any more or less skilled than someone who is right-handed . . ."

"I stand corrected," Sisko said with a wink in McCoy's direction. The aged doctor chuckled. "I'd better get back to work on that adapter," Sisko continued. "How much longer will you and Selar need to finish your collecting?"

"That will depend on the outcome of Dr. Selar's tests on today's specimens," Tuvok said thoughtfully. "Unless, of course, what disturbed the Sliwoni escalates into a situation which necessitates our abrupt departure."

"Which I can't guarantee until I can get that damn adapter to do what it was designed to do, or jury-rig something else that will," Sisko said.

Tuvok glanced around the cabin, feeling a frown form on his face. "Where is Zetha?" the Vulcan asked quietly.

Now it was Sisko's turn to frown. "I don't know."

"You want to what?" Crusher had demanded. "I don't think that's a good idea at all."

"Is there a medical reason why she can't be cleared to accompany the away team?" Uhura asked.

"You know there isn't. There's some evidence of childhood malnutrition, but she's in excellent health now," Crusher half-whispered, leaning into the screen and hoping Zetha couldn't hear. Crusher was in her office, separated from the examining room by a clearsteel partition. Just past her left shoulder, Uhura could see Zetha sitting upright and quite still on the end of the diagnostic bed, studying her surroundings with her characteristic alertness, and no doubt aware that she was being discussed in the next room. "You still haven't told me who she is or what's going on."

Medical had always had a special place within Starfleet hierarchy. Doctors regardless of their rank reserved the right to tell off their superiors at regular intervals and, technically, Crusher did not answer to Uhura or anyone in SI, but to her superiors at Medical. So if she chose to address the admiral as a peer and even, on occasion, chew her out, it was expected.

"She's the courier who brought the locket across the Zone," Uhura said.

"She came all this way through hostile space, carrying something that could have killed thousands if the inner seal was breached—" The very thought made Crusher breathless. "She's barely out of her teens!"

"And a Romulan, not some spoiled human kid. From what Tuvok's been able to gather, a Romulan with no family who grew up on the streets. Tuvok's not entirely sure whether or not she's a trained operative."

"Oh, and so you want to send her back the way she came

and hope she doesn't signal her superiors and betray the rest of your team. Brilliant!"

"I thought it was," Uhura said calmly, pretending she didn't hear the sarcasm in Crusher's voice. "Because if she does make the attempt—and I believe Tuvok's capable of preventing her from completing such an attempt—then we'd know for sure that her story's a fake, wouldn't we?"

Crusher managed to look chagrined. "I hadn't thought of that."

"Which is why you're a doctor, not an intelligence operative," Uhura said before McCoy could. The old grouch had gotten the hang of Heisenberg's holo program, and found he enjoyed virtually loitering in her office to eavesdrop whenever the fish weren't biting. "I want her along for cover on worlds where there are Romulan speakers. As good as they are, Tuvok and Selar are still Vulcans. There are circumstances under which an outright lie could trip them up, and nuances of the culture and the language that Zetha can pick up that the others might not. And I do believe that, in the custody of three Starfleet officers, there's very little harm she can do. How would you characterize her mental status?"

"She seems . . . wary," Crusher conceded. "As I would be in strange surroundings, among a people I'd never seen before who spoke a language I only partly understood. Oh, yes," she said off Uhura's puzzled look. "She's already mastered the rudiments of Standard and then some. She wanted to know exactly what I was doing, what each instrument was for . . ."

Zetha had been watchful but cooperative during most of the examination, answering questions, following instructions. "Close your left eye, now your right eye, stick your tongue out, inhale, exhale, cough. Does this hurt? What about this? This may sting a bit. Lie down, sit up, stand on one foot, hop on the other," and so on. Only the hypospray seemed to alarm her.

* * *

"What is that?" she had demanded when she saw what the healer had in his hand, her muscles tensing, ready for fight or flight. Pointless. At the weak-chinned Tal Shiar operative's nod, the injection was administered, and the healer left the room.

"Nutritional supplements," the weak-chinned lord said. "You're not a little malnourished."

"No, really? After a lifetime on the streets? Who'd have imagined?"

"Dispense with the sarcasm," he snapped. "It's very unattractive."

"Of course, Lord," she'd replied flatly. Did he know this was the greatest sarcasm of all?

"What is that?" she demanded again when Crusher approached her with the hypo. *Either side of the Marches,* Zetha thought, *it's all the same!*

"I'm not injecting you with anything," Crusher explained gently, stepping back a little at her alarmed look. Professional manner aside, she'd taken an immediate liking to the girl and wanted to put her at ease. "It's just a blood draw. Some of it will be used in our research, but mostly it's to make sure you're healthy."

"She does seem to be wound too tight," Crusher acknowledged. "But that may be normal for a Romulan. It might also be a little bit of post-traumatic stress. Did she give you any details on how she got here? I imagine it must have been harrowing. She'd need to process that."

"But would you say she's fit to travel?"

"If I say no, you'll lock her away in one of your famous SI containment rooms, at least until the away mission returns. Which could be weeks or . . . longer." Neither woman was willing to complete the thought that the away mission might not return at all. "But if I say yes, and you send her into the Zone, at least part of the responsibility is mine."

Just past Crusher's shoulder, Uhura watched Zetha slide quietly off the diagnostic table and begin moving slowly around the enclosed room, not touching anything, but examining every object she could see from every possible angle, as if memorizing it. She did not, Uhura's practiced eye noted, bother to try the door or seek any other avenue of escape, at least not overtly. But then she would know she was being watched, so perhaps she would do that later. Her actions could be equally interpreted as those of a curious child, or a spy.

"Let me worry about that, Doctor. Is there any way you can give me an objective assessment of her state of mind?"

"You mean anything that might indicate whether she's been conditioned, trained to lie?"

"Not necessarily."

"There are tests I can run, but whether they'd work on a Romulan . . . we know so little about them, and half of that's rumor laced with propaganda. I doubt a standard DSM score would work, but—"

"In English, please."

"Diagnostic and Statistical Manual of Mental Disorders score. With some modifications, it's how we've assessed human mental status for the past four hundred years. I can't tell you if it will work. But I have an idea what might." Crusher hesitated. "I'd like to take her home with me tonight."

"Doctor . . ." Uhura nodded toward the room behind her, where Zetha had chosen that moment to pick up a small mediscanner Crusher had left on a side counter. It bleeped sharply enough to startle her, and she set it down a little too forcefully as Crusher turned abruptly in her direction. Almost sheepishly, the girl moved away from the counter and retreated back to the bed.

"Some spy!" Crusher remarked before Uhura could state

the obvious. "She's just curious. It's normal. My radar would go off if she *wasn't* curious. And if she could spend an evening with Wes and me in a less clinical setting, I think I could learn more. See how she socializes, get her to drop her guard."

"Absolutely not!" Uhura said. "Don't get soft on me now, Dr. Crusher. She'd be a security risk, and you know it."

"Respectfully, Admiral," Crusher said, "you've asked me for a psych assessment; this way I can give you one. You're not going to get that with her sealed up in a windowless room with no one but Tuvok to talk to. Oh, I know, SI's containment rooms have all the amenities of a luxury hotel, if you overlook the fact that the door locks in the wrong direction. She needs socialization, not just a bunch of SI types asking her questions all the time."

"I agree," McCoy chimed in. He had the annoying habit of presenting himself as just a voice, even though he had Uhura and Crusher on visual.

Who asked you? Uhura wanted to snap at him, but she restrained herself.

"You might remind yourself that she's as strong as a Vulcan," she told Crusher. "Would you be able to overpower her if she attacked you?"

Crusher held up a hypospray. "This can. Done it before with psychotic patients. Has she attacked anyone so far?"

"She's been contained so far."

"Do you want me to do a psych profile or don't you?"

"Are you blackmailing me, Doctor?"

"What do you think? At home I can run her through DSMs and Rorschachs and anything else you'd like and give you an evaluation in the morning. I can also feed her a home-cooked meal and show her that humans aren't the monsters her upbringing has no doubt led her to believe. You want to be paranoid, fine. Have Tuvok tag along. He can bunk in with Wes; they can play *kal'toh* together. But Zetha gets the guest room."

Uhura drummed her fingers on her desk, weighing options. This wasn't what she'd had in mind, but was she balking just because McCoy was siding with Crusher?

"Promise me you'll be careful," she said at last.

Crusher held up the hypo once again. "Where the safety of my son is concerned? Always."

Sisko was the last to arrive at the briefing the next morning, and realized something at once as he glanced around the room.

I'm the only human on this mission, was his first thought. His second was, *Get over it. Not every Vulcan is like Solok!*

That particular Vulcan and his notions of racial superiority had left Sisko with a sore spot ever since his Academy days. The resentment still festered, though he hadn't seen Solok in years. Solok was one Vulcan who didn't seem to understand that it was illogical, not to mention unjust, to continually point out to humans where they were lacking in comparison to Vulcans, whether it was in physical strength, longevity, emotional control, or intellect.

All the more reason not to judge all Vulcans as a species. You're in command of this mission, he reminded himself. *You can't afford to let old baggage get in your way. Besides, no Vulcan will ever be able to throw a split-finger fastball. Console yourself with that.*

His reactions to his fellow Starfleet officers were fleeting. But then he caught sight of Zetha. A civilian. And another Vulcan? If so, something about her was . . . off, Sisko decided, but he couldn't figure out at first what it was.

"Thank you for joining us, Mr. Sisko," Uhura said evenly. "I believe some introductions are in order. Lieutenant Tuvok, Dr. Selar, Lieutenant Benjamin Sisko. And this is Zetha. She has come to us from across the Neutral Zone."

"A Romulan—?" Sisko blurted before he could stop himself.

Zetha's chin came up, her eyes narrowed, assessing this

human, but saying nothing. Uhura cleared her throat, and Sisko settled himself into the only empty chair in the room.

"I'll make this brief, people," Uhura began. "Your goal is to attempt to track this disease to its point of origin. You're to start with worlds where we have Listeners, and work your way backwards, following the disease vector Dr. Selar has plotted from known cases. We need to know where this began, even if you have to go all the way across the Zone and into the Empire to do so."

She didn't give anyone time to react, but forged ahead.

"Your cover will vary from world to world. We don't know a lot about the worlds inside the Zone. Some are Romulan sympathizers, some would prefer to be allied with us, but the majority seem, not surprisingly, to resent being marginalized to a DMZ between two enemies whose differences they refuse to recognize. So I don't think I need to tell any of you to get the lay of the political land before you speak.

"Mr. Sisko, you are in command. Your cover is as the skipper of the *Albatross*. She's your ship. The others have chartered your ship and your services. You're a Terran, but a freebooter with no loyalty to any government. Your cover name is Captain Jacobs. All the necessary documentation is in your personal logs onboard."

If he noted his sudden promotion, Sisko didn't mention it. He did notice Uhura had given him his son's name as cover, and it was enough to make him smile. Uhura read his thoughts on his face and spoke before he could.

"Don't get sentimental on me, Lieutenant. I gave you that name as a mnemonic. It's one thing you'll never forget, whatever the circumstances."

"Yes, ma'am."

"Your goal is simple," Uhura continued addressing the group. "Target the places where people gather. Talk to them, monitor news reports, listen to gossip. If possible, monitor the medical clinics. Any report of unusual illness, get in as close as you can and collect what you can, bring it back to the ship for testing, and interface with Starfleet Medical.

"Tuvok and Selar, where you believe it best to be Vulcan, you will use your true names; where Romulan cover would be preferable, use the names Leval and Vesak. You are itinerant merchants, husband and wife, and Zetha is your niece."

Selar nodded. Tuvok reacted not at all. Zetha looked as if she were about to speak, but thought better of it.

"Your course has already been laid in; the ship knows where she needs to go, but you can override if necessary. Specifics on known worlds are in the memory banks; you'll have plenty of time in transit to memorize the details. Dr. McCoy, Dr. Crusher, and I will be available to confer on holo whenever necessary. I don't have to tell you that if for any reason you're boarded, use your discretion, but if you're taken in tow, you dump everything.

"I wish I had time to go into more detail now, but the one thing we don't have is time. This thing is spreading. There are now over thirty Federation worlds reporting deaths, and the media's picked it up; we can no longer keep this quiet. People are dying. We have to track this thing to its source and put a stop to it."

She made eye contact with each of them, trying unsuccessfully to keep the emotion out of her voice.

"Dismissed," she said, "and all my hopes go with you."

"So you're Romulan?" Sisko broke what seemed like an eternal silence, punctuated only by the hum and bleep of instrumentation and the odd, ominous creak from the old bird now and then that he was determined to track down as soon as he had a moment. Even though *Albatross* had been on autopilot since she'd coughed and grumbled her way out of one of the most remote berths in the Utopia Planitia yards, he still felt a strange obligation to sit at the conn and watch the stars go by. At some point, Zetha had joined him.

"Yes" was all she said now, mesmerized by the view on the forward screen.

"I've never met a Romulan before. I don't think most humans have. What's your story?"

"Truth is always easier than a lie," the Lord had drummed into them at drills, usually during combat training. "Why?"

Zetha watched the others watching each other, none of them wanting to speak first, in case they might be wrong. Apparently it was the reaction he expected, for it made him smirk.

"Truth is consistent!" he barked to be heard above the grunting and huffing and straining in the cold, high-ceilinged room as his *ghilik*, as he called them—the word meant "mongrel"—went through their daily exercises and he stood off to one side, hands clasped behind his back, alternately berating and lecturing them. "If you must lie, remember what you've told to whom, in case you're asked to repeat your story later."

The less intelligent among them, even those who'd survived by lies, had raised their hands during the break, asking questions. Zetha said nothing, but when he challenged her, she was ready.

"Truth is also dangerous," he barked, gimlet eyes focusing on Zetha, annoyed that she didn't flinch the way some of the others did still. "Why?"

She hadn't hesitated. "Because to tell the same truth too consistently makes it seem like a lie."

He hadn't smiled, hadn't even acknowledged what she'd said. He'd merely narrowed his eyes at her, and she knew she'd won.

"So essentially we're on this mission because of you," Sisko said thoughtfully when she'd told him the most recent version of the truth.

Zetha shrugged to hide a sudden lurch in her heart rate. *Carefully!* "That's one way of looking at it."

"How do we know you're not a spy?"

"Tuvok doesn't seem to think so."

"You're not speaking with Tuvok at the moment," Sisko said, tweaking the environmental controls, which were still sluggish regardless of the work he'd done. His tone was not unkind, but it was incisive. "I'm in command of this ship."

Zetha shrugged again. She understood that her role here was no different than what it has always been—to be silent, invisible, to speak when spoken to, watch and listen. She had followed Tuvok onto *Albatross*, dutifully stowed the clothing Uhura had provided her in the wardrobe she shared with Selar in the sleeping quarters, and sat on the edge of her cot awaiting instructions. When Tuvok told her she was free to move about the living quarters and the cargo bay, she had masked her surprise and gone exploring before venturing forward to the control cabin, in hopes Sisko would allow her to watch the stars on the forward screen.

He'd been running a diagnostic prior to departure, the pilot's seat swung 180 degrees around from the controls so he could check all systems when he saw her in the hatchway. He'd crooked a finger at her and pointed her toward the copilot's seat.

"Sit if you want. But don't touch anything."

She had done just that, and watched silently as *Albatross* rumbled out of dock and made half-impulse until she was clear of the Sol system, then lurched into warp. She'd won points from Sisko for being quiet and enjoying the view, but now he seemed torn between curiosity and mistrust. Unfortunately, it was the mistrust that came through in his words.

"Tuvok knows where to find me," Zetha said now, studying the human out of the corner of her eye. Distrust was straightforward; she could deal with it.

"Three things," Sisko said. "First, you're allowed forward

only when I'm here and on my say-so, and when you're here, you sit where I tell you to sit and you don't touch anything. Second, you stay out of the engine room."

"And third?"

The lieutenant's expression softened somewhat. "Tell me about Romulan cooking. You're not vegetarian like Vulcans, are you?"

"Vegetarian?" Zetha didn't recognize the word.

"You don't just eat plants. You eat meat, fish, things like that."

"When we can find it, yes."

"You like spicy food?"

The recollection of the meal she and Tahir had pilfered from the refuse bins outside The Orchid, discarded no doubt because some centurion's wife found it not to her liking, tingled for a moment on her memory's taste-buds.

Remember the food, she told herself. *Don't think about Tahir. Either he escaped that afternoon or he didn't, and if he did, you've long been replaced in his affections by another . . .*

"Sometimes," she said carefully.

Sisko's smile appeared genuine. "This mission might not be so bad after all!"

How important is it, Zetha wondered, *to make this human accept me? More to the point, why is it necessary when the others have?*

Uhura accepted me almost too readily, because she believed I was sent by Cretak. Tuvok needed to ask his questions but, once satisfied with the answers, he no longer questions me. As for Selar, her passion—and yes, I know, Vulcans are reportedly lacking in passion, but as the distant brothers, we know better—Selar's passion is medicine, her focus narrow, and if whenever we are planetside I play to the cover story that we are kin, and emulate her behaviors, and if when we are on the ship I make myself useful by volunteering to do small, unskilled chores in her lab, she in her quiet way will accept me.

As for the other humans, the flame-haired one and her son all but apologized for being human in my presence, something I still don't understand . . .

"*Jolan tru*," Wesley greeted her when his mother, her hand proprietarily on Zetha's shoulder, introduced them. At only eleven, he was already taller than Zetha. "I hope I'm pronouncing that right."

"You are." Zetha said. *He is a child*, she reminded herself, shaking his proffered hand as she had observed other humans do. *Do not judge him.*

"I'll leave you two to get acquainted," Beverly said, heading for the kitchen.

It was after he'd shown his guest around and she had repressed her reaction to the sheer wealth of *things* that one child could possess that Wesley, running out of small talk, suddenly blurted:

"I'm glad you're here. I've never met a Romulan before. I get to meet new people a lot, but never a Romulan. My mom's always bringing home stray kittens and people with nowhere else to go . . ."

"Very nice, young man!" came Beverly's voice from the kitchen, though Wesley seemed to know he'd blundered as soon as he'd spoken.

"Oops. I didn't mean—"

"I know exactly what you mean," Zetha said without inflection, and Wesley had excused himself as if to find a hole big enough to crawl into, even though she hadn't seemed to be offended. If anything, she had wanted to laugh at his ingenuousness. But then it made her angry, that he should have the freedom to be so ingenuous, when even at his age she—

Not his fault, she reminded herself, her sharp ears picking up the heated discussion in the room beyond.

"But, Mom, I didn't mean it that way—!"

"Well, what exactly did you mean? Because from what I could hear, it sounded like—"

"I mean—I don't know—maybe because she's like a kitten? She's small, and she seems gentle, but I bet if she got mad, she'd have claws, that's all."

"That's very glib, Wes."

"I'm sorry."

Is this because of me? Zetha wondered, marveling. She could hear Beverly sigh.

"I'm not the one you should apologize to, but if Zetha has the good grace not to be offended, I'll let you off the hook. But try to think before you open your mouth from now on, please? Remember the one about walking in someone else's shoes?"

The boy didn't say anything then; perhaps he merely nodded. Zetha treated him with caution for the rest of the evening.

At the dinner table, she watched how they used their utensils and emulated them, and waited to be asked if she wanted seconds, because she was beginning to understand that humans, at least these humans, always had more than enough food. She thought of Aemetha's foundlings fighting over the last scrap, the last drops of soup in the pot, thought of the House and the rows of refectory tables, the bowls full of the same gray slop whatever the meal, and, having guessed that Dr. Crusher's medical instruments would assess her past as readily as the Tal Shiar healer's had, ate with gusto, but slowly, knowing she was watched.

She endured their efforts to entertain her, uncertain of the rules. No one had ever singled her out for such attention before, unless they wanted something in return. Assuming Crusher was monitoring her as much as Tuvok had been, she watched and waited for cues. Did she want to watch a video with Beverly, or play a game with Wes? She would do either, both, whatever was needed to get through this night until Tuvok retrieved her and she learned her fate on the morrow.

Had Zetha been amazed to learn that she would be going with the away team? There were not words enough in her vocabulary to encompass her amazement. Yet nothing showed on her face. She would find acting the part of a Vulcan, when the time came, easy enough.

So the Crushers had accepted her, and even the ancient one named McCoy, who otherwise seemed so abrasive, had found a smile for her.

"Zetha, is it?" he'd asked, deigning to appear in full for a change instead of as merely a voice or a floating head. "My, aren't you a pretty little thing! Or am I allowed to say that? My guess is both our worlds allow an old geezer like me to say pretty much whatever I want. Feel free to tell me to shut up."

"I would not do that," she said, repressing the urge to smile for the first time in a long time. Aemetha would have liked this one, she decided.

But this Sisko, Zetha thought, watching him out of the corners of her eyes. *What does he want? He is in charge, and it is a given that I will obey his restrictions. Does he think I know how to operate this ship or, more to the point, how to sabotage it? He speaks of food. Perhaps he intends to cook some elaborate meal, and I can praise it and win his trust that way. If he knew what I have had to eat or not eat in order to get to this point . . .*

"Are you hungry?" the Lord had taunted her on the third day of the survival course.

"Are you?" she shot back, for the sheer pleasure of watching his hand half-curl into a fist involuntarily before he became aware of it.

"Tanclus fainted during the forced march today," he told her instead.

"Did he? Tanclus is twice my size. He needs twice as much food as I do."

"And you think that makes you stronger?" the Lord sneered.

"If you say so, Lord," she said, waiting for the blow to fall. For once, it didn't.

I cannot do the impossible, she thought now, getting up from the seat Sisko had assigned her and heading for Selar's lab, letting Sisko have the stars to himself. *But I will do the best I can.*

They were two days into the journey before she understood what the problem was.

Crew quarters on *Albatross* were cramped; the four of them lived, ate, and slept in a single compartment. There were two bunks, one atop the other, built into each side, and a table in the center that did service for meals from the nearby replicator or the minuscule galley adjacent. At other times, it served as map table, writing desk, showcase for the one prized Vulcan orchid Tuvok had brought with him, or anything else any of them might be working on.

It wasn't the crowding. On cold nights, she and as many as a score of other street brats had bundled together under the piles of clothing in Aemetha's salon to keep warm. It was because the tidiness and order reminded her of the barracks, and it was because she dreamed.

Chapter 10

The day was overcast and chill; it had been raining. She and Tahir had finished their purloined meal in the alley behind the Orchid and were loitering in the main square near the Senate, watching vids in the window of the Bureau of Announcements, when it happened.

Scroungers' Second Law: Hide in plain sight. The shadow of the Senate was always replete with scroungers, forgers, black marketeers, operating under the premise that there were more guards per square meter here than anywhere else on Romulus, and where better to conduct one's illicit business than right beneath their noses because, in their bureaucratic smugness, the powers that were assumed no one would dare?

Thus she and Tahir, having earlier in the day relieved a priggish apothecary of two crates of simple remedies that might keep the foundlings' winter-long sniffles from becoming something deadlier, were celebrating by filling their own bellies first for once and watching snippets of the narratives that people who had vidscreens could see in the comfort of their homes.

There were two rows of screens, usually reserved for official announcements, but the Praetor was away at his winter palace and there were no official announcements that day. So the two rows of screens warred with each other, one row portraying a space battle, the other a lurid romance replete with betrayals, elopements, suicide pacts, and lamentations by both families at the funerals.

Because there were no announcements, the loudspeakers were turned off, and no sound penetrated the window. Thus she and Tahir watched both vids simultaneously, supplying their own mocking dialogue and holding each other up against paroxysms of laughter when something, and it was not Tahir's hand working its way, as if accidentally, down from her shoulder, made her entire body tense.

"Something . . . behind us!" she hissed, jabbing Tahir in the ribs to get his attention. "Go, now!"

Never run when you've stolen something. When you're afraid, act brazen. But when an unmarked black hovercar with sealed windows begins to slow on its way past you, run as if your life depends on it, because it does.

Scroungers knew every escape route in the rabbit warrens of the old city—every alley, cellar, tunnel, catacomb, roof access, secret entrance, and exit. But sometimes the escape routes simply weren't there.

"The cellar!" Tahir called out behind her, but she slewed around long enough to shout "No!" before zigzagging past it. Part of a network of tunnels through the cellars of boarded-up buildings, she'd heard rumors that it served as a meeting place for a mysterious group whose name meant roughly "unification" and, while she personally thought they were insane, she would not endanger them. Her breath coming shorter, she continued to run.

They should have split up, she thought later, then realized it wouldn't have mattered. Perhaps Tahir thought he was protecting her by following, ready to throw himself in the hovercar's path so she could get away. She would never know. They ran until they could run no more, then stopped, exhausted, in an alley where a high crumbling wall separated an ancient burial ground from the featureless rear walls of a row of warehouses.

"A lovers' tryst," Tahir said with what little breath he could catch, grabbing her elbow and positioning her with her back against the wall while he stood in front of her, ready perhaps to shield her body with his own if there was to be any shooting. The alley dead-ended a few meters beyond them. They could hear the hovercar's purr somewhere overhead as it rose above the rooftops, as only official cars were permitted, to scan the alleys, no doubt reading them on infrared. "Only reason we were running was so your lover didn't spot us. We're only stealing kisses now."

Or you're only using it as an excuse! Zetha thought with what little of her attention wasn't fixed on the hovercar, begging it: *Go on, search elsewhere. It's not us you want; we're nothing! There's nothing here to see!*

Tahir raised his right hand, the first two fingers together, and touched them to her lips. The proper way was to touch hand to hand first, but he wanted it to seem to their pursuers that they had been doing this for a while. Zetha touched her fingers to his lips in turn. Ironic, she thought, her mind squirreling, that after months of teasing each other, their first kiss should come on the verge of death! Fingers and lips were numb with terror; only her heart, threatening to pound its way out of her chest, and her eyes seemed to work. The latter were filled with the sight of the lone aristocratic figure flexing fingers gloved in expensive leather, casually making its way toward them.

"You!" the figure called out, just loudly enough. Behind him, on either side of the hovercar's open hatch, two helmed figures waited with stun batons held across their chests, more deadly weapons no doubt at the ready in those heavy belts.

As if they'd rehearsed it, she and Tahir broke apart, backs to the cemetery wall, guilty lovers caught in the act. The lone figure was not impressed. He focused on Tahir, ignoring Zetha, who wondered how fast she could climb the broken stones of the cemetery wall before the stun batons took her down.

"You do not exist," the figure informed Tahir, flicking a dismissive finger at him. The voice was almost mechanical, with that inescapably nasal upper-class accent. "Therefore I do not see you. Disappear before I assist you in doing so."

Needing no further prompting, Tahir allowed Zetha one last horrified glance that said simultaneously *I'm sorry/I can't/I love you!* before he bolted in the direction of the 'car; there was nowhere else to go. To the helmed guards he might have been a dung-fly; they ignored him. He literally leapt over the front of the 'car—there was no other way out of the alley—and was gone.

Hyperfocused, Zetha watched, at the same time assessing what was really happening here. The aristocrat was studying her as if she were a butterfly pinned to a dissection table, wings still fluttering. She drew herself up and studied him in return.

Weak-chinned, beady-eyed, the eyes half-hidden under a brow ridge so pronounced there was no telling their color. Whip-thin except for a lazy man's paunch, studied in his gestures, and, from the cold smile playing at the corners of his downturned mouth, he knew exactly who she was and had been tracking her specifically.

Only one entity tracked the mongrels. Tal Shiar.

"Name," he barked at her.

"As if you don't already know," she snapped back, thinking, *Kill me and get it over with, whether it's for robbing the apothecary or simply for breathing air that might otherwise go to a more deserving true Romulan, but you will not toy with me!*

"Name," he said again.

She sighed, as if it were a great imposition. She was shaking so hard she could barely stand. "Zetha. Nonperson. But you know that."

"Do I?"

"Oh, aside from the common wisdom that we half-breeds don't look Romulan enough, you've sought me out deliberately." She jerked her chin toward a small device blinking and chittering on his belt. "You have my codes in that little comm unit you carry around as if it were just a wallet."

"Do I?" The trace of a smile continued to play at the corners of his mouth.

"Of course," Zetha said, smirking. "You positively reek of Tal Shiar." *Now that*, she thought, *was too far*, regretting it the instant it was out of her mouth.

The blow came swiftly, a stinging slap across her cheek that knocked her to the ground. She scrambled to her feet without so much as touching her face. Her eyes were dry.

"I *reek* of Tal Shiar? What makes you say that?" he demanded.

"You mean aside from the 'car and the guards and the marks against the fabric where you've removed your rank pips?" Zetha said brazenly.

She was feeling her teeth with her tongue to see if he'd chipped any; he hadn't. She all but laughed aloud as he touched his collar absently, even though the other half of his brain knew he was wearing civilian clothes, not his uniform, and there were no marks. She was toying with him. The inquisitor was being inquisited. He liked this not at all.

"I'm joking. But your ilk wears his skin like a uniform. It's the haughtiness. You look down your nose at people, you have that superior tone to your voice. You couldn't hide that even if you stuttered like a colonial."

He watched her silently for a protracted moment, his eyes narrowed. "My mentors said the same thing of me," he said, then seemed to catch himself. "So noted. I will not make that mistake again. You have helped me become a stronger enemy. You should be afraid of me. Why aren't you?"

Zetha shrugged. "When you're told every day of your life that you don't deserve to live, you find there's very little to fear. If you'd wanted to kill me, you would have by now. Instead, you have some reason to keep me alive."

"It's not you I'm interested in," he said indifferently. "There is an old woman in the N'emoth District. Some call her Godmother. I'm told she shelters the likes of you. Dozens of you. Teaches you to steal, trades in forged documents, illicit substances, even flesh peddling."

"That's not true!" Zetha shouted. Too late, she saw the trap. Foiled by a lifetime's conditioning, she had assumed he wouldn't be interested in the likes of her, but would use her to go after Aemetha. Now she saw the hidden edge of the sword. Rather, he would use Aemetha to get at her. If she didn't do what he wished, whatever that might be, Aemetha would disappear. The villa would be razed, the foundlings scattered.

So! Zetha thought, reading it in his too-small eyes. *I am more important than I know. But why? If everything I know must be abandoned for a moment's bad timing, I will know why. Whatever he wants, I must do it. Or at least let him think I will, for Aemetha's sake.*

"My life for hers," she said, drawing her insubstantial person up to her full insignificant height.

He did laugh then, a small chuckle in the back of his throat.

"You consider that an equal trade? Aemetha is of good family. You are nothing."

"True." Zetha shrugged. "But you can't do math without a zero."

His eyes narrowed again, this time with appreciation. He crooked a finger at her. "Come with me."

She followed him to the hovercar. As she stepped between the guards and climbed through the hatch into the comfortable rear seat, she noticed that the windows were blacked out. She thought she knew where he was taking her, but she would never be sure.

* * *

Every night, she dreamed it. Dreamed she was back in the barracks with the other *ghilik*, rows and rows of them, all training for the same purpose—to be the Tal Shiar's cannon fodder, the ones sent on suicide missions, their lives post-training often measured in days. Infiltrators, agitators, saboteurs, poisoners, assassins. Every day lived was a triumph, but every day lived only brought one closer to the day when one would have to kill, and then most likely be killed.

And every night that she dreamed it there was the risk, for all her training, that she would cry out in her sleep and reveal it.

If she'd cried out on the merchant ship on the way across the Zone, no one paid her any heed. None of them spoke Romulan, and she was bunked in one of the remoter areas of the ship. She had woken with a start as usual in the containment room at SI, no doubt with Tuvok watching through the mirror wall, and again at the Crushers' residence, and again last night, her first night on *Albatross*, but no sound had escaped her lips. This second night, the sound of her own voice woke her.

To find Sisko watching her in the dark.

She had the upper bunk on one side, he the lower on the other. He couldn't see as well in the dark as she could, and didn't realize she knew he was watching her. Tuvok was taking a turn at the helm; Selar was asleep in the other upper bunk across from her, unperturbed by any exterior noise, her breathing so soft and so regular she might not have been there at all. But Sisko's deep brown human eyes, all but unblinking, were looking right into Zetha's.

She stirred to let him know she was awake. *We'll see*, she thought, *if he will say anything*.

"You okay?" he asked.

"Did I wake you?" she answered without answering.

"You must have been having a nightmare," he said. "You were shouting."

"What did I say?"

"Just sounds. I couldn't make it out."

"It's gone now," she lied. "I'm sorry if I disturbed you."

She rolled over to face the bulkhead, her back to him. Vulnerable, perhaps, but effectively terminating the conversation. She heard him grunt and roll over as well, but not before she realized: It was not Tuvok she needed to be careful of, but Sisko. Perhaps Selar as well—that concentrated Vulcan silence could disguise many things—but definitely Sisko. Winning his trust was now more important than ever.

Tenjin V was a mostly humanoid world whose position unfortunately placed it sometimes in Federation space, sometimes within the Zone. Settled during one of the Federation's more ambitious expansionist phases by colonists from a nearby system whose sun was failing, it had the advantages of being a fortified outpost on the fringes of the Neutral Zone, a trading hub for several nearby worlds, and was a good source of borite and high-grade gadolinium. However, there were also disadvantages.

"When the maps were drawn at the end of the Romulan War, nobody took the orbital apogee into account," their contact, one of Uhura's Listeners, informed them when they met her at the rendezvous point, blending in with the crowd in a bustling public square. "For roughly a third of their year, the Tenji are inside the Zone, and for the first few days their in-system traffic is gridlocked with ships heading in one direction or the other."

"We did notice considerable local activity on the way in," Tuvok acknowledged.

"In two days we'll cross into the Zone and the madness begins," the Listener went on. The Tenji came in all sizes, shapes, and colors, and there was no way for her guests to know if she was a native or a human whose hair had been replaced with iridescent feathers. "You'll want to be gone before then."

"We plan to mingle with the outgoing traffic and slip into the Zone that way," Sisko said.

The Listener thought this over. "Then we haven't much time to get you the information you need. As if they didn't already have reason to be jumpy, this time of year makes the Tenji even jumpier. They don't like either side and, for obvious reasons, they feel more than a little vulnerable out here. But this is their world, and they make the best of it."

The "obvious reasons" lay beyond the habitat domes of the planet's enclosed cities. Tenjin's axis was pointed toward its sun, leaving it a sharply divided world of barren lunar landscape, of pocked and pitted waterless wasteland, one hemisphere constantly fried by a merciless sun, the other facing the frozen void of open space. The Tenji lived entirely in enclosed habitats.

"Like so many huge glass paperweights," Sisko had remarked as the *Albatross* juddered into her assigned berth in synchronous orbit above the night side.

"Indeed," Tuvok had concurred.

Inside the habitats, night and day were internally regulated to keep the inhabitants from going mad with constant exposure to either light or dark. Outside the safety of the habitats, there was atmosphere to breathe but, depending on which side of the planet one lived on, the temperature was a constant of either desert heat or arctic cold, and dust storms or storms of needle-sharp ice crystals often obscured the stars. If they were ever attacked and their habitat domes damaged, the Tenji would not survive for long.

Still, within the tenuous safety of their domes, they had developed a rich and varied culture based primarily on trade. As one of the last free ports on the Federation side of the Zone, Tenjin flourished. Over a dozen species speaking as many languages strolled past the landing party amid a maze of kiosks and shops and restaurants exuding enticing sights, sounds, and smells; displaying clothing in more colors than the eye could see and the flashing lights of the latest personal technology; offering samples of everything from Risan massage to *domjot* games to freshly made *chorizo*. The Tenji themselves strutted and preened like so many peacocks.

"Market day in New Orleans meets Tokyo's Ginza," Sisko said, inhaling deeply. His educated sense of smell told him that someone somewhere in this place was preparing an eggplant ratatouille, and he intended to find out who and where. "Ever been to New Orleans, Tuvok?"

"I cannot say that I have," Tuvok replied. He and Selar were enacting their Vulcan personae on Tenjin. As they moved with the crowds, Selar was surreptitiously scanning each passing shopper with a medscanner equipped with an added long-range filter to record every cough or sneeze occurring within this particular dome. Tuvok would as unobtrusively collect atmosphere samples, dust samples, even samples of the soil in the potted plants displayed everywhere, whereas Zetha—

"How do they live?" she blurted out, and Sisko realized she must be practically dizzy with sudden sensory overload. "Where does all this food come from?"

"My sister's eldest," Selar told the slightly startled Listener, absolutely deadpan, slipping the still-scanning medscanner into a pocket. "It is her first offworld journey."

"And so naturally she is curious about everything," the Listener said, playing along. "There is a narrow greenbelt along the north-to-south border where sun meets void," she explained, as if Zetha were in fact simply an inquisitive young Vulcan. "The inhabitants long ago decided to reserve those areas for agriculture rather than living space, and to live instead inside these domes. Even so, most of their food needs to be imported from offworld."

"Thank you," Zetha said, lowering her eyes much as Sisko had seen Tuvok and Selar do. It was a good performance.

"Your sister's eldest?" Sisko challenged Selar as the Listener left them and went off to arrange passage on one of the interdome tubes.

Selar quirked an eyebrow at him. "My sister has three offspring, therefore logically one must be the eldest."

"But you said Zetha was—"

"I did not. I said 'my sister's eldest.' I did not say 'She is my sister's eldest.' That the Listener chose to interpret my statement—"

"I see," Sisko said, shaking his head in amazement. "So that's how it's done!"

McCoy looked up from the screen and rubbed his bleary eyes, which by now were more red than blue. It was nearly dawn. Behind him the computer voice droned on, tirelessly reciting the data on telomerases he had sent it in search of while he scanned every paper on cytokine engineering in the UFP medical database. He'd thought multitasking would speed the process, but the computer's voice was getting to him.

"Shut the hell up, will you?" he growled. "I'm trying to concentrate here!" The computer, not hearing the proper command, droned on. "Goddamn literal-minded machine. Computer, mute!"

He cursed himself for being old and absent-minded. Forty, fifty, a hundred years ago he'd been up on all the journal entries and known who was working on what, and the rumor mill would have told him who among that elite group of scientists whose talents lay with gene splicing might have gone bad. Now he had to go through reams of data comparing the ever-mutating viruses not only with each other, but with similar archived bugs, looking for a common denominator. While he searched, people were dying. He could hear the agonal final beating of their hearts, hear their labored breathing ratcheting down like so many broken clocks.

"What's the rush?" he chided himself. "It's not up to you

to find a cure, just the perpetrator. You keep charging ahead, you might miss something important. Slow down!"

In the private lake at the back of his property, he could almost hear the trout taunting him, leaping and splashing with complete impunity, knowing he was too busy to get at them now.

"Motivation . . ." he muttered. "What's his motivation? Why would someone create a killer like this? Is he psychotic? Trying to control the galaxy? Distributing smallpox-infected blankets to the natives so he can claim their land for his own? Or is it revenge? On whom, for what? Figure out his game, and you'll find him . . ."

When at last he found what he was looking for, the realization almost knocked him out of his chair.

"Why, you smarmy sonofabitch!" he muttered triumphantly, seeing the similarity between one of the mutations Crusher had isolated and an illustration from a paper presented at the Federation Medical Academy over a dozen years before. "I've got you now! I told them there'd be a signature!"

He pushed a button on the arm of his chair and it floated gently off the floor and hovered on a cushion of air. The chair had been a gift from Spock some years ago after McCoy had reached 125, an acknowledgment that the doctor's human legs were not as strong as they once were. McCoy zoomed across the room to the comm unit and, not bothering to check what time it was in San Francisco, opened a frequency.

"Nyota, Beverly?" he shouted, his voice shaking with excitement. "Come on, ladies, get on the horn. I've got him! I know who created this goddamn bug. I've found the signature. Where's Selar?"

"Nothing like what you're describing," Dr. Sekaran told Selar when the Listener had left them alone in the heart of the medical dome on Tenjin V. "The only unusual event we've had in the past year or more was a cluster of cases of a bizarre carcinoform that occurred simultaneously in several of the domes, then disappeared just as quickly."

Sekaran was in essence the senior physician for all of Tenjin. His headquarters, at the heart of a dome in the central government complex, was as busy in its own way as the myriad mercantile domes it serviced. Here Sekaran and his multiplumaged staff monitored the health of every citizen on the planet, though visiting tourists, he admitted, were more difficult to track.

Selar studied the readouts scrolling down the clearsteel walls of the medical complex, her practiced eyes searching for something commensurate with the specimens she and Crusher had thus far identified.

"Probably not at all what you're looking for, but you did say you wanted everything," Sekaran went on. "It popped up unexpectedly two seasons ago—anything transmissible is unexpected here, because the atmosphere is filtered more carefully than even on a starship. We simply can't let something contagious get loose inside even one of the domes, because they're all interconnected by the travel tubes. As a result, we've become so accustomed to the filtration systems that we've been spoiled. Even a common cold could kill some of us."

"Understood," Selar said, studying the specific dataset Sekaran indicated. "You did say the entity was a carcinoform?"

"It was quite bizarre," he said. "People turned up at clinics complaining of chills and fever but, on examination, were found to have a rapidly forming cancer that started in the lungs and metastasized to the rest of the major organs. Tests showed no evidence of unusual bacteria or viral infection. Yet people in close proximity—family, coworkers—would 'catch' this from each other as if it were a flu bug."

"When you say rapidly forming . . ." Selar began.

"Days. Often in less than forty hours of onset of symptoms. I've never seen anything move so fast in my entire career. Germs are supposed to do that, but not cancers. And cancers are not supposed to be contagious."

If Selar was shaken by this information, she gave no sign. "I believe, Dr. Sekaran, we can abandon our parameters of what is 'supposed' to happen where this entity is concerned."

"So you think it's related to the bug you're trying to track?"

"Possibly. I will need access to this data in order to run more tests."

"If your medscanner can interface with our system, you'll have it," Sekaran said.

Back on the ship, it was clear from the aromas that Sisko had found his eggplant. *Albatross*'s galley was barely big enough for him to turn around in, but, having gathered all the ingredients he needed on Tenjin, he was making magic there.

"Step right up, ladies and gentleman," he announced, spooning something savory and steaming over plates of fluffy white rice. "No replicated rations tonight. This evening's main entree is freshly prepared, completely vegetarian, and guaranteed to please the most demanding palate."

"What is it?" Selar asked, inhaling appreciatively before taking her plate to a nearby console where she could work on Sekaran's data while she ate.

"Eggplant ratatouille," Sisko explained, watching for the nods of approval as each one tasted his masterpiece. "Baby eggplant sauteed in virgin olive oil with finely chopped Vidalia onions and fresh garlic, then blended with carrots, plum tomatoes, three kinds of bell peppers, a few new potatoes, some zucchini, cilantro, cayenne, and, well, a few secret ingredients of my own, and simmered to perfection."

"Excellent," Selar remarked.

"Indeed," Tuvok concurred. "All of this from ingredients gathered on Tenjin?"

"Not counting my own secret spice blends," Sisko

grinned. "I have my own herb garden on *Okinawa*. And I never go anywhere without some. I sure hope I haven't violated the Prime Directive by comparing recipes with the Tenji," he added with a wink, "although the restaurant did call itself the Interplanetary Café, and I could swear the sous-chef with the blue feathers had a distinctly Cajun accent . . ."

He stopped himself and blinked at Zetha, who had finished her portion in the time he'd been talking. "Did you even taste what you just ate?"

"It's good," Zetha said as if stating the obvious, wiping her plate inelegantly with her fingers to get the last of the tomato sauce. "Is there more?"

"Don't know where she puts it!" Sisko marveled, doling out a second helping and watching her attack that with equal gusto. "If you're going to eat with your fingers planetside, no one will ever mistake you for a Vulcan."

"I'll remember that," Zetha said with her mouth full. "But where I come from, when there's food, you eat it."

Sisko still wasn't sure he believed she had simply been plucked off the streets of the Romulan capital and sent to them on a mission of mercy. He intended to have a little chat with Tuvok on that very subject when Zetha was out of earshot. Assuming Zetha was ever out of earshot; she seemed to be everywhere on the small ship except where he'd denied her access, mostly following Selar around like a puppy, setting up petri dishes, sterilizing instruments, tidying the lab. For now—

"Where did you—?" he began, but just then Uhura's voice interrupted him.

"Dr. McCoy's identified our mad scientist," she said, shimmering into being, flanked by Crusher and McCoy. "It may not help us much, but it's a start."

It had begun by accident, like the discovery of penicillin. Every schoolchild knows how Sir Alexander Fleming, in a bout of bachelor carelessness, went on holiday and left an uncovered dish of deadly staph bacteria lying about, only to find blue mold, no doubt migrated from someone's unfinished lunch left equally carelessly in a wastebin, claiming its turf here and there on the surface of the dish and driving the bacteria back wherever it touched. But where Fleming's random chance led to a cure that had saved millions, the man the Renagans knew as Cinchona had stumbled upon the power to kill as many and more.

It wasn't what he'd wanted. Following the rout at the Medical Academy—disgraced, family ties severed, his career in shambles—he had wanted only retreat, anonymity, to disappear into the proverbial black hole and never emerge. The family had settled a small fortune on him on condition he go away, at least for a while. He wouldn't need to work at anything. He didn't like work; it was being pushed into it that had gotten him into trouble in the first place.

But the healer's daughter Boralesh had attached herself to him, and, yes, the child born soon after the wedding was undeniably his—he'd done the tests to prove it, but how was he to have known the custom here?—visiting him with thoughts of retreating further, but where? Aside from the fact that Boralesh's kin would hunt him down and drag him back, even if he could get his small ship started again, emigration inside the Zone was not the easiest thing for someone with his past, even for a Rigelian.

"Rigel? I have never heard of this place," Boralesh said, dewy-eyed with innocence (or was it cold-eyed with ulterior motive?), the night they met beneath the stars and she began to lay her snares for him with scents gathered from the *levora* flowers. "Where is it?"

"Far away, but not far enough" was all he would tell her. "My family is important there. Too important. I needed to strike out on my own, to prove myself."

* * *

Boralesh knew about family, or thought she did. She had accepted his story at the time, even though a dozen years and three more children later, he had in fact proven himself to be little more than a teller of tall tales and a fair rider of the local *sedraz*, saddled or bareback, winning prizes that cluttered the sideboard in the best parlor and gave the children something to brag about at school.

Oh, and in recent years there was his "laboratory," which was the name he had given to the cave in the foothills where she had spied on him and watched his strange rituals. He would go there early in the morning and return after dark, but never say anything about what he did there. Boralesh half-wondered if it was a woman, and not work at all, which drew him away every day. Still, unless it was a woman from the next town distant, Boralesh would have known who she was. The laboratory, or whatever it truly was, maybe only a private cave to retreat to when the children's voices were too much for him, got him out of her way during the day, and for that reason alone, it was worth it. Even if there was also a woman involved, she told herself, only half-believing it, even as she only half-believed in this place called Rigel.

On the odd chance anyone else from outside ever came to this backward world, Cinchona would count on Boralesh's skepticism to conceal him. Renagans had heard tales of space travel, but weren't sure if they believed them. There was no reason to explore, they reasoned. There was food enough for those who obeyed the laws, healers for when they were sick, wise ones to teach them that the stars were the home of the gods and deciders of man's fate. If the occasional visitor happened along to tell them that beings like themselves also came from some of those stars, he was greeted with knowing smirks and "Oh, tell us another, stranger!"

So this particular stranger, running ahead of his own disgrace, had come to ground here when the power cells on his one-man ship had failed, hidden the ship in the hills, and walked into the nearest village purporting to be a healer from a far province. He had chosen the name Cinchona, and the healers' guild, after asking a few questions to which he apparently gave satisfactory answers, had welcomed him, particularly since one of their own had a daughter who needed a husband.

For all Boralesh knew, Rigel was a faraway city on her own world, not a distant planet that was part of something called a Federation. Even if she had believed it, it wouldn't have mattered as much as the fact that she was nearing the age where no man would want her. Cinchona had looked good in her eyes at the time, wherever this "Rigel" might be.

In fact, the Rigel system consisted of several habitable planets, though it was Rigel IV which had two claims to fame. One was the fact that its round-eared inhabitants appeared human, but the configuration of their internal organs, their heart rates, blood types, immunohistochemistry, were similar to those of Vulcans. In fact, only an expert could distinguish a Rigelian's medscan from Vulcan or Romulan.

The second thing Rigel IV was noted for was the fever.

Rigelian infants were inoculated against it at birth, and in developing the vaccine for this elusive disease the physicians of Rigel V, who had long ago emigrated from Rigel IV for political reasons, had become some of the most renowned in the quadrant. But their former neighbors on Rigel IV were a different matter. Little more than pirates prior to Federation, they were ruled by a consortium of powerful families with a reputation for luring visitors to their world or the resorts on nearby Rigel II, slipping them the live virus, then offering a cure, for a price.

Cinchona knew this very well. His family had made their fortune this way until Federation membership put a stop to it, but by then the family wealth had been diversified into other things. And, yes, his family was wealthy. The "money-less" economy of the Federation might be the norm every-where within its borders, but on Rigel IV they still used currency. Succeeding generations of the old pirate families were expected to go legitimate, to send their offspring to the universities on Rigel V and elsewhere and stop dealing in bootleg medicines.

"Set the groundwork for you," his father had said on the day Cinchona left for medical school. "Did everything I could short of going to class for you. Can't do that. Too old. They won't let me. Get out there and achieve something."

Well, he'd tried, and failed. He was in fact the dullest of his father's children, and only generous gifts to his teachers had seen him through school. But he was the eldest, and carried the family name, and this brought with it certain obligations, and those certain obligations had pushed him in directions that almost brought his career down around him before it began.

Chapter 11

"A squinty-eyed nonentity named Thamnos," McCoy announced, presenting the Three Graces, as he'd taken to calling the trio of Uhura, Crusher, and Selar, with the last-known image of their prime suspect, a pink-faced humanoid with a lipless mouth and a permanently furrowed brow that seemed to plead *Take me seriously!* "First name Crofter, though he never uses it. Thinks just being a Thamnos is glory enough. A mediocre clinician whose prior history includes a series of lackluster assistanceships in one lab or another. I overlooked him as a suspect initially because I was looking for some evil genius. Thamnos may be evil, but he's no genius."

"Thamnos?" Selar recognized the name. "Of the Rigelian family?"

"The same," McCoy said. "They all but run Rigel IV. Some of 'em are clever, but this one's about as smart as a box of rocks. Rumor has it his father endowed a new lab at the best med school on Rigel V just so they'd pass him through, and he was still in the bottom tenth of his class. Then in the tradition of the old Orion pirate families, Daddy paid for a new library, and suddenly Thamnos the Younger is styling himself a researcher. Published a few not-very-original papers on Rigelian fever, then dropped off the radar some years ago after he tried to publish a paper on Bendii Syndrome using someone else's data. . . ."

If he listened hard enough, Thamnos could still hear them jeering at him. Anyone who thought medical conferences were genteel gatherings of the thought leaders in research and new techniques, convening to exchange ideas and learn new things, had obviously never been to one. Cutthroats, ready to pounce on every datum and analyze it to the subquark level, then call it into question, they had done everything but throw rotten fruit at him.

He had paid someone to lift the data for his Bendii research from other sources, assuming those sources were sufficiently obscure so that no one would notice. Having slept through his neurology courses and cribbed the exams, he hadn't understood enough of the material to doctor it sufficiently to avoid charges of plagiarism, and he had been caught.

And fled the conference, the planet, the Federation in disgrace, some highly virulent Rigelian fever cultures in his baggage.

He'd taken the cultures with him from the family's private stock when he left home almost as an afterthought; he did not at the time even know why. Officially they did not exist, but the old Rigel families still had their secrets. A wild thought occurred to him afterwards that he might have released the R-virus into the air ducts or slipped it into the cocktail-hour punch and taken out every non-Rigelian at the conference. Too bad, really.

Because he was of the First Families of Rigel, he had his own private ship, and no need to go through transporters or sensors or baggage checks. Which, from what he heard from his sources these days (amid the equipment he had scavenged from his ship and installed in his cave laboratory was a surprisingly powerful transmitter, its signals uncrossed by others, since Renagans no more believed in radio than they did in space travel), was no longer the case. The disease he had created (yes, he, the family idiot, had done this!) was changing the rules. Not so much as a microbe could pass the filtration systems now.

Too late! Thamnos/Cinchona thought almost gleefully, his own internal laughter drowning out the voices of his accusers, at least for a little while. *The seeds are already in place, the damage already done. Soon you'll come to me for your answers, and there will be no jeering then!*

He had escaped a universe which knew him as a buffoon, some subconscious survival instinct smarter than he was telling him: *Take the fever with you!* and he did, changing his name, hiding his ship, and blending in on Renaga. Random chance, perhaps, or maybe something more. Because on Renaga, there was *hilopon*. And that made all the difference.

It was a naturally occurring bacterium in the soil that the natives had used as a folk cure for as long as they could remember, reputed to cure everything from cancer to the clap. Boralesh had taught him how to gather it, how to process and store it, how to apply it to open wounds or tincture it for sore eyes or stomach ailments. Skeptical at first, he had marveled at its all but universal applications, and wondered how it worked.

Then, a true Thamnos, born to privilege and the conviction that the needs of the reigning few precluded any consideration of the masses, he wondered how he might exploit it to his benefit. And when, just out of curiosity, he treated some of the R-fever cultures with it and watched them die before his eyes, he thought he had the answer.

He must make certain no one outside of Renaga ever heard of *hilopon*. If it truly could cure everything it touched, whoever "discovered" it and brought it to the attention of the universe at large had better make sure he owned all the rights to it beforehand. But how to do that on a world where *hilopon* was, quite literally, as cheap as dirt? As he tinkered with the substance in his laboratory cave, that one mystery eluded him. And there were other forces at work around him that, short-sighted as he was, eluded his notice as well.

Backward and lacking in resources though it might be, Renaga had its attractions for those whose empire flourished on conquest. Romulan eyes are far-seeing, and while it is assumed that they usually prefer the military solution, sometimes subtler methods are employed. Romulans are long-lived as well, and there are some who will accept as their duty to the Empire the assignment to infiltrate other worlds, go to ground for decades if necessary, and await instructions.

Thamnos was not the only outworlder on Renaga.

"So what makes you think this Thamnos character is behind our neoform?" Crusher asked. "The man you're describing would hardly have the skills to create something this sophisticated."

"Probably not on purpose," McCoy acknowledged. "But if he somehow got his hands on the Romulan Gnawing and grafted it onto certain strains of Rigelian fever . . ."

"Indeed," Selar said after a thoughtful silence.

Uhura frowned, scanning her memory for what she knew about Rigelian fever, which wasn't much. "What's so special about Rigelian fever?"

"Selar?" McCoy said.

"There are five known strains of Rigelian or R-fever," Selar explained. "The penultimate strain, R4b, can mutate into two separate strains, R4b1 and R4b2. Of those, R4b2, when acting as a host virus, could potentially cause multiple mutations if grafted onto certain other viruses with similar hydrogen-chain configurations. There have been no known cases of R-fever reported since 2339; therefore, the disease is studied as an artifact in most medical schools, but not in any detail. I should have known better."

"Don't worry," McCoy tweaked her. "We won't report you to the Vulcan Perfectionists' Association."

"With all due respect, Dr. McCoy," Selar shot right back. "Were there such an entity, it need only be called the Vulcan Association, to avoid redundancy."

"Okay, people, as you were," Uhura said. She'd been running a search on Thamnos from the data McCoy provided while they spoke. "Leonard, one question. I'll grant you a Rigelian might have access to stores of R-fever virus concealed somewhere in their system. The Orion Syndicate still has ties there, even today. But what makes you think Thamnos in particular? Dr. Crusher's right; he doesn't seem to have accomplished much in his career."

"Well, aside from the fact that no one's seen hide nor hair of him since the Bendii incident, you'll notice there's a year missing in the reportings from his private laboratory."

"And—?"

"What your reports don't tell you is that the lab, paid for out of Daddy's pocket, was shut down by the Rigelian government for about a year due to sloppy work habits and—get this—'questionable practice in the use of strains of R4b2.' Rumor has it those questionable practices included trying to breed a species of hare that would carry R-fever without succumbing to it. Thamnos's argument when he was brought up on charges was that he was trying to create a model to be used in testing, but the authorities suspected it was a not-so-clever attempt to infiltrate rival labs with these animals and contaminate their data. He was only let off because the experiment was a total failure. He'd neglected to consider that Rigelian hares can't be infected with R-fever."

"And just where did you get that information?" Uhura demanded.

"Not gonna tell you!" McCoy said. "You protect your sources, I protect mine."

"All the same," Crusher was still skeptical. "If he's such a bumbler, how could he possibly—"

"He may be a bumbler, but someone else out there might

not be," Uhura suggested. "Someone from the Romulan side."

"With access to Gnawing cultures," Selar suggested. "And enough medical knowledge—"

"Or access to a pool of medical and bio-warfare experts," Uhura interjected. "Leonard, where are you going?"

"Time to make a few house calls . . ." He drifted out of range of the holotransceivers and for the moment Uhura let him go.

"I'll need access to live R-fever," Crusher said.

"I'm on it," Uhura said, calling up access codes for Starbase 23, and seeing what ships were in the vicinity that could be diverted to act as couriers.

In the living quarters of the *Albatross*, the others watched and listened to the medical briefing. Sisko was clearing the dishes away. Tuvok was simultaneously scanning the buzz of communications above Tenjin, monitoring the holo communicator to make certain there was no leakage, and tending to his prize orchid. Zetha slipped away to prep the lab for Selar, one ear on the transmission.

"Speaking of mutations," Crusher was saying. "The majority of them turned out to be red herrings. They replicated for a while, then died off. Of course, we wasted days isolating and monitoring them, which may have been part of the design. But if we can verify that they were caused by R-fever, we'll know which ones to pay attention to in the future."

Just then Selar's console beeped, indicating that the analysis on the data she'd brought back from Tenjin was complete. She forwarded it to the others. "However, Dr. Crusher, I suggest you add at least one more active culture to your list. This one is a carcinoform."

Uhura sighed. "In English, please."

"The pathogen collected on Tenjin is a virus that mutates into a form of cancer," Selar explained. "It tracks with the

Gnawing/R-fever neoform in all other respects. Patients presented to their physicians with cough, shortness of breath, fever, respiratory compromise, unilateral or bilateral infiltrates in the lungs, and symmetrical alveolar spread. Mortality rate was one hundred percent."

"Sounds like our bug, all right," Crusher said morosely.

"With one notable differentiation," Selar said. "Autopsies revealed that every major organ was riddled with cancerous tumors . . ."

"There goes my appetite!" Sisko said quietly.

". . . despite the fact that the disease vector indicated a contagion which was passed from one person to another in close proximity."

"How many dead?" Uhura asked, ready to add this new death toll to the others.

"Sixty-four," Selar said.

"A cancer that's contagious?" Uhura frowned. "How is that possible?"

"Ordinarily, it is not," Selar explained. "But we are dealing with an artificial neoform which, hypothetically, could be. Both viral infection and cancer are inflammatory processes."

Before Uhura could ask her usual question, Selar went on.

"Most disease processes, from cancer to the common cold, are the result of normal cells going awry," she explained. "Either a 'germ' such as a cold virus or a cancer-causing agent invades the body from the outside, or healthy cells can mutate for a number of reasons—exposure to radiation, environmental pollutants. The body contains cells known as natural killer cells, which recognize these altered cells as invaders and attempt to destroy them.

"The resulting 'battle' is what causes inflammation. The patient exhibits fever, in the case of a virus, or other symptoms with the onset of cancer. If the NK cells win, these symptoms abate and the patient lives. If the mutated cells win, the body succumbs and the patient dies."

"And you're telling me this process is the same for cancer as it is for a head cold?" Uhura asked skeptically, making sure she had it right.

"Superficially, yes. Where cancers differentiate is that once they have established themselves in the host, they recruit healthy cells in order to colonize and grow. Tumors, left untreated, will create their own blood vessels and divert the blood supply from healthy tissue. They will then proceed to crowd out and scavenge healthy cells in a lung or liver or pancreas or in blood or bone until the healthy cells cannot function, the organ or system breaks down, and the patient dies.

"It is my hypothesis," Selar concluded ominously, "that someone, whether by design or accident, has discovered that grafting the Gnawing onto R-fever, possibly with other factors, can sometimes cause the resulting virus, once it is introduced into a host body, to mutate into a form of cancer. The cancer itself is not contagious but, because the virus is, the end result is the same."

"And it has somehow managed to spread in an enclosed environment like Tenjin," Uhura said.

"Correct."

No one said anything for a few minutes. Uhura's fingers ticked over her console, totting up all the casualties to date.

"We've also had a dozen new cases reported on Cestus III," she reported, "and a possible outbreak on . . ." Her voice trailed off just in time to hear Crusher ask Selar something about "squeak tests."

Uhura sighed again. "Squeak tests?"

When Zetha first volunteered to help Selar in the lab, the Vulcan had taught her how to perform viral squeak tests.

"Viruses emit high-frequency sounds," she had explained, setting up the simple wave transmitter that would do the job. "And each virus has its own distinct sound. A single copy of a stable virus can be detected in a biosample and identified on the basis of its unique sound. Do you understand so far?"

Zetha nodded. Entities so small that they were invisible, existing inside every living thing, some of them powerful enough to kill? Science or sorcery, it was all one to her. If they could kill, why couldn't they sing as well?

"How does it work?" she asked, indicating the transmitter, insatiably curious, wanting to know everything. Too, pragmatically, the more she learned, the more useful she could be.

Selar, who enjoyed instructing anyone so clearly eager to learn, explained.

"Quartz crystals transmit radio signals. When coated with particles of a virus we wish to identify and exposed to an electrical field, they will vibrate until the virus detaches and shakes free. When it does so, it emits a burst of sound.

"The crystal resonates to the sound and records it as an electrical impulse. Humans cannot hear these sounds, and therefore must rely upon reading the recorded impulse. But most fall within the range of Vulcan hearing, therefore speeding the process."

"But—" Zetha started to say, then stopped. She was not a Vulcan, but she could hardly say she was a Romulan after a lifetime of being told she was not.

It had occurred to her, once she stopped trembling and settled into the hovercar behind the silent aristocrat whose name she still did not know, that if he had in fact traced her through her codes, he also knew her origins, and which part of her was not Romulan.

It had occurred to Koval as well. In the ensuing months, he would taunt her with it.

"Don't you want to know your codes? To know who spawned you, what your parents were?"

She did, but she didn't, not from him. She couldn't trust him to tell her the truth, and what she wanted above all else was not to be beholden to him.

"No," she said.

"I don't believe you," he had said with his smug little smile. "If you volunteer for a mission, I will tell you. You will know your place before you die."

She had shrugged. "If I die for the Empire, I'll be an honorary Romulan after death," she reminded him, making sure she was beyond arm's length before she finished her thought. "By then, though, I doubt I'll care."

"I am not a Vulcan," she told Selar, "nor a Romulan. I—"

In answer, Selar placed a sample virus in the detector and activated it. Its almost inaudible hum grew in intensity as the crystals shook faster and faster. There was a single burst of noise—which sounded to Zetha like a tiny, abbreviated shriek—then a winding down to silence as Selar shut down the device and the crystals ceased their vibration.

"Did you hear that?" she asked Zetha.

"Yes."

"Can you distinguish it from this?" Selar replaced the contaminated crystal, treating the new one with a fresh viral sample and activating the device. This time when the virus shook free, the sound Zetha heard was more like the snap of a twig. She told Selar this.

"The first was the neoform, the second a mutated herpes virus," Selar explained. Was there a tinge of pride in her voice, pride in Zetha's accomplishment? "A human would hear nothing but the vibration of the crystal. You hear like a Vulcan. That is sufficient for our purposes."

Selar had taught her to codify a number of viruses. By now she could identify the Gnawing neoform by its sound, distinct from anything else Selar could test her with. The sense of accomplishment was something new and, as she listened to Selar explaining the process of squeak testing to Uhura, she savored it.

* * *

Albatross slipped into the moil of traffic above Tenjin as the planet's orbit took it out of Federation space into the Zone. Deftly Sisko adjusted her trajectory until she was running upstream against the flow of Federation-registered vessels moving grudgingly back into their own space, until he had maneuvered her into the queue of nonaligned vessels waiting to cross into the Zone, then slowed the old girl to station keeping. He could feel more than see Tuvok's quizzical look.

"May I ask—?" Tuvok began.

"There's a big old Draken multipod astern, coming up to starboard," Sisko explained. "She's going to pass within a couple of kilometers of us, and we're going to let her. When the seventh pod is parallel to us, we're going to match her course and speed. We're small enough, if we're quiet enough, to play shadow until we're out of range of Tenjin's sensors."

"And avoid any potential challenge from Romulan-allied vessels in the sector," Tuvok surmised. "Very inventive."

Sisko caught himself shrugging like Zetha. "Just common sense."

"In summary," Uhura had said before Sisko shut down the holos to rig for silent running prior to crossing over into the Zone, "we know what this bug looks like—and, apparently, what it sounds like—and we have a fair idea who created it. We still have no idea how it has spread across this much space, and so quickly, even into controlled environments. But we go forward.

"Once we've acquired the live R-fever from Starbase 23, Dr. Crusher will compare it with the neoform and possibly tease out the differences. *Albatross*, you will continue your research from space on the worlds you pass, and on the ground where possible. Set course for Quirinus."

"Quirinus," Sisko said, trying the name out on his tongue. His mouth had gone suddenly dry at the thought that they really were inside the Zone now. The danger was almost palpable, like a change in the temperature or the humidity in the creaky old ship, and he found himself sweating. Maybe if he kept talking, he could talk his fears away. "Sounds Romulan."

"The inhabitants are Romulan in appearance," Tuvok replied. "However, Quirinus's location within the Zone precludes it from seeking membership in the Empire without violating treaty. In some respects, its citizens have become more Romulan than Romulans. And there is not inconsiderable resentment toward humans and the Federation."

"This ought to be fun!" Sisko said wryly.

"It will be challenging," Tuvok admitted. "Selar and I will have to perfect our Romulan personae well before we arrive."

Part of that included learning to use an honor blade. Tuvok, adapted by training to any form of weaponry, had mastered the nuances before they left Earth. Selar, whose most powerful weapon had heretofore been a laser scalpel, was less apt. Eager to repay Selar for her trust, Zetha made herself useful.

"It is not a weapon," she instructed Selar, "but a natural extension of your hand, an extension of your soul. It is given you by your family when you reach adulthood at the age of seven, and you keep it with you from then on. A true Romulan feels naked without it."

Selar weighed the pretty but deadly-sharp object in her hand and considered this. She seemed to slip into a light trance for a moment, as if calling upon some ancient race memory that might help her become one with something she really would prefer to lock away in a display case and admire for its beauty, not its killing skills.

"I am a healer," she said at last. "Perhaps understanding too well how much damage even such a small blade can do to internal organs is what restrains me."

"Then you must free yourself of that knowledge whenever the blade is in your hand," Tuvok suggested. "Nowhere is it written that you must use the blade, wife, merely that you know how."

It was the first time he had called her that, and the layers of pretext it suggested—and necessitated—seemed to galvanize her.

"Indeed . . . husband," she said carefully, then turned to Zetha. "Show me again."

And Zetha, who had never owned an honor blade because there was no family to give it to her, nevertheless showed Selar everything she had learned by watching others, true Romulans, challenge each other even in the most refined venues, often over the most trivial things. It was not at all uncommon for two senators to be dining in one of the most opulent restaurants in Ki Baratan and fall to insults over the choice of wine. Lurking in the alleys, she had witnessed the outcome often enough.

"I've never seen anyone killed with an honor blade," she told Selar now, thinking: *Not entirely true* even as she said it. There had been weapons training in the barracks, though the Lord had pointed out that the weapons they were given—which were taken away and locked up again at the end of each training session—were not true honor blades, because *ghilik* could never truly be honorable.

She had wondered at the time why at least some of them hadn't turned on him and filleted him like the dead fish he was. Already some of their number were starting to disappear. Sent on special missions, they were told, but they all knew. Special indeed. So special that no one ever returned. Zetha would count the empty bunks each night and wonder when it would be her turn.

"Interesting," Selar was saying now, as Zetha hid her thoughts behind tales of old ones, women, adolescents up and down the castes and classes and hierarchies of Romulan society drawing knives in challenge. "How often do they kill each other?"

Zetha shrugged. "Rarely. Mostly it's bluster. You shout insults, I shout insults back, I pull my knife, you pull yours, we glare at each other, attract everyone's attention. Sometimes we inflict superficial wounds, so we can show off the scars later." She searched for a metaphor. "Like two *h'vart* in an alley. Lots of yowling and claws and fur standing on end, but they rarely actually fight."

With a skeptical eyebrow, Selar said. "Show me again."

And she did. Selar was tall and possessed of a long-limbed grace; freed of her philosophical constraints, she learned quickly. In exchange for what might prove a life-saving lesson on Quirinus, she perfected Zetha's cover identity by lasering off her freckles.

"I don't look like me," Zetha said to the face in the mirror, wondering if it was the freckles that had marked her as non-Romulan.

Without them, might she pass? Well, for Quirinus, anyway. Ironic that there were Vulcans who looked like Selar and Vulcans who looked like Tuvok, Romulans with brow ridges and without, and variations in both races to encompass ever possible color of skin and eye and texture of hair, and no one on Tenjin had questioned her supposed Vulcan ancestry, yet on Romulus there was something about her that other Romulans could see and judge that she was not one of them. Would she ever know what it was? Since she would probably never see Romulus again, did it matter?

"I have preserved their exact pattern in your medical chart," Selar told her, sensing her concern. "Once we leave Quirinus, I can restore them. Or you can remain without them until we complete our mission and then have them back just as they were."

Zetha said nothing. Why did such a minor change disturb her when so many major changes hadn't? What if she died without her true face?

"They are, after all, a part of you," Selar said mildly.

Zetha suppressed a sudden wave of what a human might call hero worship. She found herself wondering how old Selar was, whether she, like most Vulcans, had been betrothed as a child, whether she had children.

In Ki Baratan, she had often searched the crowds on the streets for males and females of a certain age, imagining any one of them might have engendered her. The little monster with the booted feet was not even part of her consideration.

She thought she had gotten out of the habit by now, but she'd been wrong. The face that looked back at her in the mirror was not only naked without its characteristic sprinkling of extra pigmentation ("As if when the gods were making you they got distracted and forgot to stir the batter properly before putting you in the oven to bake!" Aemetha used to say), but the look in the green eyes was vulnerable. She had never had a mother; why crave one now? She had Selar's trust, and she had found ways to make herself useful. What more did she want?

Everything, Thamnos had thought, balefully eyeing the stranger blocking the light at the entrance to his cave. *I am about to lose everything!*

"How did you find me?" he asked, pretending to be calmer than he felt.

"Your father sent me," the stranger said.

"But—" Thamnos began, and only then, after how many years, did it occur to him that of course his tiny ship, only one of many in the family hangar, would have had a homing device.

But the stranger was not interested in Thamnos family matters. He came straight to the point. "He owes us certain . . . considerations. Control of the *hilopon* is ours from here on."

Chapter 12

As a matter of cosmic history, one man's terrorist can be another man's freedom fighter, and if a Rigelian by any other name can pass for a Romulan to the cursory scan of a tricorder, the reverse can also true.

The path to the office of chairman of the Tal Shiar was a steep and necessarily twisted one. In the course of his climb, Koval had had to do a lot of traveling early in his career.

Everyone knows what spies do. They infiltrate a society, eavesdrop on its conversations, study its fleet movements and weapons technology, report on unrest and sedition in its streets, send encrypted messages back to headquarters on often-compromised frequencies and, with luck as much as spycraft, live to spy another day.

But that sort of legwork is largely for the young spy, and the goal is always to come in from the streets and out of the cold to a room of one's own. The secret world, like any organization, has its middle management. Those spies who survive the years of ground-level sneakery without capture, torture, execution, or, perhaps worst of all, reprogramming, eventually plateau here, unless they have the sheer temerity to step on as many necks as possible on their climb to the upper echelons.

In the world of spies, much of a middle manager's daily work lies in trying to "turn" spies from the other side, convincing them to join his cause; the rest of his time is spent in recruiting civilians to be spies. How and why the Thamnos family ended up in Koval's pocket was a tale too long in the telling. But the sins of the fathers often pass to the sons, even if the sons are not sophisticated enough to understand the agenda their fathers have created.

All this weighed on Koval's mind as he stood in the entrance to the makeshift underground laboratory, the dust of Renaga sullying his otherwise meticulously shined boots. The Tal Shiar had had sleeper cells on Renaga for decades. They knew someone had come to ground in a small private ship over a decade ago and had reported their finding to their superiors, who filed the information for future reference.

When Koval needed a front man for his latest freelance project, he had thought of a Rigelian. There was a saying about Rigelians on both sides of the Zone—"looks like a human, scans like a Vulcan"—and they had been of use to both sides often in the past. Koval recalled that Thamnos the Elder owed him a favor. If he believed in gods, Koval might have thought they were smiling on him when the senior Thamnos told him of his son's disappearance and provided him with the call signal for the missing ship.

Marvelous! was Koval's first thought. *Everything I need in one place. Pity it's such a backward, out-of-the-way place and I shall have to travel there personally, but even so . . .*

Mindful of the bewilderment in Thamnos the Younger's squinty eyes—the fool had no idea what this was all about—Koval considered the mediocrity of the material he sometimes had to work with. But the stupid ones were often the most easy to manipulate, and it was all for the glory of the Empire, was it not? Koval looked down his aristocratic nose at the man who on this world called himself Cinchona and asked:

"How would you like to be immortal?"

The poor dupe's answer was exactly what Koval expected.

"What does that mean?" he said and, on that tenuous basis, Koval worked his alchemy.

Utilizing a lifelong fascination with biological warfare, he had become a specialist within the Tal Shiar, responsible for not a few covert experiments on colonials and subject populations. Now it was time to take his skills to the next level. Since Jekri Kaleh's ouster, he was one step away from the chairmanship, and the Continuing Committee was rumored to be seeking a replacement for the current chairman, who was well past his prime. This action, Koval hoped, would prompt the Committee's hearts and minds to turn toward him.

In his research he had of course searched the archives for the Gnawing, and found its potential encouraging. In fact, he wondered why no one had thought to use it before. He now had a place to begin. One never knew when the ability to depopulate a planet without damaging its infrastructure might come in handy. And there were so many other things one could do with a manageable disease along the way.

But there were problems. For one thing, fear of the Gnawing was so entrenched in the Romulan psyche that, even after a thousand years free of it, it would be among the first things any reputable physician would test for. Further, its incubation period was too short to be effective. Within a day or two of exposure, those afflicted died. Civil authorities, faced with an outbreak of something so virulent, would quarantine affected populations, terminating the spread. One could hope at best to kill a few hundred per world. Not what Koval had in mind.

Then, of course, there was the question of checks and balances. One wanted an antidote, a way of stopping the disease from spreading to one's own troops, being inadvertently carried onto a warbird, and turning it into a ghost ship or, worse, a carrion bird bringing the disease back to the homeworld.

Problem: Create a disease with a long incubation period for which there is a cure that only you control.

Solution: the Gnawing, grafted onto R-fever (which had the added advantage of crossing species to affect humanoids as well) and other chimeric entities, to confuse anyone trying to deconstruct it, potentially curable by a substance called *hilopon*, which your sleeper cells report is only found on Renaga.

He could have done all of this himself, although obtaining the R-fever might have been problematic, but for safety's sake Koval wanted a dupe to take the fall in case anything went wrong. Who better than a former Federation citizen, who just happened to be a research physician of sorts, living in exile on the very world inside the Zone that held the cure? It was almost too easy.

Using the simplest words possible, Koval told Thamnos what was expected of him. Not that he told him everything. He offered Thamnos virtual immortality and Thamnos, being who and what he was, didn't bother with the details. The disease he would create, with the help of Romulan scientists, would simply evidence itself on selected worlds, Koval explained, with no possible way of being traced back to him. His role would be that of the great savior who offered the cure. Fame, fortune, the Nobel Prize, the Zee-Magnees Prize, all would be within his reach.

"But what if the *hilopon* doesn't work?" Thamnos asked.

"Oh, but it will," Koval assured him. "We've already tested it on the Gnawing. We assume you've tested it on the R-fever. If it kills both, it will kill the two in combination. We're certain of it."

" 'We'?" Thamnos echoed him.

Koval's answer was a cryptic smile, and even Thamnos knew enough not to follow that line of questioning further. Then something else occurred to him.

"If word gets out that I've got the cure, what's to stop anyone with a big enough fleet from invading Renaga and stealing all of it?"

"Now, there's a curious thing," Koval said. "*Hilopon* only seems to work on Renaga. We've tried taking it offworld, and it's useless. Our scientists are not certain whether it's something in the atmosphere, the sun's radiation, the climate, some interaction with other elements in the soil, or simple magic. We'll figure it out eventually, but how fortunate for you that we haven't yet, hm? And because Renaga's inside the Zone, the machinations necessary for either side to violate treaty, confront the other side's patrols, invade and conquer, are simply too costly in this day and age. Both sides will have to come to you."

But Thamnos wasn't even thinking that far ahead. It never occurred to him to ask why, if Romulan scientists knew all about *hilopon*, Koval even needed him. All he could think of to ask was "Why me?"

"Because you're here. Because you were resourceful enough to bring specimens of R-fever with you. And because if a Romulan scientist announced that we'd discovered the curative effects of *hilopon*, we'd be accused of violating the Neutral Zone, wouldn't we? Suspicions would be aroused no matter what. Romulans are always blamed when there's trouble, seldom honored when honor is due. But you're a Federation expatriate, married to a Renagan female. You'd have immunity. Do you see?"

Thamnos did, but he didn't. Ultimately, Koval knew, it was all too complicated for him. It never occurred to him to refuse. Maybe it was the echo of the words "the Nobel Prize, the Zee Magnees Prize" that crowded everything else out of his brain. He'd asked Koval what he meant by "immortality," and now he finally understood it. He thought.

McCoy wished he hadn't said anything about "house calls" within Uhura's hearing.

"You are not—repeat *not* going to Rigel IV to talk to any member of the Thamnos family," she scolded him, surprised that McCoy, who had previously resisted so much as moving off the porch, was suddenly packing a bag and arranging transport. "Someone from Medical can handle this, or one of my Listeners. There's no need for you to—"

"This is personal!" McCoy interrupted, his jaw set. "There's a special circle in hell reserved for doctors who create illness instead of treating it, and I have no doubt whoever did this has a front-row seat, but I'd be happy to hasten his journey. What was it Jim used to say about risk?" he asked rhetorically, stuffing clean socks into a travel bag.

"Leonard, I'm serious. Stop it right now! If you want to talk to Thamnos Senior, rattle his cage, that's fine. But you do that onscreen, not in person. Neither of us has time to waste on this."

"Is that the real reason?" McCoy demanded testily. "Or are you just mothering me?"

"It's not about that. I want a record of the transmission. We can analyze it, determine if he's telling the truth or not."

McCoy stood there with the last pair of socks in his hand; he seemed to have forgotten what he intended to do with them. Finally he remembered what he was doing and began unpacking the travel bag.

"Hadn't thought of that," he acknowledged. "All right, you win. I'll try to get him to talk to me on subspace. Won't be easy, but before you ask, yes, I'm up to it. Anger is a wonderful tonic, young lady. Now get off my screen; I've got work to do."

Some of the bluster had worn off by the time he'd been routed through a maze of security checks and retina scans and spoken to half a dozen Rigelian authorities, each more officious than the one before, and he had no doubt that if he wasn't who he was he'd have been ignored entirely. But even Papaver Thamnos knew better than to let Leonard McCoy talk to his automated comm system.

By the time the lanky, liver-spotted old pirate, who was not much younger than McCoy himself, appeared onscreen,

McCoy was ready for his afternoon nap. Still, they managed to exchange pleasantries and talk about the weather and what to do about arthritic knees, and McCoy was about to do his diplomatic best to lay out his case for needing to know the whereabouts of Thamnos the Younger without telling the old man why when, as if on cue, a pack of multicolored five-toed Rigelian *emilli* hounds came bounding into the room where Thamnos the Elder was, setting up a fearful baying racket.

The old pirate feigned surprise, but didn't order the dogs away. Instead he began laughing and playing with them, encouraging them, in a scrabble of toenails and a kind of breathless yapping, to race around the room in a kind of bizarre choreography as he sat back and watched McCoy's reaction. His face—an older, cannier version of his son's—was a grinning mask.

McCoy, to his credit, didn't rattle. He'd figured the dogs had been introduced in an attempt to distract him, and he was not about to be distracted. He also knew the yapping would make it difficult for the voice-print analyzers to do their job. He waited calmly until most of the hounds tired and flopped panting on the floor before he asked Thamnos where he might find his son.

"No idea," Thamnos said. "Wouldn't tell you if I did know. Wouldn't be prudent. None of your business, anyway. Can't help you. Don't know why I should. Only professional courtesy, one physician to another, letting you get this far. Goodbye."

And that was that. The two men sat glaring at each other for a few moments while the senior Thamnos sat stroking of one of the dogs, stonewalling him. Then McCoy tried again.

"There's a disease akin to the Fever," he began. "Some of the first victims were on your own world—"

But Thamnos merely held up one liver-spotted hand to silence him.

"Not interested. Someone else's problem. Isn't it?" he asked the dog, fondling its ears and checking them for ticks.

How long they sat there at an impasse, McCoy couldn't tell. He cleared his throat and tried one last time.

"Dr. Thamnos—"

"Can't hear you."

Now it was a question of who would terminate the transmission first. Much as it irked him to do so, McCoy shut it down from his end without saying goodbye. He hoped Papaver would eventually divert his attention away from the dogs and wonder how long he'd been performing to an empty room, but he doubted it.

"Tuvok? What is a 'red herring'?"

Tuvok was scanning transmissions from the worlds they passed on the way to Quirinus, searching for any report or rumor, official or otherwise, of unexplained fatal illnesses. Had they the time and the guarantee of safety, they might have come closer and scanned the worlds themselves. But Uhura sent them daily updates on the spread of the disease; it bloomed from world to world on the starcharts like the blight of fungus on an endangered tree. There was no time to refine the search process. Perhaps if there were Listeners in the vicinity, they could go to ground and search out data on the worlds they passed, but *Albatross* had to hurry.

Thus Tuvok scanned, encoding his findings and sending them back to Earth for Dr. Crusher's team to analyze.

And now this question, the sort of question one of his children might have asked when they were far younger than she, Tuvok mused. But if Zetha was what she claimed to be, her education has been incomplete at best, and such questions could logically be expected.

She was tending the orchid he had brought with him. An indulgence, he had told himself at the time, most illogical. And yet, he thought now, it provided an esthetic touch to the *Albatross*'s drab, utilitarian surroundings, and each of his crewmates had, at one time or another, admired it. Zetha seemed particularly taken with it.

There were orchids on Romulus, Tuvok knew. Perhaps it was because it was familiar that she was attracted to it. Or perhaps it was that she had never had the luxury of caring for one herself. An illogical impulse to make her a gift of the orchid at the end of their mission teased at a corner of his mind.

In any event, the sight of the young face, bereft for once of its ever-watchful sideways glance or almost as familiar scowl, complemented by the exotic shape and bright splash of color provided by the orchid, was pleasing to behold. Near space was quiet for the moment. Tuvok sat back from his console and gave Zetha his complete attention.

"A herring is a fish, often used for food on human worlds," he began. He saw her frown, wondering what fish had to do with the disease they tracked, but to her credit she waited for his explanation. "When it is smoked or cured prior to consumption, its ordinarily gray flesh turns red. It has a distinct odor. When training hunting dogs, humans traditionally set red herring in their paths in order to condition them to ignore false data and continue to pursue their prey."

He watched her process it, the fine-boned face and mobile mouth contorted with concentration. As he had learned to do with his children, Tuvok waited for the next question, suspecting it would not be about fish or hunting dogs.

"They're violent, aren't they? Humans, I mean," she said. "As violent sometimes as Romulans. Not like Vulcans."

"Some are," Tuvok acknowledged. "Just as I am certain there are some Romulans who are not. It is wiser not to judge an entire species by a few examples."

Zetha's shoulders hunched slightly, as if she wondered if she was being reprimanded.

"As for Dr. Crusher's use of the term 'red herring,'" Tuvok completed his thought in order to let her know he was not reprimanding her. "It has come to mean any false evidence set in one's path to distract one from the object one is searching for."

"I see," Zetha said and then, as this extra datum was added to her education, she smiled.

The smile was a gift, and Tuvok recognized it as such. Acknowledging it, he returned to his scanning.

"If it were up to us, we'd become part of the Empire, but we're stuck here in the middle of some arbitrarily drawn-up 'neutral zone,' and so it's not allowed!"

The speaker was an angry bureaucrat named Jarquin whose office the landing party had been referred to in order to obtain the proper travel permits. Selar and Zetha had taken the two chairs in front of his desk. Tuvok, snow dripping from his boots, stood behind them.

The office was oppressively warm, as might be expected in a region inhabited by vulcanoids where it snowed eight months out of ten. Jarquin's taste in decorating was decidedly Romulan. Despite the climate, he had somehow managed to acquire fresh hothouse flowers, arranging them in the minimalist Romulan style. The geometric light sculptures had no doubt been imported from the homeworld. A human would have called the look Art Deco. Narrow buttress windows framed by dark blue patterned drapes set high up in the thick walls looked out over a public square that might have been anywhere on Romulus, except for the ever-swirling snow.

"Our young people grow up and emigrate," Jarquin grumbled. "There's nothing to keep them here. The Empire allows a certain quota every year to complete their educations or find work on the homeworld. My own sons were among them. Most decide to settle and never return. They do it to get away from the damned snow."

"Of course," Tuvok remarked.

The three outworlders were dressed in "fur"-lined parkas, replicated to look as close to what the natives wore as possible without actually being made of fur. Their boots were also authentic, right down to the retractable cross-country skis built into the soles, the best means of local transport in a city where the snow fell so fast and so often that there was no point in clearing it. Citizens merely skied on top of it to reach their destinations. The tall, slope-roofed buildings lining the streets had multistoried windowless basements that were used to store food in the winter, because these levels were uninhabitable in the cold months; a bright-green "snow line," twice the height of a tall Quirinian in the season when there was no snow, was painted around the foundations to show how far an average winter's accumulation reached.

Jarquin glowered at the snow, closed his eyes, cleared a space amid the datachips on his desk, folded his hands and sighed. His features—the hawklike eyes and upswept brow ridges, the characteristic bowl-shaped haircut, even a tendency to fat in his middle years—were more Romulan than Romulan.

"Tell me what it's like. Is it true it's warm enough in summer to swim in the lakes and rivers? Is it true that when all the moons are in the sky, it's as bright as day? Do you know how rarely we can even see the sky on this world?" He did not give any of them a chance to answer before he went on. "I read a book about Romulan butterflies once. Can't imagine what it must be like to see such delicate, multicolored things actually flying through the air. Here they'd freeze in mid-flight!"

The mere memory of the illustrations in the book was enough to make his eyes moist. He shook himself as if shaking the snow off his shoulders and demanded once again: "Tell me what it's like!"

Speak up! Zetha told herself. *It's situations like this for which you've been sent along as cover, because the Vulcans can't provide the detail you can. He may only be making conversation, awed because he so rarely meets what he thinks are true Romulans, or it may be a ploy to test who we really are. It all depends on you now. Say something!*

Back on the ship, Sisko was less than happy. While he was willing to accept input from his crew, Admiral Uhura had put him in charge, and he hadn't expected Tuvok, of all people, to try to undermine his command decisions. But Tuvok had decided the antihuman sentiment on Quirinus was strong enough for Sisko to remain on *Albatross*.

"I figured we'd work in shifts," Sisko said when the subject first came up. "Selar and I, you and Zetha. That way there's always someone here to monitor the landing party in the event there's a problem and we need to beam up in a hurry."

"This will be the first time Selar and I have to pass as Romulans," Tuvok pointed out. "I would prefer Zetha accompany us. And, as security officer, I am compelled to point out that you would be put at unnecessary risk on Quirinus."

Disgruntled though he was, Sisko had to concede that Tuvok was right. It was ironic, though, that the Vulcans, who hated the cold, were obliged to go, but he had been looking forward to a visit to Quirinus and was forced to stay behind. He and Jennifer had gone cross-country skiing in Calgary once before Jake was born; he'd been a natural at it, and wanted to try it again.

Well, so what? he thought. *This isn't a vacation, and it wouldn't be nearly as much fun without Jennifer, anyway.*

He contented himself with running diagnostics and keeping a weather eye on the three onscreen blips among the several thousand heat readings in the city below whose safety he was responsible for. That was another thing. Except for the rare occasion on *Okinawa* when his name came up for bridge duty—and he always made it a point to request gamma shift, when things were usually quiet—he had never been responsible for people's lives before. It was one thing to make command decisions onboard a ship, particularly one as small as *Albatross*, but seeing those three small blips on his screen made him feel almost as vulnerable as they were. He liked that not at all. And suddenly he was not alone.

"Mr. Sisko?" It was Dr. Crusher's voice, soft as always, but it made him jump. Dammit, he thought he'd shut the holos down! He was beginning to feel like a Romulan, under scrutiny all the time. "Got a minute?"

He took a breath before he trusted himself to speak. "Yes, Doctor? What is it?"

"We've had a breakthrough with the Tenjin carcinoform."

"Selar's on the planet, but you can relay the data directly to her computer," Sisko suggested.

"I'll do that anyway, but right now I wanted to share that with somebody in person."

Behind her, Sisko could see the lab at Starfleet Medical, and members of her staff working round the clock on the R-fever that had been rushed to them from Starbase 23, as well as the Tenjin virus.

"It must be awfully late where you are," he said.

"It is. That's why I didn't want to disturb the Admiral."

"So you want to share it with me? I'm listening."

"Before you signed on for this mission, I did a little dog-and-pony show for the admiral, McCoy, and Selar. Mostly for the admiral's benefit, to help her understand what we were dealing with. Just at random, I compared our neoform to human HIV. I don't know if you've heard of it; it's an artifact from the twenty-first century—"

"I've heard of it," Sisko said. "Are you telling me that's what this thing is like?"

"At the time I did the presentation, it was just a lucky guess. But putting together the pieces your team has been gathering, it turned out to be an accurate guess. This germ doesn't kill by itself; it does what HIV used to do and turns the body's own defenses against it. That's why it shows up as a killer flu on some worlds, as a cancer on others."

Sisko thought about that for a moment. "I have a feeling that's not good news."

Crusher sighed. "No, it isn't, not in terms of isolating and/or treating this thing, not yet. But I just wanted you to know that what *Albatross* is doing out there is important."

Sisko didn't say anything to that.

"Want to talk about it?" Crusher asked against his silence.

"Talk about what?"

"Feeling outnumbered? Only round-ear on the mission and all that?"

How long had she been watching him? he wondered. How much of his muttering had she overheard?

"You know I am," he said, wondering if she was reading his vital signs from there and registering his stress levels as well. "And I don't appreciate Tuvok's second-guessing me about beaming down to Quirinus. I might have reached the same decision he did, if he hadn't overridden me. Maybe he doesn't think I'm experienced enough to make command decisions . . ." Sisko stopped and thought about that. "And, dammit, he's probably right. But I should have been allowed to arrive at that on my own. It seems to me Vulcans can't resist telling us mere humans what's best for us. I pride myself on being able to get along with anyone, but—"

"—but you've been bent out of shape since you were drafted for this mission, and Tuvok's second-guessing you only makes things more difficult."

"Is that an official prognosis, Doctor? Or are you just minding my business?"

"Neither. Just a prelude to asking you to put on your best face for a moment. There's someone here who wants to talk to you. Admiral Uhura arranged it especially. It's a little earlier on *Okinawa*, so it's only a little past his bedtime . . ."

"Daddy?"

"*Jake?*" Sisko couldn't believe his eyes. His son was standing there in his pajamas rubbing one eye, a favorite stuffed "critter" so raggedy Sisko couldn't remember what it had once been trailing behind him. He found himself kneeling on the deck to be at eye level, wishing more than anything that he could put his arms around the boy. But while the holos were good, they weren't that good.

Yet, Sisko thought. *Someday, maybe. But for now . . .*

"Jake-O? Son, how are you? How you feeling, little man?"

"*Daaad*—!" The kid managed to stretch the single syllable out to at least four. "I'm not little! I'm almost five and a half."

"So you are. My mistake. It's just you're growing up so fast. What's going on? How's kindergarten? How's Momma? Did Grandpa Joe call you since I've been gone?"

Shut up! he told himself. *Let the boy speak. What's the matter with you?* Jake was rubbing both eyes now.

"Sleepy!" he announced. "Goin' back to bed. Momma's here, though."

"Okay, Jake-O. I'll talk to you soon. I love you!"

"Love you, too, Daddy . . ." And, dragging his critter behind him, he was gone.

"It's my guess you miss him," Jennifer said, and this time Sisko had no words at all; he just rose to his feet and gazed at her. Had she been this beautiful the last time he saw her?

It was at that point that Crusher made her exit.

"I'll put you two on discrete," she said. "Lieutenant, you can let me know when you want to terminate."

"What?" he said vaguely, his eyes and mind only for Jennifer. "Affirmative, Doctor. And . . . thank you."

"It rains a lot," Zetha told Jarquin, as usual blurting out her words without giving anyone else a chance to speak, though this time, she suspected, it was welcome. "But, yes, it's very warm in the summer. Warm enough to walk bare-armed in the sun. And when any two of the moons rise, it's very bright, and everyone has two shadows."

"Two shadows!" Jarquin whispered almost in awe. "And the butterflies—?"

"Exquisite," Zetha told him, though she'd seen precious few of them in the dark streets of the capital. "Just as you imagine them. Sometimes if you're very still, they'll even light on your shoulders and in your hair, especially if you wash with flower soaps."

Now that, she thought, *is going too far. It was only one butterfly, and it landed on the wildflower Tahir found struggling through a crack in a cobblestone and braided into your hair. But how would this—bureaucrat—know that?* Emboldened, she went further.

"There are certain times of the year, when they migrate, there are so many of them overhead that they block out the sun . . ." Zetha noticed that Tuvok was watching her, something like admiration in his eyes. "Citizen Jarquin, can you imagine looking up at what you think is a cloud and seeing instead a rainbow of colors, flashing in the sunlight, all fluttering at once, moving as one toward a common goal?"

Jarquin did not answer. His thoughts were very far away. Tuvok cleared his throat.

"That is sufficient, Niece," he said. "Citizen Jarquin and I need to discuss our itinerary now."

That brought Jarquin out of his rapture. "I'm afraid it won't be entirely possible for you to visit every sector you've requested."

"Why not?" Tuvok demanded with what he hoped was a credible Romulan imperiousness.

"I can issue you limited travel permits for certain areas, but others . . ." He seemed to weigh something before he spoke next. "Citizen Leval, Citizen Vesak, I trust these words will never leave this room . . . but there have been outbreaks of we don't know what, except that it was deadly. . . ."

Zetha, her mouth shut at last, dared a glance at Selar, who had suddenly become even more alert than usual.

"We've had to quarantine two of the cities you requested, and certain sectors of three more. No one gets in or out until we're certain this thing is finished."

Jarquin had pulled up a map on his desk screen. Selar leaned forward imperceptibly, committing it to memory. While Jarquin was occupied with pushing buttons, she and Tuvok exchanged glances. Selar's was visibly excited; Tuvok's urged caution.

"Damnable, inexplicable, something like that occurring in the winter," Jarquin was muttering. "Every citizen receives immunizations at the start of every winter against anything contagious. Well, you can imagine, shut up indoors most of the time, we can't be too careful. But usually no one gets sick in the cold weather. Sorry, I know this will cut into your profits, but I can't let you . . ."

"We quite understand," Tuvok said before Selar could object. "But we can have permits for the other sectors we requested?"

"Oh, of course, of course," Jarquin blustered, rummaging on his desk for the proper forms. "Always happy to be of service to loyal Romulans . . ."

Sisko's chrono beeped, reminding him that he needed to check on the landing party's whereabouts every fifteen minutes, and that fifteen minutes was up.

"Jen, I have to go."

"I know," she said. "But this doesn't have to be the last time. We'll talk again, soon. You know I love you." She didn't wait for him to end the transmission, but terminated it from her end, as if afraid neither of them would find the courage to go first.

"I love you, too!" Sisko whispered to the empty space where Jennifer had been. With a sigh he checked the readings and saw his three charges more or less in the same place they'd been last time he checked, in the company of a fourth party, no doubt still arranging for travel permits. He realized Crusher was probably waiting in the wings for him to sign off, and signaled her.

"Ask you something, Doctor?" he said once he had her attention.

"Certainly."

"How do we know this whole mission isn't a setup?"

Crusher put her hands in the pockets of her medical smock and leaned back in her chair, rotating it slightly from side to side.

"I'm listening," she said.

"We're inside the Neutral Zone in violation of treaty, on the basis of data sent to SI specifically to Admiral Uhura's attention, supposedly from a Romulan official she once met on Khitomer."

Crusher waited. She obviously knew he had more, but was hesitating. "And—?" she prompted.

"And wouldn't this be just the perfect opportunity for a cloaked Romulan ship to pick us off before we even knew they were there or, worse, bring us in tow and take us back to the Empire as political prisoners for a show trial? And when we tried to tell them that we were working for their benefit as well as our own, they'd tell us there was no such disease within the Empire, and we were using it as an excuse to violate the Zone."

This time it was Crusher who held the silence.

"Am I being paranoid, Doctor? Or have these thoughts occurred to you as well?"

She sighed. "As a matter of fact, they have. But there's no question that there's a very real disease killing people on both sides. Seems like an awfully elaborate hoax to pick off just one little ship. Now, why don't you say what's really on your mind?"

"All right, what about Zetha? How do we know she's not a plant?"

"We don't. But unless she's been sent on a suicide mission, she's as much at risk as you are."

"How do you figure?" Sisko asked, growing heated. "If the ship is attacked, granted, we're all dead. But I'm thinking of her signaling to her side that we're here, or tampering with the tests Selar's running in the lab . . ." He realized he was overreacting, and forced himself to calm. "I'm sorry. I know Selar backs up all her research and confirms it with you, and I keep an eye on Zetha anytime she's in my vicinity, but I keep thinking there's something more here, something we've all missed, even Tuvok, for all his security training. Something that could get us all killed."

Crusher had the grace to wait until he was finished. "The same thoughts have crossed my mind, Lieutenant. But I wonder if we aren't all guilty of just a little bit of species profiling here. Wouldn't the joke be on us if Zetha turns out to be exactly what she claims to be? In any case, nothing we can do about it now except play the hand we've been dealt and see the game to its end."

"Now you're starting to sound like my friend Curzon," Sisko muttered.

"Then I'll take it as a compliment," Crusher replied. "Time for me to log off. Good night, Lieutenant."

"Good night, Doctor," Sisko said, and waited for the chrono's next signal.

As they were leaving, travel permits in hand, Tuvok asked Jarquin one thing more, something any Romulan might ask another.

"How often do you hear from your sons?"

He had been mindful of the small framed holos set apart from the clutter on Jarquin's desk, of two handsome young men, close in age if not twins, whose features strongly resembled their father's intermixed with those of what must be a beautiful mother.

Jarquin hesitated before he answered.

"I haven't, since they left for the homeworld. It's very common. They lose interest in their birth-world, lose touch with those they left behind. Many never speak to their families again. Maybe they're ashamed of their roots, of coming from this place. They want to blend in, give their allegiance to their new home. Then again, there could be other factors, political unrest, censorship. I can say that to you, because you're not government, but sometimes one wonders . . ."

"Indeed," Tuvok said, pulling the hood of his parka up over his ears in preparation for the cold.

"Maybe you could—" Jarquin began, then thought the better of it. "Forgive me. I was going to ask, when you return to the homeworld, if you could make inquiries about my sons. Presumptuous of me, but . . ."

Tuvok knew his reply was illogical, but he made it nevertheless. "I will see to it, Citizen Jarquin."

The door slid closed behind them, leaving Jarquin alone, watching the ever-swirling snow from his window, but thinking about butterflies.

Chapter 13

"I'll put my Listeners on it," Uhura promised. "A migration of that magnitude from an unallied world to Romulus should be easy to track. If Jarquin's sons or any concentration of Quirinians are registered on the homeworld, we should be able to learn something, however tenuous. Meanwhile, I assume you're scanning the so-called enclosed areas from orbit?"

"Affirmative," Selar reported.

"And—?"

"And several regions appear to have been abandoned altogether. There are no life-sign readings other than those indicating small animal life-forms, most likely verminous."

Rats, Uhura thought, suppressing a shudder.

"Of the other quarantined or 'enclosed' areas, most appear to be very sparsely populated," Selar went on, "and there is evidence of reduced activity among the few remaining inhabitants. Scans show elevated body temperatures, indicating the likelihood of infection. Since I began scanning the village of Sawar less than one hour ago, there have been four fatalities in the quarantined area."

"But there's no way of telling for certain if that's caused by our neoform," Uhura suggested.

"Without actually collecting biosamples? I believe not."

"It is unfortunate we were barred from traveling to the quarantined areas," Tuvok interjected suddenly.

"Yes, it really is too bad," Uhura agreed. "But of course I'd never tell you to disobey Citizen Jarquin's directive and try to infiltrate those regions illegally."

"Obviously," Tuvok said. "A pity, since we do have hazmat suits against just such a contingency. And, given the necessity for bulky clothing in the Quirinian climate, it would be quite possible for us to conceal all but the face mask of a hazmat suit beneath our parkas. Further, were we traveling at night . . ."

"Hypothetically, of course," Uhura said, her face as deadpan as any Vulcan's.

"Hypothetically," Tuvok agreed. "Of course."

Selar watched this exchange with great interest. She wasn't certain what was going on, but it intrigued her. Sisko, being human, understood entirely, and managed, just barely, to suppress a chuckle. A glance in Zetha's direction told him she got it, too. Sisko crooked a finger at her.

"You come with me," he said, indicating she was to follow him forward, out of earshot of the briefing.

Zetha shrugged. She had grasped immediately what was going on. But if Sisko felt it necessary to exert his authority, she would humor him.

"You begrudge me the knowledge that Tuvok and Selar intend to infiltrate the enclosed areas," she observed when they were alone in the control cabin, where he had assigned her a seat far away from the instruments. "Why?"

"I begrudge you any detailed knowledge of this mission," Sisko said honestly, frowning at one of the readings. The environmental control adaptor had been hinky since departure, but since when had it refused to respond? "I think the less you know, the better. There's no guarantee you won't run to the first Romulan you see with the information you already have—"

"No guarantee except Lieutenant Tuvok, who can no doubt outrun me," Zetha said, too low for Sisko to hear.

"—and no idea what disposition SI's going to make of you once this mission is over—"

"I assumed I would be sacrificed."

She also said this so quietly Sisko almost didn't hear it, but he did.

"Sacrificed? What are you talking about?"

Zetha shrugged. "I am still learning your language. 'Executed' might be a more accurate word, 'eliminated' easier on your sensibilities. But killed, in so many words."

Sisko stopped fidgeting with the controls and gave her his full attention. "Run that by me again? You honestly believe Starfleet will have you executed once this mission is over?"

"It is what the Tal Shiar would do," Zetha said.

"Then why in God's name are you going along with it?"

Does he not see? Zetha wondered. *No, of course he doesn't. His life to this point has been far too soft. When he speaks so fondly of a dead mother who loved him, a father who taught him to cook, his wife, his son—a family, a place to belong, in so many words—how can he possibly know?*

"Perhaps I don't understand," she said ingenuously, watching him out of the corners of her green eyes. "Is not the purpose of this mission to trace the origins of this disease, apprehend whoever has created it, and save the lives of those who might be afflicted by it?"

"Ideally, yes, but—"

"Then that is why I am 'going along with it,' as you say. When 'it' is over, so is my usefulness. You cannot imagine I will be allowed to return to your Federation knowing what I know?"

"That's exactly what—" Sisko started to say, but stopped himself. "You can't tell me you're just here to help us. We're strangers to you. Enemies, as far as your conditioning has taught you. There's got to be another motive."

Zetha shook her head, almost pitying him, as she had almost pitied the elites on her own world whom she had spent a lifetime mocking, eluding, pilfering from. He really did not understand.

"Every day I live is a day I live, human," she said with a coldness no one so young should possess. "It is one day more snatched from the jaws of death. Understand that, and you understand me."

At last Selar got the joke. Anyone who thought Vulcans had no sense of humor need only study her face. Her eyebrows threatening to disappear into her hairline, she did not trust herself to speak, but allowed the two trained operatives to have the floor.

"Well!" Uhura said at last, as if a decision had been reached. "My log entry will show that *Albatross* intends to remain in Quirinian space while you complete your cover mission with a visit to the village of Sawar, which is badly in need of replicator parts. I'll expect your follow-up report by this time tomorrow."

"Affirmative," Tuvok said, ending the transmission.

Selar allowed him a moment's silence before she asked: "Lieutenant, am I to assume we will have need of those hazmat suits after all?"

At least the weather favored them. Quirinus offered the landing party one of its rare sunlit days. Citizens Leval, Vesak, and Zetha wore UV goggles to keep from going snowblind as they made their way on their short skis through an untouched alpine landscape beneath a cloudless lavender sky. The air was warm enough for Zetha to lower the hood of her parka and turn her face like a flower to the sun. Emulating her—if they were truly Romulan rather than Vulcan, they would be more adaptable to the cold—Tuvok and Selar did likewise.

It was hard to believe that only a few kilometers distant

from this pristine beauty a wall sealed healthy citizens off from those suffering an agonizing death.

Tuvok and Selar wore their hazmat suits beneath their parkas, the face masks stored in rucksacks that also contained samples of the merchandise they had ostensibly come to Quirinus to sell. Zetha carried only a sample case in her rucksack, and wore no hazmat suit.

"We will require your talents as we mingle with the citizens on the 'safe' side of the quarantine enclosure," Tuvok instructed her. "Obviously we will be forbidden access to that enclosure. We will appear to acquiesce, as long as it is daylight. After dark, Dr. Selar and I will infiltrate while you return to the ship."

Their arrival in Sawar, a village sheltered in a valley surrounded by high mountains, was greeted with some curiosity and not a little suspicion. The curiosity they had expected. Offworld visitors seldom ventured beyond the major cities, and rumor had run ahead of them that they were selling not only genuine Romulan replicator parts (someday, Tuvok thought, he must ask Admiral Uhura where she acquired those) but Tholian silks, noted for their durability as well as the brilliance of their colors. Safe and warm inside their thick-walled houses, where they could remove the multiple layers of utilitarian clothing necessary to survive the climate, Quirinians often dressed quite resplendently. Orders for the silks were expected to be plentiful.

But why the suspicion? Tuvok wondered. The trio had permits from Citizen Jarquin, worn prominently displayed on their parkas. Had the effects of the plague in their village made the citizens distrust even that?

"You sense it, too?" Selar asked softly.

"Indeed," Tuvok said. "And I believe we are about to learn something of its source."

A group of citizens who had been milling about an outdoor information kiosk reading the day's news had broken

away and was heading toward them. The trio had perfected a
response to just such an approach by now. Tuvok would
speak first, Selar only if addressed directly, and Zetha only if
the conversation ventured into an area, such as Romulan
butterflies, whose nuances the other two might not be con-
versant in.

"You are Citizen Leval," the group's apparent spokesper-
son, a rawboned angry-eyed female almost as tall as Tuvok
addressed him from behind a breather mask.

The entire crowd wore breather masks, not against the
cold, but against the possibility of infection by outsiders. *Illogical*, was Tuvok's first thought, *since there is no concrete evidence that the disease is airborne*. As the crowd moved toward
them, a stout elderly man with what looked like a bulky antiquated medscanner in his hand was obviously reading them
for signs of infection. One could only hope the scanner was
too antiquated to distinguish Vulcans from Romulans.

"Correct," Tuvok replied with a touch of arrogance, wearing his Romulan persona like a second skin by now.

He noted that even with the supposed security of the
masks and the scanner, the woman still stood back at some
distance. Quirinians, like Romulans, Tuvok had noted in
their visit to Jarquin, only seemed to trust each other when
they stood closer than arm's length, a throwback, no doubt,
to the age of swords when they had needed more room to
safely draw arms. This woman and her constituents stood at
a distance, the distance one might consider safe from casual
contagion transmitted by a cough or sneeze.

"We were notified that your party would arrive today.
You'll have to wear these to go among us." The woman
thrust three face masks into his hand. Tuvok noted that she
also wore surgical gloves, which she removed after her hand
had made contact with his, and threw into a nearby disposal
painted with a bright green sign signifying hazardous waste.
"We can't be too careful of strangers after what happened."

"Citizen Jarquin has made us aware of your situation—" Tuvok began, but the woman interrupted him.

"My name is Subhar. I am magistrate here," she said as if he hadn't spoken. "Ordinarily I'd invite you into the warmth of my house to conduct your business. But even as we speak, some of our most esteemed citizens are dying without remedy behind that wall . . ."

She nodded toward the end of the street, where the landing party could see that part of an ancient wall that had no doubt once encircled the first settlement here had recently been haphazardly bricked up once again. What looked like electrified wire topped the hasty two-meters-tall construct, and armed guards patrolled the perimeter.

". . . so we will conduct our business outdoors, where the fresh air at least gives us a fighting chance against contagion."

Subhar seemed to be struggling to maintain her composure. The landing party said nothing as she blinked back tears before they froze in her eyes.

"I didn't want you here," she snapped. "It seemed . . . inappropriate. But we need the replicator parts, and one of my advisors . . ." She indicated a gray-haired elder, his hands tucked into the sleeves of his parka, who merely nodded in acknowledgment. ". . . reminded me that our future will not always be about death. So far no one outside the wall has gotten ill. This was what we did in ancient times, and it seems to have been effective. Some have said it's barbaric, but what else could we do? We have contained the damnable thing, and we will need bright colors in order to celebrate the lives of those who died, after we have mourned their deaths. So you see why we must be wary of strangers, even though bearing official approvals," Subhar concluded, her anger and sorrow having given way to a kind of weariness. "It was a stranger who brought the illness."

"A stranger?" Tuvok dared after what he hoped was a suitable silence.

"He said he was from Qant Prefecture, but his accent gave him away. Clearly he was lying, but lying's not a crime, not yet. After this, it might be. We never did find out where he really came from. By the time we investigated, the first casualties were already affected. He had no identification on him when we searched him."

"What became of him?" Tuvok asked.

"Oh," Subhar said, as if it were an afterthought. "We killed him."

Tuvok reacted to this as a Romulan might, which was to say not at all. "Then he did not succumb to the illness?"

"No. But it wasn't here before he came, and once we contained everyone he'd come in contact with behind the wall, no one else got sick. And now you've asked enough questions, Citizen. Show us your samples, and let's be done with it. This weather won't hold for long."

As if on cue, the sun disappeared behind a fast-moving cloud, and the wind picked up. Motioning her visitors toward the news kiosk, where a counter was cleared for them to set their rucksacks down, Subhar and the townspeople gathered around, though careful that none of them touched their visitors or anything they had brought with them.

"It's hit the fan," Crusher told Uhura. "I've just received a memo from the C-in-C wanting to know what the hell—and I'm quoting here—kind of progress we were or were not making on this disease. Which, by the way, I'm told they've code-named Catalyst."

"You don't have to tell me, Doctor," Uhura said wearily. "I've gotten the same memo."

"The news media's suggesting every rash or runny nose could be evidence of germ warfare. They're quoting numbers in the millions."

"At least we aren't!" Uhura said a little more sharply than she'd intended. "Yet. I've got a press conference this afternoon to try to do some damage control. Can you give me a bone to throw them?"

"Nothing I'd want getting out to the public at large," Crusher said, tossing her bright hair over her shoulders. "And, off the record, we'll never develop a serum against something where everyone dies."

Uhura thought of everything she'd learned about viruses in recent weeks. "Which leaves the genetic route."

"Hypothetically," Crusher said. "We finished mapping the human genome in the early twenty-first century. The Vulcans, not surprisingly, had their genetic codes down centuries earlier, and the Romulans probably have as well. There are some genes that all three species have in common, but—"

"Go on," Uhura prompted.

"But a retrovirus that can infiltrate all three species at the genetic level, particularly one that mutates the way this one does . . . well, it took thirteen years to map the human genome. It took longer than that to cure HIV at the genetic level, even when we knew exactly what it looked like. This is more like cracking secret codes than practicing medicine."

"So even if the away team succeeds in tracing this to the Romulan side . . ."

"There might be some political value in pointing out that they created it, but unless they've also got a cure up their sleeves, it's not going to save any lives."

"Political value in the negative sense," Uhura mused. "A chance to let slip the dogs of war on both sides." She shook her head. "Not if I can help it. I'll give the C-in-C the same sweet talk I give the press. You get back to work."

"Yes, sir," Crusher said.

Despite the citizens' unease over the deaths behind the wall, the "Romulan merchants" were doing good business. Zetha faithfully recorded several orders for Tholian silk, aware that in the corner of her eye Tuvok was assessing the wall, the guards, the odds of successfully infiltrating the enclosure. In one ear, a Quirinian matron was asking her whether she personally would choose the gold print or the green—

"Well, I'm assuming green for you, dear, because of those beautiful eyes, but I think the gold would look better on me, don't you?"

—while in her other ear, Selar was dangerously close to blowing their cover.

". . . curious about the flora and fauna extant in your warm season," Selar was saying. "The preponderance of calcareous and dolomite rocks in combination with cretaceous sandstones and marls suggests an edaphic ecology dominated by small wildflowers with a very short growing season. Am I correct?"

That's probably more words than she's put together since we left Earth! Zetha thought frantically, noticing as Selar did not that some of the citizens were watching her more warily than they had, even with the fear of contagion, on their arrival. What in the name of Gal Gath'thong did she think she was doing? Without thinking, Zetha kicked her sharply on the ankle. The Vulcan did not wince, of course, but she did give Zetha an odd look and, much to her relief, stopped talking.

"Forgive me, Aunt, but all this talk of the warm season, while we and the citizens stand here freezing. . . . And it's getting dark. . . ."

"Of course," Selar said, and they concluded their official business just as the clouds closed overhead and the snows began again.

The beam-out, Sisko thought, was one of the better ones of his career. He managed to pull all three of his charges up to the ship just long enough for Zetha to step down and Tuvok and Selar to seal up their hoods and the masks of their hazmat suits and then, while the citizens of Sawar were still talking among themselves about the goods they had just ordered—to be delivered, they assumed, on the next convoy arriving to take more of their sons and daughters offworld to Romulus—and even the guards patrolling the enclosure were momentarily distracted by the transporter sparkle, he pinpoint-beamed the Vulcans to one of the more abandoned sectors inside the enclosure, where they could do what they had to do.

"Corpses," Selar reported, shielding her tricorder from the blowing snow with a mittened hand, which also muffled its whirring sounds as she scanned what appeared to be a storehouse of some kind, a heavy lock and chain securing its only door. "Well over one hundred of them, stacked several deep and chemically preserved, presumably until they can be cremated or interred."

"One would think the cold would be sufficient," Tuvok remarked, his own tricorder alert for signs of movement in the narrow, high-walled streets, where the wind howled around corners, adding to the chill.

Selar silenced her tricorder. "A charnel house. An attempt to at least contain all the dead in one place. Doubtless waiting until everyone has succumbed before any effort is made toward disposal."

"Apparently stored here in the earlier stages of the disease," Tuvok observed, indicating the frozen corpses littering the narrow street before them. "These others were not so fortunate. Can specimens be gathered from the recently dead?"

"Perhaps," Selar said, kneeling in the snow to examine the two nearest them, an elderly woman and a child wrapped in a final frozen embrace against the perimeter wall. "Ideally, however, those still living would be preferable."

"But to trouble them when they know that they are dying . . ." Tuvok suggested. Was it only the cold that made his voice husky?

"Indeed. But if the evidence they provide can prevent further deaths . . ."

Tuvok frowned. "I would be most interested in ascertaining the identity of the stranger whose arrival coincided with that of the illness. Lieutenant Sisko has us both on locator. I suggest we split up and communicate on discrete."

"Agreed."

Once again, Sisko was monitoring life-sign readings and talking to one of the holos. This time it was Uhura.

"Not good news on Jarquin's sons," she reported. "Or any Quirinian who emigrates to Romulus, for that matter."

"From what I understand of the situation, Admiral, why am I not surprised?"

"Most of them are recruited by the military. The Empire essentially uses them for cannon fodder for the most dangerous missions. The ruling families have always preferred to use colonials on the frontiers. Looks like they've refined it to a science."

"Glad it's Tuvok and not me who has to give Jarquin that information," Sisko mused.

"Status report?" Uhura asked, bringing them back to the present.

"Tuvok and Selar have both infiltrated the enclosure and, judging from the readings, except for the occasional patrol, they're the only thing moving down there. They've split up. I'm assuming Selar's gathering specimens. Tuvok said something about wanting to find out anything he could about the stranger the citizens claim brought the disease."

"And Zetha?"

"Aft, puttering in the lab, last time I checked."

"Do you check often, Lieutenant?"

Tuvok moved like a shadow. The lock on the storehouse door proved too strong for him to break, but that didn't mean he couldn't pick it. But the mechanism was sluggish with the cold, and it took him longer than he expected. He had timed the patrols outside the walls earlier in the day, and now could only hope to be inside the storehouse and out of range of their scanners before they happened by again. His life-signs would read normal, not feverish, and the guards might consider that worthy of investigation.

At last the lock yielded to his skills, the massive door opened inward and, mercifully, did not either scrape the floor or squeak, and he slipped inside. As his eyes adjusted to the dark, it took all of his Vulcan discipline not to react to what he saw.

He had expected the corpses, but not the rats. They swarmed everywhere, feeding on the dead, hissing and squealing but refusing to give ground at his approach, swarming with the mad purposefulness of a single entity. Wondering if a rat bite would breach the fabric of a hazmat suit, Tuvok moved stealthily so as not to rouse them further. He also wondered if there was some way to warn Subhar and those outside the wall to exterminate the rats.

An enclosure in one corner of the vast, high-raftered room — doubtless at one time an office of some sort — drew his attention. Perhaps there were records, lists of the dead, even information about the interloper who had purportedly brought the illness among them.

This door was not locked. While there were indeed some cursory lists of the dead, apparently abandoned when the numbers became overwhelming and, perhaps, the one compiling the list also fell ill, what Tuvok found most significant was the corpse thrown carelessly onto a table in a corner, doubtless the interloper himself, set apart from the others as if not to defile them by his presence. Ironically, his being exiled in death had spared him the defilement of the rats.

Judging from the wounds inflicted on the body, he had not died easily. His clothing was Quirinian and so, on superficial examination in this dim light, were his features. But Tuvok's tricorder told a different tale.

"Evidence of cosmetic surgery to remove pronounced brow ridges," he reported to Selar on discrete. "On empirical evidence, I believe this individual was Romulan."

"Interesting," was Selar's muffled response. Tuvok assumed she was preoccupied with gathering evidence of her own, and ended the transmission. Then, using the techniques Selar had taught him, he took blood and skin samples from the late and unlamented stranger and, making his way gingerly among the rats, returned the way he had come.

Zetha was tidying and prepping the lab in preparation for Selar's return. She could hear Sisko and Uhura discussing her, even at this distance. Sisko might dictate where she could go, but not what she could hear. Knowing when and how to listen had gotten her this far.

"You are wallpaper," the Lord told her. "A potted plant, a desk ornament. They will speak freely in your presence, because they will not notice you are there."

I am wallpaper, Zetha thought. And it was true. Neither of the two men noticed her; they talked with their heads together as if she was not there.

Military, her instinct told her as soon as they had appeared in the anteroom of the shop, the younger of the two announcing that he had an appointment with the jeweler to look at some naming day gifts. Neither man identified himself, but there was no doubt they were military, though both were in mufti. It was in the way they carried themselves. All Romulans walked guarded in public, but these two were even more so; their very ears had ears. Erect spines, square shoulders even without the overpadded uniforms, voices correct even in whispers, that upper-caste accent they could never escape.

"But what else?" she could hear the Lord's voice in her mind. He had arranged for her to apprentice to this particular jeweler expressly because his shop was frequented by officers. For all she knew, the jeweler himself was Tal Shiar. He certainly had the nastiness. *"Observe, report. What else?"*

Student and mentor? Father and son? Superior officer and subordinate? She did the exercise for her own purposes; she would tell the lord as little as possible. Even as she pretended not to look at them, concentrating on untangling a mess of fine neck chains the jeweler had dropped, she swore, on purpose just to give her something to do, and they made themselves comfortable on the couches in the anteroom while the jeweler went to fetch his trays of rings and pendants for their consideration, her peripheral vision took them in, her senses registering every nuance.

Report: They were a generation apart in age, and the younger man—not young, but younger than the other, middle-aged, the kind of man who might easily have children her age, who might even . . . *Stop it, fool! Stop seeing every Romulan of a certain age as a potential father*—all right then, the one in his prime, square-faced, ridge-browed, graying at the temples, deferred to the elder who was the handsomer of the two—silver-haired, smooth-browed, fox-faced, patrician.

Yes, military by caste and birth, when either might have chosen differently had there been a choice permitted. Aemetha's speech about a people always at war rang in her head, and she found herself wondering if the elites as a caste would be quite as arrogant if they didn't live under the knowledge that they would forever have to send their best and brightest out to the stars and to death.

The squarish one might have been an architect, she thought, the silver-haired one a poet. *Stop it!* she told herself. *Shut off the voices in your head and listen to what they're saying! The Lord is testing you, and you'll have to tell him something . . .*

". . . always intemperate, Alidar," she heard the elder say before the jeweler had emerged from the back of the shop. Did she only imagine he was looking her way when he said it? "Intemperate in war, and now you reverse course and speak too vociferously for peace. It's going to cost you."

His eyes were so blue she could determine their color from where she stood, and she'd always had a thing for cheekbones. There were bloodlines here, Zetha thought, that were far more easily traced than hers, and something else, anger and a deep and unremitting sadness, as if in his long life he'd seen enough and more than enough of death and most of it unnecessary. *Stop it!*

"But it's too much, Tal!" the younger one said too abruptly. "Forgive me, I don't mean to be rude, but even you have to admit that these days it's war for the sake of war, because if the Romulan in the street turns his eyes away from the stars and starship battles, he'll see that the economy is in shambles, his livelihood threatened, his children poorly educated, his future mortgaged for yet another warbird. The entire system is corrupt."

"And so it always has been!" the one called Tal agreed, then stopped himself as the jeweler came prancing toward them, balancing velvet-lined trays of precious baubles in both hands. "You see, now you have me doing it!"

"Perhaps I thought to have an ally," the one called Alidar mused after a long silence spent contemplating the wares before him, waving aside a tray of silver rings, sending the jeweler to the back of the shop for more. "At least someone who agreed with me in spirit."

"We're reduced to family names now, I see," the silver-haired one said, avoiding a direct answer. "Shall I call you 'Jarok' from here on?"

Jarok, Zetha thought. *Now, why is that name familiar? Aemetha would know. Aemetha knows everyone of any importance. Knew everyone. Aemetha, how are you, where are you?*

Did the Lord leave you alone once I agreed to go with him? Stop it!

"Forgive me, Che'srik. I have become a bit . . . obsessive."

"I'm glad you said it!" Tal muttered, fingering a filigreed pendant that had caught his fancy.

"First names, surnames, what does it matter?" Jarok asked bitterly. "Mine will be anathema if I've judged the climate wrongly . . ."

"The Hero of Norkan?" Tal snorted. "That alone will protect you, but only up to a point. Leave off this line of inquiry, I beg you."

"Not this time, old friend," Jarok said.

"How many such triumphs and reversals have you and I survived?" Tal leaned forward so as not to be overheard, but Zetha heard him anyway. "That business following Narendra III, for instance? How long did that measure of peace endure before it once again was set on its head? But you and I moved with it and are here today to tell of it. These days it's not only the enemy at the gates we need to fear, but the one in the room beside us. Yet we do survive, if we're careful. We have no alternative."

Not kin, then, Zetha noted for herself, not the Lord, watching the white-haired Tal clasp Jarok's shoulder in support. A mentor advising a student who he felt had surpassed him in rank, in accomplishment. What serious thing were they talking about? Something so serious no nonmilitary half-breed could begin to guess at it.

Jarok, she thought, as the jeweler returned as if to stay this time, plopping himself down on a couch at a deferential distance from the two, nattering on about the merits of this piece or that. *If I've heard the name, or read it, it's in my mind somewhere. Why can't I retrieve it?* The stresses of the past few months, the constant drills, the lack of sleep, more empty bunks in the barracks, the sense that something was building to a fever pitch, were taking their toll. She couldn't endure this much longer.

I am wallpaper, she thought. *They do not see me; therefore, I don't exist. But what if they actually say something that the Lord wants to hear? How will I know what's of value to him? How will I know what he will use it for? Is it only because these two are so interesting that I wish them no harm? Or is it because the only pleasure left in my life is thwarting his lordship?*

". . . and your family to consider," Tal was saying, indicating with a gesture that he would take the delicate pendant after all, and motioning the jeweler off to wrap it and ring it up. "You've wed again, I hear."

Jarok smiled then for the first time. "It's why I'm here. To get her something suitable for her naming day." He produced a padd from his pocket and displayed what was probably his wife's holo. Zetha couldn't see, but both men stopped to admire it. "Something suitable for the most beautiful woman in the Empire."

"She is a beauty," Tal acknowledged. "Children?"

Even from where she stood, Zetha could see Jarok's eyes mist over.

"Not yet, but we were planning, if I could get enough leave time . . ." Jarok's voice trailed off. "Perhaps it was a mistake to marry again, considering . . ."

"Haven't you got those settled out yet?" the jeweler hissed, coming up suddenly behind her. She pretended to be startled, and dropped the tangle of chains so she would have to start over. Beyond fury, the jeweler stalked to the back of the shop to deal with the purchase of the pendant.

If the jeweler is Tal Shiar, then why do I have to listen? Zetha wondered. *He's practically sitting in their laps with his trinkets and his simpering; let the Lord ask him what he's heard. Or is that part of the trap? The jeweler reports one thing, I another, the Lord assumes I'm lying and kills me.*

She eyed the exit just beyond Jarok's square shoulder, and

wondered how far she'd get if she ran for it. One of the other *ghilik* had told her there were sensors sewn into the hems of their clothing, something in the food they ate that made it easier to track them. She didn't know what she believed anymore. Jarok, meanwhile, was angry about something. He never raised his voice, but it was clear he was furious.

"There's never enough time, don't you see, Tal? They work us to death, and for what? It used to be honor, but no more, no more. We give the Empire our lives—go here, fight there, rendezvous here, attack there—"

"Alidar, for Elements' sake—!"

Jarok seemed to remember where he was. Shopkeepers and their apprentices were not on the same plane as senior officers of the Fleet, but they had ears.

"Forgive me; you're right," he said, somewhat subdued and, resuming his seat, continued his search among the baubles for a gift for the most beautiful woman in the Empire.

Jarok! Zetha remembered at last. *Alidar Jarok, even a groundling like me knows who you are. The Hero of Norkan, Tal called you, and it's what the Praetor called you in his speech when he awarded you that medal on the vidscreens for the whole world to see, but what I've heard in the catacombs among my kind is that you're a cold-blooded killer. What harm in telling the Lord that? Takes one to know one, and none of my business.*

But what I hear you saying now suggests a change of heart. Maybe you can do some good with that. Maybe that's what his lordship is afraid of. Maybe, maybe, maybe, and all of it, if I want to go on living, is my business.

She tossed the tangled chains back in the bin they'd come from. The jeweler was too busy with his pricey customers to notice. Zetha knew what she would tell the Lord.

"Nothing!" Koval hissed. His voice became even softer than usual when he was furious, and Zetha could barely hear him through the ringing in her ears. Why was it, she wondered, picking herself up off the floor, that a blow to side of the head always sounded worse than it felt? "How dare you tell me you heard nothing? How stupid do you think I am? Get up. I didn't strike you that hard."

Zetha suppressed a giggle behind her usual deadpan ("You'd out-Vulcan a Vulcan," Aemetha always said, but Aemetha had never been offworld, and Zetha doubted she'd ever seen a Vulcan, even in a vid). *How stupid do I think you are? Don't let me speak; you'd cut my tongue out!*

"They must have said something. You were right there in the room."

"Yes, Lord. With that damned background music, which is supposed to make them think there are no listening devices—if you don't count the breathing ones—and my head still ringing from the blow you gave me yesterday. And the jeweler dancing attendance on them like a small yappy dog. Why don't you ask him what he heard?"

Koval's narrowed his eyes at her. By now she knew all his facial expressions and the threats implied by them. This one had absolutely no effect.

"What did they speak of?" he demanded. "I must know!"

"They spoke. What about I could not tell you; I didn't hear a word. They spent more than an hour examining everything in the shop before the elder bought a pendant and the younger a pair of earbobs. Gaudy ones; I can't say much for his taste. He said they were a naming-day gift. That much I did hear. Before he left, the older one clasped the younger one's shoulder, and they left." She took a deep breath before adding: "I didn't even learn their names."

I've guessed right! she thought, watching the satisfaction spread like rancid oil over his features. *At best he wanted me to report on what they talked about; at least he wanted me completely ignorant of who or what they were. It seems he won't kill me . . . today.*

Yes, joke, she thought, *for as long as you can, but the truth is the tension's killing you, however slowly. Your hair's starting to fall out, have you noticed? Your gums bleed, and it's not the food, because plain as it is, you're better fed now than you've ever been, even under Aemetha's care. It's the deciding. You have to decide, and soon, which way you're going to jump. It's only a matter of whether he kills you before you can. And then where do you go? And what becomes of Aemetha? And Tahir, because he was seen with you, and the others in the villa, and—?*

Wait and see, she chided herself, as much because she wanted to live, regardless of the circumstances. *Wait and see what the mission is, and then decide. If there's a fragment of a possibility of a chance that you can act on your own behalf, without harming anyone else . . .*

Well? What more can anyone hope for?

"You're useless," Koval announced. "I don't know why I feed you. Back to the barracks; I'll summon you when I need you."

Only later did it occur to her that perhaps the two had deliberately spoken as they did within her hearing. Had they known she was there to spy on them? Had they wanted her to report on what they said? She didn't know. She would never know. She wasn't as good at this as she'd thought.

And I'm still not! she thought, lining up retorts, setting out pipettes, checking the containers of acids and reagents, removing sterile instruments from the autoclave, checking and double-checking the sterifields, the pH meter, the spectrophotometer. *But each day I live is a triumph, and that will have to be enough.*

Her sharp ears no longer heard Uhura's voice, but a sudden commotion in the control cabin told her Sisko was not alone.

Chapter 14

"Your Citizen Leval has been less than honest with us." Citizen Jarquin's voice preceded his appearance on the viewscreen. "He led us to believe he had visited other prefectures before ours. But out of curiosity, one of my aides messaged several of the regional offices and found out otherwise. Naturally I am interested in knowing why Leval deceived us. I'm sure he has a very good reason, but I want to hear it from him personally. Kindly put him onscreen."

"I'm afraid I can't do that right now, Citizen Jarquin," Sisko said, hoping he sounded calm, also remembering to play the role of the hired ship's pilot taking orders from his Romulan employer. Below the screen's visual level, his hands were busy working the comm, trying to raise Tuvok, to at least let him hear the exchange and perhaps give Sisko some guidance. "He, um, gave me orders he was not to be disturbed, and I've learned from past experience never to disobey Leval's orders. But I'll give him your message and as soon as he's available—"

Citizen Jarquin cut him off. "That is not sufficient, Captain Jacobs. I wish to speak with him now. If you do not put him onscreen immediately, my guards and I will be required to board your vessel and seek him out personally."

Dammit, Tuvok, I know you can hear this! Sisko thought, trying to locate his reading amid a moil of small life-forms within the Sawar quarantine zone. He'd last tracked Selar moving among a small huddle of Quirinians, but now couldn't pinpoint her at all. *Tuvok, wherever you are, get your butt back up here, now!*

A voice behind him, out of range of the viewscreen, said quietly, "The lab. I'll do it."

Zetha, Sisko realized, thinking on her feet. At least closing the lab was one less thing he needed to worry about. Now, where the hell was Tuvok? Sisko put on his best smile, and stalled.

"Citizen Jarquin," he said sincerely, pouring on what Jennifer had always called the Sisko Charm ("Makes you think you can get away with anything," she'd say, "and you usually do!"). "I'd like nothing more than to help you out, really I would. But I'm just the skipper here; all I do is steer the boat. And I've learned from hard experience that when Leval tells me to do something, I'd better do it. That's what he pays me for."

Onscreen, Citizen Jarquin was now flanked by two very large Quirinians, armed and in full combat garb. His personal guard, ready to board the ship and search it from stem to stern. A telltale on Sisko's console told him someone in Jarquin's vicinity was attempting to override *Albatross*'s transporter lock. While he did his best to charm, Sisko was also changing the transport codes. He wondered how long he could get away with that before the Quirinians caught on.

He had no doubt that if he refused Jarquin permission to board, there would be a Quirinian warship up his tailpipe within minutes, and *Albatross*, he reminded himself, was unarmed.

I'll never see Jake or Jennifer again, he thought.

"Your loyalty is commendable, Captain Jacobs," Citizen Jarquin was saying. "But in Quirinian space, my orders supersede Leval's. Put him onscreen. Now."

*   *   *

Zetha watched the lab modules slip silently into place. Would Sisko be angry that she'd pilfered the control mechanism from his pocket while he argued with Citizen Jarquin? She'd deal with that later. For now, she contented herself with checking to make sure nothing had been left lying around the cargo bay that might reveal its true nature. Then it occurred to her to police the sleeping quarters as well. All the while she kept one ear on the conversation in the control cabin.

How much longer could he keep this going? Sisko wondered, wiping his sweating hands on his trousers, then realizing that the familiar shape of the module control mechanism was no longer in his pocket. He hadn't even felt Zetha take it. *Never mind that now!* he told himself. *Think of something, anything, that'll make Jarquin go away, at least until you can get a lock on Tuvok!*

"Citizen Jarquin . . ." Sisko hesitated, using his nervousness to his advantage. "I shouldn't tell you this . . . it's a direct invasion of Leval's privacy and it'll probably mean my job. Hell, strong as your people are, it could mean my life. He'll take my head off for telling you this, but after they came back from Sawar, Leval and his wife—well, how do I put it delicately? They retired early, ordered that I not disturb them. He has a favorite collection of Jandran string music, and I've learned whenever that's playing . . ."

"That they're having a little romantic interlude?" Jarquin finished for him. "Very touching, Captain. But if he's a true Romulan, he'll understand that official business supersedes the arts of love. Hail him, knock on his door, do whatever you have to do, or allow me to spare you the embarrassment and knock on his door myself. My aide will give you our coordinates. Beam us up at once."

"But, sir—" Sisko started to say when Tuvok's hail from the surface, on discrete in the small earpiece in his ear, interrupted him.

"Message received, Mr. Sisko. One to beam back."

"One moment, Citizen Jarquin," Sisko said distractedly, activating the transporter, then realizing he could hardly beam Tuvok aboard with the Quirinians watching. "Message breaking up. Some kind of interference. I'll have to—"

He terminated the transmission clumsily. *Oh, as if that's going to fool them!* he thought frantically, as Tuvok materialized and waited on the transporter pad for the decontamination beam. The specially shielded case containing the specimens he'd gathered, another Heisenberg design, would protect them from decontamination. Without a word, Tuvok handed it off to Zetha, who had once again materialized from nowhere and disappeared in the direction of the lab.

"Where's Selar?" Sisko demanded. An incoming message from Jarquin blinked angrily beneath his hand, near where another telltale told him they were decoding the transporter lock as fast as he could recode it. If he didn't answer them, Jarquin and his guards would override and beam themselves aboard.

"No doubt making her way to the rendezvous point," Tuvok said mildly, stripping off his parka and the hazmat suit and stuffing them into a disposal on his way to the living quarters. "I will attempt to distract Citizen Jarquin while you locate Selar."

"But what if he wants to talk to both of you?" Sisko demanded of his retreating back. "And how the hell am I supposed to beam Selar aboard while he and his guards are here?"

Realizing he was talking to himself, Sisko located Selar just as someone from the surface overrode the transporter lock, and Citizen Jarquin and his two guards materialized before his eyes.

"You will bring Leval to me, or I will go to him," Jarquin said placidly. "The choice is yours."

Just then the sound of breaking glass startled all of them.

* * *

"You said I could have half of every order I took myself! You promised me!" Zetha was screaming. "Father only gave me permission to come with you so I could add my earnings to my dowry, and you lied!"

The remains of a vase Selar had purchased on Tenjin crunched beneath Citizen Jarquin's feet as he and his guards, slowed by the low ceiling in the gangway, followed the racket into the cargo bay. What they saw was a furious Zetha, backed against one of the containers by an equally furious Tuvok, whom she held at bay with an honor blade.

"This is not the time!" Tuvok was arguing. "Will you carry on like this where the human can hear? It's unseemly!"

"Unseemly? Stealing my dowry is unseemly!" Zetha snarled, waving the blade back and forth as if she really did intend to cut him as he loomed over her.

As if totally unaware that they were being watched, Tuvok feinted right, then left, seizing Zetha's wrist and wresting the knife from her grasp. Snaking one long arm around her waist, he lifted her bodily off the deck as she kicked and clawed and tried to bite him. He set her down, grabbed her hair and held the honor blade to her throat.

"Will you stop now?" he demanded quietly, but with a Romulan-worthy rage still etched on his face. His eyes took in the three Quirinians, and the glare he gave them eloquently expressed his feelings at being publicly humiliated by a mere girl. "Will you?"

"Y-yes!" Zetha whimpered convincingly. She'd been clawing at the arm that held the knife, but stopped now, let her hands drop limply to her sides, surrendering.

Tuvok thrust her from him and she staggered a little before she could gain her feet. As if noticing the watchers for the first time, she stood on one foot staring at them, not knowing what to do.

"Ungrateful *veruul!*" Tuvok spat at her, tucking the knife into the sash of the sleeping robe he'd somehow found time to change into. His feet were bare, as if he really had been roused from bed. "Any girl your age would be grateful to see the worlds you've seen under my patronage, and all you do is carp about a dowry!"

"May I have my knife back?" Zetha dared, coming to her senses, straightening her clothes and running her fingers through her tousled hair, defiance on her face.

"You'll get it back when you get your honor back!" Tuvok waved her off. "Leave me! And clean up the broken glass!"

She bolted from the cabin.

Tuvok laughed, but there was no humor in the sound. He addressed his uninvited guests for the first time.

"Gentlemen, forgive me. I apologize for that little scene. Young people, hm?" Tuvok tightened the sash of his robe, folded his arms and leaned casually against a container that contained mostly replicator parts and stem bolts.

"You see why she needs a dowry," he went on. "Few men would have the patience for her tantrums if she didn't come with money. I ought to toss her out the airlock for such behavior, but her aunt would never forgive me. And to think my wife slept through all of this! Citizen Jarquin, what brings you all this way to speak to me?"

Forward at the controls, Zetha looked at the welter of lights and toggles in dismay. Maybe if Selar hailed in from the surface, the Vulcan could talk her through the process of beaming her up. The very thought of scrambling and descrambling someone's molecules visited her with such fear she couldn't move her fingers. Then she realized Sisko still had the earpiece with him. Even if Selar did hail in, she could hardly let her voice be heard aloud in the control cabin with the Quirinians on board. Damn the human, anyway! Well, maybe Jarquin would be content to talk to Tuvok and leave Selar out of it. Maybe . . .

* * * *

"This is somewhat embarrassing," Tuvok, immersed in his role as Leval, was saying sheepishly. He found an empty storage crate, upturned it and sat down, scratching his head and yawning once more for emphasis. "The tax laws on the homeworld . . . well, let me begin from the beginning. Let us say for the sake of argument that I have a business partner. Let us say he puts up the money, then sits in his lavish villa while I travel the length and breadth of the Outmarches risking my life, and when I get home, he takes the bloodwing's share. But lately his earnings have gotten the notice of the taxation advocates in the Senate, and he has instructed me to pad the expenses, claim more for travel than I actually spend, and take fewer orders than I have before.

"Quirinus was the first world where I tried it. Logged thirty prefectures, planned to visit only two or three. I'd have gone home and reported that I hadn't been able to take any orders in the other twenty-six or -seven, business was that bad. Take the write-off for the time and travel expenses, claim the loss, then we would not have to pay taxes on whatever we actually did sell. Do you see?"

"I'm beginning to," Jarquin said grumpily, so absorbed in Leval's explanation that he didn't notice the human had slipped quietly away.

"I will be honest with you," Tuvok was saying. "I am not good at deception. It doesn't sit well with me. But if my partner cuts me off without funding, I would lose everything. I thought by deceiving you, I could keep you clear of it. Now you've asked too many questions, and you're implicated along with me. If anyone from the homeworld comes asking questions . . ."

"We never had this conversation!" Jarquin said abruptly. "I am here only to examine your cargo to make sure you're not running arms or any other illicit goods."

He waved an imperious hand toward the container behind Leval, who yawned once more and, in a very leisurely gesture, began keying in the code to open it.

* * *

"What the hell are you doing?" Sisko demanded, seeing Zetha in his chair at the controls. Selar's voice in his ear, as much as his inability to listen to much more of "Leval's" explanation with a straight face, had led him back here with all due alacrity.

"Your job, if I had the skills!" the girl snapped, leaping out of the chair. "Selar's signaling. What do we do now?"

"You get out of my way and let me do my job," Sisko said, locking onto Selar's signal. He supposed he could keep her in the pattern buffer until the Quirinians left, a risky move if they stayed too long, and what if they wanted to talk to her? "Then you go back to the living quarters and figure out another diversion in case our guests go looking for your 'aunt.'"

There was blood on Selar's hazmat suit, and other stains Sisko didn't dare examine too closely. Even after she stepped out of the decon beam he hesitated before taking the sample case from her, as if the exterior might somehow still be contaminated, stashing it under the control console where he hoped Jarquin wouldn't notice it.

"I would have signaled sooner, had the patrols not been in the vicinity," Selar explained as she disposed of the suit. Something in Sisko's manner cautioned her to speak softly. "Is something wrong?"

He explained. ". . . and either I'm going to have to conceal you somewhere until they're gone or, ideally, figure out a way to get you back to the living quarters without their seeing you. And since there's only one gangway leading the length of the ship—"

Selar gestured toward the transporter.

"I'm not sure this transporter is safe for intraship beaming," Sisko objected, reading her mind.

Selar retrieved her sample case and Tuvok's before stepping back onto the pad. "We are about to find out, Lieutenant."

* * *

Citizen Jarquin was bored. There were only so many cases of silk one could examine. Now it was he who was yawning as he gestured to Leval to reseal the third of the three containers he had asked to examine.

"Your cooperation is appreciated," he told Leval. "And your rather creative approach to accounting is safe with me."

Gesturing to his guards, he headed for the gangway, only to find his way obstructed by Zetha. The girl was on her knees picking up glass shards one by one. Apparently absorbed in her task, she didn't look up until she realized one piece was directly under Citizen Jarquin's boot.

"Give it up, girl. It's probably beyond salvaging," he suggested not unkindly.

"My aunt is going to kill me!" Zetha muttered. "It was her favorite."

"Has your aunt truly slept through all this uproar?" Jarquin wondered, looking down at the girl with a smile. Skinny little thing, he thought, but those eyes—!

As if in answer to his question, the door to the sleeping quarters opened partway, and a tousled-looking Selar appeared, wearing a sleeping robe of the most luxurious Tholian silk drawn directly from their inventory. The neckline was cut invitingly low, and she held it halfway closed with one enervated hand.

"Citizen Jarquin? What are you doing here?" she asked with a bewildered smile, as if she might be dreaming and he, realizing at last that this really was beyond the bounds of propriety, merely nodded and hurried toward the transporter pads, his guards in tow. If he heard Selar's reaction to the discovery that her "niece" had broken her favorite vase, he paid it no mind. Romulans, after all, were noted for their tempers. Everything was as it should be.

Albatross was light-years out of Quirinian space before Sisko trusted himself to laugh out loud. "I'm beginning to think that, all your rationalizations notwithstanding, Vulcans are more adept at lying than humans! I heard you back there. You lie like a rug!"

His laughter masked the sense of futility they all felt. The stains on Selar's clothing were the closest Sisko had come to the reality of this thing so far, and he wondered if there was any point in going on, deeper and deeper into the Zone, increasing the odds of being challenged by friend or foe. Didn't they have enough evidence by now to connect this disease to the Romulans? And so what if they did, if there was no cure?

He couldn't get the thought of all those dead out of his mind, and naturally any such threat turned his thoughts toward Jake and Jennifer. The concept of anything so awful even touching his family filled him with such despair he wanted to hit something. So he joked instead.

Tuvok, perhaps sensing his gloom, managed to look properly indignant.

" 'Lying', Mr. Sisko? Having done as much research as is possible into Romulan tax structures, given the silence between us, I assure you that the fictional merchant Leval certainly could encounter precisely such adversities in his effort to support himself and his family."

"Oh, so you're writing fiction now! Maybe you should submit it to a publisher. Or write a holodrama. You and Zetha scuffling with that honor blade was one of the best performances I've seen in my life. Come to think of it, Selar did a damn fine job of looking like she'd just rolled out of bed, too. I'm surrounded by talent! Which reminds me . . ."

He went looking for Zetha, who was as usual in the lab assisting Selar. He didn't say anything, merely stood there with his hands out, palms upward.

Zetha, gauging his mood, fished in a pocket and handed him the master control device without a word. Selar, restored to her prim and proper self, was testing monocyte chemotactic peptide recruitment in the specimens gathered on Quirinus, but found time to watch what was going on.

"I'm not going to ask you where you learned to pick pockets like that," Sisko said. "I'd probably only embarrass myself for letting you get away with it." He sighed; his features softened. "But I did want to thank you. You saved our lives."

Zetha shrugged. "My own primarily. If Citizen Jarquin had seen through our ruse, it would have meant my life as much as yours."

Sisko cleared his throat, started to say something, wondered what it was. Compliments rolled off her as readily as criticism. Was there any way to get through her shields? To his surprise, she greeted him with one of her rare smiles.

"Does this mean I'm allowed to watch the stars on the forward screen without your permission?"

His eyes narrowed. "All right. But keep your hands out of my pockets!"

"I should thank you as well," Selar said quietly when Sisko was gone. Zetha gave her a puzzled look. "For destroying the vase."

"I thought you'd be angry."

"It was aesthetically pleasing," Selar said ruefully. "However, it was foolish of me to acquire any object which might connect us with Tenjin."

Zetha hadn't thought of that. They'd been following an erratic course through the Zone for just that reason, to make it difficult for anyone who might be tracking them to determine their point of origin or where they'd been before.

"It was Tuvok's idea to stage a quarrel to distract Jarquin until we could locate you. The vase was the first thing that came to hand."

"Fortunate for all of us that it did," Selar suggested.

"Tuvok, how do you do it?" Sisko asked him during a quiet moment. The ship was on autopilot, and he was allowing himself some downtime to whip up a soufflé with the last of the vegetables from Tenjin.

The Vulcan was adding nutrients to the potting soil containing the orchid one drop at a time. "Do what?"

"Spend months or even years away from your family? Maybe it's just thinking of all those dead on Quirinus, but all I want to do is rush home and be with my wife and son."

Tuvok found the nutrient level to his satisfaction, set the orchid under its gro-light, and gave Sisko his complete attention.

"I submit, Mr. Sisko, that all you have wanted to do since we left Earth is return to your wife and son. However—" he said before Sisko could object. "To answer your question, it was necessary for me to leave Starfleet in order to start a family. Once I was confident my sons and my daughter were sufficiently mature not to require my guidance on a daily basis, I was free to return. As I understand it, you and your spouse have been fortunate enough to be assigned to the same ships for much of your career."

"It's true, I've been a little spoiled. This is the first time I've been away from Jennifer this long since Jake was born. Maybe if he were a little older I wouldn't feel so bad, but . . ."

Uncertain what answer Sisko was looking for, Tuvok said, "It has been my experience that one of the most difficult, yet most essential, aspects of being a parent is knowing when to let go."

For some reason Sisko found himself thinking of when Jake was a toddler and first learning to walk, how he'd gone from room to room making sure everything was safe. He'd put extra carpeting in the living area, cushioned the corners of every low table, and still followed the boy around with his hands outstretched, ready to grab him any time he seemed about to fall. It had been his own father who set him straight.

"You intend to be around to cushion his fall for the rest of his life?" Joseph Sisko had demanded. Ben had some leave time and had dropped in to New Orleans so that Jake could spend some time with his grandfather and vice versa. They were in the restaurant just before opening, setting the tables.

"I just don't want him getting hurt," Ben had answered, not taking his eyes off Jake, who was toddling from table to table, and from chair to chair around each table, rocking the chairs against the hardwood floor to hear their sound and laughing at his newfound skill as he went.

"And what's that supposed to teach him?" Joseph wondered, smoothing out each tablecloth as they went.

Ben didn't answer. Jake had gotten hold of the edge of one tablecloth and was starting to pull. "Be careful, Jake-O. Don't do that; you're going to fall—"

Just then he felt his father's grip on his arm, hard.

"Let the boy go, Ben. How else is he going to learn?"

"But it's a hardwood floor," Ben started to say. "There's no protection. If he—"

But Joseph refused to relieve his grip, and Jake kept pulling on the tablecloth until it slipped off the table, knocking him back on his well-diapered bottom. Jake seemed surprised for a moment, then giggled, pulled the tablecloth over his head, and crowed. "Peekaboo!"

"Peekaboo to you, too, young man," Joseph said, letting go of Ben's arm and retrieving the tablecloth. "Give that to Grandpa, now, and go on about your business."

The boy clutched the rungs of the closest chair, pulled himself upright, and continued his exploration around the next table and the next. His father, whose every muscle had tightened when the boy fell, finally relaxed.

"He just got his first lesson in physics, Ben," Joseph said. "And you a good lesson in parenting. Sometimes you've got to let them go."

Now Tuvok was telling Sisko the same thing. Would he

ever be able to let Jake go? He guessed he'd have to learn the answer to that question one day at a time.

"The organism on Quirinus is indeed the same," Selar reported during the next medical briefing with Uhura and Crusher. "At least as evidenced in blood and skin samples taken from those quarantined inside the enclosure."

"But—?" Uhura prompted her, hearing something in her tone.

"But serum and skin samples taken from the outworlder killed by the villagers show no trace of the organism."

"What if he had nothing to do with the infection?" Uhura asked.

"That is possible," Selar acknowledged. "However, what is unusual is that his blood was remarkably free of any active organisms or even background noise."

" 'Background noise'?" Uhura asked.

"Everyone's blood is a road map of their medical history," Crusher supplied. "Immunizations, childhood illnesses, even the common cold, leave antibodies in the bloodstream long after they're introduced into our systems. That's why immunizations work. If you get a measles shot, for instance, you won't catch measles, because the old germs are telling the new germs on the block: 'Been there, done that, go somewhere else.' "

"Gotcha," Uhura said. "But you said 'remarkably' free."

"Indeed. Given the small volume of blood Tuvok was able to obtain, I cannot say with certainty that the stranger was entirely free of antibodies, but there were none in the sample."

"None?" Crusher echoed her. "That's impossible."

"Maybe he was just very healthy," Uhura suggested.

"Hypothetically," Selar said, "someone who had never received any immunizations, who had never been ill nor exposed to anyone who was ill, or someone whose entire blood supply had been dialyzed and replaced, might show such a pattern."

"But—?"

"But there's no such animal," Crusher said.

"Such an individual would not have been cleared for off-world travel without receiving new immunizations," Selar clarified. "And since Tuvok's scans indicate this individual was most likely a Romulan surgically altered to more closely resemble a Quirinian—"

"Something stinks," Uhura finished for her.

Selar, less literal minded than most Vulcans, merely said, "Agreed."

"Is it possible," Uhura said, thinking it through as she asked it, "that a person's biology could be programmed to make them immune to a disease that they could spread to others?"

"Not by our science," Crusher said. "It sometimes occurs naturally. Carriers who are immune, like Typhoid Mary."

"Not by our science," Selar agreed. "But perhaps the Romulans—?"

"That could solve the mystery of the delivery system," Crusher suggested. "Admiral, are you okay?"

They sometimes forgot that, tough as she was, Uhura was no longer a young woman. This thing had been keeping her up nights, and it showed.

"Okay as I'll ever be," she said, passing a hand over her eyes and straightening the momentary sag in her shoulders. "Carry on."

Their next stop was a world called Sliwon.

Vulcan, like many worlds, eventually entered a period of aggressive colonization, and perhaps a ship or ships from that era had ventured as far as Sliwon. Or perhaps its people were descendants of some members of the Sundering's hegira who refused to travel further. Perhaps, too, there was an indigenous population of humanoids on Sliwon when they arrived, or perhaps the legends of the Preservers populating the galaxy with humanoids could once more be given evidence here. In the event, the Sliwoni, like the Rigelians, were a bit of both.

And perhaps it was the overlarge moon that made its people moody and given to extremes of temperament, or perhaps it was the uneasy agglomeration of their biology that made them quick of temper and prone to quarrel. It was Surak himself who, according to some accounts, said "Put two Vulcans in a room and you end up with three arguments." Blessed with a mild climate, abundant rain and rich soil, in between arguments the Sliwoni grew things. They clung to certain customs, such as the use of archery for personal weaponry, even as they advanced in-system space travel. They had no desire to venture beyond their own system, though they welcomed visitors from offworld, particularly those who had things to trade, but insisted that they land their ships instead of leaving them in orbit.

Sisko set the ship down where the Sliwoni authorities instructed him to. A party of officials met *Albatross* at the designated landing area, scanned a few of the containers, issued travel permits good for three days and maps to the nearest town, then went on their way. Fascinated by their traditional use of archery, Tuvok set about gathering native materials to construct a longbow.

Once again Sisko suggested the landing party work in teams.

"I don't want to leave the ship unattended. Even sealed up she's vulnerable, no matter how many reassurances the Sliwoni authorities give us. We should either pair up, or at least Tuvok and I should take turns remaining behind."

"Agreed," Tuvok said.

More than a little surprised that this time he'd gotten no argument, Sisko organized his thoughts.

"Right now my main concern is getting that environmental adapter back online. Apparently it's the one thing Heisenberg overlooked in the refit, and he didn't leave me a spare. I can gather air and soil samples in the vicinity of the ship while the rest of you go into town. Then tomorrow I can go with Selar and Zetha while you stay with the ship."

This seemed to sit well with Tuvok, who nodded in agreement, then returned to sanding the riser on the longbow, deep in concentration.

Zetha found him testing the tensile strength of the completed bow.

"Must I go with you this time?" she asked quietly.

Tuvok unstrung the bow and considered. She had been inordinately calm and quick to react when the Quirinians were on board. Had the event taken more of a toll on her than was evident?

"Do you wish to remain here?"

Still unable to ask directly for anything, she shrugged.

"Selar and I will be employing our Vulcan cover," Tuvok said. "There is no necessity for you to accompany us. You may remain here with Lieutenant Sisko if you wish."

"I'll speak to him," she said, and was gone.

Sisko was up to his elbows in machine parts. Assuming he was alone, he was cursing in all the languages he knew.

"Not going well, is it?" Zetha asked over his shoulder.

She was sitting cross-legged in the doorway, looking like nothing so much as a mischievous elf. That was another thing about her that got under his skin. She was never outright disrespectful, but she didn't go out of her way to be anything more than civil, either. Sisko found himself glowering at her. "Thought I told you to stay out of the engine room?"

"I'm not in the engine room," she pointed out. "I'm sitting on the floor of the gangway looking into the engine room."

"It's not a 'floor,' it's a deck," Sisko said crossly, then realized how petty he sounded.

"Something's wrong with that thing," Zetha observed. "You've been fussing with it for days. Is it dangerous?"

"Not at the moment," Sisko said, turning his back on her, tinkering. "But it's failing. If it fails altogether while we're in space, it could affect the air we breathe."

"Enough to kill us?"

"Probably not."

"But it might?"

She's a kid, Sisko reminded himself. *She's concerned about her welfare, that's all.* He gave her his complete attention.

"Remote possibility. If I can't fix the adapter. Which I can. Or jury-rig a bypass. Or, worst case scenario, go into town and see if the Sliwoni have something similar I can trade for."

"Is that likely?"

Sisko returned to his tinkering. "According to Starfleet records, they trade with humans. Their tech is a little behind ours and, given the age of some of *Albatross*'s original components, I wouldn't be surprised."

"So they'd use it in their offworld ships?"

Sisko sighed. Even Jake didn't ask so many questions when he knew his dad was busy.

"It's a universal adapter. Could be used in a transport vehicle, a hovercraft, anything motorized."

"What does it look like?" Zetha asked.

Sisko gave her an odd look and pulled the adapter out of the manifold, holding it up and motioning her to cross the invisible line that separated the engine room from the gangway. "Like this. Composite polymer single-walled carbon nanotube. Semi-conductor nanowires. Titanium casing. Only without the points worn through here and here. That help you any?"

She took it from him, hefting it in her hand and examining it from all sides before giving it back, wiping her hand on her trousers.

"It might," she said cryptically.

"Mind if I go back to work now?" Sisko asked.

Zetha shrugged and disappeared back the way she'd come.

Sliwon had an extensive public transit system. One merely had to stand at designated positions along any of its vast network of highways in order to be retrieved by a pneu-mobus that joined the endless trucking convoys bringing produce to and from its multitude of small communal cities strung along the road system like beads on a necklace.

There was no currency, only barter, one commune's grain traded for another's sugar beets for another's wild fowl for another's tubers, all on an endless convoy of hover-vehicles whose hydrogen-powered engines only slightly disturbed the otherwise tranquil air of a truly beautiful climate.

Selar's tricorder was active from the moment she and Tuvok climbed aboard the bus; the hum of the engines and the chatter of Sliwoni going to market masked its sounds. She shook her head imperceptibly when Tuvok raised an in-quiring eyebrow. No sign of unusual illness so far. She con-tinued scanning as they strolled through the marketplace.

"Nothing," she reported. "The occasional cold virus, a few cases of eczema, and the sausage vendor has a precan-cerous condition."

Tuvok read what she was thinking. "You will not mention this to him, of course."

Selar gave him a studied look. "Not directly. But I see no harm in recommending he take antioxidants."

They had not gone far before they heard the disturbance. Wending their way among the fish and poultry stalls and past the herb sellers, they rounded a corner to find an angry knot of Sliwoni, most of them chatting into the headsets affixed as if permanently to the left sides of their faces, but also gath-ered around to listen to a sidewalk orator.

". . . and it is because we are too open a society that

these things happen!" he was shouting hoarsely. "We let anyone and everyone land here, and look what it gets us! This disease didn't come from one of us. It came from outside!"

Murmurs of both agreement and disagreement greeted him from the crowd. Selar's tricorder was busy. Her eyebrows told Tuvok more than anything she might have said.

"Affirmative," she said anyway. "Perhaps a dozen individuals in the crowd, including the speaker, are running a low-grade fever." She closed the tricorder. "Superficial scan suggests an organism bearing the Catalyst signature, but without specimens—"

"I submit this is neither the time nor the place to gather specimens," Tuvok suggested, taking her arm in an uncharacteristic gesture and moving toward an opening in the crowd through which to return the way they had come.

"Those two!" the orator shouted, pointing directly at them. "Do we know who they are? Do we know where they came from? Do we know the documents they carry are legitimate?" Some of the crowd were turning to stare at the Vulcans now, not quite menacingly, but with purpose. "We all know Romulans have been guilty of biological warfare in the past. How do we know that's not the case again?"

His voice faded as the Vulcans retreated down yet another busy market street where the crowd swallowed them up temporarily, out of reach of the restless mob.

"I believe we have gathered enough evidence," Tuvok said. "The sooner we return to the ship—"

"Evidence that the disease is here, but no indication of how it got here," Selar said with a trace of stubbornness. "We need to ascertain the source, the delivery system. Perhaps another 'stranger' such as the one you found on Quirinus. Further, Admiral Uhura's instructions—"

"This is not the time," Tuvok repeated. "We will return later, perhaps after nightfall, or choose another locale. Otherwise we risk a choice between being accosted by an angry mob or, since we do not yet know how it is spread, possibly contracting the illness ourselves."

Selar had no choice but to go with him. She continued surreptitiously scanning the crowd as they walked, her readings indicating that perhaps one person in fifty was affected.

The street narrowed to an alley, which dead-ended abruptly. As they doubled back and returned to the herb sellers' street, they heard more shouting.

Chapter 15

Ki Baratan was sweltering that night under an unusually early heat wave. Romulus, it was said, had only two seasons—too hot, and too cold. From the comfort of her climate-controlled suite high above the pavement, Cretak watched the streets empty of pedestrians as the curfew sounded. Soon there was nothing to see below but an occasional air-car on patrol, stirring the debris at the curb as it passed. And were those—? No, they couldn't be. Vermin, even in this part of the city? Disgusted, Cretak let the filmy drape fall over the window and moved away.

What would this city be like? she wondered, not for the first time. *This prefecture, this province, this region, this planet, this system, this empire, if we weren't always at war?*

But how can we not be, when whom we are most at war with is ourselves?

The aristocracy hid themselves behind the walls of their great estates, the Senate saw to it that the areas surrounding official buildings, the places outworlders saw, were maintained, but the rest of the city was a shambles of potholed, muddy pavements, piles of uncollected refuse rotting in alleys and banked against the sides of buildings by the prevailing wind, swirling into ever-changing tels of new piled upon old, chaotic time capsules evidencing: Here we were when this happened, when this emperor died and this war overtook us, when we invaded here and were invaded there, all the way back, it wouldn't surprise her, to the Sundering. In that case, there would also be evidence of the Gnawing buried in the debris of their past. Always, like a knife scar through the psyche, the Gnawing.

Is it only that? she wondered. *Only the Gnawing that has conditioned us so that, no matter how much some of us have, we always want more?*

She couldn't see the decay from here, but knew the signs abounded throughout the city, the broken cornices and battered facades of once beautiful buildings, windows shattered and patched and repatched with scrap lumber and great running globs of adhesive, coming unstuck when it rained. And dirt, always dirt, no matter how many times the old ones came out with their twig brooms to sweep, like some antique parody of what once was, but was still, because the sanitation bureau was too corrupt and the automated cleaners were more often broken down and in the shop than not.

Everything gray. Gray buildings, gray pavements, gray clothing, gray souls. *Why must we all dress alike,* she wondered, *affect the same helmetlike hairstyle, if not to blend in, disappear, say to the forces that can track us by a fingerprint, a breath, a smattering of chromosomes: "It's not me. I didn't do it. You want someone else!"*

Elements, Cretak thought. *I am so sick of it! It's in the very air we breathe, gray air, gray food, gray souls. We swallow down the grayness, the broken, the trashed and rubbishy; our very souls are chipped and worn and in need of replacement, replenishment, renewal.*

And now this new thing, this illness, scattering among the colony worlds but, evidenced by the new reports her sources brought to her, moving inward, toward the homeworld, even as it moved outward, across the Zone, to the other side. A hundred cases here, a thousand there, an entire suburb cordoned off on such-and-such a world. And yet, in the official news sources . . . nothing. People who have lost relatives are told it was a chance thing. There is no epidemic, and anyway the government is investigating it. Return to your homes and go on with your lives. Or else.

Only one entity within the power structure would have the temerity to experiment thus on its own citizens, Cretak thought: the Tal Shiar. And why, without any proof, when she thought of epidemics did she automatically think of Koval? He had been fixated on sickness for as long as she had known him, perhaps only because Tuvan's Syndrome ran in his family and he sensed his life would be shorter than most. Cretak had no proof he was behind this—pestilence—and even if she did, what could she do with it?

She had been offworld often enough to know that it wasn't the universe that was gray, but only those things touched by Romulans. *We left Vulcan because it was nothing but sand and logic,* she thought grimly. *Now we have become nothing but dust and deviousness!*

Yet here am I, Cretak thought, *secure in the Senate despite my early association with Pardek, currently in disfavor, with whatever power that gives me to oppose the sort of calculated chaos the likes of Koval plays at, if only I can stay ahead of the knives. Madness. If Koval loses control of whatever he's doing, I shall be senator of a dung-hill. Some distinction! But this is my world. What else can I do?*

It was late. There was much to do on the morrow. Cretak hated sleeping draughts, but took one anyway, knowing there would be no sleep this night if she did not. As she waited for oblivion, she went over the day's events in her mind.

Once word had reached her in its roundabout way that her Pandora's box had been delivered safely and its message understood, she had thought her part in this was over. She did not understand enough about medicine to know if this horror could be cured or at least defended against. Her only thought in giving the information to Uhura had been to say: *Don't let me carry this alone!*

But she was embroiled now. Even as she wanted to stop up her ears against the influx of reports, they continued to come to her, all but driving her to despair. Had she sent the messenger too late, or too soon? Or if there truly was nothing to be done, had there been any point in sending the messenger at all?

". . . guaranteed to cure what ails you, stranger!" a hoarse voice croaked. "Come try a free sample on that bruise on your arm."

"A snake-oil salesman," Tuvok concluded. And at Selar's inquiring look, he elaborated, "Terrestrial culture, pre-warp. Dealers in false medicinals. Their cures were always fake, usually harmless, occasionally dangerous. An interesting example of the placebo effect. Such individuals would sell everything from herbs to wood shavings to common soil, presented in a pleasing form."

The salesman was a scrawny, red-faced humanoid with a raucous voice worn down by a lifetime of shouting out his wares. A small crowd had gathered around his booth to listen, but no one was buying. Even after he "cured" a "volunteer" from the crowd, no one was buying.

"A common technique," Tuvok whispered to Selar. "The 'huckster' frequently planted a 'shill' in the audience to feign an illness. This person's 'cure' often inspired purchases in others."

"Curious," Selar replied. "I would be very interested in the composition of this miraculous substance."

"Indeed," Tuvok said as they began to work their way through the crowd.

The Listeners had reported an increase in the number of merchants selling 'miracle cures' in this sector. Admiral Uhura had thought it worth investigating, which was why the team was here.

"It's a fake!" a Romulan in the crowd was shouting. "And you want too much for it!"

"Too much for a miracle?" the huckster shouted. "This here, my friends, is something you've never seen or heard of before. It's found on only one planet in the entire quadrant, and I've risked my life to get it."

This got a few people's attention, and a few purchases were made, but most in the crowd began to drift away, giving Selar a chance to move forward.

"What will you take in trade for a sample of this miraculous compound?" she asked the huckster who, once off his platform, was nearly a head shorter than she. He squinted up at her and grinned.

"Whatcha got to trade?" he leered hopefully, licking his spittle-flecked lips. "That's a right fine pendant you're wearing. That Vulcan?"

"It is." Selar slipped it off and gave it to him to examine.

"Genuine garnet," he appraised it, then gave it back. "But I'd have to give you a cartload of *hilopon* to be worth that."

"Even for a miracle cure?" Selar asked dryly.

The little man's eyes shifted sideways, as if he suspected a trap. "Well, how's about I give you a free sample? Then I'll take the pendant in trade for something, shall we say, more of interest to a beautiful young woman such as you. Perhaps a love potion for that . . . um, special Vulcan time?"

Tuvok, who had been hanging back in the crowd searching for the shill, who had melted away, suddenly materialized beside Selar. His appearance was sufficient to wipe the leer off the huckster's face.

"Look, I don't want no trouble!" he protested, raising his hands as if to fend it off, backing away from them. "I can tell you're with the gov, but my permits are in order, and I ain't selling anything that's on the banned list. Okay, the *hilopon* is a little out of the ordinary line, but it ain't illegal to sell it here, and you know it. Besides, I'm not the only one selling it, and it don't hurt nobody. Want to look at it another way, I'm selling hope. There's always a chance it *might* work."

"We are more interested in what it is and where it comes from," Tuvok said sternly, palming one small packet and secreting it in his specimen case as the huckster began hurriedly packing up his booth; if the little man wanted to believe Tuvok was a Sliwoni official, Tuvok would not inform him otherwise.

"It's called *hilopon*. And if you're with the gov, you know it comes from Renaga. That's common knowledge. You're trying to trip me up, make a liar out of me, but that's the truth. And you got no jurisdiction on Renaga, so you got no hold on me."

"Refresh my memory," Tuvok said, distracting him while Selar ran her tricorder discreetly over his wares. "Why was it necessary for you to risk your life in order to obtain this substance?"

The little man had been snatching vials and jars and packets off the counter, tossing them into a carryall, lowering the curtains on the booth to indicate it was closed.

"Hey, you know how it is there. Natives are as backward as sheep. They think the stars govern their lives. They don't like strangers, and they believe if you take so much as a handful of dirt off their planet, you're making it smaller. Can you believe that? So I had to sneak this stuff off very carefully, even though it's only dirt."

He'd finished packing now, and was searching the gathering crowd furtively for a means of escape.

"But you know that!" he accused Tuvok, waving a finger in his face defiantly. "You're just toying with me so I'll leave town. All right, all right, I'm leaving, see?"

The uproar he was making was drawing a new and not entirely friendly crowd. Someone shouted, "Leave him alone!" Selar turned off her tricorder and quirked an eyebrow at Tuvok. It was time and past time to get back to *Albatross*.

* * *

Maybe it was working in the sometimes airless confines of the engine room all day, or maybe it was the unfamiliar dusts and pollens in the air of Sliwon, but Sisko had been bothered with a tickle in his throat all afternoon. Clearing his throat didn't get rid of it, drinking water had no effect. By the time the Vulcans signaled their impending return, it had evolved into an annoying cough. In the ensuing attack by the villagers with their shortbows, he had almost forgotten about it, but now it was back. He cleared his throat.

"It would be unfortunate if your display of superior fire power upset the normal evolution of weaponry on this world," Selar was suggesting to Tuvok as they came aboard.

"Dubious," Tuvok remarked. "The villagers think nothing of space travel. Their use of the bow is merely traditional. On worlds where archery is a normal part of the weaponry, for example, the crossbow and the longbow often evolve in tandem. Curious, since the longbow is a far superior weapon. At the battle of Agincourt, the English lost only 500 men to the French 10,000, because of their adoption of the Welsh longbow . . ."

"And that's the long answer," Sisko quipped, admiring the longbow. "Damn fine craftsmanship on such short notice."

"In fact, it is very primitive," Tuvok pointed out. "It ought to have been made of French yew, aged for at least thirty days. However," he said, unstringing it and stowing it under his bunk. "It has served its purpose, in that it has prevented something as inconsequential as a skirmish with the locals from endangering our mission." He frowned slightly. "Where is Zetha?"

Sisko blinked. "I don't know. I assumed she went with you."

Tuvok's frown deepened. "She asked if she could remain here, and indicated she would speak to you about it. I should have verified that. An oversight on my part."

"I've been in the engine room the whole time," Sisko explained with a sinking feeling. "I assumed, since she always goes with you . . . I never thought to check."

Was this where it happened? Sisko wondered. Was this where she jumped ship, went back to her masters, set his crew up for an attack? Was the ambush they'd just foiled part of her plan? How much of that was his fault?

"She's probably back in the lab," he suggested, praying it was so. "Although why she didn't come out during the attack . . ."

But Zetha was not in the lab, nor anywhere else on the ship.

"We would have to attain orbit in order to get clear of local comm chatter," Tuvok suggested, already preparing for departure. "But if Zetha is anywhere in the vicinity, it will be possible to put a trace on her. . . ."

"And if she isn't in the vicinity," Sisko said grimly. "I wouldn't be surprised if—" Just then the perimeter alarm sounded, and he slid into the command chair.

"The Sliwoni are back," he reported, scanning the clearing and the surrounding woods. "Not just a handful on foot, but half a dozen hovercraft, weapons powering. I'd say we've overstayed our welcome."

Tuvok had taken the seat beside him at the controls and was scanning the weapons signatures. "Standard plasma weapons. If they fire, shields should be able to handle it. But I would prefer that we not have to test them."

"You and me both," Sisko agreed. "I doubt these shields have been used since before I was born. I wouldn't want to find out—"

A shot across their bow left his thought unfinished.

"Whatever happened to 'come out with your hands up'?" Sisko groused, sealing hatches, powering up. "And is it me, or are there no official markings on those 'craft?"

"Confirmed," Tuvok reported, scanning. "Unmarked, and of several different designs."

"A posse," Sisko decided. "Vigilante justice. Well, they want us out of town before sunset, I'll be happy to oblige them."

Before Tuvok could ask the question, he gave him an answer.

"My educated guess is those 'craft are built for atmosphere, not vacuum. I just want to get high enough up to where they can't follow us, and then we'll go looking for our runaway. Shields up," he announced just as one of the hovercraft fired another shot. The shields took it with only a little protest, though Sisko could feel the drain as if it were he and not the ship who'd been hit.

"Shields down to sixty-eight percent, recharging," Tuvok reported smoothly.

"Can't wait for it," Sisko announced. The engines were fully online now. He opened the intraship to warn Selar in the lab. "Hang onto anything breakable, Doctor. We're out of here!"

With that he activated the forward thrusters and threw the big bird into reverse. She slid abruptly backward to hover above the raging sea, buffeted by the wind sheer until Sisko reversed thrusters and, like her namesake, her cumbersome shape defied gravity and soared upward, over the heads of the disappointed hovercraft, and away.

Comm was crackling furiously. Since Sisko was occupied, Tuvok monitored. A jumble of cross talk greeted him, Sliwoni authorities arguing with their attackers, who were arguing back.

"Some are insisting that they should let us go and good riddance," Tuvok reported. "Others want to imprison us on charges of bioterrorism. A third group insists they should have destroyed us while we were still on the ground." He closed the channel with something like a sigh. "By the time they finish arguing among themselves, we will be well away. Can you accurately pinpoint one Romulan life-form reading within ten kilometers of the clearing?"

"Assuming she's still within ten kilometers of the clearing, and assuming she's the only Romulan within ten kilometers of the clearing . . ." Sisko muttered, scanning. "Sliwoni have their own distinct signature, but given the interplanetary population, I'm also reading non-Romulan humanoids, what could be Rigelians and . . . hello."

The scanner indicated one vulcanoid reading, in the very same thicket from which the archers had attacked, as if Zetha were crouched and watching the hovercraft circle the now empty clearing with something like futility, wondering what she should do next.

"I guess she's completed whatever errand took her into town," Sisko said half to himself.

Tuvok raised an eyebrow, but said nothing.

"Lowering shields," Sisko said, "and activating transporter."

A rather breathless and disheveled Zetha waited for the decon beam before hopping off the pad, something hidden in her jacket.

"I tried to get back before they attacked, but they cut me off," she reported, as if it had all been part of some plan. "Thank you for rescuing me."

She reached inside her jacket and presented Sisko with a reasonably new adapter that, with slight modifications, would be exactly what he needed.

"Where did you get this?" he demanded, not sure if he was annoyed because she'd been able to find it or because he'd been so impatient with her questions about it in the first place.

"What difference does it make?" Zetha asked. "Does it fit? I know it works."

"What do you mean, you know it works? You stole this, didn't you?"

"I scrounged it. Stole it, if you prefer. Its previous owner has an entire warehouse of them, and if it works, it will help us, will it not?"

Sisko opened his mouth to say something, but nothing came out.

"Would it comfort you if I told you I meant to barter for it, but when I heard all the uproar in town I didn't have time?"

"Barter with what?" Sisko demanded. "You don't have anything worth bartering for!"

He regretted it the minute he said it but, as usual, Zetha took no offense.

"Well, there you are," she said with her characteristic shrug.

"Thank you," he told Zetha tightly. "I'll deal with this later. For now . . ." The hovercraft were dispersing, but who knew how long it would be before official sources tried to intervene? ". . . we're getting the hell out of here."

When at last they were well away from Sliwon and Sisko had repaired to the engine room, it was Tuvok's turn. "How did you manage not only to slip into town undetected, but to steal the adapter and elude pursuit on your return?"

Zetha's smile came more readily now. "Sisko thinks I'm a spy. So, in your heart, still, do you."

"Yet you claim you are not."

"I'm small, I'm fast. I've been told all my life that I'm invisible, that I do not exist. Who's to say it isn't true?"

Aft in the engine room running a diagnostic on the environmental controls, Sisko was shaking his head. "Well, I'll be damned! I don't believe for a minute that this was the only errand that took you to town, but at least the darn thing works. . . ."

"It's continuing to spread," Crusher informed Selar. "Twenty-seven planets and five starbases affected. Outbreaks confirmed on seven freighters and two science vessels, and we're following other reports. Still one hundred percent mortality in those affected. We can give palliative treatment to ease the symptoms in the final hours, but we've had no luck cracking the code on this thing. And we still haven't a clue to how it's spread."

"Giving further credence to the Typhoid Mary theory," was Selar's opinion.

"So it seems," Crusher said. "And yet, the Romulan on Quirinus tested clean. What's the word on Sliwon?"

Selar told her what she'd found. "As expected, air, water, and soil samples tested negative. Native flora and fauna, also negative. As for the putative cure . . ."

"The stuff you confiscated in the marketplace," Crusher said. "What do you make of it?"

"Structurally intriguing, but essentially inert."

Crusher sat back in her chair, hands in her pockets. She'd hailed Uhura and McCoy, but neither had reported in yet. Well, she could give them a précis later. "Structurally intriguing? I'm listening."

"At the molecular level, it would appear to be a levorotatory form of the Gnawing bacillus," Selar began. Suddenly McCoy popped into view beside Crusher. A human might have been startled, but Selar merely waited for him to say what he would inevitably feel compelled to say.

"Are you sure of that?"

"Within 99.997 percent of certainty, Doctor, yes."

The old man's eyes lit up. "That's wonderful news! We could be talking about a potential treatment, or at least a decoy. Same principle behind ryetalin treatment for Rigelian fever."

"I'm afraid it is not that simple," Selar said quietly, and suddenly Uhura was with them, too.

"Wait a minute. Back up and explain this for the layman, please."

"She means 'in English,'" McCoy supplied. Crusher suppressed a smile. Selar's news was making them all a little giddy; it was the first ray of hope in a long time.

Selar activated a holoprogram. "We are all by now familiar with the Gnawing, as seen at the molecular level," she said, as the image rotated before them. "This," she said, calling up a second shape, "is *hilopon*, its mirror image, the substance Lieutenant Tuvok confiscated from the individual in the Sliwoni market.

"As you can see, the same number of molecules, in the same order, is present. But in the Gnawing, the genetic helix rotates to the right, whereas the *hilopon* spiral rotates to the left. Thus *levo*—from the Latin, meaning 'left'—rotatory, or turning in the familiar helical configuration."

"So this could be a potential cure?" Uhura asked, not daring to hope.

"Not exactly," McCoy butted in before Selar could speak. "Since you're not dealing with the pure Gnawing, but with the Catalyst neoform, which has been grafted onto Rigelian fever. But Rigelian fever's curable with ryetalin, which is what I started to tell you about. But I'm sure with a little ingenuity we could design a cocktail of the two compounds, a little one-two punch that'd knock this damn disease right out of business."

"Hypothetically," Selar said quietly. "If it worked."

Crusher had been studying the two organisms intently. "You started to say something about its being inert."

"Correct. I have tested it against the Gnawing. It is ineffective. In fact, it does not kill even ordinary staphylococcus. There are several potential reasons for this."

"There's something I'm not getting here," Uhura interrupted. "Why would something found in the soil of a planet hundreds of light-years from Romulus cure a disease found only on Romulus?"

"You mean a disease found only in the *soil* on Romulus," McCoy supplied for her. "Who knows? Why do targeted histamines ingest some kinds of cancer? Why does bread mold kill everything from pneumonia to the clap? And why does Rigelian fever affect humans as well as Vulcans, and why it is cured by something found on Holberg 917-G? One of the universe's unanswered mysteries, one of God's little jokes. From a purely empirical point of view, it does, that's all. We'll philosophize about it later; for now, we work with it."

"It would fit with Sagan's theory about star stuff," Crusher said thoughtfully. The others looked at her. "C'mon, guys, am I the only one who knows this? Carl Sagan, late twentieth century Earth, taught physics in a way so simple a child could understand it. God, I think I can recite it from memory! 'We are a way for the universe to know itself. Some part of our being knows this is where we came from. We long to return, and we can, because the Cosmos is also within us. We're made of star stuff.' "

She stopped, suddenly embarrassed.

"Why, Doctor, you're a poet," Uhura said appreciatively.

"*Brava!*" McCoy chimed in.

"In other words," Uhura went on, "whatever cosmic forces formed this part of space might have split these two molecules out of a single matrix and scattered them across parsecs of space to form two separate, compatible entities on two distant worlds."

"Something like that," Crusher acknowledged. "Even a passing comet could have scattered biological debris on both worlds."

"Well, now isn't that interesting . . ." Uhura said, accessing something on her office screen that the others couldn't see yet.

Awake despite the sleeping draught, Cretak reviewed everything she had done since Taymor's death. It all had the quality of dream. Sometimes her own temerity amazed her. But she had been consumed with rage when she showed up in Koval's office that day, and her anger had neutralized her fear.

In the old days, she might simply have accused Koval and his office of complicity in her cousin's death, drawn her honor blade, and exacted his life for Taymor's. Then, of course, Koval's second would have had to challenge her, and

then her family—well. While some might simplemindedly
think that all disputes could be resolved at the point of a
knife, others had learned to be more subtle.

She would use the Tal Shiar's own methods against them.
She could not bring Taymor back, nor any of the others the
disease had already taken. But she could expose the plot,
and at least stop, if not bring down, the plotters, without
their ever knowing it was she.

Thus she appeared in Koval's office, flustering his aide
with her silky request to speak with him even though, oh,
dear! she had committed the unconscionable gaffe of showing up without an appointment.

Don't simper! she warned herself as the aide asked her
to wait in the soundproof antechamber and she scowled at
the official decorators' consummately bad taste. *You were
never girlish, even when you were a girl, and he'll remember
that. He also knows your record in the Senate, and that fluttering is not your style. You will appear preoccupied, but not
silly.*

"Kimora?" Koval managed to act ever so slightly surprised
without altering his face, his stance, the tone of his voice.
Cretak assumed whatever genuine surprise he might have
experienced at the mention of her name had been brought
under control well before she crossed the threshold. "What
ever brings you here? You're looking well. Flourishing, in
fact."

Then I'm a better actress than I thought! Cretak thought
as the aide brushed past her a touch too close for propriety.
Listening, taking readings, or simply rude?

"I am as well as can be expected, thank you, given a recent death in the family, as I'm sure you know."

This time Koval allowed something resembling embarrassment to touch his features momentarily. "Yes, of course,
your cousin. How stupid of me to forget. My condolences."

She acknowledged this with a brief nod, lowering her

head just enough so that he wouldn't see the fire in her eyes, thinking: *You, forget? Since when? I will see to it that you never forget, murderer! At least one result of my visit here today will be that you give orders to your purveyors to steer clear of important families from here on.*

"That is not why I'm here," she said. "As I'm sure you also know, I am part of the diplomatic mission to the Borderlands. There is much to do before we leave, and my staff is overworked as it is. . . ."

"Is there anything I can do?" Koval asked helpfully.

Cretak allowed her expression to brighten, as if with great relief. "Possibly. In fact, you were the first I thought of. I need a messenger. Someone discreet, possibly expendable. I know you are training a cadre of young people for special missions, and I thought perhaps—"

"Well, if dense as a stone qualifies as discreet . . ." Koval was ruminating. "Walk with me."

He would not bring her to the barracks; the crowding and the squalor might offend her delicate sensibilities. Instead he brought her to the official gardens, where he had sent some of his charges to pull weeds and rake up debris.

There were official gardeners to maintain the official gardens, but Koval didn't trust them. Afraid that someone might plant listening devices or introduce dangerous bacteria or poisonous plants, he insisted that only his *ghilik* work the gardens surrounding his office. He personally hated greenery and would have preferred to pave everything over to give himself a clear field of vision but, if official decree said that he must have official gardens, his mongrels could serve as the first line of defense therein.

"You may have any of these," he told Cretak with a proprietary air, as if offering her the choice of a hunting dog or a steed from his stable. "They're all at the same level of training. Most of them can even read and write."

"You joke!" Cretak feigned a smile, though her eyes betrayed something else. "I'm sure they're all as bright and able as—"

"—as a true Romulan? Don't be so sure. But, please, feel free."

There were seven of them, working with varying degrees of assiduousness. As she approached them, each one stopped work long enough to offer a bow and a murmured "my Lady . . ." in deference to her caste and office. Most looked down at their shoes as they spoke. Only one looked her briefly in the eye, and the look all but rocked Cretak back on her heels.

Nevertheless, she passed that one by and moved to the next and the next until she had completed a circuit of the gardens and studied each of them.

"Well?" Koval said airily, but with a touch of impatience, his tone implying that he really had far more important things to do.

Cretak pretended to hesitate. "It's difficult to decide. If I could speak to each of them . . ."

Koval shrugged. "Take all the time you wish. But I don't want to leave you alone with them. Not that they'd try anything. They know they're monitored constantly—" He indicated the spy-eyes set into the walls. "—but I'd prefer that you have guards with you as well."

He snapped his fingers at the nearest *ghilik*, but Cretak stayed him.

"I've taken enough of your time already," she said and, drawing upon everything she had learned about him during their brief affair so long ago, added: "Tell me which of them you can most easily spare."

He pretended to hesitate, looking them over one by one. "That one," he said finally.

Her face was a mask, but inside Cretak was gloating. She had guessed correctly! She motioned to the small one with the freckles and the jade green eyes. "Come with me."

The girl set down the basket of weeds she'd been carrying and obeyed. Concentrating on maintaining her own performance for Koval and his spy-eyes, Cretak failed to notice at the time that he was gloating, too.

Had she made a mistake? she wondered now with the hindsight of darkness and a sleepless night. Had Koval somehow steered her toward Zetha, had she misinterpreted what she took to be terror in the girl's eyes? Was it too late to do anything about it now?

She sat up abruptly, cursing herself for a fool. How could she get word to Uhura now? She could hardly go back to Koval and ask him for yet another messenger. She was certain most of the Senate's supposedly secure frequencies were monitored, if not her private comm as well, and if she sent anyone else across the Outmarches, Koval would know. And even if she could share what was only a hunch, would it do more harm than good?

Chapter 16

The three doctors scanned the report Uhura had sent them ("A New Cure for an Ancient Illness? The 'Magic' of *Hilopon*") at their own individual reading speeds. Uhura waited as they read, watching their faces for reactions. McCoy was the last to finish, but the first to speak.

"Well, well, what a coincidence!" he said dryly.

"So you think it's genuine?" Uhura said.

"Could be," the old grouch hedged. "Where'd it come from?"

"You're not the only one who's been fishing," Uhura told him. "Intercepted by one of my Listeners from a submission to the *Journal of Xenohistology and Interplanetary Epidemiology*."

"Okay," McCoy said. "I'm suitably impressed."

"Apparently the journal wasn't," Uhura reported. "They've flagged it for rejection pending verification from outside sources. Which gives us an in. But that's your molecule, all right."

"Confirmed," Selar said.

"I agree," Crusher chimed in.

McCoy was still ruminating. "It's still got the Thamnos cartel written all over it," he said. "That old pirate knows damn well where his son is!" he blustered. "There oughta be some way we can turn the screws on him."

"Probably not necessary," Uhura said coolly. "We have ways of monitoring him. If he tries to get in touch with his son or sends anybody looking for him, we'll track it. You rattled his cage; that's sufficient."

"I'd like to rattle more than that!" McCoy steamed. "What about the author of this article? Who or what is a Cinchona, and where's it located?"

"A logical assumption would be, at the source of the *hilopon*," Selar suggested.

Koval's inner sanctum was virtually soundproof, not only because it was thick-walled and deep underground, but because those walls contained the most sophisticated baffling and jamming equipment known to Romulans. A good thing, too. At the moment, Koval's voice was shrill enough to shatter glass.

". . . because by publishing your findings this soon, you idiot, you've risked antagonizing an entire planet full of xenophobic Renagans who are apt to kill you for it, that's why!" he was shouting.

"But I didn't tell anyone where to find it!" Thamnos protested. "When the *Journal* publishes my article, they'll have to come to me."

"*Hilopon* has been touted as a folk cure in that region for generations. You might have at least had the imagination to call it by another name!" Koval's voice dipped down into a lower, ominous register. "Oh, they'll find you, all right, and in so doing they'll save me the trouble of killing you. Aside from that, your research is full of holes because you've once again paid someone else to write it for you!"

"That's not true!" Thamnos protested. "I put this report together myself."

"Only because no one on Renaga can read!" Koval ground his teeth. If he'd owned a sense of irony, he'd have burst out laughing at this juncture, if only from futility.

"How *dare* you publish without my permission? What were you thinking?"

"I didn't expect so many people to die. You never told me so many people were going to die."

"So one death or a hundred is acceptable, but not thousands or tens of thousands, is that it?"

Thamnos was silent. At least, Koval thought, his anger spent, his mind already ticking over with alternatives, the transmitter was audio only, so he was spared the sight of that nauseating pink face!

"You were supposed to await my instructions," Koval said tightly. "We're still trying to determine why *hilopon* only works on Renaga. By defying my orders and publishing now, you may well have destroyed any future with us."

"My father won't let you hurt me!" he heard Thamnos say, and if he could have reached through the transmitter and wrapped his fingers around the man's throat, he would have done so. "What if you never find a way to make the *hilopon* work off Renaga?"

Then I persuade the Continuing Committee to send a warbird to Renaga to lay claim to the hilopon, *and I personally kill you!* Koval thought, shaking with anger. He listened to Thamnos mouth-breathing, the only sound from Renaga at the moment.

"What do I do now?" Thamnos asked at last when he realized Koval was not going to answer his question.

"You do nothing. Absolutely nothing, until I tell you otherwise. Can you manage that?"

Koval didn't wait for an answer.

"Idiot!" he added once more for emphasis before terminating the transmission.

Albatross was en route to Renaga. McCoy had gone offline to take a nap. The holos were no longer broadcasting to the ship, but Dr. Crusher had something on her mind, and she was talking to Uhura on discrete from her office across the quadrangle.

"Admiral? Mind if I ask you what the hell we're doing?"

Crusher's office faced east, but Uhura had a view to the west. The sun had just set behind the Golden Gate Bridge, and the clouds were entertaining themselves with shades of slate blue edged in fuchsia and salmon pink before a turquoise and cobalt twilight won out over all. Uhura was visited with a sudden memory of a moment in time when the bridge had been awash with flood waters, a Klingon bird-of-prey foundered bobbing in the ocean beneath it, and Earth thought it would never see the sun again. So long ago, and yet it seemed like yesterday.

And I'm still at my post trying to save the universe, she thought. *Just this one more mission, and—*

"Go ahead, Doctor."

"We've got more than enough evidence now to hang this on the Romulans."

"No argument there," Uhura acknowledged. On her desktop, reports on a half-dozen new crises were streaming in from Listeners flung across two quadrants and she watched them slot into different categories of crisis awaiting SI's attention. "Now why don't you say what's really on your mind?"

"Lives are being lost, and we seem to be wandering around in circles. How much longer do we continue sending the away team from one planet to another to another before we bring the evidence we have to Command and to the Federation Council and whoever else we need to and—"

"And accomplish what exactly? Alerting the Romulan Empire as a whole to what we know won't cure this disease, Doctor."

"We can just ask them if they're experiencing anything similar inside the Empire. Suggest we work together on a cure. Let them take all the credit if they offer one. Because if they created this, they must have a cure."

"What makes you say that?"

"Because it would be suicide to do otherwise. The odds on something this deadly spreading throughout the entire Empire—I can't believe they'd do that."

Uhura sighed. Every generation had to be taught anew. "Then you don't know Romulans. Granted, there have been no official contacts since Tomed, but go through your archives and see how many instances we know of where Romulan medical personnel have used experimental drugs on subject populations . . ."

"That's different," Crusher argued. "A drug can be targeted and controlled. A contagion without a cure can't." She shuddered, stuck her hands in the pockets of her smock. "Every time I have to work with this thing, no matter what precautions we take, I keep thinking of what could happen if it got out of the lab somehow, if I accidentally brought it home, if a ship whose crew is infected pulled into Space-dock and somehow brought it to Earth. I want a universe in which my son will be safe!"

"Don't you think I want that as well?" Uhura demanded. "But we ask the Romulans if they know anything about it, and then what? They deny any knowledge of it until they can produce enough evidence to say we created it. How will that make the universe safer? Answer me that. You're young; I don't know if you've ever been in a combat situation, but—"

"I lost my husband to one."

That shocked Uhura into silence. She'd forgotten the circumstances of Jack Crusher's death. She closed her eyes and took a deep breath before she spoke again.

"I'd forgotten that. And I am sorry. But let me try to explain something to you." She deactivated the incoming messages screen—it would be waiting for her the next time she accessed it—folded her hands, leaned forward, and gave Crusher her complete attention. "The reason I am still at this desk instead of off on my own private island somewhere

where there are no comm screens, is because I want to do as much as I can to stop the screaming."

"The screaming? I'm sorry, Admiral, I—"

"I won't presume to burden you with my experiences, with the number of times in the course of my career that I sat at that communications console listening to the screaming. Because that's what a comm officer always has to contend with, is the screaming. You have to keep the channels open, keep listening in case the enemy wants to surrender, but mostly what you hear and keep on hearing is the screaming. Until the moment comes when you don't hear it anymore, you merely watch the debris field scatter across your forward screen. And then you listen to the silence, but it still sounds like screaming."

She paused for breath, more exercised than Crusher had ever seen her.

"I would like, very much," she said slowly, "to live the rest of my life without ever again having to listen to the screaming.

"Now, then," she said, changing gears suddenly, all business again. "This is what we're going to do. The away team is on its way to Renaga to collect samples of this *hilopon* and see if it works. If it does, Q.E.D., we bring in the diplomats and the away team comes home. If it doesn't, I recall the away team anyway, and I get word to Cretak about what we've found so far. Then she and I decide what happens next."

"You'd send Zetha back to her?" Crusher asked for want of anything better to say. "And what about this Thamnos character?"

"Let's wait and see what the away team finds," was all Uhura would say.

"And Catalyst?"

"Catalyst!" Uhura repeated bitterly. Why had Command dreamed up such a beautiful name for such a deadly thing? "We keep on looking for a cure. I don't have a better answer than that, do you?"

* * *

"Shooting fish in a barrel," Sisko muttered as he and Tuvok scanned through several hundred meters of rock to find Cinchona's laboratory deep inside the mountain and read one solitary life-form within.

"I beg your pardon?"

"It's too easy," Sisko said, suppressing the cough that still plagued him despite Selar's having given him a complete physical and finding no physiological cause. "Nothing else about this mission has been spelled out in big block letters for us. Something in my bones tells me we're being set up, and I don't like it."

They had scanned Renaga from space, registering a predominantly agrarian society on a temperate but thin-soiled Class-M planet. There seemed to be no large cities, only narrow-laned villages clustered atop steep-sloped mountains, most of them walled and fortified.

"It appears to be a preindustrial society," Tuvok observed. "I note the equivalent of oxcarts, and some faster indigenous steeds vaguely resembling horses. Unpaved roads, no motorized vehicles or machinery of any kind. Agriculture is conducted by manual labor or with the use of draft animals."

"Wonder why most of the settlements are clumped on top of the hills like that?" Sisko wondered. "Even if they use most of the land for agriculture, you'd think they'd build a farmhouse in the fields now and then. Floods, maybe?"

"Perhaps they were originally fortresses," Tuvok suggested. "Possibly suggesting a long history of fighting among local warlords."

"Of course!" Sisko said. "You think there's any centralized government at all?"

"Not our concern," Tuvok said, homing in on a particular sector where something had caught his interest. "We are here to gather *hilopon* and, if possible, find the individual who submitted the paper to the *Journal*. The less attention we attract, the better."

"Agreed. But I meant to ask you about that. How can we be so sure he's here, if—" Sisko began, but then he noticed what Tuvok had picked up on his scanner. "That can't be right. You said this was a preindustrial society."

"I did," Tuvok acknowledged.

"Then what are they doing with a subspace transmitter? And am I imagining things, or is that a Romulan signature?"

"You are not imagining things," Tuvok assured him.

A scan of the entire planet in fact revealed three Romulan transmitters, two of which were being intermittently used by a handful of Romulans to send strings of code, probably to a warbird lurking somewhere on the fringes of the Zone. Tuvok would send samples back to Starfleet Command for decoding. The third transmitter, sending from a cave beneath one of the hilltop cities, might have been a Romulan transmitter, but it was not being used by a Romulan.

"The difference is subtle," Tuvok reported. "But unless I am mistaken, this individual is a Rigelian."

That was when Sisko began wondering why it was all suddenly so easy. The sight of Cinchona's life-form reading, alone within his unguarded mountain fastness, was making him twitchy. Not for the first time, he suppressed the urge to cough.

"You'd think someone sitting on what could be one of the greatest medical discoveries of the century would at least have a security system in place," he suggested.

Traditionally, the Romulan military loathed the Tal Shiar, and the feeling was mutual. Officers of the Imperial fleet were, at least by training, straightforward and direct; they preferred action to talk, the shortest distance between two points. Military strategy had purpose, they argued; the Tal Shiar's sneakery, they maintained, was more often than not spying for spying's sake.

The Tal Shiar in general, and Koval in particular, considered the military to be weapons-happy dunderheads, the product of too much upper-caste inbreeding, incapable of original thought.

Nevertheless, when he needed to commandeer a warbird, even to enter the Outmarches, Koval had sufficient clout to hold his nose and do so.

"Cloak engaged," Admiral Tal announced. He gave Koval a look that would have frightened most men. It bounced off Koval's mental shields like a badly aimed phaser blast. "I wish I knew where in the hells we're going and why."

"The where I can answer," Koval said indolently. "The why is none of your business."

It was no easy feat to land a space vessel unnoticed near a populated area on a planet where the sound of an engine had never been heard before. It would be one thing if they were an anthropology team simply studying the inhabitants; they might have set *Albatross* down anywhere in the hinterlands and hitchhiked into town in the back of an oxcart. But in this instance they needed speed as much as stealth. The ship had to be close to their objective.

"I'd be happier if this were a shuttlecraft with a starship for backup," Sisko muttered, searching the terrain near where they'd picked up the Rigelian's signal for a safe place to conceal the ship. He was reluctant to leave her in orbit at station-keeping and beam down, but this time thought he'd ask Tuvok for his input before he made his decision.

"I figure there's too much likelihood that we'd be noticed beaming out. More to the point, I don't like leaving her alone up there in case someone should get curious."

"Agreed," Tuvok had said. "However, landing the ship will necessitate our splitting up into shifts again."

"Logically, Lieutenant Sisko," Selar suggested, "as the two best trained for alien terrain conditions, you and Lieutenant Tuvok are the optimal choice for first reconnaissance.

Further, I am in the middle of an experiment which requires my complete attention. Zetha can remain with me."

It was what Sisko had had in mind. Now all he said was: "You'll keep her sealed up until we signal you."

"Of course," Selar said, turning her attention back to her scanners.

Albatross waited until sundown before gliding into atmosphere on thrusters and, in a daring maneuver he'd never tried anywhere but in simulations before, Sisko cut the engines entirely for the last hundred meters and let her momentum carry her until he swore he could count the blades of saw grass skimming by beneath her belly. Just when it looked as if he could reach out and grab a handful of that grass, he activated the reverse thrusters in a series of short bursts which, if all went well, would neither scorch the grass nor awaken the neighbor's dog, and *Albatross*, once more true to her name, bumped awkwardly but unhurt to ground. Only the sheen of sweat on Sisko's brow revealed just how uncertain he had been that she would.

Selar and Zetha were holding things down back in the lab, oblivious to how dangerous the maneuver had been. Tuvok, still hoping to pick up more signals from the two Romulan transmitters, was also monitoring the Rigelian's underground lair, and had barely noticed the descent.

"The cave is deserted at present," he announced once he and Sisko had left the ship, scanning once more with his tricorder as they prepared to go exploring. "Doubtless its owner has returned to hearth and home."

"Let's hope it's for the rest of the night. Don't suppose a longbow is any use inside a cave?" Sisko mused, absently groping at his hip where a phaser ought to be. "Oh, well. There are two of us. How strong can one Rigelian be?"

The cave was indeed deserted, but if the two Starfleet officers expected to find a laboratory, however primitive, they were disappointed. What they found was a dirt-walled cavern only partially excavated from a natural formation, dimly lit by a few overhead lamps. Several rustic tables against the walls of this crudely formed room were cluttered with jars of various sizes and colors, obviously made by local craftsmen, as well as the transmitter which had led them here, which was indeed of Romulan design. There was also a computer terminal which seemed to have been cobbled together from modules salvaged from a vessel augmented with Romulan components.

"Hybridized Rigelian computer," Sisko announced, just looking at it. "That particular style of interface is something they use."

There was a refrigeration unit, also of Rigelian manufacture. Instead of specimens or test samples, the refrigerator was cluttered with containers of half-eaten food, much of it spoiled.

"Likely solar powered," Sisko said, indicating the generator. "Might be able to find the collectors out there in the daytime."

While he searched the fridge for anything resembling research samples and ending up with nothing more than moldy stew, Tuvok attempted to gain entry to the computer, something which proved not at all difficult. There were some rags and what looked like parts scavenged from a ship piled against one wall, covered in dust and cobwebs, and Sisko began picking through these as well.

"Clothing's synthetic," Sisko reported. "Modern stuff, not something you'd find woven on a handloom in a preindustrial society. Food looks local, though." He heard the Vulcan's indrawn breath at something on the computer screen. "What is it?"

"Pornography," Tuvok said, repressing his distaste. "There seems to be nothing on the computer but that. I find no records, no experimental data—"

"Nothing but dirty pictures, huh? Maybe he's got the data stored somewhere more portable. This is a hideout," Sisko decided. "The kind of place a man goes to when the wife and kids get on his nerves."

"Indeed. Perhaps Cinchona's laboratory is elsewhere."

"I'd be surprised if he had a laboratory at all." Sisko picked up a few of the jars, opening the lids and alternately peering inside or sniffing at them. "*Hilopon?* It looks like dirt."

Tuvok ran the tricorder over the jars. "*Hilopon.* As Selar suggested, a natural compound found in the soil of Renaga, just as the original Gnawing bacillus was found in the soil of Romulus."

So saying, he ran the tricorder over the walls and the dirt floor of the cave and came up with the same readings. "The substances in the jars may have been refined to remove gravel and other debris, but it is essentially no different than the soil beneath our feet. Curious."

"Or just plain dumb." On a hunch, Sisko rubbed the contents of one of the jars on a small cut on one finger he'd acquired while chopping the last of the Vidalia onions he'd purchased on Tenjin. The cut healed instantaneously. "Cinchona was right about one thing. It does work for small stuff, at least on its own planet."

"Cinchona was right about more than that," a voice said behind them.

Selar motioned Zetha to join her in peering at the specimen under the microscope. The girl's eyes widened in astonishment.

"Is it the *hilopon?*" she wondered.

"Negative," Selar replied. "After our departure from Quirinus, I derived a serum from the blood of the Romulan who was killed because the Quirinians believed he had brought the disease."

"The one who had no . . . germs," she pronounced the word carefully. ". . . in his body at all."

"Correct. I treated several of the Catalyst mutations with the serum. These are the results."

Zetha examined them again, just to make sure she understood. Before she could speak, Tuvok's voice on the intercom interrupted.

"Dr. Selar? Can you beam into the cave at once? Your expertise is required."

Selar brought Zetha with her. It seemed the logical thing to do. Besides—

"Please don't leave me here by myself," Zetha pleaded. "If anything goes wrong, I won't know what to do."

"Dubious," Selar said. "You have managed quite well so far. However, for Lieutenant Sisko's peace of mind as well as your own safety, it might be best if you did accompany me."

"Did my father send you?" was the first thing Thamnos asked his two unexpected visitors. Then something seemed to tell him that was not the appropriate question, so he asked another. "How did you find me?"

"Is that of consequence, Dr. Cinchona?" Tuvok asked, suppressing any sign that he knew who Thamnos was; Sisko had suggested he do most of the talking when they first confronted their suspect. "I am Tuvok. This is Dr. Jacobs. We have read your paper on *hilopon*. We wish to learn more."

First captain, now doctor! Sisko thought, trying to hold a deadpan in the face of his most recent promotion.

Thamnos's beady little eyes lit up momentarily. "Are you from the *Journal?*" he asked hopefully. Suddenly the dread that had set in after his last conversation with Koval seemed lifted from his shoulders. If someone from the Federation side was willing to foster him, maybe he was safe after all.

Tuvok did not exactly answer the question. "There is another physician in our party who would be better able to address your research. May I summon her?"

Not many men can affect a swagger standing still. Thamnos somehow managed it. "Sure. Be happy to talk to her. Tell her to beam on in."

Selar's arrival alone might not have set him off. But something about Zetha's presence made him suspicious.

"You're a Romulan," he said.

Before Zetha could answer, or even decide what to answer, Thamnos began to laugh.

"Okay, I get it! You're not from the *Journal*. You're not from the Federation side at all. I thought he'd come himself, but this is even better. He wants me to test it on you, to back up my article to the *Journal*. Of course, it all makes sense now . . ."

His voice and manner grew suddenly manic as he pushed past Sisko and went rummaging amid the debris in the corner until he had scattered all of it to reveal a case of datachips, which he set beside the jury-rigged computer, shoving the jars of *hilopon* aside.

"Oh, he's clever! He doesn't come himself, he sends one of the seeds . . ." Thamnos was muttering near-hysterically, fumbling through the chips in search of a particular one. "Let's see, which seeding was it? This one? No. Perhaps this one . . . let's see . . . yes, I think this is it."

Silently Sisko gave Tuvok an inquiring look. *Recommendation?* the look said. *Do we let him run amok or do we corral him now before he tries to destroy evidence?* Tuvok shook his head imperceptibly: *I recommend we ascertain what it is he is searching for first.*

Thamnos inserted a datachip into the interface. "Computer, correlate retina scan of subjects present with extant files."

The computer answered him with a code, and Thamnos turned to Zetha smugly. "I knew it! Sample 173. The photo on file makes it look like you have freckles, though. Or is that part of your cover?"

Perplexed, Zetha looked from Selar to Tuvok to Sisko,

then back to Selar. "What is he talking about?" she demanded.

"I believe," Selar said, "he has just provided us with the
source of the disease vector."

Cretak had read Koval's character correctly. Knowing
Tuvan's Syndrome ran in his family, he had been obsessed
with illness—and immunity to illness—all his life. When it
first occurred to him what a marvelously versatile illness the
Gnawing could be, he recalled what most people had forgotten—that some rare few Romulans were immune to the
disease. Once his scientists were able to tell him why—
possession of a particular rare gene sequence, extant in less
than one tenth of one percent of the population—the rest
seemed self-evident.

At first he thought he would simply gather together as
many of those with the immunity sequence as possible, secretly infect them with the Gnawing, then scatter them like
seeds throughout first the worlds on his side of the Zone, then
on certain worlds on the Federation side where vulcanoids
were common. He would choose as his "volunteers" Romulans who traveled frequently, many of them his own operatives.

The first stage would have the effect of spreading panic
and compelling both his Empire and the other side to accuse each other of biological warfare, always a good ploy for
keeping the balance of power unbalanced. Anything that
sent the Federation side into a frenzy, as long as it was done
subtly, was something Koval's superiors welcomed. Many in
the Tal Shiar, as well as the military and the Senate, hun-
gered for an end to the Empire's half-century of self-imposed
isolation, and a return to expansionism. If Koval's scheme
worked on this level, he could present the expansionists with
a game plan for conquering worlds and eliminating their indigenous populations without deploying a single warbird or
firing a single shot.

So, how to disguise the Gnawing, and render it dormant until its purveyors could be spread across two quadrants? That was the easy part. When carried by the immunes, it could incubate for weeks, sometimes months, before spreading. Koval's physicians did not know why the incubation period varied from one immune to another, but it wasn't that important to them. The difficult part was not making the vector so obvious that it attracted attention too soon.

Then there was the awkwardness of having important Romulans suspected of being carriers. It was at this juncture that Koval began not only training the *ghilik* who were already members of his expendable cadre, but searching the Imperial Census files for those who lived in the back streets and whose disappearance would go largely unremarked. The day he cornered Zetha and Tahir in the alley near the cemetery had been only one of many.

Tahir was not an immune, and so of no use to him. But Zetha, once she had been injected with a series of "nutritional supplements" which, had Selar been there to examine them, she would have recognized at once as Catalyst, became Sample 173. The rest was only a matter of time.

Sisko cleared his throat. The annoying dry cough, which had not bothered him while he and Tuvok had at first been poking around among Thamnos's belongings, had returned. "What are you saying?"

"Oh, come on, don't play innocent with me!" Thamnos had deactivated the computer, closed the case full of datachips. "He's more clever than I thought he was. I never realized he had humans and Vulcans in his employ, but then why wouldn't he? He has the resources. But as soon as I saw her, I knew. All right, you're branching out on your own, trying to get to the vaccine before he does. I know how that works. Fine, no problem. Only take me with you. He's as much as threatened to kill me. You have a ship? I want out of here, and fast. I give you the vaccine, you take me with you. Deal?"

"You have perfected an actual vaccine?" Selar asked. "Derived from *hilopon*, as described in your paper to the *Journal*?"

Beside her, Zetha had covered her mouth with her hand and was backing away from all of them.

"Sure!" Thamnos said brightly. "Not here. Of course I wouldn't keep it here. I knew this would be the first place he—or you—would look for it. It's in a safe place. But I need to go alone. If any of the villagers spotted any one of you, even a human . . . they're suspicious enough of strangers, but your clothes . . ."

"Your vaccine," Selar said. "Will it work offworld?"

Thamnos's eyes shifted from side to side.

"I don't think you're going anywhere," Sisko said softly.

He nodded to Tuvok, who moved, catlike, encircling Thamnos's neck with one long arm, the fingers of his other hand set at the precise point on his shoulder where the briefest pinch would take him down. Thamnos, recognizing the maneuver, did not fight.

"You knock me out, you don't get the vaccine," he said. "And you really don't want to waste any time, you know. You're all going to need the vaccine very soon. If it isn't already too late."

"What the hell are you talking about?" Sisko demanded, moving toward him ominously. He wasn't sure what he'd do once he got there, but he made the move anyway.

"How long have you had that cough?" Thamnos demanded. He jerked his chin toward Zetha. "She's the carrier, don't you see? She's immune, but she's been incubating the disease for months. Once it's triggered, you'll all get it. That cough tells me you already have!"

It wasn't a collapse, exactly, Uhura insisted. She'd gotten up from her desk while she was talking to Crusher, and simply misjudged her footing. The fact that she was walking across a level floor that suddenly seemed to undulate and buckle beneath her was beside the point. She was fine, really.

"The hell you are," Crusher said, pressing the hypo against the side of her neck. Seeing the older woman literally fall off her feet, Crusher had used a priority override and beamed directly into Uhura's office, then ordered a backup team to escort the admiral home. "You're this close to exhaustion. You're to stay in bed and away from that desk for at least eight hours if I have to strap you down in order to enforce it."

Annoyed at all the fuss, Uhura was sitting very straight with her arms folded, wearing The Look, by the time Crusher had sent the backup team on its way and returned to the bedroom. But The Look, she discovered, only worked on the male of the species. *Damn!* she thought. *Either I'm losing my touch, or it's whatever tranquilizer Crusher's shot me with, but this evening is not going the way I'd planned!*

"Doctor's orders?" she managed, resting on her dignity amid the pillows of her queen-size bed.

"Bed rest. Watch a movie, listen to some music, read a good book," Crusher said. "Anything but work."

"May I answer some mail?" Uhura asked sweetly. If The Look didn't work, maybe her best smile would.

"Only if it's not work-related," Crusher scolded, halfway out the door. "Want a cup of hot milk before I go?"

"Get the hell out of here!" Uhura snapped. If the smile wasn't going to work, either, she'd save it for another occasion. "Go home to your son; I don't need you here."

"Good night to you, too," Crusher said, and was gone.

As soon as the outer door slid shut and locked behind her, Uhura activated the beside console. Riffling through the usual office memos and notes from friends and family members she didn't have the energy to answer, she found a message from Curzon. She unscrambled it.

"*Called in on emergency diplomatic mission, effective immediately. Hush-hush, rush-rush, top secret. So I won't tell you I'm aboard* Okinawa. *Will comm you when I get back. Thanks for the memories, Curzon.*"

Ordinarily, if Curzon was off on a top secret mission, he kept it secret. By its very presence, his message bothered her. Following her refit, *Okinawa* had been scheduled to go on maneuvers in the Mutara sector awaiting a new assignment. Where had she been diverted on such short notice, and why would Curzon specifically want Uhura to know?

Memo to self, she thought sleepily as she turned off the bedside lamp and the combination of the sound of foghorns on the bay and whatever it was Crusher had given her took effect: *Ascertain* Okinawa's *official destination, then extrapolate.* Tranquilizers or no, a familiar tingling at the back of her neck said it had something to do with Catalyst.

Chapter 17

Zetha backed away from the others until she reached the far wall, one hand covering her mouth, her eyes wide with terror. Thamnos was still smirking.

"Do we have a deal?" he demanded. "The vaccine and your lives in exchange for my freedom? I'd say you've got the better end of the bargain."

Again a look passed between Sisko and Tuvok which was too quick for Thamnos to notice. The human let the Vulcan know he was about to create a diversion.

Sisko appeared to crumble while they watched. He clenched his fists against his temples and seemed to stagger. When he straightened up, tears welled in his eyes.

"I don't want to die!" he cried with all the passion of a Shakespearean actor. "I've seen what this disease does to people!" He turned on Zetha. "If this—this Tal Shiar plant has infected us all, the only thing that matters is the vaccine! Tuvok, let him go."

"But, Dr. Jacobs—" Tuvok interjected, playing along.

"I said let him go, dammit!" Sisko snapped. "Dr. Thamnos, we'll agree to your terms. We need that vaccine."

As if reluctantly, Tuvok released his hold. Thamnos was swaggering and smirking at the same time.

"Now, there's a sensible man. Maybe once we get out of

here, we can be business partners. We can sell *hilopon* to both sides. I'll still want full credit for the research, of course, but—"

He never finished his sentence. The knife that severed his windpipe prevented it.

Admiral Tal got up from the command chair to pace the warbird's bridge restlessly. Few realized how much of a warbird commander's life was spent just sitting. Sometimes, especially times such as this, a person needed to stretch.

This place had been hard won, and over a long and storied lifetime. That incident when he was a subcommander had almost ended his career if not his life; the climb back up had been arduous, to put it mildly. Tal had gotten as far as commander without tarnishing his honor or his morals—no mean feat in the service of an Empire not always committed to either—only to find himself subordinate to that butcher Volskiar at Narendra III.

He still had nightmares about that, though it was sixteen years past. It made him wary of all orders from above, and intent on scrutinizing their origin and their purpose. As he'd tried to tell Jarok, the headstrong fool, the important thing— well, the next most important thing after honor and morality, was moderation.

The next most important thing after that was to stay off-world, and out of politics, as much as possible. Such caution had won him an admiralcy, but at the cost of rarely seeing sky above him. He had no doubt he would die someday within the confines of a ship, in the service of a world where it was not safe for the moderate to live.

Tal would fight when he believed the cause was just. But, after Narendra III, he would not fight unless he knew precisely what he was fighting for.

The admiral did a circuit of the bridge stations, communicating by a glance here, a nod or touch on the shoulder there, that he knew he could count on his crew to give him their best, for they never got less from him. As for his crew, their respect for him bordered on adulation.

Tal saw that all was in order, then settled back in the command chair.

"Well?" he demanded of Koval. "We're almost there. What happens next?"

"There" was a world Tal had finally managed to correlate between their course and existing starcharts as Renaga, designated unallied and "to be observed." It was the only thing in the vicinity even the Tal Shiar could possibly be interested in. Tal knew other ships passed this way occasionally in spite of the treaty; he suspected Federation ships did as well. Was that the point of this Tal Shiar effort, to provoke accusations of treaty violation and stir up trouble for no particular reason? Did the Empire not have enough else on its mind? Whatever happened, he and his crew would take the brunt of it, and Tal was not amused.

Koval had had ample opportunity to observe the admiral on their journey here as well as earlier. He knew Tal's history, and knew from his own investigation that the admiral was politically beyond reproach. He had been seen more than once in the company of Alidar Jarok, who was under surveillance for reasons owing to a possible shift in orthodoxy, yet the content of their conversations, beyond talk of women, had never been substantiated.

Koval knew as well that Tal was no ordinary commander. Intelligent, patrician, fit and energetic despite his years, not quick to anger but, once there, implacable, this one would not be bullied. He had also reached an age where he was beyond fear.

Koval was forced to consider him a peer. Very well; it would be a challenge. Had he known how much Tal despised his soft-bellied self, he would have found the challenge all the more exciting.

In answer to Tal's question, he said: "We wait."

"For what?" Tal asked incisively.

He got no answer.

On *Okinawa*'s bridge, Captain Leyton had just asked his helmsman for an ETA at Renaga.

"Approximately 2.5 hours, sir," the helm reported not a little nervously. "Barring interception by a Romulan patrol."

"They won't intercept us, Ensign," Leyton said confidently. "Ambassador Dax assures me they want us to get there."

This earned him puzzled looks from some of the bridge crew. Leyton was not about to resolve their puzzlement; he wasn't entirely sure what they were doing on this mission himself. Beside him, Curzon Dax was as opaque as stone.

Unbeknownst to Uhura, Dax had been following as much of *Albatross*'s progress as he could by way of his special diplomatic access to intelligence matters. When the C-in-C informed him there was reason to believe a Romulan warbird was heading toward Renaga, reason or reasons unknown, but in the first overt violation of the Zone in a very, very long time, Curzon's logical conclusion was that it had something to do with *Albatross*.

Curzon knew that Tuvok had reported there were Romulans on Renaga sending transmissions back to the homeworld. Once he was given access to the decoded transmissions, he could extrapolate from their very existence and the excitement they had generated at Starfleet Command that the Romulans were interested in something other than crop yields and weather reports on this backward little world. Curzon knew, as perhaps not everyone on *Okinawa* did, that by the time they arrived at Renaga, they would find themselves nose to nose with a decloaking Romulan warbird.

Back on Earth, Admiral Uhura was having words with the C-in-C.

"Never mind how I found out *Okinawa* was en route to Renaga. I want you to tell me why. Sir."

She didn't expect anything but the usual obfuscative need-to-know speech. She was floored when the C-in-C told her there was reason to believe a Romulan warbird was also moving toward Renaga. Had someone else fielded that while she was out of commission last night? If so, why hadn't she been informed?

"Has Captain Leyton been briefed on the presence of my away team?" she wanted to know, grateful it was *Okinawa*, with Curzon on board, that was on its way. But on its way to do what? "I don't want them getting caught in the crossfire."

Assured that Captain Leyton and Ambassador Dax knew as much as anybody did about the situation, Uhura signed off, not a little perturbed. If there was a warbird about, it was essential to have a starship there for balance, but she'd rather *Albatross* had been well away before that. *Albatross* had not responded to her hails for over an hour now. It could mean nothing. It could mean a great deal. There was nothing to do but wait.

"There is a story about a river," the woman who had thrown the knife said, her voice echoing off the walls of the cave. She stood in the long narrow passage that led perhaps a thousand meters downward from the entrance to the cave, her hands limp at her sides. Her eyes were glazed and she wore a fixed and eerie smile. Selar, surreptitiously running her medscanner, noted the presence of strong hallucinogens in her bloodstream.

"The river fed all the farms in the valley where it ran, and the people in the valley were content," the woman said dreamily. "But a greedy man bought the land high in the mountains where the river rose as a small spring between the rocks. And the man dammed up the river and diverted it so that only his farm benefited from it."

"It's an interesting story, ma'am," Sisko said cautiously. He'd made note that, having thrown the one knife in her possession, really more of a meat cleaver, with remarkable accuracy, she was otherwise unarmed. "How does it end?"

"One would think," the woman said, "the way such stories usually go, that the other farmers would rise up against the greedy man and destroy the dam, or kill him so they could have their water again, but no. Instead, it was the river itself, meaning his own greed, that rose up in time of flood and drowned him."

"A parable," Sisko said, still humoring her. "Who are you?"

"I am the river, of course," she replied, her manic smile widening. "I am also Boralesh, widow of the man Cinchona, who was killed by greed. A vision led me here. When he rose from my bed tonight, I took the dreaming drugs, and they led me here.

"No one man can control the river. No one man can claim the riches of our world for strangers. We do not want you here. You must leave."

"That's our intention, ma'am," Sisko said. "But the vaccine your husband spoke about—"

"You mean the potions he was always concocting in my kitchen?" Boralesh's voice was laced with sarcasm. "None of them ever improved upon what the gods have already given us. *Hilopon* is our mothersoil, our life's blood. It cannot be made better. And it will not be taken away from us."

"But you wouldn't mind if we took one of—Cinchona, did you say?—one of the potions with us?"

The woman shrugged. "These things are nothing to me." Something seemed to penetrate her drug-induced fog, and she frowned. "The children . . . I must not leave them alone for long. . . ."

With that she drifted out of the cave, and they let her go.

"We should follow her," Sisko said after she had gone. His anxiety was not feigned now. "If Thamnos was right, if we're all infected, we do need to get ahold of whatever it was he was working on, however crude."

"I submit we have more urgent things to deal with now, Lieutenant," Tuvok said tautly, preparing to take the case full of datachips with them, indicating the dead Thamnos crumpled against one wall. "Speed is of the essence. If we are discovered here . . ."

"Agreed," Sisko said. He was already disengaging the Romulan transmitter, and selecting which Rigelian artifacts he would take with him. The more evidence they had of the connection between Thamnos and the Romulans, the better. "But it might not hurt to see what Boralesh has in her kitchen."

"I doubt it is anything more than what we have found here," Selar suggested, gathering several jars of *hilopon* just in case. "And if the vaccine is indicative of its 'creator,' it may be as ineffectual as the raw materials it is derived from. Further, something Zetha and I were working on just before we came here . . ."

It wasn't as if the others had forgotten Zetha, but in the wake of Thamnos's bizarre revelations, the suddenness of his death, and the eerie apparition that was Boralesh, their focus had been elsewhere. At the mention of her name, Zetha whimpered quietly. All eyes turned to her, and those eyes held questions.

She had sunk to the floor in the half-dark, and huddled there as if she didn't know what else to do. She looked up at Tuvok, tears streaming down her face.

"When you asked if I was Tal Shiar, I told you no. It was the truth. They took me off the streets, threatened to kill Godmother if I didn't go with them. I was trained, but I never took the oath. All *ghilik* have to take the oath before they're sent on their mission. I had made up my mind I would not take the oath, but I could find no means to escape. If Cretak hadn't taken me away from them, they would have had to kill me."

Tuvok was solemn. "Is this, now, the entire truth?"

"Yes!"

"You might have told us this from the beginning."

"Would you have trusted me if I had? I wanted—I needed you to trust me. The only way I could think of was to tell you only part of the truth."

Concerned with getting back to the ship before the sun rose, Tuvok said: "We will speak further on this later."

"No," Zetha whimpered. "There can be no 'later.' I have killed all of you. Leave me here! Seal up the cave when you go. Leave me with this . . . murderer, this eater of souls! I will not be the cause of any more death!"

"There is no evidence that you have caused any deaths," Selar began.

"Thamnos said I was!" Zetha cried. " 'Sample 173' he said, and Sisko believes him. How can it not be true? The datachips . . . they gave me the injections, said they were nutritional supplements . . . I never had enough to eat when I was little. . . ."

"Hey, I never meant that!" Sisko said. Her accusation struck him so hard, he winced. He wasn't sure what he believed anymore. He went to her, crouched down and took her hand as if he were talking to Jake. "It was a diversion, to distract Thamnos, like what you and Tuvok did with Jarquin. You didn't really think—? My God, little girl, how awful it must be not to be able to trust anyone!"

In the meantime, Tuvok had gone up to the entrance of the cave, estimating the time until sunrise, then returned. He and Sisko had walked in under cover of night, but there was no time for that now.

"You and Selar beam out first," Sisko instructed him. "Zetha and I will follow."

Carrying the Romulan transmitter as well as the data-chips, Tuvok signaled the transporter on *Albatross* to beam them in. As the transporter beam engulfed the two Vulcans, Sisko took Zetha's hands and gently pulled her to her feet. He wrapped his arms around her and she clung to him like a child. Her bones felt as fragile as a bird's.

Hell, he thought, *if I've caught the disease, it's too late to worry about it anyway. And Selar seemed awfully confident none of us had. Guess I'll know more once we get out of here.* Not knowing what else to do or say, he rocked Zetha in his arms until the transporter grabbed them both.

"I was beginning to worry," Uhura said a short time later as Sisko settled in at the controls and answered her hail. It was a little disconcerting seeing her as just a face on a viewscreen after so long using the fully dimensional holos, but the away team was in a bit of a hurry right now.

"All present and accounted for, Admiral," Sisko responded as Tuvok locked into the seat beside him. He barely noticed Selar touching the hypo to his arm to draw blood. "We have a lot to tell you."

"Hold that thought for now," Uhura said crisply. "There's a warbird in the vicinity, and *Okinawa*'s on her way. Curzon Dax is aboard. *Okinawa* will be looking for you. Rendezvous soonest."

Sisko didn't know whether to be elated or alarmed. Having *Okinawa* come to them meant he'd be reunited with Jennifer and Jake that much sooner, but he was disturbed at their being inside the Zone and potentially in harm's way.

"Acknowledged," he said, keeping rein on his thoughts. "Tell *Okinawa* we're on our way.

"Easier said than done," he said to Tuvok as soon as Uhura had signed off. His cough forgotten, the possibility that he might be infected with Catalyst forgotten, his main concern now was how to get the clumsy bird off the ground. "Recommendations, Mr. Tuvok? Tiptoe out the way we came in, or push the afterburners, go up like a rocket, and risk frightening the neighbors and, maybe, signaling our position to a warbird?"

Tuvok had been scanning for any energy displacement that might have been a warbird under cloak. So far, so good.

"I submit we cannot reveal our position to a warbird that is not yet here."

"Agreed," Sisko concurred, powering her up full. "Maybe the natives will think it's just thunder . . ."

With a shudder and a roar, *Albatross* took wing.

Selar had gathered serum samples from everyone, Zetha last. The girl lay on her bunk, no longer weeping, but curled up into herself in stony silence.

"I will need your assistance with the next phase of the experiment," Selar began.

"All those people—!" Zetha whispered hoarsely. "Everywhere I went, I carried it with me. Cretak, the crew of the ship that brought me, Admiral Uhura, Dr. Crusher and her son. Other 'seeds' may have started the outbreaks on Tenjin and Quirinus, but I must have brought it again to the domes we visited, the survivors in Sawar, Citizen Jarquin, the Sliwoni when I went into town to steal the adaptor . . . we wondered how it spread so quickly there . . ."

"You have not infected anyone," Selar said. "Of that I am certain."

Zetha sat up, rubbing the tears off her face with the heels of her hands. "How can you be sure? Thamnos said—"

"As with everything else, Thamnos was incorrect. Admiral Uhura is quite well. She and Lieutenant Sisko were in communication minutes ago. No one else on Earth has been infected."

This seemed to give Zetha hope. "Then maybe the disease was still . . . incubating? Perhaps it's only active now. But still, you and Tuvok and Sisko, even that madwoman on Renaga . . ."

"Lieutenant Sisko shows no signs of the illness. His cough, I believe, is psychosomatic," Selar said.

"Psycho— What does that mean?"

"It means, and you did not hear me say this," Selar said, in a rare moment of confidentiality, "that Lieutenant Sisko is uneasy with the responsibilities of command. The emotional stress is taking a physical toll."

Zetha remembered how her gums used to bleed in the final weeks in the barracks. She understood about stress. For a moment she almost pitied Sisko. Then she remembered about Catalyst.

"So I didn't infect him? Does that mean—?"

"Will you assist me in continuing my experiment?" Selar asked again.

Puzzled, emotionally spent, Zetha could think of nothing else to do. She followed Selar to the lab.

Many in the village on the hilltop were awakened by the rushing sound of *Albatross*'s thrusters, and some ventured to their windows in time to see the fiery orange trail soaring upward, but none dared venture outside to investigate. Some prayed, others simply went back to bed. In the morning, some would venture into the woods from which the demonic sight had originated, see the scorch marks in the grass, and pray again. The only one who might have offered some explanation, however incredible, was Boralesh, who slept through it all.

Speculation might have entertained the villagers for days if they had not soon had newer marvels to concern themselves with. For that morning Boralesh informed her neighbors that she had dreamed her husband had been murdered

by a demon, and this was of far more interest than some unexplained fireball in the sky. Perhaps the two were somehow
connected?

When Thamnos failed to reappear that same evening—
the villagers were accustomed to his seemingly aimless pere-
grinations, but he always returned for supper—some would
whisper behind their hands that perhaps he had deserted the
woman who had forced him into marriage. Others would
speculate that it was not a demon that had killed him. The
buzz would last for several weeks, then dissipate. It was all in
the stars and the gods' hands, anyway, and there was nothing
anyone could do about it.

"Well?" Admiral Tal demanded yet again, wishing Koval
would get out of the habit of standing just between his peripheral vision and the forward screen every time he was on
the bridge. "We're here. Now what?"

Koval did not look at him so much as address him over
his shoulder. "I beam down. You wait."

"Alone?" Tal demanded, though not with any great passion. If a Tal Shiar operative chose to beam into a possibly
hostile environment without a security team, who was he to
stop him?

"Yes, alone," Koval said. "Where I'm going, no one will
even see me. I will instruct your transporter crew. You will
stay in constant contact with me and await my orders."

The sight of the knife in Thamnos's throat almost made
Koval wish he'd brought guards. But there was nothing living in the cave, and Koval was confident he could beam out
before anyone might come shuffling in from outside.

He had already silenced the other two transmitters and
their operators, ordering the warbird's transport officer to
beam him from site to site. He'd planned to silence Thamnos next, but someone had beaten him to it.

The fact that the murder weapon was a native kitchen knife might almost have led him to the obvious conclusion that Thamnos had been killed by a Renagan, for whatever reasons Renagans killed each other. Jealous husband, embittered wife, cheated business partner—what did he care? But when he realized that the Rigelian's transmitter and the datachips were gone, Koval arrived at a different conclusion entirely.

A Renagan killer might have opened the case looking for valuables and, not finding anything but datachips, meaningless to an illiterate, dumped them on the floor, smashed the transmitter as being equally useless, trashed the place, and gone away. The fact that the only things missing could directly link Thamnos, the seeds, and the Empire was disquieting. Whoever had done this knew exactly what they were looking for. Using a native knife to kill the Rigelian was just a sardonic twist.

Seething, Koval searched the cave once more to make certain he'd overlooked nothing. Knocking carelessly against a table, he overturned several jars of *hilopon*.

"And we never even figured out how the accursed stuff works!" he muttered in disgust, rubbing the fine powder between his fingers before wiping them fastidiously on a handkerchief, which he wrapped around the haft of the knife and, not without tugging, pulled it free. He touched the dead man's neck. Not that he expected to find a pulse, but he wanted to determine how long ago he had been killed.

The corpse was still warm, the limbs limp as a rag doll's, not yet stiffened with rigor mortis. Thamnos had been dead for less than an hour. Whoever did this could not have gone far.

With a humorless smile, Koval wrapped the knife in the handkerchief, which he concealed in his tunic before signaling the warbird.

"Scan the planet for any sign of transport," he ordered Tal. "A ship, a shuttle, a transporter signal. At once!"

"Acknowledged," Admiral Tal replied, nodding to his science officer to run the scan. Tal himself was watching something else on the forward screen with the intensity of a predator watching a mouse. The schematic showed him a smallish, lumpy shape that did not match the configurations of the military vessels of any enemy he knew. A civilian ship, then, streaking away from the surface of a pre-industrial world as fast as its engines could take it, which wasn't all that fast.

She cannot see us, Tal thought, checking the cloak anyway, *yet she somehow knows we're here. I wonder if she's what Koval brought us all this way to find.*

Admiral Tal allowed himself the luxury of a yawn. With the indolence of a predator who's already eaten a full meal, he let the mouse go.

"Admiral?" Sciences had completed her scan. "There is no sign of any alien vessel on the planet."

They had all seen the small awkward ship streaking away from the planet just moments before Koval gave his order for a sensor scan. But if Tal said they hadn't, then they were prepared to swear on their mothers' graves that they hadn't.

"Admiral?" Helm was more nervous than usual. None of them liked it when Tal Shiar was aboard, and no one needed to tell them Koval was Tal Shiar. They knew. "Colonel Koval is signaling to beam aboard."

"Yes, yes, by all means, beam his lordship aboard!" Tal said dryly. "And quickly now! He needs to know we found nothing on the planet."

Whatever smiles or titters the bridge crew might have indulged in were well gone before Koval strode onto the bridge.

"We're leaving orbit," he announced.

"Are we now?" Tal's expression was just this close to a sneer. How many scars did he bear in service to an Empire that had spawned . . . *this.* But Koval was oblivious to the admiral's disdain. Whatever he'd found on Renaga had locked him into killer mode; before Tal could give the order, Koval took over.

"Helm, come about. Set scan to widest possible range and scan for any and all vessels in the area. The rest of you, to battle stations!"

"Energy distortion," Tuvok reported evenly. "Port side aft."

"I'm told no matter how often they redesign the cloak, there's always some leakage," Sisko mused, hoping he didn't sound as anxious as he felt. "Damn! Just a few minutes more and we'd have been able to put the planet between us and hide out. She's seen us, and she's in pursuit."

The icy silence between the Federation and the Empire had begun before he was born. He'd never seen a Romulan warbird before, and would have been perfectly content to live a long and fruitful life without ever having the privilege. He raised *Albatross*'s ancient shields and opened the intraship.

"Sisko to Selar and Zetha. Assume battle stations. We've got company, and we may have to do some fancy maneuvering between now and when *Okinawa*—uh-oh!"

Tuvok correctly interpreted that as "Romulan vessel powering weapons and decloaking." At Sisko's nod he opened a channel and, in the most imperious Romulan he could muster, announced: "Imperial warbird, this is a civilian vessel. Documentation is in order. We are prepared to be boarded and searched if you desire."

The hell we are, Sisko thought, trying to push the engines to give him a little bit more, but they were already giving him everything they had.

"Imperial warbird . . ." Had to give Tuvok credit for trying. ". . . why are you powering weapons? I repeat, we are a civilian vessel. We are prepared—"

The answer was a phaser blast that, had Sisko not flung the clumsy bird into evasive, would have blown them into smithereens. Instead it swatted the ship off course, drained the shields down to forty percent, and set off an alarm somewhere that Sisko hadn't even known the ship had.

"A little better aim and we're finished," he told Tuvok un-necessarily, readying to throw her into a new evasive pattern before the next blast. "C'mon, *Okinawa*, where are you?"

It was a peculiar artifact of Romulan ships that they were rather poorly designed acoustically. Depending upon the class of ship, they all made some sort of sound. Some hummed, some whined, some expressed themselves in a kind of low waspish buzz, but they all gave voice. One would think a species so acute of hearing would have reme-died this long ago. Or perhaps the ships were designed that way deliberately, to keep the crew always on edge, always combat ready.

As if the background noise weren't annoying enough, sea-soned veterans swore they could feel the weapons fire vibrate through the soles of their boots before they heard it. New re-cruits usually scoffed at them, until they felt it for themselves.

Some commanders, it was said, could feel the weapons even before they fired, the way a cat senses a thunderclap or a bird an earthquake long before a human does. After more than a century in space, Tal could feel the weapons in his bones. Even as Koval said, "Weapons, target and fire" he was out of his chair shouting "Belay that!"

But if Helm was nervous, Weapons was more so, and he'd triggered one phaser blast, however badly aimed, before he could stop himself. But Tal's wrath was not for him. He fixed his glare on Koval.

"Weapons, stand down!" Tal addressed his crew, though his eyes had locked with Koval's and he did not break his gaze. "You obey no order but mine. If Colonel Koval has a problem with that, he will have to speak to me. Now, you," he said to Koval. "What, by the Elements, do you think you're doing?"

"What am *I* doing?" Koval asked quietly. "Destroying a ship that should not be here in the first place."

"Admiral?" Comm said, opening the channel so he could

hear the voice from the merchanter demanding to know why they were being fired on. Tal listened, still glaring at Koval.

"That's one of our own aboard. If you kill him without knowing who or why—"

"A Romulan? On that rattletrap?" Koval waved the idea away. "Weapons, overtake and fire."

The weapons officer placed his hands on his knees, turning to look at Tal as if to say *I can be killed for less.*

Tal stalked over to stand all but nose to nose with Koval; they were about the same height, but Koval's very posture spoke of inbreeding, decadence, where Tal was disciplined to the bone.

Technically Tal Shiar of Koval's rank could commandeer the vessel and remove even an admiral from the bridge, but he'd find precious little assistance from Tal's handpicked crew if he did. Concomitantly, Tal could see to it that Koval fell down a turboshaft or did something else equally stupid that might be expected of someone not used to a warbird's hidden dangers, but he who had thus far had more lives than a *h'vart* might this time not survive. Stalemate.

"This is my ship," Tal told Koval quietly, biting each word off distinctly. "We don't fire unless I know why."

Koval held Tal's gaze, though the blue eyes were fierce, but his words were for the weapons officer. "Weapons, I told you to fire," he said, his words as distinct as Tal's.

"Admiral?" Helm sounded almost apologetic. "Unidentified vessel approaching at 107 mark 4. Configuration . . . Federation starship."

Chapter 18

Now this was a target Admiral Tal would have no problem firing on if need be. Shrugging Koval off, he locked into the command chair.

"Engage cloak and come about. Bring us in line with her and maintain." He looked at Koval "Did you know about this?"

"No," Koval said. "But it makes matters more interesting, doesn't it?"

It seems self-evident to describe space as three-dimensional, but it's something to keep in mind when talking about tactics. During the Romulan War, analogies to submarine warfare were often drawn, but they could help only so much. Yes, two submarines can confront each other up-to-down as well as sideways-to-sideways, but both would still be dependent upon the planet's gravity for maneuverability, and could never have approached each other upside down.

But there is no "up" in space.

Cultural historians often found it interesting to study old twenty-first-century space operas and note that two ships or even two fleets facing off for battle inevitably arrived at the point of confrontation right side up. No one ever dropped out of warp upside down or perpendicular relative to the observer.

In this particular instance, those on the warbird saw *Okinawa* emerge from the void at a 45-degree angle. If the warbird hadn't been cloaked, she would have seemed from the point of view of *Okinawa* to be listing acutely to starboard. From Sisko's perspective on *Albatross*, they were both askew, but his mind adjusted for it even as the ships themselves corrected for the discrepancy. What worried Sisko more was that *Albatross* had ended up smack in the path of both of them.

"An interesting tactical dilemma," Tuvok observed. "On the one hand, the warbird could simultaneously incinerate us and give *Okinawa* a glancing blow. But in doing so, she would have to decloak, and leave herself open to return fire from *Okinawa*. If we attempt to escape the line of fire, we risk giving the Romulans a clear shot at *Okinawa*; however—"

"Save it for the debriefing," Sisko said tightly, racking his brain for a tactical maneuver that would solve this. "I'm getting us out of here, and then I'm going aft to see where that alarm is coming from."

He threw the ship into a dive that structurally she shouldn't have been able to manage, and the clumsy bird juddered and groaned and squawked in protest, but she somehow managed it.

"What do they think they're doing?" Captain Leyton wondered. He'd been just about to hail *Albatross* when she suddenly began to plummet like her namesake after a fish. A glance at the energy distortion just behind where *Albatross* had been gave him his answer. "Oh, I see."

He began issuing orders calmly. "Yellow alert. Send standard challenge on all frequencies. Raise shields. Weapons at ready; stand by. And let me know if *Albatross* slows down long enough to engage a tractor beam."

* * *

"I can give you something for space sickness," Selar suggested, seeing all the color drain from Zetha's face as Sisko pulled the ship out of the dive, under *Okinawa*'s belly and, in a roller coaster ride of evasive maneuvers, out of the line of fire.

Zetha shook her head. "I'm fine. Tell me again about the test results. Is it really true?"

"Affirmative," Selar said. Battened down or not, she had completed an analysis of *hilopon*, and was now downloading all the data she had gathered on this mission into her tricorder, in the event they needed to abandon ship. "We have a potential cure, and perhaps the rudiments of a vaccine as well."

Despite her terror, Zetha managed a weak smile. "But if we die here, without letting the admiral and Dr. Crusher know . . ."

Selar had no answer. They had the Romulan datachips, and she would continue to copy her research in hopes of transferring both to *Okinawa*. Worry was illogical.

Too many Romulan commanders are trained only to fight, not to negotiate. Admiral Tal was not one of them. Looking daggers at Koval, he instructed his comm officer to answer *Okinawa*'s challenge at once.

"I can't help thinking that that starship is here because of you," he remarked to Koval as Comm fiddled with codes and frequencies, "I don't know what you did on Renaga, but I do know where you went. It seems to me that ever since we crossed into the Outmarches, my crew and I have risked our lives for the privilege of becoming an interplanetary incident at the behest of the Tal Shiar. And I find that most irritating."

"Admiral . . ." from Comm; he raised a hand that indicated: *Wait!*

"You may have power enough to commandeer my ship, but once on my ship, you are answerable to me," Tal continued, his eyes boring into Koval. "I have survived far greater threats than you. If you speak, if you so much as inhale deeply while I am speaking to their captain, I will give them the coordinates you beamed to. I wonder what they'd find there?"

Koval said nothing. He simply met Tal's gaze squarely. It was so seldom anyone challenged him that he found it refreshing. For a moment a pair of defiant green eyes flashed across his memory and he frowned slightly. Who might that have been? He had touched so many lives, watched so many die, so many beg for mercy, so many realize at the last moment how completely he had invaded and controlled their lives without their ever realizing it, that sometimes it was hard to remember them all. Ah, well. If the admiral wanted to run this part of the show, let him. He had other means at his disposal.

Tal nodded to Comm to open the channel.

"Commander Federation vessel," he said to the bearded human materializing on the forward screen, "challenge acknowledged. But you are as much in the wrong place as we. I await your explanation."

Ultimately the standoff took on the aspect of a chess game. Admiral Tal dropped the warbird's cloak (necessary after this much time, if he intended to have full power for weapons) but not her shields; Captain Leyton stood fast. For the next several minutes the two commanders traded accusations of trespass into the Zone, treaty violation, and whether there were Romulans with transmitters on Renaga. Tal made note of the frail-looking humanoid standing behind the bearded captain's shoulder occasionally whispering something into his ear. Each time he did so, the human would frown and go on speaking.

And where was *Albatross* during all of this? She had come to station-keeping just within transporter range of *Okinawa*, her situation precarious in all senses. She couldn't outrun a warbird, and even if she tried, it would only set the warbird in pursuit and *Okinawa* after her, and what a mess that would be. She couldn't hail out and *Okinawa* couldn't hail her without the Romulans hearing and knowing for a certainty that she was allied with *Okinawa*.

But Tuvok could monitor whatever conversations went on between the two larger ships, and he was doing that now.

Sisko, meanwhile, was getting itchy. *Albatross* couldn't budge until the two larger ships had finished their business, and whatever had set off the alarm was not reading on his instrument panel; he'd have to check it out onsite.

"I'll be in the engine room," he announced, never more glad to get out of the center seat, and headed aft.

"I thought so!" he said ruefully, seeing the readout from the port nacelle. The phaser blast had winged her, and all those subsequent fancy maneuvers had only made the damage worse. Hairline fractures spidered out from a ruptured conduit that leaked coolant ominously. Left alone, it would eventually go critical. Sisko was confident he could patch her up well enough to get her home, but first he'd have to let her cool down.

"Steady as she goes, old girl!" Sisko comforted her, shutting down the portside matter/antimatter pod and watching the temperature monitor begin to drop back within normal parameters. An hour or so from now, he could begin to make repairs. If they were still here an hour from now.

He took his time walking back to the controls, stopped to look at the magnificent ruse of the storage containers lined up monolithically along the narrow passageway. The holo transmitter was hidden away in one of them. Only the main lab module was open and active, and Selar and Zetha were at work there, their heads together, deep in concentration on . . . something.

Sisko almost approached them; he wanted to ask Selar about the results of the blood tests. But he wasn't sure he could face Zetha right now. Besides, he'd felt a lot better since they'd returned to the ship; the mysterious cough was gone. If he did have Catalyst, he didn't want to know until he absolutely had to.

"Tell me that freighter isn't yours, Captain Leyton, and you wouldn't mind my destroying it," Tal challenged. Dax took it as a hopeful sign that the Romulan was opting to talk.

"I could never sanction the destruction of a civilian vessel. . . ." Leyton began, but Dax decided it was time to intervene.

"May I?" Dax interjected and, without waiting for an answer, somehow deftly diverted attention to himself. "Admiral Tal, I am Ambassador Curzon Dax. The freighter *is* ours," he said, eyes on the forward screen, grateful he couldn't see the look on Leyton's face. "Sent as a scout to investigate reports of Romulan transmitters on Renaga, just as your government sent a similar vessel to Imago IX some months ago to see if we had established a footprint there. Your scout found nothing, ours has found something."

He let that sink in for a fraction of a second.

"Now, then, we both know there's something on Renaga we are both interested in, the very reason you sent infiltrators, and that something is *hilopon* . . ."

Tal seemed to hesitate. "Yes," he said. "Yes, of course."

"Let's not waste time then, Admiral. The Empire wants *hilopon*; the Federation wants *hilopon*. There are currently no official communications between our governments, but you and I can initiate contact with the Renagans and work out a solution that will enable us both to obtain what we want without involving our respective bureaucracies."

Tal's eyes narrowed. Finally, he said, "Agreed."

"Excellent!" Dax smiled benevolently. "Then we can beam down together. But first, a tradeoff. If we say we never detected your transmitters, you overlook our little freighter."

"I need to consult with one of my . . . aides . . ." Tal said, his eyes sliding to something or someone off screen.

"Of course," Dax said, and both sides muted comm while they consulted.

"Well, I'll be damned!" Sisko said, returning to the conn in time to hear some of this exchange. "The Old Man comes through again. We may get out of this alive after all."

"*Hilopon?*" Tal demanded of Koval.

"An absolutely essential medicinal," Koval assured him. "You've heard rumors of a resurgence of the Gnawing on some of the colony worlds?"

Tal wondered how much Koval knew he knew. "Perhaps."

"Our scientists have reason to believe *hilopon* could be the cure," Koval said evenly. He watched a momentary doubt cross Tal's hawklike face. "Or did you really think we came all this way because of a couple of transmitters? Be careful what you do here, Admiral. Diplomacy is not for amateurs."

A lesser man would have lost his temper. Tal almost did. But unless he could make the Tal Shiar operative's death look like an accident, his crew would be forfeit. The thought stayed him. It was the only thing that could.

On *Okinawa*, Captain Leyton was scowling at Curzon.

"What in blazes is *hilopon* and why do we want it?"

"Bacteria. Occurs naturally in the soil here. May have some use as a topical medication," Curzon said, his back to the screen so he couldn't be lip-read. "We want it because the Romulans want it. It's called diplomacy."

Admiral Tal had made up his mind.

"There will be no mention of an alien freighter in my logs, Curzon Dax. And if I make no mention of a freighter, neither will any member of my crew," he said for Koval's benefit. "I'm sure you'll agree that what you thought were

Romulan transmissions were really only artifacts. Natural occurrences prevalent in this region of space."

"Agreed!" Curzon smiled. "Isn't it fortuitous that we both arrived here on the wings of rumor? Shall we discuss when and how we shall make contact with the Renagans?"

Albatross was too bulky to fit through the shuttlebay doors, so *Okinawa* took her in tow.

"Tell your crew to gather their personal belongings and prepare to beam aboard, Ben," Leyton told him. "That damaged engine isn't going to hold for long."

"But, sir, she's not—" Sisko started to say, before he realized that of course the Romulans would be listening in. "I mean, yessir, we're on our way."

It only now occurred to him that there was no way they could bring the ship home with them. *Okinawa* could hardly tow her all the way home, and even under full power, it would take her far too long to limp out of the Zone in her present condition, unarmed, and with the Romulans now alerted to her presence. The contingency plans they'd had in place to protect Heisenberg's little modifications from prying eyes would have to be enacted, and Sisko would have to be the one to enact them.

"Dr. Heisenberg's going to be heartbroken," Sisko said disconsolately, closing the channel.

"Are you in need of assistance?" Tuvok asked. His carrybag slung over one shoulder, the orchid balanced precariously atop the case of datachips, he was prepared to leave without so much as a glance backward.

"Negative," Sisko said as Selar and Zetha also arrived, ready for transport. "You all go on ahead. I need to initiate an antimatter breach. And I'd like a minute alone to tell the old girl goodbye."

He watched first Selar and Zetha, then Tuvok shimmer away in the transporter beam, then went aft to work his magic. When the ship blew, it had to look from the Romulan point of view as if it were an accident. He had no doubt they realized they'd damaged the port nacelle. All he had to do was make them think the damage was enough to cause the antimatter pods to lose their magnetic containment, causing the antimatter to release, interact with the normal matter, and annihilate the vessel structure.

Sisko implemented the sequence just as he'd learned it in reverse at the Academy. He estimated he had about three minutes to get clear before she blew, and hurried to the sleeping quarters for his kit.

Tuvok had left the Romulan transmitter behind.

They had the datachips as evidence, not to mention Zetha. Sisko had overheard Curzon's agreement with the Romulans to ignore the two transmitters if she ignored *Albatross*. There probably wasn't any reason to bring this transmitter along, but for some reason Sisko couldn't get his mind off it.

Just then he felt the tractor beam release. *Okinawa* was about to put some distance between herself and the doomed *Albatross*, he had less than a minute left, and he'd better get moving.

"*Okinawa* to *Albatross*," he heard Leyton saying tightly. "Let's go, Ben, let's go!"

Koval watched the starship moving away from the disabled freighter, then watched the freighter implode. Minutes before tactical had informed him that the starship had lowered her shields and made use of her transporter, not once but three times, the third time several minutes after the first two. Koval would study the data later and decide whether he believed the intercepted comm signals, or whether the ship had been destroyed deliberately. Why did he care? he asked himself. Doubtless whoever had beamed onto the starship had taken their evidence with them. Still Koval was not overly concerned. He had enough fallback positions to erase all trace of his involvement in this venture once he returned home. Didn't he? For possibly the first time in his career, Koval was visited with a little trickle of doubt.

Just his luck that the only ship available to bring him here had been commanded by one of the few officers in the Imperial Fleet who had the intestinal fortitude to defy his order to destroy the freighter and damn the consequences.

What bothered Koval most was how the ungainly little freighter, followed by the starship, had known to come to Renaga. They must have had far more to go on than Cinchona/Thamnos's sloppy academic paper touting *hilopon*. Had the idiot's father blabbed?

That thought led Koval to another uneasy thought: He would have to notify the old man personally that his son was dead and, if necessary, instruct him to remain silent. An unpleasant duty, but one he must perform.

And as he knew his Rigelians, he doubted the lockjawed Papaver had talked. There was something here he wasn't seeing. What was it?

Leaving the warbird's bridge, where Tal's relief, a sardonic old veteran who had lost family to the Tal Shiar, was more than happy to see the back of him, Koval repaired to the safe room hidden in the bowels of every warbird, equipped with everything a Tal Shiar officer might need, whether one was assigned or not, and sealed himself off for the duration. He had much work to do.

"What took you so long, Ben?" Leyton had come down to sickbay personally. "For a minute there, we thought we were going to lose you. No one said you had to go down with the ship."

"Just saying goodbye," Sisko said. He nodded toward the transmitter. "And wanted to make sure we brought all the evidence."

"Not worth risking your life for," was Leyton's opinion.

"You're an innocent, Ben. Don't you know if there isn't enough evidence, you can always invent some?"

"Sir?" Sisko asked, but Leyton had moved on.

Under orders from Starfleet Command, the away team had been beamed directly into quarantine in sickbay. Selar assured them it would not be for long.

Curzon Dax and Admiral Tal had a less than productive encounter with the Renagan Council of Elders.

"Isn't this a violation of your Federation's touted Prime Directive?" Tal remarked once they'd finally beamed down to Renaga and met face to face.

Curzon smiled as they strode together up the broad steps of the Council building. "Not in this instance. The Renagans have had outworld visitors before. Some have actually beamed down in their presence and been ignored. The Renagans simply refuse to believe that anyone lives on the lights in their sky. You'll see."

The meeting, if such it could be called, was exactly as Curzon said it would be. The nine doddering old men studied the two visitors, then conferred among themselves before their leader spoke.

"You say you are not of this world. That is not possible. Therefore we know you are lying, and we do not acknowledge you."

As one, the Elders turned their backs on them.

Tal took a step forward, as if to argue, but a gesture from Curzon stayed him.

"They did actually speak to us," he whispered. "It's more than they've done for anyone else. It's a beginning; let it be enough for now. If we try to push it, they'll interpret it as weakness. There will be other times."

Tal clenched his teeth in frustration. "Fools!" he growled as he and Curzon walked together down the broad steps of the Council building, completely ignored by the passersby, and returned to where they had beamed down. "To stand there and speak to us, yet tell us we do not exist—! The urge to knock their rotten old heads together . . ."

"Try negotiating with Klingons sometime," Curzon muttered. "We shall report back to our respective governments and let them decide what to do."

He and Tal eyed each other with mutual respect. "*Jolan tru*, my newfound friend," Curzon said. "Perhaps someday we'll meet again."

"After half a century of silence?" Tal snorted, but then thought about it. He shrugged. "Who knows?"

There is an art to leaving the battleground when no battle has taken place. In a graceful maneuver worthy of a Strauss waltz, warbird and starship pirouetted away from each other under impulse and, their navigators having plotted the quickest route out of the Zone, turned their backs on each other, and catapulted into warp and away.

No way of knowing what happened aboard the warbird. Aboard *Okinawa*, a medical conference was under way.

"This is the result of introducing a serum derived from the blood of the dead Romulan on Quirinus into a sample of active Catalyst virus," Selar was saying, her data safe in *Okinawa*'s databanks and being relayed to Starfleet Medical on Earth. "This, the result of a similar serum derived from blood samples Dr. Crusher took from Zetha before we left Earth, also interacting with live Catalyst virus."

There was no need to give a play-by-play. Everyone watching, from McCoy to Crusher to Uhura to the away team to *Okinawa*'s medical staff, who had cleared the team to leave quarantine once they'd seen the test results, could see what was happening. Dr. Selar's two experimental sera were gobbling up the Catalyst virus faster than it could replicate.

"There's your vaccine," Crusher said with a nod toward

Zetha. "It's you. For whatever reason, probably something at the mitochondrial level, the disease didn't have time to activate in your bloodstream before it mutated. We've had the solution right under our noses all along."

"Not entirely, Dr. Crusher," Selar said as Zetha wondered where to put herself. "We still have to ascertain why the same gene sequence that renders some individuals immune to Catalyst also mutates from a deadly form to a killed form suitable for vaccine, given enough time."

"Not something its creators anticipated, I'm sure!" McCoy growled, then reconsidered. "Or maybe they did. Be convenient for some Romulan bioterrorist to have the cure handy once the disease had killed enough people to create panic. I knew Thamnos hadn't done this on his own!"

"It's convenient for us, too," was Uhura's opinion. "With the help of those datachips, we can track down any additional 'seeds' in Federation territory. I'm sure at least some of them would be happy to serve as *in situ* providers of vaccine."

Tuvok had in fact already begun tracking. "An interesting addendum to the mystery on Tenjin," he reported. "Two seeds were in fact deployed to two separate environmental domes. Both eventually met up in a third dome and were killed in a transport accident before they could spread the disease further."

"And Sliwon—?" Uhura wanted to know.

"It seems our snake-oil salesman was the vector there. A Rigelian by birth, who had traveled extensively in Romulan territory, and claims he has no idea how he became infected."

"Oh, I'll just bet!" Uhura said, making a note to have the man extracted from Sliwon. She was going to enjoy interrogating him.

With her away team safe and *Okinawa* on its way home, the source of the pestilence identified and a cure being implemented, Uhura found herself breathing normally for the first time in days. Had they actually solved this? There were a thousand loose ends to tie up, not least of which was somehow getting word back to Cretak so that she could take steps toward tracking down the seeds inside the Empire and stop the spread of the disease before both governments officially got involved.

And then what? What was she going to tell the C-in-C and what would he do with the information he gave her? Whoever had initiated this on the Romulan side was still at large and could easily do something like this again. But was it worth hurling accusations back and forth and perhaps making the already uneasy detente with the Romulans that much more uneasy? Uhura had no answers.

That's why you're a spy and not a diplomat! she told herself, halfway tempted to contact Curzon and ask him what he thought she should do. Should she risk that while *Okinawa* was still in transit? Perhaps best to wait until her team had returned home. As if she needed an excuse to see Curzon again.

"It's ironic," Zetha told Tuvok.

"I beg your pardon?"

Finally tired of roaming the corridors of the starship, marveling at everything, the young Romulan had come to rest in *Okinawa*'s crew lounge, where a helpful ensign who had a weakness for girls with green eyes had initiated her into the marvels of something called a hot fudge sundae. She was scooping the last of the sticky confection out of the bottom of the dish and licking her fingers while she spoke.

"This whole situation," she explained. "My being programmed to be some sort of killing machine, and ending up providing the cure instead. Aemetha would call that irony. Would have called that irony." The green eyes suddenly welled with tears. "I don't even know if Aemetha is still alive. . . ."

She let the spoon drop into the bowl, suddenly nauseated by what she had been eating. Tuvok watched and took note.

"You did this, all of this, in hope of protecting Aemetha?" he began.

"And the little ones. So many little ones. She helped everyone who came to her. I hoped I could live long enough to be like her. . . ."

"You have already helped more people than you know," Tuvok suggested, alluding to the vaccine that Selar was even now replicating in *Okinawa*'s sickbay. "And will serve to protect countless more for the foreseeable future. Ironic, indeed."

Neither spoke for the next few moments. Behind Tuvok's shoulder, Zetha could see the phenomenon of stars slipping by at maximum warp. On the table in front of her, the unfinished sundae seemed as much a miracle. She pushed the dish away.

Tuvok rose to go.

"Doubtless Admiral Uhura will question you in greater depth when we arrive on Earth, about your training, about those who trained you."

Zetha shook her head. "We *ghilik* were housed separately from 'true' Romulans. There was only one man. We were instructed to call him 'Lord.' I never knew his name."

"Another irony," Tuvok decided.

The lecture Zetha had been dreading never came. Instead, Tuvok let his hand rest for a moment on her head, the gesture of a loving father. Zetha did not look up until he was gone.

From his safe room deep within the warbird, Koval had been busy. Reports from Imperial worlds where the seeds had been planted were uneven at best. In some places, thousands had died before the entity infecting their bodies had been identified and they were quarantined. Once quarantined, all those infected died, but no new cases were reported. In still other places, the numbers of dead ranged from a few hundred to a score or less. In some places, the infection never "took" at all. The same was true for the worlds within the Outmarches so affected. And there had been no new cases reported in nearly a week.

Ah, well, the experiment in and of itself had been interesting. Koval wondered what the final numbers on Federation worlds would be. He would know soon enough, even as he would know how the revelation of the datachips would affect interplanetary relations.

There was no way the datachips could be traced to him. He had liquidated the remaining *ghilik* before he'd left the homeworld. Their barracks had been converted to a storage facility, all trace of habitation removed. The datachips would reveal the identities of beings with Romulan-sounding names who had never existed. Should the Federation be foolish enough to reveal those names, the Praetor, the Imperial Senate, and even the Continuing Committee would enjoy a good laugh at their expense.

Still, Koval was disappointed. He had hoped the experiment might continue until the number of dead had reached critical mass. There was a point in the bureaucratic mind, Koval had discovered, where the body count was deemed unacceptable. A few thousand dead was dismissed as a misfortune, but a few hundred thousand was judged an obvious conspiracy. It was from that point that he had hoped to operate, until that idiot Thamnos had ruined everything.

If only the fool had focused on the goal a little longer! The Federation would have rattled its sabers and accused the Empire of bioterrorism, and then, while they were still recovering from the embarrassment of being told those datachips were meaningless fakes, perhaps created by the Federation itself, since there were no such Romulans as those catalogued on the chips, Koval would have produced his trump card.

The source of the datachips? An overly ambitious Federa-

tion citizen trying to grab at a little glory, falsifying documents—as witness his earlier debacle with a paper on Bendii
Syndrome! Koval had kept copies of all Thamnos's "research," and if the Federation operatives denied they'd found
the datachips in Thamnos's possession, he could produce
the knife, no doubt containing traces of the murderer's
DNA. The accusations and counteraccusations could go on
for years.

It would also have served as a test case for creating a
larger pandemic at some point in the future. Ah, well. The
only thing for Koval to do now was to make sure all traces of
involvement were removed.

Which reminded him. Best get the call to Papaver Thamnos over with before they reached home.

"Go to bed?" Benjamin Sisko echoed Jennifer's words as
she grabbed the front of his tunic and began to tug him
along with her. "It's the middle of the afternoon! I'm not
even tired."

"Who said anything about sleeping?" Jennifer wondered
whimsically, still tugging. Laughing, Sisko found himself
being pulled toward the bedroom. "Jake's on a class trip to
the arboretum this afternoon; I don't have to pick him up for
another hour and a half."

"A man can get into an awful lot of mischief in an hour
and a half. . . ." Sisko mused as the bedroom door slid softly
shut behind them.

"Don't owe you anything anymore!" Papaver Thamnos
said stonily once he fully understood Koval's message about
his son. "Don't know what your involvement was, but he
wasn't dead before you went looking for him. Got nothing to
say to you. Had nothing to say to that other fellow, got nothing to say to you. We're finished. Go away."

"What 'other fellow'?" Koval said, more sharply than he

intended. But Papaver Thamnos was playing with his hounds. A moment later he terminated the transmission.

The ensign who had brought Zetha the sundae approached her table after Tuvok left, but his smile reminded her too much of Tahir's, and she excused herself and left the lounge. There was something she had to do.

Wending her way through the corridors to find sickbay on her own without asking for directions, she found Selar conferring with *Okinawa*'s chief medical officer. Seeing Zetha, the Vulcan raised an inquiring eyebrow in her direction.

"When you have time," Zetha said, a little shyly, "may I have my freckles back?"

Epilogue

It was mop-up time.

The planet Renaga was placed under joint Federation/Romulan jurisdiction. A Romulan warbird and a Federation starship would become permanent fixtures in orbit for the next little while. In addition to a raft of diplomats, teams of observers from both sides, including a joint medical team, would be stationed down-planet. Their final report would indicate that *hilopon* was in fact not the panacea Thamnos had described in his paper. It worked only under specialized conditions—the missing "ingredient" turned out to be exposure to a particular rare element in Renaga's sun—which meant that the stuff was useless once it was taken offworld. And if the Renagans didn't want visitors on their world—the Council of Elders was still ignoring them, but some of the ordinary citizens from the villages nearest the observer site had made friendly overtures, though it was too soon to tell whether the Elders or the villagers would win—the curative effects of its only valuable resource would remain limited at best. Those in the know were of the opinion that Renaga would eventually prove of little interest to either side and, given the costs of maintaining a presence there, abandoned to its own devices.

Upon condition of his donating a half-liter of blood to be transformed into a vaccine to inoculate the citizens of Sliwon against the Catalyst virus, the noisy Rigelian huckster whom Tuvok had confronted in the Sliwoni marketplace was eventually released after a very thorough questioning. He steadfastly denied any involvement with Romulan authorities or any member of the Thamnos family. He left Sliwon immediately after his release.

Unbeknownst to him, a subcutaneous transceiver, legal under Sliwoni law, was injected at the site where the blood was drawn, making it possible for the authorities to track his movements throughout the Neutral Zone for a period of half a year. If he kept his nose clean for that amount of time, the transceiver would go dormant, and he'd be free to disappear once again into the hordes of itinerant peddlers the galaxy over.

Citizen Jarquin of Quirinus received a carefully worded document from one Citizen Leval of Romulus, which informed him, with regret, of his sons' deaths. Soon other Quirinians began requesting information about their lost kin, but received no answer, and Citizen Leval's sources for the information were never revealed. While some Quirinians steadfastly refused to believe that everyone who had ever emigrated from their world to Romulus was dead, conscription and further emigration trickled to a standstill, and most Quirinians began to rethink their relationship with the Empire.

The mysterious illness that had caused pockets of death in several Quirinian provinces burned itself out and did not reappear. The walled up districts were razed, and memorials to the dead were soon buried under a new fall of snow.

Tuvok's preliminary research on the identities of the seeds on Tenjin was confirmed by a thorough census of all persons arriving in the domes over the past three years. It was decided that the two Romulans, both posing as Vulcans, who had died in the tram accident at about the time the first cancer patients began appearing were most likely the only seeds sent to Tenjin, but the entire indigenous population was inoculated against the Catalyst virus all the same.

The earliest casualties on the Federation side, the seventeen Rigelians from a single extended family, were discovered to be members of a clan that had been engaged in a land dispute since the time of Papaver Thamnos's great-grandfather. Uhura thought that sufficient to at least begin an investigation into the Thamnos family's recent activities, but she was warned off by the Federation Council. The Rigel worlds were deemed too valuable, and the Thamnos family too deeply embedded in the governments of those worlds, to risk offending them. Despite her objections, Uhura was told, "Hands off," and was obliged to comply.

She had been pondering secure ways to tell Cretak everything her team had discovered, when she received even more infuriating news.

It arrived in the form of a bland-looking young man from the C-in-C's office, who handed her a padd whose contents were retina-scan classified, and waited silently and at attention while the padd scanned the admiral and she read the cover page.

"Did Commander Starfleet tell you why he was sending you with this instead of simply messaging me?" Uhura asked the young man, wondering if he had any idea what was in the document.

"Security, sir. All he told me. And I'm to await your reply."

"I see," Uhura said carefully. "It may take me a while to read this. Would you care to sit down? What's your name?"

"Thank you, sir, no. Luther Sloan."

He sounds like he thinks I'm interrogating him even when I'm just trying to be friendly, Uhura noted. *Very well, let him stand.* What she read in the C-in-C's memo made her all but forget the young man was there.

No! she thought. *He can't do this to me! Hands off the Thamnos cartel—well, fine. Local politics, nothing I can do about it, except maybe plant a few extra Listeners on Rigel*

*and see what if anything they came up with. But if I comply
with this, thousands more Romulans may die! And the source
or sources behind Catalyst may never be stopped.*

She was too seasoned and too well trained to let her
thoughts show on her face. She could feel Sloan's eyes on
her, though she knew if she glanced up at him she would
find him contemplating the view out the window. He was
one of those people who knew when he was being watched,
and could glance away a millisecond before the person he
was watching attempted to make eye contact.

A natural spy.

So why was he working for the C-in-C and not for her?
Uhura wondered, determined to do a background check on
him soonest. For now, she deactivated the padd and glanced
up at Sloan, who was in fact looking out the window, though
he did make eye contact with the admiral once he heard the
beep of the padd recoding itself.

"Message, Admiral?" he asked, his voice absolutely devoid of inflection.

Uhura put her not inconsiderable acting talent into a
show of reluctant compliance when she said. "Inform Commander Starfleet: Message received and acknowledged. No
further action contemplated."

It was apparently the only message Sloan was prepared to
take back to his boss. He accepted the padd from Uhura's
hands, and all but clicked his heels before turning on them
sharply and going back the way he came.

The door had not entirely slid closed behind him before
Uhura had pulled his file.

Name, rank, serial number. Sloan, Luther, born on Earth,
near Pretoria, South Africa. Academy graduate, though from
one of the satellite campuses. Now why, Uhura wondered,
did someone born on Earth choose to attend the Academy
on another planet? It was the only quirk in a record that was
too perfect, but impossible to challenge.

No, check that. One more odd thing. Under "personal statement/goals," Luther Sloan had written "to someday be Head of Starfleet Intelligence."

If she hadn't met the man, Uhura might have taken that for what it was obviously meant to be—a brash young man's egotistical fantasy, a little bit of top-of-the-world-Ma showing off. But there was nothing brash about the Luther Sloan who had just walked through that door.

This was no fantasy. Behind that bland mask of a face was a man driven by ambition. He'd meant every word. The very statement was a dare. He was showing his hand in the most blatant way possible, and daring anyone to challenge him.

"Head of SI? Not while I live and breathe, Mr. Sloan!" Uhura said very quietly, wiping the screen and any trace that she'd been prying into his file. Then she focused her attention on the message from Starfleet Command.

The virus heretofore designated Catalyst, it stated, did not exist. The entity which had claimed 1,076 Federation lives was judged to be a rare and self-limiting mutant off-shoot of R4b2 Rigelian fever, and precautionary vaccinations were just that, precautionary. No additional outbreaks of said R-fever had been reported effective this date, medical experts (Uhura wondered if Crusher, Selar, or McCoy were among them) were on record indicating no further outbreaks were anticipated, case closed.

Any rumors about an unusual fever affecting Romulans were just that, rumors, and had no connection whatsoever with R4b2 R-fever or the mythological Catalyst. There was no reason to suspect bioterrorism, and no information about the R-fever outbreaks would be relayed to any individual within the Romulan Empire or elsewhere, end of report.

Even as Sloan stood there pretending he wasn't looking at her, Uhura had been running scenarios in her head, trying to think of a way around the interdict. There weren't any. Once she gave the C-in-C her word, her hands were tied.

Now, if Sloan had arrived five minutes earlier . . .

Luxury, Zetha decided, is a hot shower. Not just a mob of you lined up to make a quick pass under the sonics to kill the bugs in your hair the way we did in the House, not the rusty lukewarm trickle that was all the plumbing in Aemetha's house would ever yield, but hot running water coursing down your body, first thing in the morning, every single day. Maybe again at night before you went to bed, or any time you wanted. A real hot-water shower, the water pulsing so hard it hurt, or caressing you, flowing over you, washing away all the bad things, so that you always looked forward to the new day.

Luxury is clothes that fit, that have never been worn by anyone else. Luxury is knowing that you can fill your belly without anyone else going hungry. Luxury is knowing you have a right to live, a right to your own identity that no one can take from you.

But with that luxury comes uncertainty. When you have something to push against, the pushing becomes everything. When the fear is taken away, it's as if the ground you're standing on has suddenly slipped out from under you.

Who am I? What am I? Where do I go from here? She had never had time to ask those questions before, and now that she did, she wasn't sure she wanted the answers.

Dr. Selar had restored her freckles exactly where they belonged. She was still a *ghilik* with no family name, but that didn't seem to matter here. She still wore the sash Aemetha had given her; Tahir's smooth stone was still in her pocket. And she had an important piece of information, courtesy of Dr. McCoy.

"Whoever told you you're a hybrid never really studied your codes," he told her, having completed one last favor for Uhura and double-checked the initial tests Crusher had done by performing a complete genetic scan. "Or else they flat-out lied. You're as Romulan as I am human."

And? she thought. That bit of knowledge was at once a shock and an indifference. Had someone, perhaps the lord so aloof she never learned his name, manipulated her data from birth so as to control her all her life? Did it mean she could return to Romulus and demand her birthright as a fullblood? Did she care?

"If you were human, I'd recommend counseling," was Crusher's opinion. "After a lifetime of being told you don't exist, you're suddenly faced with a lot of choices."

"Am I?" Zetha asked. It had never occurred to her that she would be free to decide. She assumed the reason Admiral Uhura had asked to see her was in order to give her instructions for her next mission. Wasn't it obvious that she must now be used as a weapon against her own people?

Don't anticipate, she told herself. *Wait until you hear what the admiral has to say.*

For what seemed like the thousandth time, Uhura reread her resignation letter, fiddled with the commas and semicolons, saved it, and considered. Her perfectly manicured finger hovered over the Send button and almost came down. She thought of her Listeners still in the field, the numberless spiderweb threads flung out from this office across two quadrants, constantly sending information her way and resonating to her guidance. Not for the first time, she wondered what would happen to all of them if she resigned.

What makes you think you're the only one who can do this? she asked herself. *Offhand you can think of half a dozen people you've handpicked and trained yourself who could do as well or better.*

But what guarantee did she have that the C-in-C would take her suggestions and replace her with one of those handpicked agents? The answer, she knew, was no guarantee at all. For some reason, she couldn't get Sloan out of her mind.

Her finger hovered over the Send button yet again. *Who do you think you're kidding?* she asked herself ruefully, before putting the resignation letter away for another year just as Thysis buzzed Zetha in.

"You wanted to see me, Admiral?"

Uhura motioned her to a chair. The girl sat on the edge. She was as petite as Sisko was large, but her coiled and waiting posture at the end of this mission was a mirror image of his at the beginning.

"I have some news for you," Uhura began. "It's about your Godmother."

"When . . . how—?" *Please!* Zetha asked whatever gods or Elements might be paying attention. *Please tell me . . .*

"Before the away team even left Earth, I sent word back to Senator Cretak that you and your message had arrived safely. I told her what you'd told Tuvok during your interrogation, in an attempt to get confirmation from her that your story checked out. At the same time, I had one of my Listeners search for Aemetha."

Admiral Uhura paused and smiled. "Your Godmother is alive and well. In fact, my Listener reports that Senator Cretak has given the truth to your original story and more or less adopted her. I'm told she intends to put forward some legislation to pay some attention to the street urchins. She's doubtful it will pass the full Senate, but she indicated that if it doesn't, she will at least see to Aemetha's house."

Zetha said nothing. If Aemetha had escaped the Tal Shiar's reach, likely Tahir had as well. Did she dare ask? If the admiral knew, she would have told her. *Don't ask for too much*, she thought. She heard Uhura sigh.

"It's been a luxury being able to communicate with Cretak this far," the admiral said, almost to herself. "I'm afraid what happened on Renaga—even though officially it never happened—will make communication that much more difficult from now on. But—" Uhura seemed to remember she was thinking out loud. She stopped herself and smiled again at Zetha. "Neither your problem nor your concern, my dear. Do you have any idea what you would like to do next? Or have we yet convinced you that we don't intend to kill you?"

Zetha suppressed a small smile, then grew serious. The question frankly puzzled her.

"I assumed I would now serve you."

"Is that what you'd like to do?" Uhura asked. "You don't have to, you know. You're free to do whatever you want."

"But—" Zetha started to say, then stopped herself. She didn't even know what she was going to ask.

"You can go back home if you want. We can arrange for Zetha's 'death' and give you a new identity, in case you're concerned that the Tal Shiar might go looking for you . . ." Uhura began, ticking the suggestions off on her fingers.

To see Godmother again, Zetha thought, *and maybe find Tahir. To create a life for myself as—what? I have a scrounger's skills, and what Selar taught me in the lab, and I now speak Federation Standard, a skill I would hardly boast about on Romulus. Where would I go; who would I be?*

". . . you're welcome to stay on Earth as long as you wish," Uhura was saying. "We owe you immeasurably for giving us the means to stop Catalyst. You're free to go wherever you wish, be anything you wish to be."

And have Sisko invite me to share dinner with his family, as he did on the ship, and make me jambalaya. To learn from Tuvok's wisdom, perhaps to count "the three doctors" among my friends as well. And to have Admiral Uhura's gratitude. This is something I must consider. . . .

"Someone has to speak directly to Cretak before the wall of silence grows thicker still," she said. "If you wish, I will be that someone."

"You're under no obligation—" Uhura started to say.

"I know that, Admiral. But it is what I wish to do."

"Are you certain?" Uhura asked. "Because once you're inside, we may not be able to get you out again. If you wanted to get out."

This time Zetha did shrug. "I will not know that until I go back in." Then she smiled. "But, Scrounger's Second Law: Hide in plain sight. If there's a way out, I will find it."

Uhura hesitated. Was this the right thing to do? Zetha's life had been commandeered from the very beginning. She hadn't asked to be abandoned by her family, recruited by the Tal Shiar, transformed into an instrument of death, not even to be sent by Cretak as an exile among strangers. What right did anyone have to ask her to return to that world?

But by volunteering to return, wasn't she saying "I choose!" and wresting control from those who had presumed to control her? Zetha needed this as much as Uhura needed a messenger inside the Empire.

"Very well, if you're sure," Uhura said now, making arrangements even as she accepted Zetha's offer. When she'd done, she beamed at the girl. "Whatever you ultimately decide, I'll see to it. Hailing frequencies open, young lady, always."

Zetha beamed right back at her. Her parting words were, "Tell Lieutenant Sisko I'll be back for the *jambalaya!*"

Yes, word was already on its way to Cretak. While it might take weeks or even months to reach the senator's pointed ears, oh, well, the genie was out of the bottle and no way for Uhura to stop it. She wondered if Sloan had made particular note, during his carefully trained scanning of her office that, like a psychiatrist's office, there were two doors, so as each new visitor arrived, the previous one could, if necessary, leave by a different door to avoid being seen by the subsequent one.

She had sent Sloan out the way he'd come in. Zetha had left in the opposite direction.

Who will spy on the spies? Uhura wondered as, with a bitter smile, she considered the order she'd just received. She was pleased that Catalyst would have no diplomatic or military repercussions, but furious at the thought of its perpetrators' escaping unscathed. Had she not been able to dispatch a Listener to Cretak, she'd have been more furious still, but a Pyrrhic victory was better than none.

And it wouldn't surprise her, months or even years from now, to receive a return message from Cretak saying that her government, too, had informed her that Catalyst did not exist.

We and the Empire are more alike than different, Uhura thought, *but equally perverse!*

How many such "nonevents" had she had to countenance in her intelligence career? How many more could she stand before she snapped? With a sigh she again opened the resignation letter she'd kept on file since the day she took this job.

Sisko couldn't bear to look at Dr. Heisenberg's face once he'd told him how *Albatross* had met her death. He thought at first that the older man was going to cry. He did turn his back on Sisko for a moment, and Sisko thought he saw his shoulders shake. Then Heisenberg straightened with a sigh and said wryly: "Oh, dear!"

"Dr. Heisenberg, I'm really sorry . . ." Sisko began.

"No, no, dear boy, it's I who should be sorry for you," Heisenberg said. "*Albatross* was just the prototype. I've much more interesting gadgets up my sleeve. I'm more concerned with the amount of paperwork this will generate. Forms, requisitions, explanations . . ." The old man sighed. "But you, to have to sacrifice your ship on your first command . . ." He clapped Sisko on the shoulder sympathetically.

"But she wasn't—that is, I wasn't—" Sisko said, but then he realized Heisenberg was right. He'd wondered why, even with the relative success of the mission, even reunited with

Jennifer and Jake, he'd still felt a niggling sadness. He'd have to think about that some more. "Guess I'll think twice before accepting another command, sir. But I'm honored that *Albatross* was my first."

Long after he'd left Heisenberg tinkering with his latest gadget and returned to his post on *Okinawa*, Sisko realized what he'd said. *Accepting another command?* he thought. *Me? I'm an engineer. I've ducked the command track all my life. What was I thinking? What bizarre Freudian slip of the tongue made me say that? Could Curzon have been right?*

He'd barely arrived in the engine room when a Level-2 diagnostic soon occupied his entire attention. He never noticed Curzon observing him from the upper level, a knowing smile on his otherwise angelic face.

Uhura left the resignation letter on one screen and opened another to her to-do list. Notify all members of her away team, plus the medical team, of Commander Starfleet's instructions, each of them individually so as to keep cross talk at a minimum. Brace for the howling she knew she'd get from Dr. Crusher's direction. Maybe she'd talk to Crusher last.

Tuvok was already back on the *Billings*, Selar on her science vessel, Sisko in *Okinawa*'s engine room. McCoy was out on the lake communing with the trout. She'd probably have to bark at Crusher to make her settle down, or let her oversee the vaccination program on the starbases to keep her too busy to be angry but, ultimately, all was well.

Uhura reread her resignation letter one more time, and one more time her finger hovered over the SEND button. With a sigh, she filed the letter for another time and went back to work, for now.

About the Author

Margaret Wander Bonanno is the author of *Dwellers in the Crucible* and *Strangers from the Sky,* as well as two s/f trilogies, *The Others* and *Preternatural.* Born in Brooklyn, New York, she now lives on the Left Coast. Visit her website at www.margaretwanderbonanno.com.

STAR TREK®

STARGAZER: THREE

MICHAEL JAN FRIEDMAN

WHEN A TRANSPORTER MISHAP DEPOSITS A
BEAUTIFUL WOMAN FROM ANOTHER UNIVERSE
ON THE *STARGAZER*, GERDA ASMOND SUSPECTS THE
ALIEN OF TREACHERY.

BUT SHE HAS TO WONDER—IS SHE FOLLOWING
HER KLINGON INSTINCTS OR SUCCUMBING TO
SIMPLE JEALOUSY?

GERDA NEEDS TO FIND OUT—OR PICARD AND HIS
CREW MAY PAY FOR THEIR GENEROSITY WITH
THEIR LIVES.

AVAILABLE AUGUST 2003

STST

STAR TREK

ACROSS

1 Bajoran col
5 Medic for a colony at six-Borg in "Unity" [VGR]
8 Author Bombeck
12 Use ser energy-containment set
15 Kind of openness in "Rhodendrop" [DS9]
16 First-flot crewperson as "The Apple" [TOS]
17 Arachnid with half-meter-long legs
18 Bee mysteoid over sacceeaded Jessia
20 Teen on Capella IV in "Friday's Child" [TOS]
21 Be a broadcaster
22 Spanish wave
24 2024 San Francisco problem
26 Science station Tango ....
28 PG abbreviateret abbr.
31 Seattle
33 Year
34 Like 17 Across
36 Omicron .... star system
39 Assault weapon
40 T'Lar's government envoy in "Armageddon Game" [DS9]
45 Opposite of dep.
44 Widthspreaded
46 ... Targ (Klingon delsver)
47 Shotgun capital
49 Bajoran scout Aldovon in "Accession" [DS9]
50 Elevator inventor
51 Homeworld of two assassins sent to DS9 in "Babel"
52 Lessor before Lessie
55 Aldoran beverage served in Ten-Forward
58 Moon, mostly seed
60 ___ wing dog
61 ___ vacco si Ha'dka
63 Lifeform indigenous to the Celten Homeworld
66 Lt. Pade agent Steo toen
67 Radiate
68 Ferenco mercenaries who offered Kirk booze
69 Klaang escaped from one in "Broken Bow" [ENT]
70 Care for Scotty
71 Billard's Prella

DOWN

1 Royal letters
2 Samoan friend of Jessie's Dax
3 Chess castle
4 Doanea on "Star Trek: The Next Generation"
5 Planet who played Drex
6 Used a bowel pool
7 Restless
8 "Enterprise" supervising producer Howard
9 Brannon in "Violations" [TNG]
10 Fantascape imaginary friend of Chakon as a child
11 Melbourne actor bothered to Khan in "Space Seed" [TOS]
13 Sultan center
14 Actor Morales
18 "... lest I rest" [DS9]
22 Alpha-current ___
25 Bebop
26 Supercosme secret
28 Meadow of Klingon intelligence in "Visionary" [DS9]
28 Regical on Elios in "Patience of Ferox" [TOS]
30 Denation creafast Kocea compared to Kirk
32 Parent of F'Chan in "Survival Instinct" [VGR]
35 Mecinetned
37 Doanea on "Star Trek: The Next Generation"
41 Fiscal accents
45 Warp core injector output
42 Captain of the U.S.S. Equinox also in the Delta Quadrant
47 Author's tribes
47 Techoid office on stage stell in "Rightful Heir" [TNG]
48 Bajoran grain-processing center
51 Sets as kidnapped to this planet in "Maodaal" [VGR]
52 Tanackeara Bay, for one
54 Show-horse
55 Finally ruines
58 Bear of the Keiton Collective
60 Miles O'Brien's softena-ocsed hour
62 Of roll
63 Digatoras: Abbr.
65 Fight Searcher

50 ACROSS: Puzzles worked on for amusement

CROSSWORDS

by *New York Times* crossword puzzle editor John Samson

Available Now!